I0819963

The Ballad of
Titha Mae
An Epic Fantasy Written and Illustrated by

JON B. DALVY

Series Edition

"To my three little sisters and the light they hold"

written and with illustrations in print by
Jon B. Dalvy

Contents

In the cradle of darkness,
by light of the Moon...

CHAPTER ONE

The Middle Child

Titha could hardly believe it. Every year she counted the Moons 'til her favorite holiday, the *Festival of Dawn*. "No more waiting!" she squealed, merriment finally overtaking impatience. A smile spread from one indigo cheek to the other as she dreamed of what this Festival would bring. Who would meet their Bear-brother deep in the forest? Could she ace another tree-climbing competition? Or, *oh*! Maybe a *mountain* climbing com-petition? Her white hair sparkled above green eyes, each buzzing with endless possibilities. Her toes couldn't help but wiggle into the grass below as the stars beamed above. Excitement bubbled over into dance—or what she called dancing, anyway. Titha wasn't one to care for the thoughts of others, specifically on topics such as dancing, or frolicking, or anything, really. She was a child of her own making; a young lady of the dirt and leaves, made evident by her tattered pants and flowing, grass-stained violet tunic.

Nothing brought out Titha's youthful, jovial spirit quite like the *Festival*, either. Not even wee, squeaky otter babes (and that's saying something), and so her dance-like trot continued. As her view of the forest began to disappear behind bounding locks, she stopped to take the shortest of breathers; tying her hair up with a leafy vine before continuing along her way.

Such mirth became contagious within the forest. Nightingales sang alongside her melody as she hummed and jumped and skipped, trotting about in the dense blue night. Titha smirked as she neared a hedge of purple-berry bushes cleared of all their berries. She imagined every black bear she knew chubby and full, their mouths stained with purple, red, and blue juices. The young Luna laughed aloud as she bounded along, eventually tripping over a tree root and landing in the dirt. She shot right back up and clapped her hands together, sending swirling dust into the air. Dirt already caked the knees of her tattered pants anyway, and she wore it like a badge.

A huge smile brightened her face as she looked up. Ahead of her in the middle of the trees was the Meadow— a vast expanse of lush forest floor that formed the center of her home, Yythengrey.

The ancient forest was a sight to behold. All indigo-skinned Lunas lived in Ythengrey, and the Meadow was of particular importance. The trees formed a thick canopy around its core with an opening overhead just wide enough to let the stars and Moon shine through. Lunas loved the night sky; the Moon especially. It was their whole world—their entire existence was in pale darkness, for they slept during the Day. And this particular night was to be a grand one.

Titha's had woken up extra early, her excitement too much for sleep to contain. The other Lunas, however, were just now rising from their Day-slumber within enormous white flower. Her own excitement overflowed as she pipped between them, brushing nimble fingers along each glimmering petal she passed. As each Luna awoke—either by choice or Titha's not-so-quiet passing— their grand flowerbed would bloom, slowly curling out from the center into a full blossom. Some opened gracefully, others looked quite irregular as Lunas pulled the petals shut, trying to sleep *just* a bit longer. Titha smirked as she passed these struggling stragglers, or "pansyblossoms", as she called them. She skipped and hopped along the Meadow, as much in love with it as she ever had been, admiring the Lunas that chose to sleep in the Meadow's moonflowers the day before the festival (instead of their own tucked away in the forest). It was tradition, and traditions always felt right. She hopped past the shimmering white flowerbed she had chosen the night before. Its vines were grouped with two others—both still closed. Suddenly, she stopped. A twinkle filled her eyes as she burst from her chuckling into full-belly laughter.

"Rise and shine, pansyblossoms!" Titha shouted amidst her laughter. No response came from either flower. "Don't make me sing the song alone," she yelled, her hands immediately covering her mouth to fight back more chuckling. "I guess I'll have to sing the song of the Festival all by myself and *really* loudly..." she laughed. Still no response. "Here it comes," she whispered through her hands as she planted her feet.

Still no one chirped in response. It was time then, she thought. Without further hesitation Titha Mae spat forth a song as as old as the trees themselves with all the gusto her little Luna lungs could muster:

This day each year, One time each year
We wake up in the mooooorning
To greet the day, to celebrate
The Dawnfather is cooooming!

His sunshine glows, ev'ryone knows
The Festival is neeeeeear
So wake yourselves for Day this day
And si—

"You little brat!" a muffled voice shouted as the two unopened flowerbeds stirred. Luna heads popped out from each flower, both groggy, puffy-eyed and belonging to a sister. "I knew we should have slept at home," the older sister growled.

"You have to let me finish the song!" Titha spouted.

"No one cares about that stupid song, Titha," her older sister quipped. This was Gilly, and her slouching frame was the sole reason the phrase "pansyblossom" existed. Gilly glared at Titha, shoving and kicking at her flowerbed as it attempted to open, her spindly long arms and legs jerking about like a spider.

"Finish the song, finish the song!" a tiny voice peeped out of the adjacent flower. The smallest of the three flowerbeds rolled open as Titha's younger sister sat up. The tiny round Luna grabbed a blue dress and wiggled her way into it before crossing her teeny legs. She looked up to Titha, wide-eyed with anticipation.

"See, Beebee knows I have to finish the song. Don't you, Beebee?" Titha smiled.

"Finish, finish!" Beebee shouted with her tiny voice, waving her hands. Titha looked to Gilly, returned her older sister's glare, and cleared her throat with a harsh gargle. She stood up straight, shouting the final line to the song triumphantly:

Aaaaaand sing the song of Mooooooooorrnniiiinng!

"Thank you, thank you," Titha smirked as she bowed to her sisters.

Beebee cheered, clapping her wee hands. "Again, again!"

Gilly frowned even harder as she put on her velveteen green dress. She stomped down from her flowerbed and flailed her spindly legs right up to Titha, who was at least a full-fox shorter than her.

"Sing the song again and I'll throw you into the river," Gilly threatened. Beebee giggled behind her. "Stop laughing, Beebee. I will *so* throw her in the river! *Won't I,* Titha Mae?"

"Only one way to find out," Titha declared. She took a deep breath and opened her mouth wide. Before she could begin singing the song again Gilly scooped her up, marching her toward the edge of the Meadow. "Ooh, I'm so scared Gilly! Please don't throw me into the river! What ever shall I do?" Titha spouted sarcastically.

"Hope you like otters," Gilly retorted.

"Very much so, they're so cute and curious and quite polite as far as animals go—"

"Uuuugh, I am going to drown your stupid face!" Gilly screamed.

"Are we there yet?" Titha chuckled. Gilly's marching

picked up pace. Titha smiled as she flopped all of her weight down onto her older sister's green dress. She could hear the brook babbling in the background behind her as Gilly's pace quickened. "Okay, I get it. I'm annoying, I *know*. I'm the worst little sister in the world and will never wake you up to the sounds of my beautiful voice again. Can we go back now? We have to get ready for the festival!"

Gilly stayed silent as she marched on.

"Seriously, Gilly. Put me down!" Titha spat. No response came from below her, just the sound of her sister's big flat feet plopping in the mud as they neared the river. Titha squirmed, she was fast becoming upset. "Gilly!" she shouted, but her sister wouldn't reply. Without warning Titha grabbed two handfuls of her sister's long silvery hair. *"I said put me down!"* she yelled as she yanked the locks backwards. Gilly screeched, dropping Titha with a hard *plop* straight into the mud and sticks.

"What is your *problem,* Titha? That really hurt!" Gilly shouted, both of them covered in mud.

Titha sat up, fighting tears as she spotted a long rip in her rolled-up magenta pants, a stick sticking straight through the tear.

"You ruined my favorite breeches!" Titha spurted out through the huge lump in her throat.

"Good!" Gilly shouted back angrily, "Maybe now you'll

put on a *dress* for once!"

"I was going to for the festival! Why are you so mean to me?" Titha shouted, her eyes welling with tears.

"Whatever, you little brat! You started this! You *always* start it!"

"Stop calling me that! I am not little anymore!"

"But you are the *definition* of *brat,* aren't you? You are an *intolerable, spoiled little—*"

Titha screamed as she jumped over to her sister, slapping and punching wildly as mud flung every which way. Gilly grabbed Titha's arms, holding her down. "I wasn't going to before but now I'm *really* throwing you into the Daenu!"

Titha let out a blood-curdling shriek as her sister lifted her into the air over the River. Just then, a voice like thunder boomed forth from behind them; its mighty tone echoing off the churning waters like the coming of a storm.

"Put down your sister!" the voice commanded.

Both Lunas froze in their tracks. Gilly turned around to see Beebee sobbing and holding the much larger hand of their father, who was none too pleased with their behavior. Theole stood like a statue; the moonlight twinkling atop their father's bald head and weaving through his long, magnificent white beard.

This was bad. Quite bad. The girls loved him fiercely, and to see his bushy eyebrows furled in such a way was the worst of punishments.

"She started it!" Gilly blurted instinctively.

"I did not, father!" Titha shouted, tears streaming down her face. "I was just singing the Festival song to wake them up in time!"

Theole sighed. Beebee clutched the bottom of his flowing draped robes as he lowered himself to their level. "Such passionate daughters, I have" he spoke, his voice deep yet soothing. "Your little sister is right, Gilly. You should both be ready for the Festival of Dawn by now."

Gilly's face twisted with disgust at her father's words. "You always take her side!" she pouted. "I would've been ready by now if she—"

"—I didn't walk *myself* down to the river, dung-breath!" Titha shouted as the sisters went at it again.

"Titha Lilly Mae! *Enough*!" Theole's words swiftly snuffed out their bickering. "I am not taking anyone's side. If I *were* to take sides it would be Beebee's. She was wise enough to fetch me. Look at the two of you! You should not upset your youngest sister so." Beebee hiccupped through her crocodile tears as she covered up with the deep olive-toned fabrics of Theole's robes.

"Sorry Beebee," Titha said meekly.

"I believe you owe an apology to your older sister as well, young Luna," Theole spoke gently.

"Sorry Gilly," she said, her apology ringing sincere.

"Whatever," Gilly quipped, still visibly upset as she attempted to remove the mud from her velvet green dress.

Theole looked to his eldest daughter, her aura all too familiar to him. He knew arguing with her proved fruitless, as it did with her mother. He liked to think she didn't get *any* of her stubbornness from him. "Apologize to your little sister, Gilly. Then we will make sure your dress is perfect for the Festival together."

"Thanks," Gilly said quietly, "but I'll do it myself." She huffed up, walking past her father silently.

Theole's heavy brow furrowed as he bowed his head. Titha scoffed, knowing exactly what her sister was doing. She shot up after her, but to no avail.

"Let her go," Theole spoke swiftly, his wide hand stopping Titha in her tracks. "She is upset. She will find her own way." He cradled Beebee with one arm as he pulled Titha close with the other. "The Festival is very hard for Gilly," their father continued, his voice thin. "She misses your mother. I miss her too. We all miss her. But she is still with us, always. Right, Titha Mae?"

"In the trees, in the wind, and in the sky," Titha said, her damp eyes looking toward the Moon.

Theole hugged his daughters tightly. "The Festival carries deep memories of your mother for all of us," he said softly. "You should not be so hard on your sister."

Titha fought back the urge to cry, fed up with emotions for the evening. Yet as the silence set in and the crickets took over, she could not help but let her mind wander to sadder places.

"Why did mother have to go?" Titha asked, her voice quivering through the quiet.

Theole smiled. "Because only she could, my sweet child. Your mother saved us all, and now she is one with all the beauty that surrounds us." The family sat together for a moment in silence.

"I still see her sometimes," Titha said quietly, "she sings to me in my dreams."

Theole's heart swelled with love. "And she always will, little Luna. If you ever need her—"

"Just follow the wind," Titha smiled as she finished her father's words.

A single tear dropped to Theole's beard. "That's my girl," he said, lifting her up beside Beebee and hugging them both. "Now let's go get you two sprouts ready for the best Festival of Dawn yet! I hear there will be a *mountain climbing* contest this year. Now who do I know that requested *just that* this past festive?"

Joy shot back through Titha's body like lightning. She wiped the tears from her face, looking over to Beebee.

"Can you believe it, Beebee!?" Titha shouted, bubbling over with excitement. "It's finally here! We're going to play games and meet new Bear-brothers and climb mountains! We get to stay up and watch the Sun shine!"

"The Sun! It's yellow!" Beebee replied, her little indigo face turning bright pink with excitement.

Titha laughed, "Yes it is, Wee Bee! Good job! It's so beautiful isn't it? Everything has to be warm and golden and incredible during the day! Is it father?"

Theole frowned. "You are the most curious creature in this forest, little Luna, and even the otters would agree with me on that," Theole's words were lighthearted, yet his tone carried concern, "and I love this about you. But we Lunas are people of the Night, children of the Forest and of the Moon. The Day is bright and harsh and full of perils. It burns hot and fierce. It is no time or place for us."

"I don't see why not. Plenty of animals live in the Day, Father. I've seen them on the edge of Wood Gate past the Tree Hall.

They seem alright."

Theole could not help but chuckle at his daughter's matter-o-factness. She always spoke bluntly, another of her many qualities he cherished. Yet his own mind raced with violent scenes of Daylight from the past–all of which he would never let his daughters bear witness to (if he could help it). "Our forest friends are not welcome in the Daylight any longer, my child. You must never venture out into the day, Titha. Nor should Paw. The Festival should be enough, which is why we have it. Please trust me on this. I only tell—"

"—Me this for my own good, I know. I know," she interrupted playfully, "I won't, father. I promise. Even though I want to really, *really* badly."

"That's my girl," he said with a hearty laugh. As Theole released his daughter from a mighty hug he spotted a rather nasty tear in her breeches. "How did that happen?" He inquired. "Are you alright?"

"It's nothing" She replied. "I'll stitch them up at home. Again."

"One of these Nights you are going to have to put on a new pair of pants, Titha Mae."

"Why would I do that when these are all nice and worn in?" She smirked as Theole attempted to lead her by the hand back toward their home.

Yet as they headed for the mountains behind the Meadow, a strange rustling caught their ears.

"What was that?" Theole stopped cold in his tracks, his arms locking around both of his girls. The old Watcher was not accustomed to anything surprising him. Beebee buried her face in her father's arm.

"What is it, father?" Titha asked as she wrestled free of his protection. "What do you see?"

"Nothing. Which is what concerns me," Theole's words were sharp and heavy. He nudged Titha behind his leg, bracing himself as his eyes began to glow bright blue.

"Uh oh," Beebee murmured, her little eyes peeping up at her father's.

Without warning, a massive black shadow leaped forth from the bushes, berries and leaves flying every which way. The shadow let forth a roar that split the blades of grass beneath their feet. Before they knew it, Theole and his daughters were on the ground, the massive shadow grumbling as it pinned each Luna to the earth. The black mass slowly leaned forward, then *schloop*! Out popped a huge pink tongue, licking each Luna's face jovially as they wriggled beneath it.

"What in Mother Nature's...?" Theole was completely taken aback.

Titha burst into laughter as her arms shot up and wrapped around the shadow's fuzzy neck. "Paw! You bad bear!" she shouted through her laughter, "that was a *good* one!"

"What is the meaning of this?" Theole shouted as he wrestled the now-revealed black bear from atop himself and Beebee. "I ought to have you banished, you foolish cub!" Theole was not amused. He stood up right, dusting his robes and checking on his smallest daughter. Crows began to caw in the foliage. Such a riled-up reaction only made Titha laugh that much harder.

"Paw! Paw!" Beebee shouted as she jumped from her father onto the bear's back.

"He's just playing, father," Titha chortled as she frazzled the fur atop Paw's round head. "That had to be the best one yet. I had no idea it was you, fuzzybutt!"

Paw licked her face again as he stood onto all fours. He was big for such a young black bear, his shoulders standing much higher than Titha's head. "Oh, how we are meant for each other."

"That you are," Theole scoffed, his robes almost dirt-free. "I hope your Bear-brother is ready for the Festival as he should be?" He plucked Beebee from Paw's back.

Paw groaned, his chestnut eyes rolling at Theole's sternness.

"Come along, you two troublemakers," Theole continued. "At this rate we will never make our duties on time."

Titha grabbed Paw's cheeks, mushing them together as she pressed her nose against his. With an enthusiastic grunt, Paw swooped his head underneath Titha's knees, flinging her onto his back. She wiggled and wailed as she turned herself around and clutched two big handfuls of black fur. Paw always knew what this meant, and without so much as another grumble, shot off down the forest path with Titha hooting and hollering through the trees.

"At least everyone will be awake for the Festival," Theole groaned to Beebee, echoes of his middle daugh-ter's bounding bouncing through Yythengrey. "Are you ready for the pretty party, Sproutling?" he asked Beebee as he tickled her little Luna belly.

Beebee's arms fluttered as she laughed. "Party time!" she squeaked.

"Party time, indeed," Theole smiled, "and I have a feeling this will be one for the *ages*."

CHAPTER TWO

A Festival to Remember

It was almost dawn! Luna feet scurried about every which way; joyous chatter filling the air. The grand stairs leading up to Theole's chambers had been transformed into an impressive layered stage. Paw and a few other bear-brothers carried Theole's throne to its traditional spot at the center of it all, which overlooked all of the Meadow's mirth. Deep violet flags bearing the Mark of the Moon flew in every corner of the clearing as tents accented in white and earthen green were erected last minute by busy Luna hands. Banners of intricate design strung from tree trunk to trunk, each featuring the birds of old: Crows, Owls, Hawks, and their kin. Everything from tent poles to the Luna's festive garb was laced with shimmering gold trim; a rare treat as Lunas only used this captivating color during the Festival. Indeed, the entire forest beneath Mount Meri was *alight* with gold.

Theole began to make his way down from the mountain, the sound of his broad feet flickering haste into every Lunish heart. His right hand held his staff— The Ozark staff—an ancient instrument of great power and beauty. Atop its rigid wooden pike shone a magnificent orb held in place by twisted vines. To compliment this grand instrument, Theole had switched out his traditional indigo and green robes for lavish, gold-trimmed fabrics that shimmered in the Moonlight, their loudness offset by the pale olive sash he never took off. A grin swept from one ear to the other as his eyes met his festival throne—a golden sight much different to behold than his traditional silver throne. Its four feet were golden elk hooves, the legs leading up to an equally splendid chassis that intertwined like forest vines around an old tree trunk. Atop the chassis were the most inviting velvety-purple cushions any Luna had ever seen, complemented by an ancient pale green sash (much like his own) draped down the long back of the chair. Each piece of the throne's composition had to be placed *just so*—as was tradition—and Theole always insisted upon tradition. His Crows, tireless servants of their Watcher, began to land on the tiers of the throne as it settled in the shadow of the mountain.

"A bit to the right," Theole instructed, the bears grunting in compliance as they nudged the heavy chair's position. Paw swiped at the Crows with his free paw. He hated the loud little buggers.

"Be sure the sash does not drape too close to the seating!" Theole barked. "If only your kind had thumbs, this would all move much more swiftly," he laughed, amusing himself.

"Having trouble with the bear-brothers are we, Sire?" a robust and hardy voice interjected. The frame of a portly, burly Luna with an almost pinkish color to him stepped forth onto the stage. The wrinkled, round figure clutched a scroll tightly in one hand and scratched the top of his thick matted hair with the other. He sported a comically large white moustache that obstructed words from his mouth and left any who did not know him to wonder if he even had a mouth at'all. It's thickness and curl was impressive nonetheless, and their arches reached up almost to his bushy eyebrows.

"Ah, Cypress! Timely as always," Theole said as he smiled at his oldest friend's arrival. "You look particularly festive!"

"A squire is always ready, Watcher. And I do believe these robes once fit me a tad less... *snugly,*" Cypress quipped through his huffing. He adjusted his gold-trimmed green garb as a nervous look crossed his face. "Though I never quite cared for the golden trim over our traditional silver. 'Tis only once a year, though, so I digress," Cypress was clearly nervous and making small talk. "In all earnest I do have an urgent matter to discuss, if you have a moment. I just received word from Aspen, Sire, from our Cedar Guard at the far edge of the forest. They say they bared witness to something *troubling*."

"Is everything alright?" Theole asked, concern in his voice; though his eyes still combed the majesty of the Festival coming together.

"No one is hurt—it is nothing of that like, Sire. An oddity, it is, instead. The guards say they witnessed—and I know this will sound preposterous, but— they say they saw the Sun rising early… and then setting again just moments later into the horizon as if it had never risen." Cypress's tone was alarming to Theole, as his friend and Squire was one to jest at times, but never on serious matters such as this.

"Rose and set? In a moment's time? That does not sound right. Has the Dawnfather finally forgotten his duties? Surely not, and as such our guards must not be certain of what they saw?" Theole questioned.

"Not a hint of uncertainty from any of the guards, I am told. Serious as a serpent, Aspen's report was. Ten of our best gazed upon the same event, and your Crows report the same: They say the night sky lit up as if Dawn was upon them like fire to the Amber Fields, and at the center of the blazing inferno rose the Sun as bright and hot as ever. Then—as soon as it had risen—it fell again under the horizon not to return. The whole of it vanished, and that was that."

"This is *impossible*, though we both know well that word holds no meaning..." Theole stroked his long beard, his brow furrowed in discomfort. "I... this is most concerning, if true, Cypress. Send reinforcements to the Wood Gate, and have Aspen come speak with me. It may be nothing at all, but luck favors the prepared."

Cypress bowed to Theole's words and turned to call his Bear-brother—a huge, greyish-black bear with long wily tuffs of fur—and the two rode off with haste.

Theole's mind now raced with grim possibilities as he stood alone. The Sun did not, and does not, simply rise and set as it wills. Its ancient keeper, however...

Theole stopped his line of thought there, firmly. Surely he was being ridiculous; the excitement of the Festival allowing his mind to be carried away with flights of terrible fancy. He shuttered to think of halting the Festival of Days over any sort of false alarm or simple mishap. But his Cedarguard was always to be trusted: they had proven themselves so. Perhaps those dreadful Vikingmen were at war again across the fields; their ignorance causing a heinous display. Surely that was all there was to it. Surely.

He would wait for word from Aspen, then, his leader of the guard at the Wood Gate, and from her an explanation could be found.

From behind him Paw stepped forth in concern, leaving his fellow Bear-kin to finish adorning the stage. He nuzzled Theole's hand with his sandy brown muzzle, wary of the Watcher's own weariness.

"You are kind to worry for me, Paw. But all is well. Continue with your final touches, rascal. Everything is looking magnificent thus far."

Paw gave Theole another glance, then returned to the other bears.

Atop Mount Meri, Titha struggled to get ready in the daughter's quarters of Roostwood. She could hear the orchestra setting up at the foot of the grand stairs and was working herself into quite a tizzy because of it. She was going to be late, as always, at this pace! She looked at herself in the mirror, her face crinkled with freckled disapproval. This one second of broken concentration was all it took, and her foot became caught in the lace of her magnificent green velvet dress again—which she could *never* get on right and was struggling with terribly at the moment. Dresses (and the like) were, in her opinion, immensely impractical for playing in and/or enjoying the mountains. Whenever she had to suffer one it always looked too long, or too wide, or crooked or lumpy or all of these things at once. She rolled her big green eyes as she pictured Gilly looking marvelous in a long, glorious and flowy dress of the exact same color and design.

"If I had beanpoles for legs, I'd look good in this stupid dress too," she thought, reassuring herself, though it just made her even more mad. With one big huff and puff she shoved her leg down through the lace of the dress.

Rrrrrip... Titha looked down to see green lace in between her toes and dangling from the bottom of her festival attire.

"Father's going to *love* that," she said with a grimace, "this dress is older than Cypress." She grabbed the scraggly lacing and began to yank at it, tearing the entire pattern from the bottom of the dress. "There! All better!" she trumpeted into the mirror. As she did, memories of her mother's gentle, helping hands began to straighten her outfit. Titha closed her eyes and took a deep breath, remembering every detail of her mother's equally freckled skin and gorgeous bright violet eyes. She opened her own to behold another set of curious peepers reflecting back at her. A tiny little pair of yellow eyes shone out from the door behind her. She turned, laughing excitedly under her breath.

"Beebee, come out and let me see your dress! The orchestra is starting to warm up, it's time to party!"

Beebee slowly stepped out from behind the door, her little

body bobbing inside an identical green velvet dress like a bell. She was not at all happy.

"Begonia Bee Mae you look absolutely stupen-dous!" Titha shouted triumphantly. "How do you feel?"

"Like a phrog," Beebee replied, serious as the Moon.

Titha burst out laughing. "Like a frog? Bless you, Wee bee. You look great, I promise. Now come on, it's time to go!" Titha grabbed her little sister's hand and led her down the halls toward the front of Roostwood, their deep'forest home.

As they approached the entry of their father's hall the double doors swung wide open. Their ears were flooded with beautiful music as the Festival Procession rung like magic through the forest trees.

"Where is Gillian?" Beebee asked.

"I don't know, but she'll have to meet us down there. We're late as it is." Titha pulled her little sister along with enough fervor for the both of them, as there was no containing her excitement. Her green eyes widened as they began walking down the grand steps. They could see the entire Meadow: all of the lavish tents and towers, gold-laced ribbons wrapped around every tree trunk in sight, moon flags flapping in the commotion, and every Luna in existence gathering to await their arrival.

Theole rested his left hand on the arm of his throne, his body propped up parallel to his mighty Ozark Staff. Titha could see Cypress whispering something into her father's ear as a guard stood stoically beside them. They hushed immediately as she began to pass.

"Good to see you, Titha Mae," Cypress greeted, "and you, young Master Begonia Bee. And may I say you look particularly ravishing this fine Festival day."

Beebee blushed as her tiny legs hurried to catch back up with her sister. Theole did not notice them at first, his grim facial expression focused outward into the evergreens as the rest of his Cedarguards took their places along the borders of the Meadow. Their starkness was a harsh contrast to the joyous Lunas socializing below. Their chatter turned to excited whispers as the maestro took his place for the orchestra's Festival Procession. Each Luna hushed and huddled shoulder to shoulder as they awaited the official beginning of the ceremony: the *Song of the Festival of Days*. And Theole's speech, of course.

Each year, the simple yet poetic tune was sung by the sproutling Lunas, and it was to be Beebee's first year in the choir. Dark thoughts finally left Theole's mind as he remembered this. He turned to look over his shoulder, and his two youngest daughters passed looking regal in their velveteen dresses. His eyes squinted as he beheld Titha's dress. "Your sister is already in place," he smirked. "Where is the lacing on your dress?" he followed, eye-brows bending.

"I don't know what you're talking about, father," she replied with a smile as she walked past, Beebee in tow. Her smiled turned to a full-toothed grin as she looked upon the assembled choir. She led Beebee around the other sproutlings, scoping out their spot front and center.

Behind them, Cypress began to whisper to Theole again. "If you are going to call it off, Sire," he said, "now would be the time to do it."

This Titha heard. "Call it off?" she wondered. Surely they were speaking of something other than her favorite day of the year. But just at the right moment Titha and Beebee's appearance was met with thunderous applause, and her excitement became too great to ever ben cancelled by 'what-ifs'.

The sisters took their spot at the apex of the sproutling choir, holding each other's hands and sharing a smile.

"Nervous, Titha Mae?" a voice questioned from behind.

"Never," Titha replied with a smirk. "We are going to make this song sound the best it ever has," she explained triumphantly. As she turned back 'round, though, hundreds of Lunish eyes stared back at her, each above impatient smiles. A lump caught in her throat. "Are you nervous, Maple?" she asked.

"Oh, very. Very much, I am," Maple croaked as she wiped the fog from her glasses. Titha looked the choir over behind her fair-skinned friend and finally spotted Gilly standing in the back with the boys, most of whom were considerably shorter than her. Titha stuck her tongue out at her sister, who smiled and returned the gesture.

Gilly looked great in her dress, as expected, and was ignoring the boy standing next to her who apparently had developed a staring problem. Theole walked down from his throne to their side, smiling at all of the little Lunas as he passed. He winked at Titha as he took his place beside her for the opening speech. His blue eyes looked outward, and the Cedar Guard stood to attention.

"My dear Lunas, Bear-brothers, and Tree-kin, this Golden Day of which we observe once a year is finally upon us; The Festival of Days!" Theole stomped the Ozark Staff's base down onto the ground and a flash of light burst forth from the orb atop it—illuminating the festivities. Each Luna erupted in cheer, the crowd hollering and clapping with spritely exuberance. Theole tried to soak in the joy of his people, but paused a moment once more... He thought again of cancelling the festivities. His mind was so heavy.

Titha looked up to her now silent father, her eyes glowing with glee; and that was all it took. Theole couldn't bear the thought of cancelling such a sacred tradition on a whim—let alone crushing his daughters' spirits. Regaining his composure, he took a deep breath and rose his head to speak again as the cheering subsided:

"Every Night is a gift to us from the great Duskmother, whose loving wings embrace us still and forever on in her memory. On this day each year, how-ever, we must celebrate the Sun and the Day; both spawn of the Dawnfather. He gives life to our seedlings and to us as we sleep. Let this day also stand in remembrance of those we have lost, for they are forever in our hearts."

"Forever in our hearts," The crowd repeated in unison. Theole could see his fallen wife Thea's smile amidst the foliage. He paused for her, bowing his head before continuing:

"Today we do not mourn death, we celebrate life and those who made it worth living. We celebrate the Duskmother and her Moon for lighting our paths, even in her absence. We celebrate our fallen Beacon, Thea Celtica Mae, who nurtures us still through Mother Nature. We celebrate each other, for Lunas are kind and pure and true. And above all on this day, we celebrate The Day itself. Have mirth, my Lunas! The Dawnfather is coming!" Theole stomped his staff once more, and the crowd erupted into an explosion of jovial cheer that eclipsed even the one before it. This was the cue for the orchestra, who played a quick yet triumphant excerpt from the Festival Procession to footnote Theole's rousing speech.

"Oh, here we go, Titha. Good luck!" Maple babbled nervously, her glasses fogging up again.

Titha squeezed Beebee's hand in excitement as the girls and boys of the choir all turned to face the crowd. All fell silent with the orchestra; even the crickets. The anticipation was palpable. Then, like the winds of a storm, the orchestra swelled back into play with the swirling opening of *The Song of the Festival of Days.*

As the strings rose to a fever-pitch, the sproutling choir began to sing:

This day each year, One time each year
We wake up in the morning
To greet the day, to celebrate
The Dawnfather is coming!

As the young Lunas sang out these words, the sky opened up with a wondrous amber glow. Was the sun rising before the song finished? This had never happened before. Everything was timed meticulously. Titha's eyes became glued to the flaming orange sky. "That's the most intense sunrise I've ever seen on a festival!" she thought to herself. She could not believe the intensity of the brazen glow. A few of the orchestra's musicians fumbled their notes as the sky's magnificence grew in intensity. Theole looked to Cypress, whose hand was on his sword hilt already. Theole signaled for Cypress to stand down. "It is just an intense, beautiful sunrise," he whispered to the squire. "The Dawnfather must be pleased."

His sunshine glows, everyone knows
The Festival is near

With these words, the sunset retreated as quickly as it had vanished. Audible gasps escaped the mouths of the crowd as astonishment swept the Meadow. The Crows cawed and cacked, flapping their wings nervously. Aspen, Captain of the Guard, rushed in amidst the crowd, supporting swords behind her. She took for Theole, but became blocked by roused citizens at every turn. The Cedar Guard looked to one another, some clutching their weapons in confusion. The orchestra fell completely out of sync as the children kept singing:

So wake yourselves for Day this day
And sing this song of Morning!

Like lightning the sunset retuned to the sky, shooting across its dark canvas like fire through a burning field. A thunderous boom rustled the treetops as screams erupted from the Luna crowd. Waves of heat the likes of which the Lunas had never experienced burst forth from above the trees, blasting ash down into frantic crowds. Titha's eyes squinted in the heat as she grabbed Beebee, the heat wave pushing her hair back with hurricane intensity. Fire erupted across the tree tops as the deafening crackle of splintering wood pierced each Luna's ears. Gilly shoved through the panicking choir to get to her little sisters, grabbing them both. She opened her mouth to speak but was cut off by a second thundering *BOOM*! Trees began to fall in the meadow as the tents and banners caught fire. The Cedar Guards hurdled through civilians, scooping up sproutlings and rushing elders to safety amongst fierce confusion. Titha screamed for her father as smoke began to rise all around them. She screamed as loud as her voice could possibly scream, but couldn't hear herself above the bellowing flames and the ringing of her own ears. A massive indigo hand shot through the smoke and grabbed the girls. They looked up to see Theole as he pulled them in, his eyes glowing as intensely as the sky. "Father!" they cried, but their screams could not be heard. Cypress leapt to their side, his sword drawn and his scowl fierce. Theole secured his daughters with one arm and flung the Ozark Staff forward with the other—pointing it directly at the sky. A beam of white light shot forth through the smoke, clearing a tunnel through which they could see.

Two great red eyes rose up through the flames and into their narrow view. A snarling maul of jagged teeth pierced through the scorching flames, greeting them with a smile.

"The words ring true, Sire!" Cypress's heavy voice cracked as he yelled above whirling flames. "The Dawn-father is *here*!

Vulduun is upon us!"

Enormous bone claws shot through the treetops, crashing the crackling Meadow's walls to the ground. Theole watched in horror as waves of nefarious creatures swarmed his beloved home from all angles, bursting through the flames with twisted grins and knotted weapons. Enormous, hairy Ogres swept in from the North —their gnarled fists bashing through burning tree trunks with ease. From the South rose an entire platoon of Reeks, fierce lizard-men with scaly hides and fanged jaws.

"Cedar Guard! Attack!" Cypress commanded from amidst swelling fire, his sword rocketing forth into the air.

Theole whipped around, grabbing Cypress. "Get my daughters to safety. I will handle this!" he exclaimed with fierce determination.

"Sire, no! I cannot leave you behind!" Cypress decreed.

"You will not subject my daughters to any further danger. Do as I say!"

Gilly took Beebee from her father as she rushed toward the grand stairs. Cypress looked to Titha. "Come, young master! We must get you to safety!"

"I am not leaving you, father!" Titha cried. Theole smiled as the light illuminating from his eyes intensified.

"My dear Titha Mae," he spoke softly as he placed his hand upon her cheek. Titha gasped as her father's hand began to grow, his fingertips spreading before blossoming into grand silver feathers. She stepped as the light in her father's eyes shone brighter than the flames dancing 'round them—his Crows circling him like a halo. Theole's neck cracked backward, his arms shooting forth as he let out a triumphant cry. Wings burgeoned forth, his robes thrashing and tearing as shimmering silver feathers overtook his entire body. The mighty leader of the Lunas threw the Ozark Staff into the air, jumping after it; his indigo feet twisting into crystal white talons as he leapt upward. With great agility, his newly sprouted wings swooped downward as he snatched the Ozark Staff into one of his talons. Theole turned back to his daughters as he flew above them, his now enormous eyes glowing with the blue intensity of the Moon. They beheld their father anew as the Grand Silver Owl—Yythengrey's savior.

Cypress wrapped his arms around Titha as her father nodded without a word. Flapping his glistening silver wings amongst the flames, their beloved Watcher turned to meet the source of such torment.

"Father!" Titha screamed, her arms stretching as far as they could. Smoke forced tears from Cypress' eyes as he held back the thrashing young Luna, turning with her to retreat up the steps to Roostwood.

The raging flames were deafening. Theole shot down through the engulfed treetops, scooping up any civilians he could into his enormous talons as Reeks and Ogres ravaged his lands below.

A particularly ugly Goblin shot forth from the chaos. "Bring down the owl!" he gurgled, spit flying from his craggy maw. Like living flames a troop of Ogres shot forth from the wreckage, their hairy knuckles wrapped around jagged spears.

"Hurl, worms!" The foul invaders reared back, leaping forward and launching spear after splintered spear at Theole. The gigantic, god-like owl clenched the taloned civilians close to him as he thrust forth his silver wings, splintering each spear mid-air with his shimm-ering feathers. He swung his Ozark Staff 'round with his other talon, letting loose a piercing cry as a beam of white and blue light shot forth from the staff's round stone, vanquishing waves of the twisted soldiers below. Bear-brothers barreled in from the stairs, mauling and slashing back the Ogres.

Theole took this chance, dashing forth and blazing through a trail of his own making to the border of the Meadow. The civilians were released by the river; safe for the moment.

"If you can fight, stay and fight!" Theole pro-claimed, his words echoing through his mighty beak. "Elders, guide the sproutlings to safety across the River Daenu. Call to any Otters, Beavers, or river-kin you see for help extinguishing these flames. Hail every Bear-brother, Hog, Buck, and Doe to vanquish these terrible foes! Protect the forest! We will not let these foul creatures

win!" Theole's vast wings whooshed through the smoke-filled air as he turned back to the flames. His eyes squinted as he peered through the chaos, searching for the master of this death and destruction.

"Show yourself, Dragon!" Theole shouted forth into the twisting fire, his Crows flanking him. "Be known to me! Cease this misery and *show yourself!*"

The flames grew silent. For a moment the deaf-ening chaos stilled. Theole cringed as a booming laugh broke through the quiet. Smoke whirled beneath the smoldering trees as a serpentine head drew itself up from the ashes of the forest. Flames shot forth from two flared nostrils at the tip of a mighty golden maw. Glaring red eyes pierced through the smoke, their gaze breaking Theole's resolve as the enormous dragon unfolded his amber wings—toppling what trees were left standing. Horns of golden bone protruded from every side of the terrible beast's crown. All stood still as the dragon's fiery eyes met Theole's icy blue gaze.

"*Such arrogance,*" the dragon quipped, his voice barreling like thunder. "*'Dragon,' he beckons me. Do you not know to whom you speak, Watcher*?"

"I do not," Theole decreed, not breaking his gaze. "The Great Drakes that *I* know do not slaughter the innocent nor burn their homelands. I do not know who stands before me, for you are not the Dawnfather we so deeply cherish."

With those words the behemoth shot forth, slamming Theole to the ground. "*There are no more Great Drakes, wretched owl. I am all that remains—a truth your precious Nightfall will torment me with 'til the oblivion takes us all!*"

"We tried to save her, Vulduun!" Theole spoke through the mighty dragon's crippling grip. "*She*—"

The dragon's grip tightened at the incinuating of her

hallowed name. "*Do not speak of her*!" he cried out.

Theole whipped forth his wings, slashing the dragon's arm, loosening his grip. The Grand Silver Owl swooped into the air, pointing the Ozark Staff down at his golden foe as he spoke:

"The Duskmother sealed her own fate! Meriduun lusted for power—she could not be satiated! And now you come before me, the once mighty and infallible Drake of Dawn—desiring the very same! How our Drakes have fallen."

"*You wield her Moonstone at me, Luna?*" Vulduun cackled, spitting ferociously. "Fancy yourself a worthy replacement of the Duskmother, do you? I will have your *head*, Owl, but not before burning every child of the night to ash and ridding this world of darkness and Night for *all eternity*! I will not stop until every memory—every *remnant* of her existence is cleared from these lands, and each creature who failed her suffers for their treachery! This world will *burn* in eternal Daylight, Watcher, and your precious Lunas will perish in its flames!"

Without warning, Vulduun leapt forth with a searing roar, his mighty jaws splintering the Ozark Staff into a thousand pieces as the orb atop it fell to singed grass below. The golden dragon lashed out at Theole, his claws ripping into silver feathers. Sparkling dust filled the air as the megalithic creatures clashed amidst burning tree tops. Their battle became a whirl of talons and fangs, each crashing and clanging off the other's brilliant armor of gold or silver—and it became clear they could not pierce each other's armor. Theole thrusted himself upward with the wind and lunged at the dragon's throat with his talons, whipping Vulduun 'round and tossing him into the canopy. His blue gaze shot around to the burning floor of the Meadow, searching for the orb—the precious Moonstone. As Theole's glowing blue eyes locked onto the artifact, Vulduun's enormous tail slammed into his side, knocking him from the sky. The terrible Drake thrashed about within splintered trees, jostling himself from their grip. He charged t'ward the downed Theole, bouldering through debris; his wings like battering rams. Rearing his head, Vulduun bashed Theole aside with his great crown of horns, then retracted, towering proudly over his foe—when a gleaming object caught his eye.

"There you are... *Moonstone,*" Vulduun muttered as he snatched up the glowing orb. He reached down for it, gloating with pride. Yet as soon as his golden paws met the ancient object a searing pain ripped at his flesh. Unbearable burning took over the Dragon's body as he trumpeted in agony—immediately dropping the now intensely glowing orb. He growled in disgust as he grabbed his singed hand, looking around at the awestruck Reeks and Ogres.

"*Does this amuse you, imps?*" He spat. "*Cease your staring and conceal the orb! Bring it to me!*" All manner of foul creatures stirred as they grabbed whatever unburnt cloth they could find amongst the festival debris.

"You cannot wield it," Theole cried, his voice wavering amidst great pain.

"Which is why you are coming with me, Owl," Vulduun snarled, flames shooting from his maw.

Without hesitation his enormous clawed hands raked forth, slashing his own soldiers away from the now wrapped orb. Air and smoke whipped into a hurricane as Vulduun cackled, his tremendous wings flapping and battering anything and everything from his path. He grabbed the shrouded Moonstone with one foot and Theole's neck with the other, showing no mercy, and as quickly as the Dawnfather had appeared—he vanished with both prizes into the sky.

CHAPTER THREE

The World Outside

Cypress slammed the doors of Roostwood shut. His mind raced feverishly; hands still gripping his sword's hilt as he fought the voices within. He would not let harm fall to his Master's daughters, but the sound of the forest burning outside penetrated his mind like shards of glass. A gentle indigo hand fell onto his back. Cypress turned to find Titha in her usual tattered pants and tunic, her demeanor matching that of his own as she held her singed festival dress, clutched like a ruined rag. Both attempted to hold their composure as their eyes met. "I am so happy you three are safe with me," Cypress muttered through his charred moustache. "You are not to leave your father's halls, do you understand?"

Titha snapped at the words, however, catching Cypress off-guard. This was, she thought, the absolute opposite of what she planned to do. "We have to go after him!" Titha cried. "I can't sit in here not knowing if he is okay! I can't lose him! I—we can't lose father, too!"

"Yet stay we must!" Cypress returned. "My duty is to your father's word and to you sproutlings. We will be safe in Roostwood until he returns."

"*Returns*? How do we know he will return? We must go after him! *Now*!" Titha elbowed and kicked Cypress's armor, trying to break his embrace as she flailed toward the doors.

"Listen to me, Titha. *Titha*!" Cypress shouted, gripping her shoulders. "My heart aches for your father as well, but I assure you he can take care of himself. We *must* preserve what is left of Yythengrey and have faith in the Cedarguard to do their duty. I cannot abandon you girls—and you girls cannot abandon the Lunas! You three must step forth to lead our people to recovery in the absence of—if your father were to—" He stopped, not wanting to say too much. "Our people will *need* you, Titha. They will need you and Gilly and Beebee... rays of Moonlight in these trying hours. This is much bigger than our wants and fears, young one, and it is time to stand strong and grow up. The line of the Maes cannot be broken."

"He's right, Titha," a soft voice spoke from behind. Gilly

stepped forth out of the darkness, cradling Beebee in her arms. "We have to help our people and their families. That is most important right now."

"Father is *our* family! Why do we always do this? *Always* tucked away in the forest, ignoring the rest of the world? The Dawnfather… he burnt our home, ruined our Festival, took *our* father and we are going to sit up here and let him get away with it? *Why? Why are we not going after him?*"

"This is hard for all of us!" Gilly retorted. "None of us want this to be happening, Titha, but we cannot abandon our home. We are *Daughters of the Watcher*. We are the Maes. We must take care of our people. You want us to stop treating you like a child, right? Stop acting like one and think of everyone else right now."

"When did you start to care about any of that, Gilly? You never want to help with anything! Ever since mother died you've done nothing but think about yourself!"

"Hold your tongue," Cypress barked sharply. He leaned down onto one knee, meeting Titha eye to eye. "That was a vile thing to say. Your sister is only trying to do what's right. And so am I. Gilly is a young woman now, and she is only abiding by her duties."

"That's not good enough!" Titha shouted. "If this is what being grown up is, then I want no part of it. *Paw*!" she trumpeted down the hall, her voice booming with a gravitas not heard before.

Without hesitation her Bear-brother barreled down the hall, sliding to her side in an instant; albeit quite confused.

"What are you doing?" Cypress cried as he attempted to stand between the two. Paw lowered his head to Cypress, growling in his face. "Growl all you want, cub, but I am not moving. You will not allow a daughter of the Watcher to come to harm! Now stand down!"

Titha jumped onto her Bear-brother's side, climbing the packs she had already placed astride his broad shoulders.

"We lost our mother. I am not going to lose our father, too," she decreed, her brow unwavering.

"And you know how she died, Titha!" Cypress yelled over the commotion. "She perished defending us all from Meriduun! Your mother, Thea, sacrificed herself and saved every creature of the night from annihilation! Annihilation at the hands of our precious Duskmother! And what did your father do? He stood his ground and let her go—for it meant the safety of you three and of our people. It was what they both *knew* to be right. It *was* right. You must learn from their tale and do the same for Theole!"

"Mother would still be here had someone gone to her. So if you will not go after father, I will." Titha looked down to Paw who snorted in agreement.

Gilly ran up to her, begging her not to do anything foolish as Beebee cried, their tiny sister waving her arms for Titha to pick her up.

"If you go after father you abandon Beebee! You abandon me! All of us! You have to think of where you are *needed* most, not *what you want* the most!" Gilly cried. "You are acting like a brat! A spoiled little girl!"

Her words rattled inside Titha. Oh, how furious her sister made her; she wasn't truly ready to leave before this little outburst—but she was now. Gripping to Paw's fur, she tightened the straps on her makeshift baggage and braced for takeoff.

Paw looked back, licking the tears from Beebee's face. He turned again to Cypress, staring eye to eye with the worried old Squire with his Luna sister astride him. Titha's bottom lip quivered with both anger and sadness as she turned from her sisters, her focus now locked on the front doors of Roostwood.

"Titha, dismount!" Cypress pleaded furiously. "Dismount at once! Tell Paw to stand down! Listen to your sister! Listen to *me*—that is an order! You cannot do this! You are just a girl!"

There it was again. Yet this time it was worse. Harsher. More severe as it splintered her. Those last five words from Cypress shot through Titha like pine'needles. Her fists clenched as they did every time a Luna boy picked on her for wearing pants or collecting bugs or climbing trees. She wanted to reply with something profound, something monumental and defiant… but before she could, Cypress pleaded yet again:

"You are just a girl..."

"Yes, I am," she replied, her green eyes glowing as the words fell out of her mouth. Cypress stood silent. Titha kicked her heels into her Bear-brother's sides. Paw wound up, charging past Cypress for the doors, bursting through them with a mighty roar as Cypress yelled behind them.

"Titha, *please* don't do this! Come back this instant! *Come back*!" Cypress screamed until he was hoarse, chasing them to the edge of the steps before collapsing.

But Titha Mae did not look back. She gripped her Bear-brother's black mane tightly, riding down the enormous stretch of grand stairs—back into the chaos beneath Mount Meri.

"Just a girl," she murmured to herself as Paw leapt through the flames, clawing and dodging the straggling Reeks and Ogres obstructing his path. Otters spat water onto the flames surrounding them, extinguishing large blazes throughout the Meadow as brave Lunas fought alongside their Cedar Guards to take back their home. The chaos surrounding Titha filled her with rage, but also with a fierce determination.

"Just a girl," she said aloud to herself again, her brow lowering to the horizon. "Father never would've said that to me."

As they neared the Forest Hall at the far side of the Meadow, Titha spotted something shimmering amidst the ashes. "Stop!" she cried, Paw sliding to a halt. She jumped from his back, running over to find a large, shiny silver feather. "*Father…*" she whimpered, her voice trembling as she looked at the magnificent remnant of Theole, the Grand Silver Owl. She lifted the feather from the ground by its stem, immediately noticing its weight. "Wow," she whispered. A smile replaced her frown as she swung the long, serrated feather forward like a mighty sword—the blade reflecting diminishing flames as they danced 'round her. She turned to Paw who looked at the artifact as if it were very-much a weapon, his chestnut eyes twinkling with amazement. "We are going to find him, Paw. We're not going to stop until we do. Right?" she asked.

"*Raaaaaaugh*!" Paw roared, his head rearing up with the same foolhardy excitement.

Titha took one more look at the impressive blade. Not having a proper sheath, she placed it into her pack astride Paw and climbed back to his shoulders.

Both turned their gaze to the Forest Hall, its end culminating in the mighty Wood Gate that now stood open. Titha had never seen it ajar, let alone stepped outside its protection. She took a deep breath. "Are you sure you're ready, Paw?" She gulped as she asked.

"Grrrumph," he replied, snorting at her.

"Me? Oh, I am definitely ready. Very ready. Just wanted to be sure *you* were, is all. To be fair. To you." A gulp followed.

Paw let out a deep bear-chuckle as he took off without warning, barreling down the Forest Hall toward the Wood Gate. Titha snatched up handfuls of his fur as she held on for dear life. The young, mighty forest bear leapt over fallen tree trunks with ease, dodging splintered wood and bounding left and right. Before they knew it, they had arrived at the Wood Gate, which stood halfway open still.

Eerie tingles rushed through Titha as her eyes met such a sight for the first time. Paw began to second-guess his resolve, his posture leaning backward. Just as Titha began to do the same, a mighty wind picked up—its breath gusting ferociously as it propelled them both straight through the Wood Gate. As quickly as the gust had mustered, it sucked back into the forest, slamming the Gate behind them.

The pair's eyes squeezed shut and their hairs stood straight up as the burning light of the Sun met their bodies. Disoriented and dazed, Paw shuffled backward to the shade of the trees… and Titha Mae sat in the Day.

Paw let out a concerned grunt as he inched forward, biting the back of Titha's tunic, dragging her toward him into the shade. She rubbed his snout with one hand and placed the other above her eyes, peering into the silent distance. Shapes and colors slowly swirled into a landscape that made sense as her vision returned, the blinding light of day eventually loosening its hold over her squinting eyes.

"We should have thought about this a little harder, Paw," she sighed.

Paw looked back to the pack on his side, lifting the flap with his muzzle to shuffle through. He snorted as he grabbed a cloak with his teeth, rearing around and placing it on Titha's head.

"Did you put that in there? What would I ever do without you?" she smiled, the deep purple cloak engulfing her entire body. She wiggled into its welcomed protection, placing the large hood over her head. "This should help until we get used to the Sun. Will you be ok, Paw?" he nodded his head to her, having a bit more tolerance for Daylight than Titha (or any Luna, for that matter). Titha fiddled with the cloak 'til it was *just right*. Once it was, her eyes left the inside of its hood to meet the rest of the world.

Colors Titha Mae had never seen filled her young, sparkling green eyes. Directly outside the Wood Gate rested the Amber Fields, a barren prairie amidst a valley void of trees or any wildlife—or so it seemed at first glance.

Tall pale grass persisted as far as the eye could see, occasionally interrupted by a brown shrub or protruding craggy rock. Titha could see small rolling hills off in the distance, each covered with leafy trees of red and amber. "That must be Autumnhill!" she exclaimed, Paw looking on in bewilderment. "Father always speaks so terribly of the Barbarians that call it home." Paw scoffed. "Vikings, whatever," Titha retorted, correcting herself. "If what father says is true, the race of Man has no love for us either, fuzzbrain." She gripped the edges of her flowing purple cloak, taking a deep breath as she stepped out away from the tree line that separated all she'd ever known from everywhere she was about to be. Her eyes surveyed a landscape that might've appeared painfully boring to any other— but to her it was fascinating.

"Everything is so... *yellow,*" she decreed. "This place is nothing like home. So close, yet so far away. It's amazing, isn't it Paw?" She looked back to her Bear-brother. He had caught a rather large field beetle and was gnawing on its backside, beyond pleased with himself.

"Don't play with your food!" she exclaimed. Paw paused, slurping down the beetle before slumping over to follow in tow.

As Titha looked around, she couldn't help but feel that the Day and its lands were far from the foreboding terror her father had painted them as. Tales of blistering sunlight seemed accurate, but where were the Moglins? The bloodthirsty sabertoothed lions? The great cities of ash and stone... The *violence*? As she pranced about, brushing tall dry grass to the side, a clearing met her eye.

"Look at that dirt patch, Paw!" she exclaimed. "It goes on for a while, it must be a road!" She squealed with glee, grabbing Paw's fur and tugging him after her.

Paw galloped in front, running his nose through the dust to sniff out any danger before letting Titha continue. He stood back as his eyes widened.

"What? What is it?" Titha cried.

Paw's face twisted into a horrible grimace before – *aaaaAAACHOO*! He let out a tremendous sneeze, kicking up a billowing dust cloud around them. Titha laughed and coughed at the same time, waving her hands in attempt to clear the air.

"Thanks for that." She brushed off her satin cloak as the dust began to settle.

Paw shook his body vigorously, attempting to rid his black fur of the sandy mess. Just as the air cleared, a little brown wren landed in the middle of the dirt patch with a grub in its beak. Titha's eyes grew wide as she gasped in excitement.

"Look at this little guy!" she exclaimed, taking in every bit of the tiny bird's chestnut brown and peppered white coloring. "I have never seen a bird like you before, pretty little chirpie." The wren hopped about finishing its grub, but flew off as Titha stepped too close. "Huh," she sighed, "not like the birds back home, are you?"

She watched him fly off into the distance, spotting the continuation of the dirt path underneath the wren's wings. "That way!" she exclaimed. "We're heading that way. The road leads the same direction I saw the Dawnfather fly off in with father, right?

It was over the Wood Gate, and out into the Horizon. Yes, it's this way. I am sure of it. But which *way* is this way?"

She reached down, scrambling through her things to pull out a moondial, before noticing the harsh amber shadows on her hand.

"Ah—nevermind," she muttered, realizing her Night'tool was unlikely to work with the pattern of the Day's Sun. "I remember Father and Gilly speaking of the humans to the 'East', and Autumnhill is—That way. East it is, right?"

Paw shrugged.

"You're no help," Titha scoffed, smiling. "My heart tells me it is east, so—onward and eastward, Paw!" Titha commanded with a huge grin overtaking her face, her finger pointed mightily into the distance. Paw lowered his head in a harrumph, scooping Titha up. She slid backward onto his shoulders and off they walked into the *(hopefully)* eastward distance.

CHAPTER FOUR

Legends Old and New

The dirt road let on for hours, harsh Sunshine beating down upon cloak and fur relentlessly. Titha's fascination with this whole new world began to slip as every shrub-like tree they passed ended up as barren as the last, and every rock looked like the one before. No bright flowers. No twinkling dew. Nothing but skinny yellow grass for miles. Not another bird flew past to peak her interest. Even her curiosity, in this instance—in this place—had its limits.

As boredom wholly took hold, she looked back for the first time—and her heart sank. Longing crept into her bones. Her father's mighty mountain, Mount Meri, the most gigantic *anything* she had ever seen, now looked tiny off in the distance. The tree line surrounding her home was barely visible now. Her head whipped back around, eyes wide and weary. Paw looked up to her without breaking his slow stride.

"I'm fine," she reassured him, "we can't turn back now." Paw grunted in reply. "No, I truly don't want to." She exclaimed. "I want to find father. We *will* find father. Let's just hope this road is leading us in the right direction, or I don't know what I'll do." Paw grumbled again, his expressive tone weaving a sentence for his Luna-sister. "I know. Me too, bud. I have a feeling it does, too. Which is good, because there is a slight chance we have no idea what we're doing."

Paw stopped for the first time in hours, coming to a sudden halt as his eyes met a dark shape in the near distance.

"I see it, too," Titha said as she petted Paw's side. "What do you think it is?"

Both focused in on what appeared to be a very small wooden building, though it was hard to tell from such a ways away. Titha refused to turn back, thought, so they would have to approach it—whatever it was. Her mind began to race; was this to be the first big discovery of their journey? Sharing a glance, the two marched forward. Paw's footsteps were heavy, his shoulders high. Titha covered her eyes from the Sun as she squinted, trying to make out details as they drew closer. Her adrenaline kicked in as the wooden object became clear: it had wheels on both sideS but not on the ground, which was odd. Very odd. Some of the structure was splintered and torn apart, as if something had wrecked this… Aha! It was a kart!

"A wooden kart!" she exclaimed loud and proud. Just as she did, a pointy head popped out from within the structure. Titha and Paw gasped in unison. Paw lowered his head, his eyes locked onto… whatever was staring back at them. The creature shrieked and popped back into the overturned kart, its wooden structure shaking and creaking as the inhabitant noisily shuffled back in. Paw drew closer, Titha bringing her legs to one side preparing to dismount. She slipped her hand down into her bag and grabbed the stem of her father's silver feather. Paw briefly paused, sidestepping off the path into the tall grass as he looked back to Titha. Their eyes locked, and both nodded.

Like a lion leaping to its prey Paw pounced from the tall grass, crashing through the front of the kart and landing onto the creature. Titha jumped from his side, landing atop a barrel and brandishing her father's feather as a short'sword. Books and papers flew into the air as the small, pointy *whatever it was* squirmed in terror, squealing and kicking and pleading up a storm inside the creaking kart. It looked—and sounded—far from dangerous.

"Oh! Oh, please do not eat me!" it screamed from beneath a long nose. "I shall give you whatever you wish — just please do not eat poor old me! I am foul and bony and surely to be dreadfully sour!"

Paw, completely taken aback, looked over to Titha, whose amazement was broken by spontaneous laughter. She jumped down from the barrel into the shelter of the wooden kart, placing the silver feather at her side as she flung ragged book pages and maps from atop the mysterious stranger.

Clearing of the debris revealed a scrawny, knobby-horned yellow Goblin of about the same height as herself. "Of course you're yellow," she exclaimed. "We've seen nothing but yellow for miles. Is everything yellow outside of the forest!?" Titha had worked herself into quite a tizzy amidst the excitement.

"I… I beg your pardon?" the wrinkled old Goblin replied, combing back his stringy brown hair. "I am indeed of the yellow-skinned Crater Goblins, if that is what you're inquiring, but could *you please tell your beast to stand down*!?"

"Oh! Sorry," Titha laughed again as Paw smiled. "That's just Paw. He is my Bear-brother and a big baby, don't worry about him." Paw plumped backward onto his rump. "Who are you, though?" Titha inquired of the stranger, leaning in intently.

"A question I shan't answer until I know the same of you, young traveler," The Goblin replied, his long sharp ears perking up. He stood to his flat, leather-wrapped feet, dusting off his green shirt and pants which looked to be of lavish background—but had long since lost their sheen and edges. "By the looks of your supplies, this is your first attempt at a journey, is it not? This bodes well for me, as you are not likely to have traveled enough to know of the dreadful misconceptions concerning Craglins and our society, though—my, my, listen to me I've gone off and said entirely too much."

"You like to talk, don't you?" Titha asked as she smirked, her curiosity leading her all over the piles of books and papers.

"Too much, I am afraid. Which is how you've found me here. Stranded. *Inconvenienced*, really," the stranger replied.

"Nech," Titha barked, interrupting, "your name is Nech."

"Gracious me you are of Westlyn tongue, indeed," the Goblin smirked, laughing at her pronounciation. "That is how some pronounce it, yes, depending on their dialect. But I prefer Nech," he clarified. "Like a loch. You are familiar yes? A loch is a body of water, one specifically—"

"Yes I get it, geez you're like a crow once you get started, aren't you?"

"Indeed I am. But I must ask... how do you know my name, young one?"

"It's scribbled on most of these books and maps. I'm guessing you wrote all of these?"

"I did. You are certainly observant."

"I like new things," Titha smiled." I like to talk, too, so we should get along just fine!"

"Get along? Young lady, considering the horrid, billowing smoke and catastrophies of this morning I really should be hastily on my way to Yythengrey before there isn't a Yythengrey to commune with! I am afraid there is but no time at all for 'getting along'!"

"That's my home! Oh, what a coincidence!"

"This is the only road for miles, young one, it is hardly a coincidence," Nech replied. "But your home, you say? Are you of Lunish decent? Out here? That cannot be!" The Goblin's eyes grew wide as he grabbed Titha's hand, examining her pale indigo skin beneath her silken purple cloak. "Hohoo! But you are! Oh this is simply marvelous! Stupendous, even! In all my years… not once have I encountered a Luna in the flesh. Most wonder-mous, indeed! But child, what in Vulduun's name are you doing out here in this harshest of Sunlit Days?"

Titha cringed at the sound of The Dawnfather's true name. "*Vulduun…*" she whispered harshly. "*He* is the reason for the smoke and flames you speak of." Titha replied. "He attacked us during our Festival. He… The Dawnfather burnt my home to the ground and took my father. Paw and I aim to find him."

"My word. If Vulduun took your father he must be of some importance. But you are just a girl!" Nech replied in earnest.

"If I hear those words one more time," Titha fumed. "I am

Titha Lilly Mae. Daughter to Theole. And there is no such thing as *'just a girl'*."

"Daughter of Theole? The Watcher? Theole The Great?" The Goblin spoke, bewildered. "That must be his grand silver feather, yes?"

"It is," Titha replied sternly. She stepped closer to the stranger, removing her hood to reveal her shimmering white hair. "You must know my father, then, if you know that feather belongs to him. I didn't even know he really could turn into a big silver owl until this morning."

"All learn'ed individuals know of your father, child—er, Titha, if I may call you by your given name. As a scribe, I have weaved many grand tales into my history books and your father has played quite the role in most. The Watcher, as we scribes and scholars refer to him, daring not assume to be on a first-name basis with such a renowned individual, is *legendary*. And he has taken his owl form again—simply *fascinating*. I would imagine that has not happened for a full generation in this world, young one. A full century, at the very least. This considered, your unfamiliarity with it is not surprising. Such a treat that you have one of his mighty feathers with you! I would very much love to study it and—"

"Don't touch that!" Titha cried, leaping out to grab the stem of the long feather. "That belongs to me. It's— it is all I have of him now." As her grip tightened around the base of the feather, a great confidence began to replace her sorrow. She swiftly pulled the blade up out of the dirt at her feet. Titha's brow lowered as she raised the long, silver-bladed feather into the air, revealing its full splendor.

"Remarkable. Simply stupendous, it is. A Feather-sword. *The* Feathersword, I would say, yes." The Goblin spoke with splendor in his voice.

"Feathersword," Titha repeated, "I like it."

"It is a fitting name for such an artifact, young one," He exclaimed. "Though I am saddened by how it came to your possession, and by the rising smoke... and most gravely the abduction of your father. For my journey was to seek out his council. It began evenings ago, and as I drew nearer to your home of Yythengrey I was ransacked by passing Ogres and Reeks. Aside from these foul marauders... *eating*... my mule and donkey companions, they left my kart in shambles— and I believe they may have been looking for something. Regardless, I have been stranded in this very spot all of the past Day and Night. Come this morning, however, the Sun rose early in the most peculiar manner—Only to reveal itself as Vulduun—the Great Day Drake. His fiery terror descended swiftly upon your people, then, didn't it? Oh, how it was sudden and terrible to witness, even from afar. Though I am to assume from the extinguishing of the flames that your people have survived?"

"Mostly, yes. But The Dawnfather—*Vulduun,* I mean—he took my father and flew off in this direction. That is why we are out here. We are going to find my father. And we are going to save him." Titha looked to Paw, petting underneath his chin. He tucked his legs in, laying down inside the kart to rest.

"Gracious, I have lost myself in this tale already and have not offered a proper introduction. My name is Nechalec, or Nech for short, as you previously observed. I am a Council Scribe of the Craglins—or Crater Goblins as we are known to others—and quite a storied one if I may say so myself—though others may mumble in disagreeance." Nech looked down to his tired feet, then cleared his throat to continue. "To return to the matter at hand, however, is rather unnerving—for I had hoped to find an audience with your father concerning my most recent and worrisome discoveries. And now my fears have been confirmed as he certainly seems to have been... displaced."

"Are you a friend of my father? I know he has lots of old, and I mean *old,* friends," Titha asked as she sat down, cuddling next to Paw in the kart.

"Well I certainly am old," Nech chuckled, "but a personal friend of The Watcher? No. Heavens, I wish!"

"I figured as much," Titha retorted confidently. "Father never spoke highly of Goblins, and my older sister really hates them. Says they're all dep... dip... deplorable—that's the word.

Are you?"

"Am I what?" Nech stuttered.

"Deplorable?"

Nech stood firm at the strong words of such a young sprite. "On the whole, concerning my peoples, I happen to agree with your sister," He decreed, his words turning to much-needed laughter. "She is not wrong, young one, if that is what you ask; I am considered 'soft' for my kind. Many factors led to our meeting on the Amber Trail, my new friend, and dare I say that my unusual nature as far as Goblins are concerned is one of them, but that is a whole other barrel of grubs, young Luna. Your father, Theole, however—I have transcribed many of his valiant tales, yet have not had the honor of making his acquaintance, or any of your secretive kind for that matter. If my bewilderment moments ago was not telling enough, you are indeed the first Luna to have crossed my path. Craga knows how I would have reacted had I made it all the way to your Mount Meri!"

"Neat," Titha quipped, followed by a long and hearty yawn. She leaned back into Paw's warm, lush fur. The big bear was already fast asleep. "Why did you want to talk to my father?"

"It is a long story, child. Important, but long."

"I want to hear it," she replied, her bright eyes fixed on Nech.

"Now is hardly the time for stories!" Nech bumbled, the

severity of his situation crashing back down upon him. His guests had, however, already made themselves comfortable in a corner of the kart's makeshift structure; cuddled up and comfy.

"Feels like storytime to me," Titha replied. The wooden, rickety planks blocked out the Sun above them and made for quite the peaceful safehaven amidst the Barren Fields.

"Well, things have quieted down outside for now, I suppose," Nech responded, wearily. "Very well, though you may be familiar with some of what I recount. I will spare you the most drab of details, if I can help it. The condensed version must suffice. Yes, I believe it will. I tend to forget if I am speaking or writing where history is concerned, you understand, so if it all blends together after please forgive me. It has been so long and I tend to ramble... as is evident. *Ahem*. Where was I? Ah, yes. Your father:

Long ago, before the shaping of the mountains or the painting of the seas lived the Great Dragons...

This land was their land—all of its splendor belonging to them. The Great Dragons each wielded a stone from the dawn of time, two of which relate directly to our story—The Sunstone and the Moonstone. With their power, they created all we know today. Vulduun, though it is hard for you to imagine now I am sure, was once the kind and gracious Guardian of Light—Creator of the Day and all its thriving creatures. *The Great Day Drake*, my people called him! Some still do. His counterpart, his love, was Mother of the Night, Bringer of Peace and Darkness: Meriduun. Her watchful grace kept the nights of our world quiet and nurturing underneath the Moon, for her love of its kin—such as yourself—was fierce and unwavering. Once they were satisfied with their creation, they forfeited their ultimate power and gifted their stones to two cherished pupils—one of Night and one of Day—giving them the power to seed civilizations. Thus began the Age of Mortals as we know it. The Great Dragons watched over this world for the entire beginning of the First Eon; their beloved peoples protecting their stones and spreading far and wide… until the Night brought forth a rival."

"A rival?" Titha asked, her cloak now wrapped around her like a blanket as she tucked herself further into Paw's arms.

"Yes… *your mother,* young one. So beautiful and enchanting was Thea Celtica Mae that all of Meriduun's Lunas turned their gaze to her—especially your father, Theole. Thea's elegance was of Nature itself; as if the trees and the mountains, the waters and the wind, had birthed her outright. Slowly, all people and beasts of the night, not just Lunas, turned their admiration and devotion to Thea and her loving embrace. She was known for endless generosity, your mother. For this, and many other reaons your father became consumed by the love he and your mother shared. He desired a gift worthy of her purity, I am told. Perhaps he believed it was Thea who was to take Meriduun's place in the world, as the Elderdrakes had long been in resting since the exhausting task of creation. That much is not clear, as only your father knows what his thinking was in such a time—but by whatever reason Theole took the Moonstone from its ancestral resting place atop Mount Meri and gifted it to Thea. This enraged the Night Mother—your ancestors, too, I would imagine —and understandably so, as they had entrusted your father with the Moonstone's unrivaled power and unimaginably important protection. To feel this trust broken, even if not purposefully so by Theole, drove Meriduun out of her rest. All writings tell that her anger grew tenfold once she beheld Thea's beauty as well; as Meriduun's glistening purple scales had allured all prior to Thea's gaze. Fraught with jealousy and the sting of betrayal, Meriduun lashed out at Thea, taking back the Moonstone; regaining a terrible power the Great Dragons had forfeited after the task of creation."

"So this is all my father's fault?" Titha asked, very confused. She was familiar with Meriduun and the creation of their world, Gaela, but not much beyond that. Was this because of her father's mistake? Was it even a mistake? Or was it her mother? Perhaps the very shifting of admiration from Meriduun to Thea that Nech mentioned is why few spoke of Meriduun in these times. Titha placed a very tired finger on her chin. "I don't really understand. This is the first time I've heard the rest of the story, I think."

"I do not find that terribly surprising, my child," Nech responded gently. "It is no parent's wish for their child to find them fallible."

"Fallible?"

"It means that one is capable of making mistakes, Titha Mae."

"Well then we are all fa-lli-ble, aren't we?"

"Absolutely," Nech replied, sureheartedly. "No one is perfect, not even our creators."

"Then who are we to judge my father's mistake? Who are the Elder Dragons to do so, either? They clearly made mistakes, too, and we still give the Dawnfather his festival every year! Though I doubt we ever will again— "

"—You may want to hear the rest of the tale," Nech interjected.

"There's more?"

"Oh yes, child. Much more. And it is of grave consequence."

"Okay then, wait," Titha questioned. "What did Meriduun do with it? My father's—or our—or her— Moonstone?" Her hands gripped her cloak in both suspense and frustration as the Sun began to set outside.

"Asking the right questions, you are," Nech smiled, "a true

sign of intelligence and not curiosity for curiosity's sake. Though I am afraid the answer is not a pleasant one, as Meriduun had become blinded—no, *enraged*—by jealousy and heartache."

"Did she turn on us?" Titha asked.

"She was to destroy *everything*, child. For the Moonstone and its counterpart, the Sunstone, hold the power of time and existence itself. No such artifact had ever been wielded by a hateful dragon before, you understand. For Dragons, like all the rest of us, are not born inherently good or bad. But oh—oh—what dreadful power was unlocked by such a coupling of grief and magick... If she, Meriduun, could not have the devotion of her beloved night children—the very ones she breathed life into—then no one would, especially Thea. Blinded by jealousy, Meriduun lashed out at the lands she once held so dear and unleashed a dreadful power onto Ythengrey. But there was great opposition!"

"She fought back!" Titha grinned wide.

"Indeed she did! Your mother, why not only was she fair and giving, but brave and valiant, as well. She raised an Army of the Night to end Meriduun's jealous revenge—their goal being to reclaim the Moonstone. Her warriors, your mother's companions, are known in legend as *Celtica's Champions*!"

"Celtica... Her middle name."

"Yes, yes, a name no other has been given before or since. To many, Thea was—and is—Celtica, Daughter of Gaela. And champions those who fought alongside her under such a hallowed named were, for they stopped Meriduun from wiping Yythengrey and all the Duskridge from the map. Your father stood firm to protect your people as the Duskmother's onslaught continued, but they were unable to prevent all her wrath. Nothing but Vulduun could do that. By the time Celtica's Champions could best her, The Night Mother had scorched half of the forest with the burning-cold of the mighty orb, creating the very fields of barren-not we sit in now. Vulduun fell into deep grief and denial, unable to cope with what his love had become. Vulduun could not bare to end her himself… No, he could never do such a thing. And so he withdrew from the Daylight, leaving his kin to discord and abandonment, and the lands to further decay. In his absence, Meriduun's power grew once more, and she would not be satiated. Fearing the worst in the wake of Meriduun's madness and Vulduun's abandonment, the great peoples of this world raised their own armies… and the *Ever-war* began. Lunas, Goblins, Gnomes, Ogres, Giants, Beasts, Reeks, and Men alike all fought to end Meriduun's tragedy.

In the end, it was your mother, brave Thea and Celtica's Champions, who in final conflict bested the Night Mother with her spear and leafshield, but the undeniable power of the Moonstone claimed both their minds and bodies in conflict—leaving their souls in ruin as they continued to tear at one another. Wrought with grief over what he had caused through the gifting of the

Moonstone—and what horror played out before his eyes— Theole took his beloved's spear and drove it into the Moonstone, ending its outbursts and merging the two objects—both spear and stone—as one. Such a clash created the Ozark Staff in a mighty flash of light and loss… It is said, my child, that there was no other way. Neither, nor Meriduun or Thea, by this time, would listen to reason… an in their struggle neither survived the utter destruction such a release of power caused. Neither was ever seen again… I cannot imagine the grief your father must live with, Titha Mae. Theole has kept that staff by his side ever since, I am told, never to let his grave mistake cost another life. Thus, he became The Watcher, as we call him—an ever-vigilant protector of the Night."

Nech paused, shaking his head. "Of course, all of this is legend now and has been passed through the ears and mouths of many races to reach my pen and parchment—but alas, it is all true. Every last word, for its stories are matched in the lores of each culture's ancestors and in the scars of our lands."

He took a deep breath—the impact of this grand tale and its events weighing heavily on him. "This may all sound like ancient history to you child, but the Ever-war has long unfolded, and even continues as we speak. What seems to be mere years in the mists of your forests roll on as a lifetime in the lands outside your tree-halls. Meriduun's tragedy and the loss of your mother is now a century's past for us true mortals. For one hundred years all had thought Vulduun withdrawn forever… yet this calamitous War has raged on in secret. *Twisted* the Dawnfather has become… The agony of his loss and utter despair driving him to madness. I have seen the signs of this… costly, dreadful casualties of his growing heart-ache… his growing malcontent. Slowly his foul whispers have taken over the day, estranging the vile creatures of Daylight to his cause. It all seems to match up perfectly with every text concerning Meriduun's descent into madness… But now, just as then, some resist. Vulduun's planned return is what I had hoped to reveal to your father. But we now know that I was all too slow—and far too late."

Nech waited for Titha's response, but nothing came. He looked over to find her fast asleep, curled up with her Bear-brother in a deep, peaceful slumber. Nech smiled. "Fascinating," he quipped to himself, reaching over to cover her up with another cloak. "They *are* day sleepers, after all." The old Goblin looked around the wreckage of his kart; his long, pointed nose swaying about every which way as he searched piles of his damaged belongings. A tattered knapsack revealed itself from beneath another pile of books. From it Nech pulled his own brown robes, arranging them into a makeshift bed on the other side of their dwelling. His finger shot into the air as an idea hit his tired brain, one he was quite thankful for. Pushing barrels together to guard the entrance, the old scribe created them refuge, and for the first time that Day breathed a sigh of relief. "Much better," he thought as he looked over to his new counterparts, smiling once more before tucking his old bones in for a desperately-needed mid-morning nap.

CHAPTER FIVE

Companions in Trust

Outside, the Sun hung high over a much more peaceful horizon. Its heat overtook the lands as the world around the wooden kart had awoken for the afternoon. Woolly Rhinos herded next to Nech's overturned things, grazing on the tall wheat grasses that filled the Fields. Tiny Speckled Wrens, just like the one Titha had spotted, roosted on the Rhino's horns awaiting the bugs that would periodically flee from the hairy beast's munching. Such serenity did not last for long, however, as the ground began to quake with feverous ferocity—its strength gaining like the beat of impending heavy footsteps. The wrens fled their hosts as each rhino turned their gaze westward, anticipating the cause of such thundering. A great swell of ash overtook the lands outside

Yythengrey as screaming hordes of charred Ogres and Reeks swarmed outward from the battered Wood Gate. The Cedar Guard charged swiftly behind them, striking down any straggling attackers they could. Many Ogres fell, but the reptilian legs of the twisted Reeks were too fast for even the swiftest of Lunas. Dust filled the Amber Fields as soldiers were lost on both sides in their race to the East; spears, arrows and blades flying every-which-way.

Paw shot to his feet as the inside of Nech's kart began to rumble, flinging Titha onto a pile of books.

"What!? I didn't do it!" she cried out in confusion. Snapping to her senses, Titha looked up at her Bear-brother, recognizing his visible concern as the cart shook around them. Paw roared and grunted, pushing her further into the pile of books before running outside. Planks of wood began to fall inward, one of them knocking a still-snoozing Nech square on the head. He snorted painfully, shooting up in a panic. He wiped his eyes and looked around as their world quaked.

"What is happening? What time is it?" he shouted, his kart creaking and thrashing. He looked up through its cracked topside. "Afternoon! Thank Craga," he sighed heavily, grabbing his chest. "We only slept but a few hours young Luna, but I fear we must be on the move with great haste!" The rumbling intensified as Nech lost his footing. "Stampede?" he cried, running outside to check.

He spotted Paw crouched down and staring westward. Before him, a great cloud of dust and noise rushed their way.

Slowly, Nech began to make out soldiers in the distance. Hundreds of them. "My word! Reeks! More bandit Reeks! Ogres, even!" he exclaimed. "And are… are those the Cedarguard? They must be! Oh my, they are just as described—would you *look* at that shimmering silver armor? Splendid! Simply splendi—"

Paw roared at Nech, scraping his claws into the dirt.

"Right, right! We must hide, Paw. Those horrid creatures will kill us all! But the Lunas, ah! The Cedar Guard will protect us, yes?"

Paw shook his head *no* vigorously, nudging Nech back into the kart and following him inside. Nech scrambled over the debris, looking back to Titha whose head peered out of a pile of scriptures and maps in the corner.

"Titha! The Cedar Guard is headed this way, chasing Reeks and all sorts of foul invaders from your homeland! And no doubt they will be looking for you—we must go to them!"

"*No*!" she shouted in dismay, signaling for him to come fully inside their shelter. "They will take me back and lock me up in my father's halls, we must hide!"

"That is foolish youth talking, Titha! Surely they will help the daughter of The Watcher!"

"You don't understand, Nech! If they find me here outside

of our forest they will bring me back and lock me up and *no one* will look for my father! Lunas do not go far from our flowers, *ever*! We must hide until the Sun fully rises and they retreat to the forest. *Please*, Nech. You have to help me!"

"That is preposterous, child!" Nech shouted. His heart, however, told him otherwise. The old Goblin's pale brown eyes met with Titha's, and at that instant he could almost feel their destinies bond. He flung his brown overcloak from his shoulders. "Here!" he blurted, "hide beneath this and the books! You too, Paw. I shall provide a distraction!" He piled maps, scriptures, and all manner of papers on top of Titha and Paw, creating a mound enormous enough to cover the big bear and his little Luna sister.

The battle outside raged much closer now, and Nech's hands begin to quiver as he returned to the front of the kart. Just as he stepped outside—*THWIP*— a spear flew straight over his head. "*Bwah*!" he shouted, ducking and grabbing his pointy ears. The Reek that such a speedy spear had missed charged directly at Nech from the Fields. The old Goblin's eyes widened as he tripped backward, bumbling up against the outer wall of the quaking kart. He couldn't bare the horrid thoughts welling within him, and clenched his eyes shut as his entire body recoiled in fear. This was it, he thought. The nasty, gurgling maw of the Reek careened open as it poised to strike Nech full speed, then—*THWACK*—the gangly lizard's head flew forward clean off its neck, splattering against the western wheel of the kart. Its now-headless body slammed to the ground, sliding directly up to Nech's feet as he peeped through his fingers. As the dust cleared, the creature's slayer stepped forth, his silver armor shimmering brilliantly. A long, dramatic purple sash flapped in the wind behind the portly figure as he flipped his bloody sword like a throwing knife, sticking it blade-first into the ground before him.

"Who are you, Goblin?" the stout Luna barked from beneath a masked, leaf-patterned helmet. "*Speak*!"

Nech fumbled, removing his hands to reveal eyes as wide as saucers, his knees knocking together. Finally finding the words amidst his mumbling, he spoke up. "I am Nechalec of Cragoa, Council Scribe and Ambassador to my people. A Crater Goblin, if that term reaches you in a more familiar manner, mighty one."

The soldier raised his face'mask, revealing rosy cheeks and a glorious, curly white moustache. "Your name would have sufficed, Goblin," the proud soldier retorted, no longer muffled by his helmet's shield but by his facial hair instead.

Titha squirmed inside the kart beneath her pile of books as tears welled in her eyes. She knew that voice anywhere.

"I am Cypress, Commander of the Cedar Guard and Squire of Our Lord and Watcher, Theole The Grand," the soldier replied, adjusting the silken purple sash around his torso's silver armor. "These putrid lizardmen invaded our home alongside Ogres and... *other foul beasts* such as yourself."

"Oh, heavens please!" Nech snorted. "I wtinessed those who attacked your mighty home. I am no green-skinned Swamp Goblin, sir!" he cried. "Your quarrel, if it be with any Goblins, is with the *Moglins*. I am a *Craglin* of the Craglands. Our home lies over the Fells to the East and—"

"—Enough," Cypress commanded. "You are not of the same kind. I am no fool." He stopped, straightening his armor and regaining his regal composure. "I would not step foot in these putrid, barren lands if it were not for—Nevermind that."

"Vulduun you mean, certainly," Nech quipped, trying desperately to keep up the distraction.

Cypress hesitated, caught off guard. "Yes," he replied, "how do you know this, goblin?"

"I witnessed the attack from afar this past dawn, as I was on my way to seek the council of your master, The Watcher. My travels were cut short as your assailants, well, assailed me as well. They had their devilish way with my belongings, ate my steeds, and I have been stranded here since."

"I see. Even more misfortune befalls you, then, as the council you seek is now impossible. The Watcher has been... *taken* by our once great Dawnfather. He has fled to the East to his home beyond the horizon."

"Hah! East," Titha chirped from within her hiding spot. "I

knew it!"

Cypress's ears perked up. "His daughter, Titha Mae, is also missing," he growled, eyeing the kart. "She is a small Luna sproutling of fair indigo skin and the most luminous bright green eyes." Cypress paused, fighting his emotional responses as he thought of dear Titha Mae. Regaining his composure once more, he continued. "She fled, foolishly, after her father with her Bear-brother. He would be but a forest black bear to your eyes. Titha is a brave but reckless little Luna who has no business outside of our walls. She is just a small girl. Their tracks led outside the Wood Gate, but their trail was trampled by Vulduun's vagrants. So if you have seen either of the younglings I describe I would have you tell me."

For a brief, and most inopportune moment, all fell silent.

"Speak, Goblin! I haven't got all Day," Cypress scoffed impatiently.

"No I have not, Commander," Nech replied without hesitation, his back still against the kart. "I have been stranded here gathering what remains of my belongings and awaiting assistance. Can you grant it?"

"I cannot," Cypress decreed, also without hesitating. "My business is with my people. I must be off before the Sun's rays overtake my guard. If you see either The Watcher's daughter or her bear, you are to travel to Yythengrey to find me atop Mount

Meri immediately. Understood, goblin?"

"Positively, Commander," Nech spoke, bowing before Cypress. "Though, if I may ask—"

Nech's words were cut short as without warning a lone Reek soldier burst forth from behind the kart, leaping for Cypress and taking him by surprise. Cypress wailed, the nasty reptile biting and slashing at his resilient armor. Before long the mighty Luna commander found himself pinned to the ground. Nech jumped, staring into the fray unable to break from frozen astonishment.

"Grab my sword, you imp!" Cypress shouted as he punched the snarling Reek square across its narrow jaws. Nech looked over to Cypress's sword, its blade still shoved into the earth. Grabbing its hilt, the old Goblin's yellow hide shook as he pulled with all his strength, releasing the blade from the ground. Clumsily wielding the large weapon, Nech fumbled toward the wrestling combatants as they tumbled on the ground. Cypress was still pinned, his hands alternating between choking the Reek and keeping its jagged teeth from his own throat.

"Now!" Cypress shouted. A great energy shot through Nech's body, his arms rushing forth like waves behind the blade. The sword pierced the reptile's abdomen as it let out a gruesome cry, falling over to the side of Cypress.

"Thank you... *Scribe,*" Cypress smirked, his girth still fully planted on the ground. Beside him the Reek still wriggled, its maw foaming as it began to cackle. Cypress, disgusted, rose to retrieve his sword from Nech's grip. He turned, raising its thick blade over the reptile's head. The Reek's laughing intensified.

"You cannot stop him," the foul lizard gurgled, blood mixing with his saliva. "The Great Day Drake will not stop until every remnant of the night is wiped from this world. He will see you all *burn*." The Sun rose directly above them, glaring within the Reek's eyes. "And the humans are next."

Cypress snapped, dropping his sword and choking the Reek with his bare hands. "I would remove your head from your shoulders as I did your comrade, reptile, if it were not to free you from your agony. For now, use what putrid breath remains in your lungs and tell me: What could your 'master' *possibly* hold against his humans, his *Men of the Day*? They are his alone. They are *no* children of the Night and have no place in this quarrel."

The Reek's twisted laughter intensified, which in turn tightened Cypress's enraged, strangling grip. A painful, screaming gurgle escaped the lizard's maw as he fought Cypress's hold. Able to take no more, the Reek began to murmur sounds in a plea to end his anguish.

"What did you say, snake?" Cypress shouted, loosening his grasp. "Speak clearly and I will make your death swift!"

"The Sun—*ack*—The Sunstone—*cough*—Master needs the

Sun… stone…"

Before Cypress could inquire further, life left the creature's eyes. He released his grip, calmly returning to his feet. "Sunstone…" Cypress thought to himself, his brow heavy with concern as his eyes moved Eastward.

"We must warn the humans!" Nech shouted, interrupting the momentary calm.

"I will do no such thing," Cypress replied, his voice full of vicious hatred. "I owe the world of Men *nothing*."

"You cannot mean that!" Nech pleaded, "You will return to your forest and watch innocent people perish beneath the flames of the twisted Dragon just as your own did? Do the old treaties mean nothing to you?"

"Hold your tongue, Scribe!" Cypress barked. "Those treaties failed long ago! Do you see any Vikingmen slain on this battlefield? Do your eyes behold any Houndsmen coming to your aid? I thought not!" he barked furiously. "No aid came from *Men* as our forests splintered and burned before us this past night! *Men murdered* within our woods and exploit our precious nature… *Men* butcher our beast brethren and throw their carcasses upon the floor to be enjoyed in front of a *fire*. Those barbaric Daywalkers, even now, as the Sun rolls on with smoke still rising from our halls, send no messenger to answer our smoldering homeland. I will return to *my* people and I will keep *them* safe. The humans will suffer their own fate."

Cypress slammed his sword into its sheath, turning his back to Nech before giving him a chance to reply. "Cedarguard!" Cypress shouted. "To The Wood Gate and out of this wretched Sunlight!" He marched away, his men gathering along the path that led back home. As the battered Lunas retreated, Cypress yelled to Nech without turning back. "I will look for your word concerning the daughter of Theole, Scribe, and her safe return. If you can bring her back to me, you will be greatly rewarded."

Nech stood still as the Sun rose over a marching mass of shimmering silver armor. Even as a Goblin accustomed to his own kind's harshness, he could not shake the cold, abrasive tone of Cypress's words. He returned to the inside of the kart, his long nose pointed to the ground. The world was silent again. Titha, already half-removed from her mound of papers, shoved a few remaining tomes from atop herself and walked over to an obviously weary Nech.

"Lunas keep to themselves," she offered up, breaking the silence. "My people want nothing to do with the outside world. They fear it. Cypress… he is my family, but he is worse than my father ever was. He *hates* the outside world—especially the Vikingmen. I told you he would not help us." She stepped back, weary of what was to happen next after Cypress' departing words.

"It is much worse than all that I am afraid, my dear Luna,"

Nech replied, grimly, "for I cannot get what that ghoulish Reek said out of my head. We must warn Autumnhill at once, for doom is certainly upon them!"

"You're not going to take me back to Yythen-grey?" Titha smiled.

"Of course not, dear child. While Cypress may care deeply for your safety, his heart is heavy with hatred. Your heart is heavy too, Titha Mae. But with love for your father. And I could never stand in the way of such a thing. I do not believe any reward is worth that."

Titha burst into happiness as she ran to Nech, wrapping her arms around him. Nech froze, not accustomed to such gestures. After a moment, he relaxed into a glowing smile, and embraced sweet Titha Mae.

"Come, child," he commanded as he stepped back. "Fate has led you from your own halls and out into the world! We must warn the Men; The Vikings of Autumnhill must be made 'ware of Vulduun's impending treachery!"

Paw burst forth from his pile of books with a determined smirk on his face. Titha walked over to help him from under the mess as she chuckled with glee.

Nech smiled, placing his hands on Titha's shoulders. "This task falls to us alone it would seem, young one. It is no small feat nor mere jaunt that I speak of."

"I will do anything to save my father," She yelped without hesitation, "and you're coming with me!"

Nech laughed, taken again with her spirit. "I have traveled this far," He thought. "It would be a shame to give up now, would it not?"

Titha bounced and skipped at the thought of an adventure, thinking only of the excitement—too naïve to fear what else may lie ahead.

"Wait!" She exclaimed. "If Vulduun is to attack Autumnhill, does that mean he will have my father there with him?" Titha inquired as if a light had switched on inside her head.

"I would not hope for such, young one," Nech replied solemnly. "If I were to venture a guess, his advance on the Vikings has no doubt been slowed by the *imprisonment* of your father. Theole is too important for Vulduun to risk losing him in a battle with Men," he said as he stacked a pile of books outside the entryway. "Hand me those red books behind you, my dear, would you?" Titha complied, helping Nech gather his belongings as they stacked books outside the kart and organized papers into stacks, talking along the way. "There is no doubt that he travels to his horizon now with Theole, imprisoning him there and resting until the next Dawn. It is only then that he may rise again! Several theories as to why Vulduun may require your father *alive* spring to mind though, my child, so perhaps that may give you peace for the moment."

Titha exhaled. Anything of the sort hadn't crossed her mind, but hearing it aloud did truly help.

Yet each theory involves the Luna's precious and guarded Moonstone... Let me see..." As they sorted through the debris, Nech became more and more manic; as if he were looking for something he still could not find. His eyes scattered and scoured his belongings. "No–" he muttered to himself as he began to fling the few remaining scriptures. "No, this cannot be!" Nech's hands began to rip up papers as he tore them from the dirt, his arms flailing with anger. Titha, shocked, ran to him from outside the kart.

"What is it?" She asked gently.

"Oh, how ghastly! It appears I was right and have not misjudged the ransacking of my kart as a mere coincidence—Those Reeks meant to find me here on their way—and I believe they found what they were looking for—And took it! By Craga's breath, this is most disheartening, indeed. Their pillaging seems to have left me without my tome concerning the Stones and the Crown—The Crown of Elk Kings!

"The Elk Kings? I know of them! They were in one of my favorite bedtime songs when I was but a seedling! I'm not sure what a tome is, though," Titha questioned sincerely.

"It is a fancy word for a book, child. A very large, very

important book. Oh this is much worse than I feared..." he cried. "Did Vulduun escape with your father *and* his Moonstone, child? *Did he*?"

"Yes," Titha frowned. "He broke my father's staff and took the stone along with him."

"By Craga..." Nech collapsed to his tired knees. "It now seems as if Vulduun is after *both* orbs *and the Crown*… There will be no stopping him if he acquires all three. No, no this cannot happen! It *shall* not happen! To Autumn-hill! We must leave at once! Leave whatever we have not organized. Paw, my new furry friend, would you be so kind as to flip my tattered kart back onto its wheels? Quickly? Post-haste?"

Paw looked to Nech, then back to Titha, who hesitated—but only for a moment.

"Do it," she pipped, Paw nodding in compliance.

The threesome exited the kart as Paw reared back, lunging forth and lodging his head beneath the kart—flipping it over in an instant. Nech cheered as he patted Paw's side, thanking him before immediately retrieving his papers, scrolls, books, and maps from the piles they'd made. He reached over to Titha, motioning to the now-apparent, mostly-intact seat at the front of the kart. Paw, catching on, lifted Titha by her collar up into the seat, plopping her atop its bench. Nech finished placing the remainder of his largest tomes within the back, then climbed up behind Titha into the driver's seat.

"Would you also be so kind as to use your impressive musculature to pull my humble kart, Sir Paw?" Nech quipped.

Paw frumped and groaned, fully accustomed to Titha's own sweet talking when she wanted something from him. Titha stared down at him intently without saying a word. The big bear rolled his eyes, stomping his feet as he stepped in front of the kart. Nech clapped his hands in excitement, reaching down quickly to retrieve a harness.

"I do believe this was made solely for mules, but beggars cannot be choosers now can we?" He laughed nervously, tossing the front ropes of the harness over Paw. After fastening all needed straps to hinges on the kart, Nech patted Paw's rump and looked out into the East. "To Autumnhill, Bear-brother!" he shouted triumphantly. "We ride forth as companions—for we have a Dragon to best!" He turned to Titha, who sat excited at his side. For the first time Nech truly took note of her youth, both envying her naevity and immediately feeling responsible; wishing wholeheartedly to assist her if he could. "Many forces will move to aid Vulduun during the daylight, Titha Mae" he spoke, his tone serious yet still excitable. "Which gives us many enemies. The Ever-war is far grander than what has transpired here and in your forest home. But we must not speak of it openly in the Barren Fields, as your people call them, for we are at the mercy of Daylight and all its kin. I am grateful that you found me and that I may have earned a piece of your trust—but do not give it freely to others. Too much is at risk now. Does this make sense?"

"Of course," Titha replied.

"Trust is like glass, my child," Nech told her. "Well worth the effort for its beauty, but forever fragile."

"You're just full of wisdom, aren't you?" Titha chirped.

"I believe I am." He chuckled. "Wisdom aside, I will try to explain more of the facts to you when I can, I promise. But for now we must raise our hoods and travel discreetly forward. No matter what happens, dearest Luna, stay close to me, and do not speak to anyone." Nech lowered his head for a moment as his own memories feverishly gripped his mind. "There are many selfish beings in this world, and once they glimpse the spark of your fierce determination they will all covet a piece of it; a role such a magnificent tale, if you will. Nothing more, though, which is why you must always be on your guard. These are the worst of people, Titha Mae, and we mustn't indulge them—for they work only for themselves and not for friendship."

Titha nodded. She liked Nech already, but his candid nature–and the fact that he talked to her like a person and not *just a girl*, was deeply appreciated. "Glass or no glass, I'm pretty sure I trust you," she said aloud, smiling.

Nech's demeanor instantly improved. "And I you. I know

that we have only met this day—but I care deeply for this world, its fascinating people and absolutely stirring history—and I do not wish to see it end. I see this same passion in you, Titha Mae. In this and all else I believe we shall be good friends."

The old Goblin smiled once more to his new companion, and off they rolled deeper into the Amber Fields toward the greatest of Men's settlements.

CHAPTER SIX
Of Truth and Men

"I am sorry, girls," Cypress muttered from beneath his frazzled moustache. His Bear-brother, Arbor, lumbered behind him, the old beast's scraggly gray hair singed with ash and blood. Cypress hastily removed his silver helmet, flinging it to the ground before thrusting the doors of Roostwood shut. Two small gasps met his ears, and he sighed—looking up to find Gilly sitting in her father's throne—clutching Beebee to her chest. Arbor nudged his lifelong friend with his nose, but Cypress could not bring his eyes from the floor… For there he stood as they all had the night before, but now *two* Maes short.

"We vanquished what remained of the foul invaders," He finally spoke, choking on his words. "We chased them beyond our borders and struck them down. I led the Cedarguard outside our own trees, into their unknown, yet still nothing." With these words Cypress sank to the floor, defeated. "I have failed," he whispered pointedly, stewing in strife.

"You have not failed, Cypress," Gilly returned, her voice unwavering and strangely mature. "You had no choice but to make us all safe. You led many brave Lunas to victory, going beyond our wood halls and the Wood Gate—something no others dare! I cannot imagine going beyond our world, even for this. You are *valiant*, Cypress. You are brave and you saved our people!"

"You will make a fine Watchress someday, Master Gillian," Cypress replied, regaining some resolve, "but what you say is untrue. I vowed to protect you girls with my dying breath, but cannot do so if one of you is beyond my grasp. I am sorry I left you two behind, even if briefly… Like a fool, I thought I could bring your sister back—but she is gone. Your father can take care of himself, but Titha is *just a girl*. She knows nothing of the evils that lie outside our tree halls."

"None of us do!" Gilly shouted, her emotions bubbling over as she thought of her sister.

"Let me finish," Cypress retorted. "Your father and I did our best to keep you girls from harm, and your mother, but the Ever-war that claimed her life and half of our beloved forest was not ours to best." His words grew heavier as he sat down beside the girls, a strange gleam in his eye. "I have traveled to the edges of our lands and beyond. This was not a Luna's first time outside our walls, Master Gillian. The Ever-war required much of us all, and we each brought our own histories to it. Theole… your father and I fought many great battles as young Lunas, before the time of The Watcher." Arbor lumbered to Cypress's side, all too familiar with the tale that was unfolding. Cypress scratched underneath Arbor's chin, smiling into his old friend's eyes as he continued. "You girls never knew your father's Bear-brother, or my first. Boldin and Aldin they were called, and they were the finest, fiercest forest-kin to ever walk these lands. They were brothers, much like your father and I in spirit. Many battles led the four of us beyond our borders, but from each we would return proud and victorious. Until the first *fires*. The Men that lived in the hills outside our tree halls began burning and cutting our precious timbers to build their own halls. They hacked and slashed and singed countless living trees, only to build homes that housed horrors beyond your imaginations. We could not allow this, we *did not* allow this; and so your father and I rode out on the mighty backs of Boldin and Aldin to meet these wretched men head on. The Vikingmen were… large, cunning—unwavering. They were an enemy unlike wolves or wyrms or anything we had bested here in our wilds. Their enormous axes brought down Lunas just as they brought down trees, and as your father and I became overwhelmed, our Bear-brothers became enraged. Boldin defeated hundreds of Vikings in defense of your father… before they struck him down. Aldin lashed out at the sight of his fallen brother, and met the same fate. Though I miss them dearly, this is not what seals the evil in the hearts of Men. All wars have casualties. It is what they did *after* our Bear-brothers had fallen. It is what was *left* of them that I will *never* forget. And I will *never* forgive."

Cypress looked back to Arbor. He could still see his face as a cub; the tiny ball of fur he reared in the absence of Aldin, the dear beast they were both robbed of. His mind began to race and he turned in haste, looking away from Arbor as the memories flashed before his eyes. "You know and love Arbor as I do. He is our family, as are all Bear-brothers. But you never knew his ancestors, and you never will... For the skin of his father and his father's brother now *decorate the halls of Men*. Hung on walls like trophies, and flung over floors like doormats to be walked upon. I have seen their evil first hand, girls, and when Vulduun burns their cities to the ground *I will sleep peacefully again*."

Gilly held Beebee tightly as she shuttered at the horrors of this tale, now in the presence of a Cypress she had not witnessed before. Her young mind still struggled to wrap itself around the images such a story conjured. How could any living thing be so cruel? So vile? Hanging dead bears on a wall like some sort of lifeless tapestry? Burning sacred trees? Murdering her forest-kin for sport? Her thoughts then turned to Titha and Paw. Was her sister really barreling ignorantly into such a vile world? Every disagreement she had ever had with her younger sibling vanished in an instant as her mind was taken over by a solitary wish: that Titha and Paw would return home safely and unharmed by the treacherous world outside their own.

Back across the Barren Fields, evening was upon Autumnhill. The end of Mid-Day brought the Sun's strongest rays to its terrain, their unshielded heat soaking into the enormous stone wall that protected the mighty city. Bouldergate, it was called. The Houndsmen, comprised of the fiercest of Vikingmen, stood guard; each a muscled man or woman of more grizzled stature than the last. Nothing got through Bouldergate, least while the Houndsmen stood at its walls. Their heavy brows held oversized helmets in place—each adorned with the bones, horns, or fur-lined scalps of a different beast. Their shields, however, were all identical: blood red with a white dragon skull painted face-forward, as if to stare directly into the hearts of their enemies. A smaller, shrill Viking lad atop the gate's highest stone tower lowered his drake-clad shield, raising a curled goat-horn in its stead. From it rang a loud trumpeting, signaling the rest of the Houndsmen below that something of note was fast approaching.

Over the flat horizon rolled a rickety kart, steered by two small hooded monks of brown and purple. The monks and their ride were pulled in a most unusual fashion; a similarly-cloaked beast with enormous paws dredging forth through swirling dust. The runt Viking atop the watchtower signaled again, his curved horn releasing a shrill alarm. Each Houndsmen below him stood to attention, their massive shields locking forward in tandem. Slowly a grumbling chatter built amongst them, each guard alight with curiosity over the approaching strangers. An unusually well-groomed Viking emerged from the ranks, his beard much shorter and tighter than the others.

"Stodva!" he cried out, his chiseled jaw letting forth this solitary word with both grace and force. "Who approaches Bouldergate unannounced? Show face, travelers!" The approaching monks looked to one another as their kart slowed to a halt.

"We come with scrolls, tomes, and maps for your Jarl, guardsmen. We mean no harm—as is made obvious by our exposed cargo."

"Nothing is obvious from beneath a cloak, stranger," the handsome Viking replied. "Remove your hoods and then we talk."

He squinted his gleaming brown eyes, staring directly at their shrouded faces.

"As monks, you know well our sanctity does not allow us to do such a thing, guardsmen. Please, let us be on with the important papers your Jarl has requested. You do not want to be personally responsible for their delay, do you? If you will excuse us, we await an audience with your mighty Jarl Angvar," the brown-robed monk replied. His small violet-robed companion sat silent.

"My Jarl made no mention of papers or maps today, monk. But you will see him none the less. *Men, Hondla*!"

With these words, each of the Vikingmen whisped their shields onto their back, storming down and out of the Bouldergate to immediately surround the kart. A deep growl came from the cloaked beast, his claws digging deep into the dry earth. The handsome guard removed his helmet, brushing back the long auburn hair from his lightly-freckled face. "Tie up these 'monks' and their beast, search their kart, then bring it to Skaldhall along with them. We will see what Jarl Angvar makes of their claim."

"Do not fight them," the small purple-cloaked monk whispered to the beast. "Let them take us in, okay?"

The beast grumbled in compliance, dropping over onto his side like an upset toddler. The guards looked at each other, confused but immensely relieved. They tied up the enormous cloaked beast, binding his paws before doing the same to the two hooded monks. As the knots 'round their hands were finished Bouldergate slowly lumbered open.

Within its walls stood the First Refuge of Men in Westlyn. Humans and strange animals walked along dirt roads that led from one stone structure to the next. Their buildings and homes were laced with intricate wood carvings, each unique and detailed as if to tell a story. Most structures stood adorned with carved stone statues made to resemble boars, wolves, and other intimidating beasts of the wild.

The Houndsmen dragged their three bound captives down the wide dirt road bringing them straight from Bouldergate's stone doors to the distant front steps of *Skaldhall,* a grand and massive hall the likes of which Man had never built before it. It stood like a mountain, casting a shadow over the rolling hills of Autumnhill and its citizens, with an enormous spire tower protruding from the south side up into the clouds. Each Viking stopped to stare at the passing captives being escorted by their guardian warriors. They were accustomed to seeing people bound and dragged through their streets, but something about these hooded strangers had their attention.

The showy transport of said captives came to a halt at the foot of Skaldhall's gigantic front steps. The grand, tall front gate opened wide—its yellow brazen doors creaking and howling.

With this a roar of cheering, hollering, and strange calls erupted from the people of Autumnhill. The two hooded monks looked on in wonder as their eyes beheld who they could only assume was this people's leader, Jarl Angvar, stepping forth from Skaldhall's grand halls. His round, thick face was covered by a glorious red beard beneath two enormous brows of the same color, their fiery glow hiding deep-set eyes beneath them. His helmet was gold and bronze and grand like a crown of dragon's horns; his kingly attire made of the finest warm-colored wools and furs, topped with brass-scaled armor fashioned like red dragonhide. To his side came Sigrid, Autumnhill's Shieldmaiden. She was Angvar's partner and equal of all in life and stood as such beside him on the towering stone steps; her braided golden hair shining like a beacon in the harsh Sunlight. Her face was also round and tough like his, yet welcoming and beautiful at the same time. Two small but striking ice-blue eyes shone as bright as her hair above rosy cheeks and lips. She wore a grand circlet of brass and gold dragon's horns around her forehead that pierced up through her hair, and a flowing cape of wolves'fur covering her entire physique—concealing red dragonhide armor every bit as phenomenal as Angvar's, if not moreso. Sigrid raised her hand, her wolves'fur drapings ascending with it. The crowd fell silent with but a few mumbles remaining. Jarl Angvar looked to Sigrid, then to the Houndsmen with a curious smile.

"Who've we bound?" he asked jovially. His words left his throat at an immensely deep yet soothing pitch. "What 'raff do you bring from outside Stonegate?"

The strong-jawed leader of the Houndsmen stepped forward, followed immediately by audible swooning from the young women in the crowd. Angvar's smile widened. "Rainer, my oldest son," Angvar said cheerfully, "What is their story?"

"They claim to be monks with papers, Jarlfather," Rainer spoke, his voice wooing the Viking women simul-taneously. "They say you asked for books, scrolls, tomes, and maps, and they've come to deliver them."

"Is that what they carry?" Angvar asked.

"Yes, Yarlfather. Only papers and what they need for travel."

Angvar paused, as if to notice for the first time the enormous, black-haired beast that was also hooded, bound, and tied. "That… is a magnificent beast," he said, his beady eyes growing wide. "How did you ensnare it? I see no signs of struggle!"

Rainer laughed, "The small monk has tamed it, and it laid down at her command. For that we were thankful. Though the men would not have minded a fight!" The Houndsmen clamored, beating their fists against their shields and each other.

Angvar could not resist approaching the beast. He slowly

descended the stone steps, his eyes fixated on its impressive stature. "I… I should very much like to tame this beast for myself, my son," the Jarl spoke in an almost trance-like state, his hands reaching for the axe at his side. "If only to prove… my strength… once more—"

"—*You will not touch him*!" the small hooded monk cried, her robes falling back as she lashed out from her captors. All of Autumnhill swelled with gasps of awe as they beheld not a monk, but a shimmering young Luna with wild white hair as bright as the Night's Moon, green eyes like leaves in the Sun, and pale indigo skin like nothing they had ever seen—only heard about in far older tales.

Angvar stumbled backward, his axe falling to the ground. He took a moment to compose himself, steadying his breathing in the dead silence. A great whisper over-took the crowd, then he spoke. "Child, you are from the forest. You are from Yythengrey!"

"I am Titha Mae, daughter of the Watcher: Theole The Grand, and you *will not harm Paw*!" she barked, her words laced with a feverish maturity completely foreign to her usual stature. "This is Nech, he is a Goblin Scribe and my friend."

Everything hit her at once as she realized what had just happened. She looked to Nech, who was shaking so hard he could barely stand straight—fully aware of how Vikings viewed his kind. Titha impatiently removed his hood, pushing him forward.

"Say something smart," she whispered to him.

Nech blurted out a nervous laugh, his knees knocking together as he attempted to raise his head amongst the low growls of the crowd that was now privy to his Craglin heritage.

"A Luna and a Goblin! Here in Autumhill!" Angvar boasted jovially. "My, my! The daughter of Theole, no less, and her companion from the Craglands. Well, this has become a day history will remember!" He placed his hands on his belly, walking forward and leaning down to meet Titha, tipping his grand helmet back. "Forgive my disposition, Daughter of Theole. None have hosted a Luna within these walls since—oh, before my grandfather's time! And you must also forgive me for approaching your beast, won't you? I am sure you have heard many unpleasant things about we Vikingmen within your forest halls and our... *disagreements* with your animal kin, but it is very bad manners to approach a Viking's gate unannounced, especially ours. Right boys?"

The Hounds-men eruped in grunts, laughs, and hearty hoorahs.

"You will understand if I keep your beast tied and bound, yes? For the safety of my people," Angvar added, a hand still poised for his axe.

Titha turned to Nech, who nodded. She was not happy about this suggestion, and tried to remain strong as Paw looked at her wide-eyed—his maw, arms, and legs still restrained. "You're okay, little boy. Promise," she whispered to him, rubbing his cheek with her hand as she pulled back his robe.

"Little boy?" Angvar laughed. "Why, that's the biggest forest bear I've ever seen in all my days! And not a gray hair on him—still a young lad, he is! Incredible... What a day! You must come inside and tell me everything. There is quite a story within the three of you—I know it."

He signaled to his Houndsmen. "Rainer, my son. Don't just stand there! Untie our two guests and make sure their beast is comfortable while bound."

Rainer nodded in reply, his men snickering as they approached Paw, who began to snarl in protest. His discomfort manifested as growling, which began to instinctively rile the Houndsmen. Their hands all grasped to their weapons; each taken over by the same instinct as Angvar moments before. Titha's eyes widened like saucers. She could feel the situation tipping toward a point of no return; her heart racing as if it was about to be ripped from her chest and thrown off a cliff with her after it. But she didn't know what to do! Everything kept happening so fast outside the forest. Her knees began to quake as she swelled with confused anger.

Paw's snarling turned into full, ferocious growls as his eyes narrowed, focusing on the Houndsmen and their hands. Rainer drew his axe, raising it into the sky–its double blades gleaming in the Sunlight. A great howl rumbled from within the Houndsmen as they all encroached upon Paw, blinded by instinct.

"Put down your weapons, *now*!" a commanding yet feminine voice shot through the crowd from atop Skaldhall's stone steps. "Shame falls on each of you. Shame! Leave the beast's side immediately. All of you!"

It was Sigrid. And with her voice came the complete obedience of every Houndsman.

Titha was entranced; enchanted. The fierce, tall, commanding Shieldmaiden had stayed silent to this point, but could no longer tolerate the ignorance before her. She stepped down each stair with hard grace and regality; her ice-blue eyes fixated on her son, Rainer. Her hide boots kicked up dirt as she stepped down from the last stair, standing equal to him in height. She grabbed her son's weapon-clad wrist.

"Return with all of our men to Bouldergate—"

"—But mother!" Rainer cried, his strength all but disappearing. "This beast could maim us all! You cannot do this to me here—"

"—Do as I say. Houndsmen, away with you!" She commanded once more.

Each warrior wished to listen to Sigrid's decree (much moreso than her own son) and departed with haste. Rainer slammed his mighty axe back into its hip-holster, turning from Paw to return to Bouldergate.

As he turned, his eyes met Titha's. "I am sorry, Luna," he grumbled, "I am not accustomed to seeing such beasts *alive* within my borders. They have a habit of *killing* my men, so we tend to *kill them first.*"

Titha shuttered at his pointed words, stumbling back as strange flashes overtook her mind. Sigrid leaned down to her, shaking her head at her tempered son. She met Titha eye to eye, placing her hands onto the young Luna's shoulders.

"Come with me child," she spoke caringly. "We must get you out of the Sun."

The mesmerizing Shieldmaiden rose to her feet; blonde hair glistening as the Sun shone down directly behind her, making her appear most heavenly to Titha. Why, Titha would've done anything Sigrid commanded in that moment, to speak true. She was mesmerized. Fascinated. Inspired.

Sigrid extended her right hand from beneath her wolves'fur drapings and Titha took it without hesitation. They turned to Skaldhall's stone steps together.

"I will have my maidens and my youngest son untie your beast and keep him company in the gardens. There he will be happy and safe. He will not be comfortable inside our halls. Come."

Titha was not sure what was meant by this, but felt it was true. The Shieldmaiden led her by her pale indigo hand up the many, many steps to the grand golden doors as Nech silently trailed behind. She turned over her shoulder to Paw, who was already surrounded by fairy-like maidens, each adorned with colorful flowers from the gardens, prancing and pampering the big baby of a black bear. Paw smiled at Titha, the grin stretching across his face as the maidens led him around the left side of the stairfront up to the gardens on the North side of Skaldhall. Titha smirked as she could hear her Bear-brother emitting what sounded like 'the cooing of an overgrown, spoiled rotten raccoon'. Yes, Paw would be just fine. For now.

Would she?

CHAPTER SEVEN
The Fate of Autumnhill

"**Welcome to Skaldhall,**" Jarl Angvar announced with gleeful pomp, Sigrid smiling beside him. The mighty Man greeted their guests with silent wonder, his beady brown eyes glistening with all the excitement of a child adorned with too many gifts. He motioned with his left hand, extending a welcome to Titha and Nech into the grandest hall Viking'kind had ever built. Sigrid rolled her eyes.

Titha's vision grew wide as she beheld a place the likes of which she'd never seen. The walls were lined with carved wood and stone with grandiose rafters stretching as high as the treetops in Ythengrey. Great hanging chandeliers crafted of iron and bronze hung from the apex of the ceiling, shining amber light onto each surface. The enormous, woodburning stone hearths added to the warm glow, as did many'a horns filled with burning wax candles. Nech, just a step or two behind, looked as if he was in a newfound paradise; his eyes combing every foreign surface for new information and glimpses into the structure of a place he'd only written about or known from grand tales. Together the two ambled on behind the enormity of Angvar's silhouette—his shadow so great that it took them many moments to notice what caused Sigrid's reluctance to bring Paw inside.

Titha's bewilderment slowly turned to angst as she began to make out familiar shapes on the tall walls and hearths. Wild shapes began to form in her sight between the dancing firelight; each taking the form of animals she knew and loved. She gasped, her breath leaving her as her eyes met the lifeless gaze of a Woolly Rhino, its head and neck mounted above a burning fireplace. Her hands began to shake as she turned from the horrific sight, only to be met by the lifeless stare of a once beautiful pair of buck and doe across the hall. She stumbled backward, tripping over a bench before landing onto a table, her hands knocking over candlesticks held up by the skulls of forest beasts and she screamed in terror again. Then again—she was surrounded by it—by them! The whole hall spun around her, each corner adorned with the head, skin, antlers, or full body of a lifeless creature. Nech ran to her, trying to help as he might but Titha would not be comforted. The terror was all too real; all too consuming as everywhere she looked the dead eyes of forest-kin met her own.

Sigrid was mortified, blaming herself for the wild Luna's horror. She left her guests, running ahead of the party to grab the two warriors guarding the thrones.

"Take the elder-bear pelts into our chambers. Quickly!" she commanded, ripping their hides from beneath her and her husband's thrones.

The guards looked confused, as those two grand bear hides had laid at the foot of these most honored seats for generations.

"Do as I say!" she barked at their hesitation.

The guards scrambled, rolling up the enormous pelts—one of dark black and the other peppered with white and grey. Sigrid sighed as the guards took off down through the halls, knowing if Titha's eyes had met those ancient pelts there would be no hope of reconciliation—and she was smart to think such. Angvar barreled forward, breaking Sigrid's somber stare.

"What are you doing, my wife? The Elder-Bears are our greatest—Oh..." he stopped mid-sentence as the realization hit like a boulder. "You are most wise, my dearest," Angvar spoke somberly as he stroked his red beard. "To us they are mere wild and dangerous beasts to be bested. But to her... they are Paw. Look at this poor girl."

"I will bring her forth when she is ready. We still have much to discuss," Sigrid replied, slowly walking forward to console Titha.

Nech met her halfway. "She will be alright," he reassured Sigrid, his brow also heavy with grief. "Such sights are common to Man or Goblin or Gnome, but not to Lunas. If she did not see it first here, it would have been somewhere else down the path, and perhaps much worse. I have talked with her, and I think she is reaching an understanding within her youthful mind. Titha may be naïve to the ways of the world outside her forest—but she is sharp as a boar's tusk. If she asks you why these animals are mounted as they are, please be frank. She will know otherwise."

"We have much more important things to discuss I fear, Scribe. Though you are unusually caring for your kind," Sigrid replied, "it is not every day that a Luna and a Goblin show up at the gates of Autumnhill, and your arrival here is not by chance, is it?"

"I'm afraid not," Nech agreed as he hung his head. "We come with the gravest of news, and our unsorted entry has made us even more late to the cause."

Sigrid nodded. Her instincts always served her well. Her blood began to pulse hard through her veins. She brushed her hand across Nech's shoulder as she passed, walking to Titha and taking the seat beside her at the enormously long table in the middle of their hall.

"Dear child, I know we must seem brutish and horrible to your eyes, but the world is much different for us here outside your trees. I feel your terror, and my heart tells me something far worse has brought you here to me. I am sorry for the pain this has caused you, yet you must remain strong. So please, tell me; Why have you come to Autumnhill?"

Titha's eyes welled with tears. She scoffed as she fought them, wiping each away with a finger. "My father is gone," she hiccuped. "He is gone and we must find him."

"The Watcher is no longer in Yythengrey?" Sigrid asked, shocked. "What has happened?"

Titha tried to speak, but as strong and stubborn as she was, the one thing she could not bear again was the loss of family. Sigrid wrapped her arms around the pitiful Luna, bringing her to her chest and swaddling her in wolves'fur. The Shieldmaiden's brow sunk with worry. Angvar walked up, placing his hands on his beloved wife's shoulders. She looked to Nech.

"What has happened?" she asked.

"Surely you saw the fire and smoke erupt from the forest this morning?" Nech replied.

"How could we not?" replied Angvar. "But the Lunas have held their grand festival this first day of Summer for as long as we Vikingmen have settled Autumnhill."

Nech shook his head. "Those fires were not of any festival nor merriment. No, no… They were of *Dragon* and *Death*."

"What? What do you mean by this?" Angvar gasped.

Sigrid cut him off, words then leaping from her mouth. "I told you the flames were too great!" she shouted. "And the Sun! The Sun this morning rose twice. You know this can only means one thing… The Sunrise came only to roll back into Horizon and sleep for minutes to then rise again."

"Precisely, Shieldmaiden," Nech decreed. "What you saw was no mere illusion or strange Sunrise, but the return of Vulduun!"

Angvar slammed his fist on the table, knocking every goblet, plate and candlestick into the air then to the ground. "Do not come into this hall and tell me that our Dragonfather has torched sacred lands, Goblin. I will not hear it!"

"But what you hear rings true, Jarl! Does it not?" Nech steadied himself, for he knew this would happen. "The days of the once benevolent Great Drakes are gone. We know the Ever-war cost this world Meriduun; She may not have been a precious Dragonmother to you but she was Duskmother to the Lunas before your time and she is gone! An eternal Drake… *Perished* as we mortal beings do. For many years has Vulduun riled in anguish and grief and loss, and he has returned vengeful. He blames this world for the loss of his precious love—however corrupt she may have become—and he will not stop until he sees us all *burned* for it. This is why we have come. You are all in *grave danger*!"

Titha sat up, her tears finally subsiding. "He took my father. Vulduun broke his staff and he took the Moonstone. We think he's coming here next for the Sunstone."

"Sunstone?" Angvar replied, "We have no such thing here."

"Yes we do, my dear," Sigrid said as she turned to her husband. "Secrets will do us no good in this hour. All of this—every last detail—explains my dreams of late."

Angvar darted his head down to her. "I will not expose the Skaldstone to strangers. Not until the walls of Skaldhall fall before us!" he said, his voice low and harsh. "It is *our* legacy. *Ours* to protect."

"Forgive me for snooping," Nech interjected, "but I have written the words of these lands far longer than any Vikingman in this room has been alive. I know the legacy of which you speak and I know to whom The Day Drake entrusted his stone."

With these words, a fierce rumbling overtook the hall without warning. Each being braced themselves in confusion. Titha looked up as the grand chandeliers began to sway back and forth. "Look out!" she cried, leaping to Nech and tackling him out of the way. Angvar grabbed Sigrid, thrusting them both backward as a chandelier crashed into the table, splintering its wooden planks.

"This cannot be..." Angvar whispered as he rose, his mind struggling to comprehend. "We must leave Skaldhall at once! To the People!" He commanded, grabbing Sigrid with one hand and scooping up Titha & Nech with the other. Angvar ran for the golden doors, the trinkets of their grand hall crashing and crumbling behind them whilst the walls rumbled.

"Head for the gardens and get to your Paw, Titha Mae!" Sigrid cried out. "My son will lead you all to safety! Go!" Titha nodded silently, her ears ringing from the commotion surrounding them. She ran as fast and as hard as she could to the doors, pushing with Nech to fling them open. The doors burst apart, sending flame and smoke swirling in. A huge plume of ember-filled ash swept into the hall, blinding them. Sigrid threw off her wolves' fur, revealing her impenetrable Dragonscale armor. She barreled through the smoke, grabbing Titha and Nech and leaping out to Skaldhall's front stoop. Chaos had overtaken her beloved Autumnhill, but she had no time to notice. She took off down the stone steps, protecting her newfound companions with her life. Wood pillars and stone bricks fell all around her as she ran to the North side of the castle. Sigrid finally paused as she beheld her beloved gardens engulfed in flame; her eyes swelling and locked onto the tragic sight.

Amidst the flames in her gaze burst forth an enormous

shadow, and atop it rode her youngest son, Audun. The shadow revealed itself to be a bear—then more specifically Paw—who had just finished saving the maidens and his new friend from the raging fire.

"Paw!" Titha cried, leaping from Sigrid's grasp and running to her Bear-brother. They embraced one another fiercely. Titha wrapped her arms around Paw's neck, looking up to see someone *else* riding him for the first time in her life. Sigrid's son smiled, silent and shy. He slid down from Paw's back, walking over to his mother, who embraced him immediately. She thanked Paw, drawing her sword and pausing to listen for any sign of a Dragon, but none came; only the sound of flat feet and crooked weapons closing in outside the walls.

"It is the first wave!" Nech cried out as his eyes beheld a sky heavy with the colors of Sunset. "Cowardous Reeks and Goblins invade as the evening gives way to Night! Vulduun is drawing us out with his armies! He aims to weaken your peoples before his final strike with the rise of tomorrow's Sun! We must get everyone to safety before the Dawn!" He looked up to the sky as smoke billowed into a darkening Horizon. Sigrid turned at the sound of Angvar's grizzly, snarling call—his yell signaling the Houndsmen into battle as they clashed with Goblins and Lizardmen amidst the walls. Townsfolk scrambled to extinguish the flames and aid any injured Vikingmen they could, some scaling the stone walls surrounding the city to best any barraging marauders. Sigrid looked back at Angvar who stood on Skaldhall's steps hoisting an injured Houndsmen, their eyes locking with the same confused expressions.

Nech shouted over the sound of flames, his voice hoarse. These leaders of men were not heeding his warnings still, even hafter witnessing such surprise-destruction with their own eyes. "Dusk is upon us now!" he shouted, "but come the end of night and the rise of tomorrow's Dawn he will reign a terror upon us much greater than this. You must heed my words!" The wary Goblin looked up to the sky again as the burning Sun began to set on a long, bloody day. Angvar looked about, his eyes met with destruction and smoke, though he had seen worse—which led him to doubt yet again.

"Bandits!" Angvar cried in reply as the battle raged on around him. "It is nothing but bandits and marauders, my people. Help each other now, and we will rebuild as we always have!"

"I am no trickster, Jarl Angvar," Nech growled. "Yythengrey's same fate awaits you and your people if you cling to foolish pride! Autumnhill must be saved and the Sunstone must be taken far, far from here. The Last Great Drake now has Theole and his Moonstone. We cannot allow him to gain your sacred stone, too! You must listen to reason!"

Angvar, as jovial as he was at heart, never stood for being

questioned in front of his people. "If what you say is true, would you have me tell them?" he barked. "The Houndsmen of Autumnhill have faced many foes in their lifetimes—but never an Elderdrake! I heed your words, Goblin, but I will not succumb my lands to the panic and terror of a Dragon, for I see not one before me!" Angvar regained his composure, raising his chin and turning back to his people. "The Skallstone is the heart of Skaldhall, frail Goblin!" he shouted, so his subjects would hear him. "It has not moved for an Age and will remain in its rightful place!" he boasted proudly. "No Raider or Reek or wretched foul creature will ever lay hands on its majesty! *Kill them all*!" With his words the crowds cheered and roared loudly as they continued to clash with invaders. Angvar dropped his demeanor.

"Their cheering brings me much disdain, Jarl Angvar!" Nech yelled amid clashing blades. "They have no idea the horrors that await them! Theole is *gone*— and Autumnhill shall meet the same fate as Yythengrey come the rising of the Sun!"

Angvar rushed over to Nech, grabbing his collar and pulling him in for a word. "You do not think I know why the Dragonfather would torch Theole's lands and take him prisoner? You do not think he deserves this fate after all these years—after all the legends you spit so proudly? That *fool of a sprite* plucked the Lunestone from its rightful place at the heart of Ravenwood and gifted it to his bride only to watch them both fall because of his *arrogance*. Theole plunged our realm into discord and peril the moment he placed his bride's needs above that of the Dragonmother and now we all suffer for it? And if I hold Theole in contempt do you not think that Vulduun would, too? I will not make these same mistakes, no matter what your books or scrolls tell you. The Skaldstone stays in the Tower and my people stay safe. I will not damn Autumnhill to the ashes of our Dragonfather's wake. I will not make the same miscalculation that cost this world Meriduun, Lady Celtica Mae, and countless innocent ancestors of all races!"

Nech could not believe what he was hearing. "That is precisely what you are doing if you choose to do nothing! You are damning your people!" he continued, refusing to back down. "Vulduun is no longer concerned with your loyalty or your people or your worship, Jarl Angvar, you have just seen this first hand! And have you not all felt his presence fading? Your Amber fields now turn to Barren Fields! All has been dry and bleak for decades! Your once bountiful provider and protector has become blinded by sadness and consumed with hateful vengeance and would have his twisted armies *obliterate* Autumnhill to prepare for his taking of the stone. His only purpose now is to unite it with the captured Moonstone and to do so he will *end you all*! If you tell your people to stay here you are damning them to death!" He looked to Titha, who knew this to be true. The young Luna looked over to Sigrid, weary of the truth and all she had seen first-hand.

"He's right," Titha spoke over the sounds of flame and ruin. "Vulduun was nothing like the tales my father told me before bedtime. He is horrible and cruel now. There is just as much black to him as there is gold! He wanted the Moonstone as much as he wanted my father, so I know he wants your stone, too!"

"Together the two stones, or orbs, can control the very heavens themselves!" Nech continued, stepping beside Titha, shielding her from embers. "I have done a great deal of thinking on this, mighty Jarl, and the coming of darkness every night must do nothing but remind Vulduun of his beloved Meriduun! He must experience her loss again and again with every coming night, doomed to an eternity filled with relentless, cycling pain under the Moonlight. This is no mere struggle for the power of the Orbs, Jarl... I believe Vulduun aims to *rid the world of Night forever...* ending his anguish and pain once and for all! He can only do so, however, by joining the orbs within their hallowed Crown! If he has taken the Moonstone and Theole to control it, then he is surely coming for the Sunstone and whoever can wield it by their blood'right! If we can stop him from retrieving even one piece of this trinity, he cannot succeed!"

"And how are we to stop the mighty Dragonfather from enacting his will?" Sigrid asked sternly, leading the party from the fray.

"Hide the stone! Encase it! Toss it into the sea! Something! *Anything*! Is there nowhere safe it can be kept? Nowhere it could be shielded? As we stay here and debate these trivialities Vulduun's plan moves closer to reality! I have no doubt he took Theole and the Moonstone to his resting place over the Horizon. That day has passed and it will only take him another night—*tonight*—to *return* here to Autumhill from the horizon and nightfall is upon us now! His minions reign fire upon your homeland, sending it into chaos, making his impending siege all the easier. Do you not see all of the pieces lining up perfectly for him? The first day is halfway to a close and when the next Dawn is upon Autumhill he will come forth to destroy you all and take the Sunstone—regardless of how you *feel* about it!"

A pause fell over the group, each of them heeding Nech's passionate words as they moved to safety. Sigrid seemed most troubled. She slowed her pace, looking to the bronze dragonclaw pendant that had hung about her neck since she was a girl, then out to her burning homeland around her. She ran her fingers down the smooth curve of the claw, then snapped her hand forward, breaking the pendant from her neck.

"I believe them," she spoke out, grasping the ancient totem. "We cannot afford not to. All that we have seen—all that they have said—rings true within my heart. Our people come first, Angvar, as we always say. Look here. Look now to your sons and myself and your people and tell me you value your pride above them. If the Dragonfather is after the Skaldstone, he will return here no matter what. The least we can do is heed these warnings now before it is too late—and if we can—spare our people and stop our Dragonfather from plunging this world into endless, burning Daylight."

Angvar looked to the dark skies over Autumnhill, a bit too ashamed to meet any of his kin eye to eye. He lowered his gaze to the ground, then to the broken leather cord of his wife's dragonclaw pendant covered in ash, clenched in her hand. "My trust in you never wavers, beloved wife," he spoke softly. "If this is what you truly believe… What would you have me do?"

"Call upon the Houndsmen and my Maidens and bring them to Skaldhall's doors. Our people are to be led out of the city and into The Fells. Tonight we will climb the Spiral Tower and retrieve the Skaldstone from its resting place," Sigrid commanded. "And we will guard it with our lives."

Nech let out an enormous sigh, as if he hadn't breathed for years. Titha looked to her comrades, each showing their own relief. She knew the same fate awaited Autumnhill as had befallen her home, but if they could save its people and keep the Sunstone from Vulduun they may stand a chance of maintaining some sort of balance for their world. She still couldn't believe all that was happening. It was almost too much for her to imagine. Hope, however, was in her heart once more, and just in time. The Sun was peeking its last behind the distant silhouette of Yythengrey to the West as the rolling lands of Autumhill fell into darkness…

Dusk was no more. The Night had come.

CHAPTER EIGHT
A Most Curious Pairing

Titha stood as the stone door creaked open, the once beautiful garden behind them now reduced to ash. Before her a completely separate and secret entrance to Skald-hall awaited. It led to a candlelit, tunnel-like hall void of the throne room's lifeless beasts and horrid trophies.

"Better so far," Titha thought to herself.

Sigrid walked ahead of the group, her height almost too much for the narrow passageway. "

This way," she motioned at an impasse, leading them down a larger hallway to the left. The Shieldmaiden paused in front of another unassuming stone door, her torch bouncing harsh light off the old, smooth stones. Then she whispered "Rhofo". Slowly the door gave way, revealing a wondrous chamber. It was colorful and full of delightful items. Sigrid ducked through the doorway, leading Titha and Nech inside. The ever-curious Luna grinned as she beheld playful things she'd never seen before; a wooden rocking horse, stuffed dolls made to look like her animal friends from the forest, and plenty of golden-bound books. She ran over to a stuffed toy made in the image of a forest black bear, picking it up and running to show it to Paw as he squeezed his way through the small doorway.

"Look, fuzzybutt! It's a baby you!" she smiled.

Paw wasn't amused, as his actual *fuzzy butt* was stuck in the doorway. Suddenly his facial expression changed; a pair of small hands began pushing on his backside. The big bear garumphed loudly as the hands pushed as hard as they could. Finally he came careening through the opening, landing on his face at Sigrid's feet. Titha and Sigrid shared a good laugh, their first in a while. Paw, not amused, rolled out of the way to reveal whom these hands belonged to. It was Audun, Sigirid's youngest son.

Their eyes met for the second time: Titha and Audun, the first being amidst chaos and confusion. Titha wasn't sure how she felt about him—this young child of Man—as her only impression of him so far was of a pale boy cocky enough to ride *her* Bear-brother. Paw, however, had finally realized who pushed him through the doorway and smiled wide, flopping over to lick Audun's face with a smile. They had spent a lovely while in the garden together before the burning chaos, and it showed. This only made Titha even more curious, as she'd never seen Paw act this way around anyone but her and her family. If Paw liked him, though, then perhaps she could give him a chance, too. She did like his hair, after all. It was much wavier than hers, ending in rather drastic curls of a bright warm auburn color. His eyes were round and expressive just like hers, but of a much deeper amber shade. He had a very kind face with an upturned button nose, big ears, and appeared to be the same age as her. Come to think of it she really liked his tunic, too. It was bright golden yellow and adorned with wonderful knotted patterns on its reddish borders. His waist was wrapped with a tattered brown wool sash, and as she looked the young Viking boy over she noticed all of his clothing looked to be in the same shape as her own heavily-played-in attire, which made her smile wider.

Sigrid laughed to herself as she watched the two youngsters' wide-eyed bewilderment. "You haven't been introduced!" she said happily. "This is my youngest son, Audun."

Audun waved timidly, his shy stance opening up a bit.

"Audun, this is Titha Mae, a Luna from the Great Forest. She is a very special girl, and I need you to protect her, okay?"

Audun agreed with a nod and a smirk.

"Thanks Shieldmaiden, but I can protect myself," Titha replied heartily.

Sigrid laughed, "I am sure you can, young one. We are strong ladies, are we not?"

Titha's heart swelled at the thought. Sigrid was everything she wanted to be and more: beautiful yet tough, strong yet kind, wise yet fierce. If the Luna's were to be believed, all of these things were opposites, and one person could not be all of them at the same time. Little Luna girls were expected to be graceful and never harsh, pretty and not muddy, and above all: mindful but never *curious*, as she so feverishly was. Yet here stood *Sigrid* before her. Suddenly Cypress' words galloped back into her mind... *"Just a girl,"* she thought to herself—and her determination grew once more.

"We must go, my companions," Sigrid added, remembering the task at hand. "Come, Nech." She turned to the old Craglin, whose fascination had led him to a far corner of the chamber, his old hands thumbing through colorful books.

"Yes, of course!" He replied fumbling.

Titha was caught off guard by this. "You're going with them? she asked.

"I believe I must" her dear friend replied. "I know the old tales of the Ever-War better than any, I should say, and would like to be of council. You have seen enough dreadful peril these last days, dear child, so please allow yourself to rest a bit and we will return to you soon."

Titha leaned over, hugging Nech tightly. He hugged her back, realizing for the first time how quickly their bond had formed, and how much his life was changing. Sigrid kissed her son on the forehead, running her hand through his curly auburn hair. No more words were spoken as the elders exited the room through the same stone doorway they all had entered.

Titha and Audun stood in their own silence, both refusing to think this would be the last time they saw those leaving. Audun twiddled his thumbs, then sat. The room fell quieter still. Their eyes would meet, then dash away immediately. This repeated for some time.

"I… like your hair. It's very shiny," Audun finally blurted, immediately regretting breaking the silence. He hiccuped, darting away to nab a few old books and scribbled notes that looked to be of his own making.

"So you *do* talk!" Titha replied excitedly. "I was beginning to think you were a bigger weirdo than me."

"Weirdo?" Audun responded. "What's that?"

"You don't know what a weirdo is, weirdo?" she laughed. "It just means you're odd. So we have that in common. "

Audun frowned.

"No, don't be upset—it's a good thing. A great thing! In my

opinion, at least. Who wants to be like everyone else? Sounds so boring to me."

"Yeah, I am that, I guess," he smiled back. "Different, I mean. Vikings like fighting and eating; I don't, really. But I don't mind it. I mean I like to eat when I'm hungry but fighting is really pointless. I'd rather read or write or—"

"Or what?" Titha asked, bubbling with wonder.

"Explore, I think. I really want to see what's outside of Autumnhill."

"Yes!" Titha squealed. "Me too! All my life my father and my older sister told me how dangerous the world was outside our forest, but that just made me want to see it *more*. I want to see the whole world! I want to see all of Gaela and her beauty!"

"Really?" Audun replied, lighting up with an overdue grin. "I think my father *likes* how dangerous it is outside our walls. He is really protective of me, though. I'm small, he says, and father is always telling me not to go outside Bouldergate because it's '*treacherous and full of wild creatures that will eat a lad up!*' But how am I supposed to learn anything else if I stay here all my life?" he added, quite serious. "I'll get out someday—and get more books! I think I've read mine a hundred times over and over. I've started to draw and write my own but I've run out of things to draw and write. That's why I like—well— I *did* like mother's garden so much. She would bring back new things every year, and we would plant them together. Then, when they grew I would draw them." The young boy paused, saddened by the loss. "It was beautiful and unlike anything else in Autumnhill. There have to be other gardens—amazing flowers and trees and animals I've never seen. I know there is so much more outside because I see it on pages and my brother tells me amazing stories when he comes back. But not me, I'm too 'little' and "defenseless' and all I get to do is walk around the halls or mess with stuffed toys here in my room. I love to read, but I think I'm ready to see things for myself."

"Oh so this is *your* room! I like it a lot. You would love my home, Audun." Titha sat down in front of him, giddy with excitement. "It's full of flowers and leaves and wonderful friends like Paw. It's where I live so I've never really thought about what others would think of it, but it is truly beautiful, I'd say." Paw grunted beside her, rolling over in his rest.

"We have animal friends here too!" Audun replied enthusiastically.

Titha paused. She didn't want to offend her new acquaintance, but with his mention of their own "animal friends" images of the horrid dead creatures seen in their grand hall flooded her mind. She couldn't hold her tongue. "You mean the dead ones you hang in the halls? That is the most disgusting, awful thing I ever–"

"No, no!" Audun laughed. "I hate those, too. I don't get

that at all. What good is an animal if it is dead on a wall? I mean our *livestock*! We have hogs and cows and chickens and dogs a—"

"—Dogs? What's a dogs?"

Audun laughed harder. "Not 'dogs', just 'dog'. I have one, he is my best friend! They're like a wolf, but have floppy ears and they don't eat you. Mine even lets me ride on his back just like Paw does with you. Wanna meet him?"

"Do I *ever*!" Titha shouted gleefully.

Audun jumped to his feet, placing a few fingers in his mouth to let loose an impressive whistle-call. Without warning a huge, lanky and shaggy beast came bursting through the main doors into the chamber. Titha laughed and pranced amid the excitement—she had never seen anything like a 'dog' before! The scraggly gray beast was shaped like a big wolf, sure, but had wavy, coarse hair and impossibly-floppy ears atop a huge, friendly muzzle.

"This is Haldor! Mother says we were born at the same time and have been inseparable ever since. My father named him after a great Viking warrior which is kind of fitting, I guess. He can be really overprotective."

Titha was positively squeamish with delight. She hopped over to Haldor, grabbing his cheeks and fluffing up his face. "Well aren't you the cutest thing ever!?" she cried.

Paw was not happy. He jumped to his feet, lumbering

cautiously toward the foreign beast. Each furry companion smelled the other, matching scents for the first time. The hair on their necks stood up as they circled, eyeing suspiciously.

"Boys, behave!" Titha spurted, stepping between the beasts.

Paw grunted, taking a few more steps before sitting back onto his round bottom (never taking his eyes off Haldor). Haldor, oblivious to Paw just seconds later, ran to Audun and licked his face from top to bottom. The tiny Viking laughed and rolled with Haldor as Titha turned to Paw, who was still frowning. "Boop," she said as she poked his nose, accompanied by a "please calm down" side-eye. Paw slouched over, resting his enormous head in her lap. With that, she realized how droopy her own eyes had become, and how tired her young bones were from what her waking hours had been.

"Are you tired?" Audun asked sweetly.

"Very," Titha replied, yawning, before Paw let out an identical one.

"You can have my bed," He said without hesi-tation. "I like to sleep on the floor with Haldor anyway."

"Is a bed like a moonflower?" she asked, her curiosity in no way stunted by utter exhaustion. "Because I really miss my moonflower right now." She crawled into the enormous wooden bed one limb at a time, mumbling all the way. "We sleep in big white flowers," she muttered, pulling covers over her like petals. "They're really comfy…but if this is a bed, then I like beds, too 'cause holy *wow*…" And just like that, Titha Mae drifted into dreams.

Audun smiled. He was terrifically happy with his new friends, though very tired, as well. He grabbed a swaddle of blankets and fur pelts from under the bed—thinking not to fetch or show them until Titha fell asleep as he knew she'd hate seeing—well, fur that wasn't *attached* to anything living. "What she doesn't know won't hurt her, right Haldor?" he whispered, yawning as he curled up with his companion into the mass of comfy blankets. Haldor harrumphed and placed his head beside Audun's. They too, were off to sweet dreams.

High above the children there was no sleep nor rest for Nech, Sigrid, nor Angvar, as they drudged up the stairs of Skaldhall's Spiral Tower, nearing the top. They climbed the steep spiraling steps upward along with their eldest son, Rainer, who led brave Vikingwomen and men behind them. All were safe so long as the sky kept dark. Surmounting pressure of the coming

Sunrise weighed heavily on each of them, Nech's knobby knees struggling to master the last few rounds of stairs. Rainer patted him on the back.

"You can make it, you old imp," he chuckled, his cheekiness lost on Nech.

Just then the darkness of the stair hall began to give way to a glistening light. Nech panicked. "Dear Craga!" he cried, "are we too late?"

Rainer laughed. "That is not the Sun," he replied. He took a few more steps, rounding the final bend as the top of the tower opened up to golden splendor. "It is the Skallstone."

There it stood: the Sunstone of legend. Its chamber was laced with the finest golds and coppers, each rafter carved with the history and lore of the stone. Seasoned warriors stood still in its presence, each in utter awe of the honor of traveling to the resting place. Rainer basked in its glory, too. His parents stepped forth, holding hands. Staring into the stone they'd sworn to protect, they shared a moment—each troubled by the weight of what was to come—and the possibility of true harm befalling each other. The room fell silent with them—only the strange, otherworldly *hummm* of the Skallstone could be heard. Every soul stared with baited breath, waiting for Angvar to step forth and claim its light. Hands clenched as eyes widened; but it was not the Jarl who approached.

Sigrid stepped forth, her eyes locked with the golden light, and gasps broke out behind her. With one hand she let go of her husband, dropping her dragon'claw necklace with the other. It hit the stone floor, shattering into a thousand pieces. With it, her bloodline's allegiance to the Elderdrakes was broken. She took one last deep breath, then leaned forward into the intensifying *hummm* of the ancient orb. Then she grabbed it. The Skallstone. No harm came to her, as it was *her very make and blood* that was tied to the ancient stone—not Angvar's. The loudest gasp of all came afterward, and it was born of the breath of her own son. Rainer had no idea. Nech, however, stood smiling. He had known all along.

"Let me take it for you, my love. I would not have you bear such a curse," Angvar pleaded.

"It is my blood's to bear," she said, smiling at his tenderness. She turned to meet her eldest son's eyes, giving a look she hoped he would interpret. His bewil-derment stayed, though.

"Come, everyone," Sigrid commanded. "Now is the time for haste. We have but minutes before the Sun rises, and doom is upon us."

A warm glow overtook the horizon as she spoke, cutting her short.

"We may not even have haste on our side, Shieldmaiden," Nech shouted, "The Sun rises!"

A fierce, fiery glow overtook the horizon, a sunrise the likes of which no party there had seen before. With it rolled a wave of despair over each companion.

"Go!" Nech cried. "*Run*!"

Just as it had the day before the Sun dove back into the horizon, letting stars retake the sky. "

This is it," Nech spoke aloud. "He is coming."

The companions practically dove down into the stairwell. Each small window they passed as they ran gave another glimpse of a dark sky that had just been a fiery display or oranges and reds seconds prior.

"How can this be?" Rainer thought aloud. "It can only be

the end of all things!"

Titha shot up in the bed, her eyes wide. Its wooden rafters began to shake as books fell from shelves around her. She had awoken by Haldor's bark, who was staring out the window relentlessly howling at whatever was happening outside. She jumped from the covers, landing on Audun and shaking him vigorously. "Wake up!" she cried. "I think it's happening!"

"What's happening?" Audun grumbled as he rubbed his head. "What's wrong, boy?" he spoke, getting up to go to Haldor.

Titha looked to Paw, who was still dead asleep. "He would sleep through the end of the world," she thought, leaping to him and smacking his head. He wouldn't be stirred, as per usual, so Titha did not hesitate to pry one eyelid open—and that was all it took for him to take in the chaos outside. He stood up immediately, running to meet Haldor at the window. The two beasts shared a glance and turned to their beloved companions. They all knew they had to leave. But what of Nech and Sigrid and the others?

What of the *Sunstone*?

More and more steps and windows passed amidst the clanging of the warrior's weapons and armor. Sigrid and Angvar barreled downward, followed closely by Nech, Rainer and his Houndsmen. With the passing of another window a great flash took over the Tower; light pouring through the tiny arched openings and blinding them all. The stairs began to quake below their feet. Rainer fell forward, the weight of his Houndsmen behind him pressing him down—and hard. Nech braced, stopping his fall as they continued on. Rainer scoffed, smiling at the Craglin's surprising strength. As the rumbling grew worse, though, so did the party's intense dread. Angvar and Sigrid hend hands once more as she cradled the Skallstone underneath her left arm, leading the party into the hope of safety.

But it was not to be. A horrendous boom rolled forth from the sunrise. It curdled first into the brazen, trumpeting roar of a Dragon—then twised into one single foul word.

"TRAITOR!"

He knew.

Sigrid collapsed under the weight of the booming word, her blood turning cold. Angvar panicked, hoisting her up as he drew his mighty axe; Autumnbringer. Though as he lept to defend his beloved, he did not think of the Skallstone, and for this he cursed himself. The stone slid from Sigrid's weakened grasp and hit the stairs, cracking the steps below it. It bounced and pounded down, crumbling every stone that met its majesty. In a split second its light escaped them, and all hope was lost. Or so they thought.

"Rainer!" Sigrid cried, refusing to be bested by whatever curse had taken hold by the thundering voice of Vulduun. "Go after it, my son. *Go*!"

He stopped the warriors behind him and looked to his mother, confused.

"My blood runs through your veins, Rainer!" she cried out again. "You must retrieve it! Fight whatever it may do to you, and know that I love you!"

With that a blood curdling scream left her mouth, and a great, fiery claw swiped the tower above them; obliterating it. The party pushed and shoved downward as a reign of stone and ash pelted like meteors from the sky. Rainer grabbed Nech, hoisting him under his arm. He jumped down the stairs, slamming into the wall and sliding down it—his feet moving as fast as they possibly could. He no longer had time for fear nor doubt.

Above them, Angvar turned back. "Protect your Shieldmaiden!" he shouted to the Houndsmen. They immediately surrounded Sigrid, cradling her weakened form, their weapons drawn.

"I will not let you take her…" Angvar growled beneath his singed red beard. "You hear me, foul drake? *You will not have her*!" He shouted into the fire.

Jagged teeth shot through the flames, snatching Angvar from the stairs, tossing him into the sky. Sigrid cried, for she had not the breath to scream. The flaming maw turned back to the stairs, lunging for her. She drew her sword with what strength she had left, ramming it into the scales above a gigantic crooked smile. The dragon let out a horrid cry, flailing backwards. Flames shot from his very being as he rose higher, his eyes smoldering like grand fires as they met her own icy stare. He bellowed a trumpeting roar once more that unfurled yet again into the word that broke her…

"TRAITOR!"

Another set of golden claws ripped through the tower, swatting the Houndsmen into oblivion as Vulduun took Sigrid for his own. No sooner did he grab her then let out a screaming fit of severe pain. Angvar, stumbling at the drake's foot, had driven the wide blade of Autumn-bringer deep between two enormous toes. He withdrew the axe, met by another crackling yelp from the mighty dragon, and then swung again, sending golden scales flying into the surrounding wreckage. Vulduun snarled, flames shooting from his nostrils as he looked down to Angvar from the sky, clutching an unconscious Sigrid in one hand and pure hatred in the other.

"*You have lost*!" Angvar shouted, his words hitting Vulduun like spears. The Jarl looked back to the bottom of the tower to see Rainer and Nech escaping with the Skallstone—its glow wrapped within a cloak. Rainer turned to his father's words, seeing things as they were. One last smile radiated from below Angvar's beard as the flames of Hel itself filled the sky behind him.

Rainer panicked, screaming for his Jarlfather. "Look ou—" he wailed, but his words were cut short by a swirling inferno so hot he could feel it within his own throat.

Angvar smiled at his son, withdrawing his axe yet again from the drake, clutching it to his chest. At peace, he closed his eyes—and Vulduun pushed forth a rage of fire from his maw unparalleled by any creature's fury. It overtook Angvar, and all that surrounded him, in an instant.

Nech lowered his head as Rainer collapsed. "Father!" he screeched through tears, but not a word could be heard above the flames, even as every fiber of his being reached for his fallen hero.

Vulduun's rage was so great that fire continued to spill forth from him, even after nothing was left below but scorched earth.

"Rainer, the stone!" Nech yelled. "We mustn't waste your father's sacrifice!"

But he would not be swayed from his grief. Rainer shook,

the shrouded stone sitting in his lap. As he wept, two beasts shot around the back corner of Skaldhall; and much to Nech's unimaginable delight it was Titha and Audun atop their brethren, escaping Skaldhall as it shattered!

Audun peered around the stones of their home, curious as to why his brother was kneeling so. Titha screamed as she beheld Nech. The old goblin turned, thanking whatever Gods he could name that his young companion were safe astride their beasts. In the light of their eyes he saw the potential of both Night and Day reignighted, and was hit with a wave of utmost duty.

"Get up Rainer, Son of Angvar!" he cried, turning back to the fallen son. "You are now Jarl of Autumnhill, and by all the strength left within, you mustn't let it fall!"

Audun furled his little brow, confused. The tiny Viking drove his heels into Haldor, and they galloped toward his older brother, their approach guarded by the massive pile of rubble that was once the Tower. Audun lept down, taking his brother's face in his hands. Rainer's chin slowly rose. As their eyes met, Audun *knew*. He felt his brother's pain, the loss of their father, and their mother's strife as they wept together amid the swirling flames. Rainer took his baby brother's hands, squeezing them tightly. He felt a rush of life, and looked to Titha Mae, the little Luna who had come so far and seen so much. Reaching down he cradled the shrouded Skall-stone, standing slowly.

"Take it, little brother," Rainer commanded. "Take our family's sacred stone and get you both as far from harm as possible. It is up to us now. We must both be men! I will stay and tend to our people—but you—you must protect the stone! Whatever it takes. And thank you."

"For what?" Audun asked.

"For returning my strength."

Rainer thrusted the shrouded stone into Audun's small, scar-less hands. "You must be strong now, little brother. And above all you must be brave—like mother and father. Trust in Nech, let him guide you both to safety! The Skallstone will not hurt you; Mother's blood flows through our veins!" He leaned down, quickly kissing his brother on the forehead as he drew his sword. "Look after them, Goblin. Or you will have me to answer to."

"Of course, Mighty Jarl! I shall not let you down. The Sunstone will be—" Nech fumbled nervously before Rainer cut him off.

"Get out of here, imp! All of you! And do not look back—no matter what horrors meet your ears!"

"Yes, of course!" Nech blurted before letting himself be off. He rushed Audun along, the boy seeming even smaller now as he clutched the fate of the Sunstone. Titha motioned for them to hurry up, their time for escape growing less than thin.

And she was right to hurry them. Vulduun raged on, his

mass ebbing and flowing through the wake of his flames as he searched for the Sunstone on the other side of the Tower's rubble. Titha reached for Nech as the Drake's mass pointed away from them, grabbing his hands and pulling him astride Paw as Audun climbed Haldor The beasts made haste, and off they went while they still had a chance.

Autumnhill, though, was falling. Amidst chaos Vulduun rampaged on, but one fist remained clutched. It held the still unconscious Sigrid, a soul he needed un-snuffed if he was to control the Sunstone. But where was it?

Waves of his gurgling henchmen began to scale the north walls surrounding the city just as they had done before, but this time they were met by the readied weapons of Vikings.

. "*Where is it?*" Vulduun cried, his grumbling voice booming through the fire. Surely none could be so cunning as to escape *his* wrath? And with the Sunstone? An immense displeasure took him, his neck recoiling like a snake as he looked to the limp Shieldmaiden within his palm. He had its heir to control it, but not the ancient stone itself! "*No*!" he spat, flames igniting what shrubs remained in the city, and with each passing moment his rage ignited tenfold.

The battle prowess of the Vikingmen only added to his plight as they made short work of the invading Goblins, Reeks, and Ogres under Rainer's command. The dashing lad, now destined to become Jarl much sooner than he had hoped, turned ever so briefly from the fires. But he was not to flee. No. Instead, he let out a great whistle, and to him ran a horse so beautiful it could've been born of the All'father's halls themselves. Rainer mounted his trusty steed, whispering her name, Kelliah, as he greeted her in open flames. Together they galloped into death, into *war*—the Ever-war—and there they bested everything Vulduun had to offer. Kelliah was known as much for her speed and strength as she was the beauty of her long white hair, and it was not long before it's shimmer caught the eye of one very infuriated Dragon.

Vulduun cackled and spewed hateful ash their way as he flapped his enormous golden wings, rising into the air over the battle. But his mind's eye hunted for another prize. He surveyed the lands with peering red eyes, examining every nook and cranny for the glow of the Sunstone. It was nowhere to be found! As the flapping of his wings began to clear smoke, a small band of creatures escaped his gaze. It was, of course, a bear, a hound, and three tiny beings fleeing Autumnhill with all the haste a living thing could muster.

"*Auugh*!" Vulduun cried out. "*Stop them*! *Stop the beeeeasts*!"

Reeks broke from battle, slinking like the lizards they were to the eastern side of Autumnhill. They gave quite the chase, but it was not enough to please their master. Goblins then broke rank at his command, too. The Ogres, knowing they were too slow to obey their over-lord's command, doubled down on the Vikingmen with their clubs and maces. Rainer and Kelliah whipped around, breaking into a grand stride—the gorgeous white horse whisping through the carnage like a white streak. Rainer did his best to cut down every Reek he could, but the reptiles were too many. Nevertheless, he kept at them. Vulduun snarled, and gave chase himself, flying right past Rainer with eyes only for the Sunstone. As Vulduun dove into pursuit of Titha and her companions, Rainer pulled at Kelliah, her hooves grinding them to a halt. His eyes had spotted a keen opportunity—one that would allow him to take advantage of what appeared to be a weakness of the timeworn Drake.

"Houndsmen! Aim for the underside of the his wings! Do it now, but take care not to throw for his clutched hand—for it holds the fate of our beloved Shieldmaiden, my mother!" He cried out, pointing his sword to the sky.

Every able warrior fired an arrow—hurled a spear —or flung an axe—reigning a fury of steel into the drake's tender under'wings. Many projectiles were bested by his golden scales, but the few that were able to puncture by the heaving throws of Men made quite an impression.

Vulduun screeched in pain, flapping every-which-way to rid himself of the piercing blades, and in conse-quence stopped his pursuit of Titha Mae. This made him panick. He had never experienced the full wrath of Men, for they had ever been his worshipers and kin. Rainer wished the Drake would relinquish his grip and drop his mother, but there would be no such luck. For as long as Vulduun held Sigrid, he retained a half-victory.

The enormous, weary dragon looked to his wings, seeing his own blood for the first time in an Age as the weapons of Man hung splintered his hide. His wounds, he was discovering, were grievous. A gurgling shriek left his throat, and the Elderdragon finally turned tail.

"He is fleeing! The dragonfather flees!" Rainer cried out.

Goblins and Ogres recoiled, great confusion taking them—but the Vikings were not to show mercy toward their murderous onslaught.

"End them," Rainer growled, the faces of his fallen father, captured mother, and fleeing brother all before him. And with such a cry, the end of a great battle began.

CHAPTER NINE

Into The Abyss

Nech looked over his shoulder as the Sun warmed their backs; the smoke of war was slowly dispersing. Paw ran as fast as he could, his paws thumping up dirt in dry slopes. He carried his companions eastward once more— Autumnhill was now far behind them. In the distance, the enormous silhouette of Vulduun could be seen retreating for his Horizon. A brief glimmer of hope washed over Titha as the Elderdrake fled, though Audun and Haldor could think only of their family. Looming clouds of smoke gave way to the shadows of the mountains to the east, their peaks emitting shades of red or gold or orange like the very fires they had just escaped. These were the Fells, and their beauty was treacherous. Vikingmen considered the mountains as one with their ancestral Gods—their range a fiery pathway from Autumnhill into the Horizon. Even the bravest Houndsmen, however, would rather traverse the Fells than venture *below* them.

Titha knew she should be tired, but she was not. Never in her wildest dreams did she imagine so much could happen so fast outside her forest. A small flock of wrens flew past her, breaking her deep thoughts. She smiled at the familiar sight; the first birds she'd seen since the chaos began. Her smile turned to wide-eyed glee when behind the wrens tailed a Crow. Its wings flapped hard. It was an old crow with singed tailfeathers, and she knew it immediately.

"Look!" she cried. "A Crow! One of my father's Crows!"

"Is it? How splendid!" Nech decreed. "Why, your father will know you are coming for him now, Titha Mae!"

"We must follow it!" she yelled, thrilled at the chance.

"No, dear Luna! No! We cannot! We have the Sunstone! We cannot take it straight to Vulduun! We must take it into Mydlan and beyond! Your father would bid us so!"

Titha looked down to her side, Feathersword glistening from beneath bumbling gear. Her whole journey had started as an effort to bring her father home. She would not abandon him then, and would not now—but she had no choice. Events had unfolded she'd never expected, which she had come to learn was simply the way life worked. Her eyes traveled skyward, the wind and air rushing past her as Paw galloped further into their destiny with Nech astride behind her.

"If you make it back home, little Crow, please tell my sisters and Cypress that I am okay, will you?" Titha asked of the beast; a faint glimmer escaping its pitch black eye. A sharp caw echoed back to Titha, and with it she knew her message would be carried. White clouds swirled in the blue sky above the Crow's path, reminding her of her loving father's gentle gray face and flowing white beard. "I'll save you, father. I promise," she whispered. Haldor and Audun picked up their pace, coming again into her view as they rode side by side. "...But we've got to do this first. You would want me to do this, right?" Theole's Crow was almost out of sight. It looked to her from the sky one last time, then turned back to its northern flight to disappear into the clouds. "I thought so," she responded, knowing her father kept watch over her even now. He was the *Watcher*, after all. She'd be disappointed if he wasn't, even from such a debacle as this.

"We're going the right way?" Titha asked Nech as they galloped. "We have to get the Sunstone away from here and to the Elk Kings."

Nech pondered a bit and then leaned up to her. "To the Elk Kings indeed, my child!" he yelled, the words filling Titha and Audun with energy. "The Vikingmen cannot provide safe-keeping for their sacred stone nor its inheritors any longer. It is up to us now, and we must not fail, my companions! Firstly, it is imperative that we be as far from Autumnhill as we possibly can. From there we must continue eastward, for the Elk Kings reside far over sharp mountains and thick forests from the lands of Westlyn you both know. Immediately and unavoidably, this takes us to the Druidunes with haste." Nech's eyes squinted as he stared ahead over Titha's shoulder. "Into the Abyss..." he added deftly.

Audun galloped beside them astride Haldor. "Where's that?" he asked, yelling over their sprinting beasts.

"You know very well, young master Viking," Nech quipped. "The caverns open up before us—the Mouths of the Mountains! Past these hills and into their gaping gullets we go, for they are the great cave dwellings between your people and my own: The Druidunes beneath The Fells!"

"The Fell Caverns!" Audun cried. "We can't go in there! Father says to never go in there! 'Always follow the light of the Sun!' he would say."

"We have no choice!" Nech barked back. "And I struggle with the thought myself, young Man, but I dare say we are now within an age in which the Sun is no longer our ally."

"We can go into the mountains above," Audun replied, "or back to—"

"There is no turning back, master Viking. And we certainly cannot take the Mountains to the North—that much closer to

Vulduun's horizon. Most importantly we cannot use the open passages of Westlyn any longer! Not while we are hunted for such a prized possession! We must remain hidden and far from the sight of Day at all times! I understand your disdain, child, as I am aware your people's fear of the dark and its creatures. Your family's distaste for my kind is not unfounded either, as I know you have heard many an unpleasant thing about Craglins. But you must trust me now, as I think I have earned it—and not be weary of my yellow skin. Long have the Fells stood as the border between our kinds, and many battles have our peoples fought, but our task does not concern those petty squabbles or meaningless bloodshed. No, it is much greater than all of that; and you must now place your confidence in an old Goblin and his forest friends! We must get your Eternal Stone as far from Vulduun as we can get it - and as close to the Elk Kings as fate will allow! Such a task leads us into the Abyss. May Craga guide us!"

"Okay," Audun responded, "but who's Craga? Will she be in the caverns?"

Nech smiled. He tugged at Titha's cloak. "There! The path!" he pointed. "Let us enter there before we are found again!"

The young Luna's eyes grew wide at the sight. They crossed over the apex of a large amber hill—and the world disappeared below them. It was truly an utter abyss. The rolling foothills of the Fells sank into the cavern's mouth and darkness swallowed them whole. An ancient dirt path much like the Autumn trail led from atop their hill directly down the slope into the deep. "This must go somewhere," she thought, amazed at the opening. She was, as all Lunas would be, completely unfazed by the darkness awaiting her. She removed her cloak as the cool air from beneath the land caressed her skin. It felt familiar, and she vastly preferred it to the relentless heat of the Sun. As they traversed the path down into the deep dark the Day ceased to be, and Titha's green eyes shone once more—out into the blackness. The dark called out to her, and she answered, commanding Paw to continue.

"Wait!" a voice cried out from behind. "You may be able to see in here, but we cannot, little Luna!" Nech decreed, running down the path into the cavern to meet her. She had been in a trance, an utterly unbroken bewilderment with the depths; so much so that she had failed to notice Nech dismount, or Haldor and Audun's absence. Nech and Audun both returned to her side, each holding a bright burning torch of sticks and wheatey grass. Titha's entire face wrinkled as she squinted. She'd be fine if she never saw fire again in her life, but there it was in her face. Again.

"Are you alright, younging?" Nech asked.

Titha's face had turned grim. "I'm fine," she stated calmly. "The darkness feels so… familiar," she whispered as her hands trailed the cold walls away from the fire. "But that's bull-croak! It's not familiar here because don't know where I am. And I'm tired of not knowing things. It's exhausting."

"Oh, Titha Mae," Nech replied. "How far you've come, and how far you'll go. Home must feel ages away for you. It does for us all, I am sure. But it is for home that we must travel on, and for home that we must not give up hope."

"I never give up if I can help it," Titha responded matter'o'factly, "I just need you to tell me more than you are. I really, really don't like not knowing things. Ruffles my branches. We are all in this together, right?"

"Indeed we are—and a fair request," Nech responded thoughtfully. "Though I am afraid I must disappoint you, my dear, for I have told you all that I know. While I am not too shy to admit I am quite the intelligent historian, for all my efforts the location of our journey's intended end still eludes me. Igdrasil has forever evaded my efforts, and those of all great scholars, I might add."

"Igdrasil, yes! The Tree of Life!" Titha shouted. "Everyone knows that's where the Elk Kings live—or *reside*—father would say. Fancy word for live, that is."

"Yes, young lady, but do you know where Igdrasil herself lies? Did your father ever mention a precise location for her majesty?"

Titha paused, cocking one eyebrow. She had sung the song of Gaela's mythic tree a million times over, heard its heralded name practically every Night of her life, yet... she had no idea where it actually was! No one truly did, it turned out.

"See?" Nech fluttered his hands. "Do not feel discouraged, for no one knows where she takes root! Not myself, my old Council, the Peregrine Order, none of us—and we have explored every ruin possible; inscribed every piece of ancestral song or lore. One would think a tree larger than life itself would not be so hard to find!"

"Maybe that's on purpose," Titha responded. "Maybe we aren't meant to see Her."

"History and legend both support your statement, bright young Luna. But if we are to save our world, *see* her we must."

Titha stopped, her keen vision beholding somet-hing outside their conversation. A tiny spotted-something scurried along the cave floor in front of her. "Sally!" She squealed. She bounded out of the torchlight and straight into the pitch dark, her indigo hands plopping down onto the rock. She placed her chin gently onto a wet slag, and her green eyes revealed a slippery lizard stopping to acknowledge her.

"My gracious, who is Sally?" Nech squealed, startled.

"No, no," Titha laughed, "Sally-mander—it's a beautiful salamander, I mean." Its adorable black eyes blinked back at her atop a bright orange, speckled body. Titha turned back to Audun. "Salamanders can breathe in water, too. Did you know that? I wonder if there's a stream in this cave. That could lead us out!"

"Sallymanner?" Audun repeated. "My people just call them longfrogs. My books say they're newts, though, which sounds a lot better. It really is pretty, isn't it?" He wished in that moment for a scrap of paper to draw the black-spotted salamander on, but all of their belongings were packed up tight.

"It is creatures like this splendi-ferous, fiery little newt that Vulduun threatens with extinction as well, my young masters," Nech added, his pointed fingers on his equally-pointed chin. "If the world were to burn within his desired Eternal-Day, no creature of darkness would survive, not even down in these depths. I fear the Daykin would soon perish, too; for we are all dependant on one another. The Elderdrake has been blinded to all sense or reason for many Suns and Moons, however, and I do not think he knows nor cares what will happen if he gets his horrid way. Such is why we must stop him, and why we must meet with the divine!"

"I'm gonna shove my sword right into that Dragon's eye. The pointy end, too," Titha quipped amid a very serious moment. Audun chuckled, breaking the silence. Their merriment bounced and echoed down into the caverns, making them seem much less daunting for a brief moment. Titha picked up the tiny orange 'longfrog' and set him safely to the side. "You'll be safe, little fella," she spoke softly. "I promise."

With Sally safe for the moment, the companions were on the move again by torchlight. Titha's eyes followed their path down the cavern. It looked as if it went on forever.

"Do you know the name of this path?" Audun asked Nech.

The Craglin thought for a moment. "I am not certain, but I believe we are in luck," he replied. "Though I cannot recall the exact names of all the paths that lead through the Druidunes from my writings, I do know with certainty that all in Autumnhill's domain lead out of their abyss and into Cragoa—the treacherous province of my home—and that is where we shall go."

"Sounds pleasant," Titha groaned. "I thought you didn't like your home and we shouldn't either?"

"You are correct, young one," Nech replied, gulping. "But we have been left with no choice. Fate led us to the East out of a crumbling Autumnhill, and my home happens to be just East of the Fells. It would not hurt for us to seek council there, either, if I can find those who remain loyal in these trying times. I would very much benefit from the wisdom of an old colleague or two on any possible locations for the Tree of Life. Oh, how I hope others have survived. We will need all the help we can get! Besides, we Craglins are no friend of Vulduun's cause, either, understand, as we and our creature comrades held against his will til the last!" Nech paused, these words leaving his dry lips like an old habit. So much had changed since the last time that statement was still true, including much that led to his banishment. "We will be safe on the outskirts" he re-thought. "Yes, safe as the Elderdrake tends his wounds and regains his strength over his Horizon. Yes, yes, to the outskirts alone we will keep. Perhaps there we can visit an old friend, and eat... Oh, how I miss Gupper's stew."

"We have food, Nech," Audun smirked. "Titha and I packed as much as we could into our sacks before leaving Skaldhall. Here!" he shouted, tossing a roll to Nech through the darkness. The bread landed with a *plop* in the Goblin's craggy yellow hands. Nech immediately stuffed his face, crumbs flying every-which-way as he gobbled it up.

"That will have to do," he responded. "Thank you, young master."

"He's a weirdo, too," Audun said straight-faced to Titha, who chuckled at his use of the word. Paw harrumphed, his stomach growling.

"You already ate!" Titha spouted as she rubbed his side. "Don't get greedy, fuzzybutt."

The enormous bear groaned, rolling his eyes at Titha, then plumped his round behind firmly down into the dirt trail. Haldor followed suit, flinging himself down onto the cool ground. Audun landed atop him with a thud.

"These two need some rest," he said, scratching behind his

hound's floppy ears. Audun loosened his gear from Haldor, laying his provisions and torch out as he cuddled up into the hound. "Why do you call these Caverns the Druidunes?" he asked Nech out of nowhere.

"That's what we call them, too," Titha interjected. "Though it was the name for the caves behind Mt. Meri at home. These do feel the same to me."

"All caverns of this nature are called Druidunes by the old races of the world, younglings," Nech clarified. "They are not named for their location, but for the beings that created them." The three looked into the distant dark as they paused, letting their beast brethren rest.

"The Druids…" Titha whispered.

"Yes," Nech replied. "They are the first race, the eldest beings made of rock and earth and root, and know all the teachings of the world. Druids are, in essence, the keepers of us all; good, evil, it matters not. They are as ancient and wise as the soil beneath our feet. Your people call them Cave Giants, Audun—and know this place as the 'Fell Caverns' or 'The Abyss' more crudely. But they are one and the same. We should not rest long, young ones. Not so far into the dark, at least."

"That makes more sense. I read about Cave Giants all the time," Audun added, unfazed. "But my books say they left a long time ago. So where are they? Do you know? Where did they go?"

"Everywhere," Nech responded, his torch raised above his head. "They are the land, the stone, the trees and life itself." A deep silence fell over the caverns as heads turned, hoping to catch a glimpse of a Druid or Giant. But nothing came. Just as the old Goblin lowered his torch, a tiny glimmer of blue shone out from up ahead. "What is that?" Titha growled curiously. "Is it a Druid?"

"Certainly not. No, no. That is not possible, sproutling. As young master Audun said, they left our lands ages ago…" Nech spoke, thought there was unease within his voice.

Slowly, and together, they walked toward the blue shimmer. With each step another tiny twinkle revealed itself in the abyss, until the cavern around them shone like the night sky full of stars. Each rough surface began to bounce sapphire light back and forth, revealing more and more sparkling, etherial stones.

"It's beautiful!" Titha cried, her breath heavy.

"What about our stuff?" Audun yelped clutching the shrouded Sunstone—but the others were entranced.

"It can wait," Titha replied. "Just look at all the blue!" Their torchlight began to glimmer brilliantly off blue crystals, hundreds of glistening geodes protruding from the cavesides and ceiling.

Nech was enraptured. "Such a tremendous display of—well—*Magick*… I have never seen a sight quite like this," he proclaimed, his yellow face shining in the blue light. His eyes, as were Titha and Audun's, became fixated on the crystals. The harder they stared into them, the brighter they seemed to glow, until a swell of sapphire filled their minds, overtaking their sight. And as suddenly as the lumination had begun—it dispersed—darkness taking them once more.

Titha snapped up, her head jolting as she looked for her companions. But she was alone. She tried to cry out for them, but no words came. A great panic washed over her troubled mind—her chest tight and heaving— when from out of the darkness shot forth an ancient face made of rock and root; Its features weathered yet harsh. Vines intertwined the face, creating a long beard before twisting up into a pointed set of wooden, branched antlers atop its head. Two enormous earthen hands reached out to her from the darkness—then wiped its blanket away like black paint from a canvas. All became white, and a great vision overtook Titha Mae…

At first, there was nothing. Just a blinding white light made up of all colors. Slowly, its glow retreated into an orb as it floated into the sky. It was the Moonstone. Next to it, a warm, harsh golden light joined it, before subduing into the Sunstone. Each stone sat still in thin air, before three Elk stepped forth from nothingness. The greatest of the three stretched outward, his glistening crown of horns embracing the stones. Each antler grasped to a stone like a hand, fusing them into place. The mighty Elk let out a shrill cry, and ran. His fellow kings joined him, and they lept into the air, swirling up until all three landed as one enormous Black Bear. The bear's eyes shone differently, one of the white Moonstone – the other of the golden Sunstone. As the Black Bear ran gnarling and gnashing, its mass began to ebb and flow away until its fur shed to reveal a Red Wolf. But the eyes remained the same; One of white and one of Gold. The Wolf turned back, making eye contact, then howled as it turned to run. Its fierce pace took a toll on its body until its fur shed yet again, revealing a smaller Snowy Fox. Its white and gold eyes darted maddeningly as it fled, its energy almost spent. As it took off into the distance it shook snow from its fur, then stumbled. From below it a spring of water rushed forth, consuming the white Fox until it drowned; its fur shedding way to the slippery scales of a Salmon. The Salmon sped forward into the water, its body rushing upstream vigorously until an enormous long shadow overtook it. Massive jaws snapped forth and swallowed the Salmon whole, consuming it and inheriting the white and gold eyes. Out of the water a multi-colored Serpent now slithered into the light. The snake's body continued to grow until its own shadow consumed it. Then, out of the bright nothingness above swooped a Great Eagle. Its regal talons snatched up the Serpent, tossing it into the air before swallowing it whole. As the Eagle consumed the Snake, its eyes changed color, too – one to white, and one to gold. It let out a magnificent cry, looking back again. It paused, revealing its full splendor, then flapped its broad wings downward, lifting it up into an unfolding sky before splitting in two – each half flying away until it could no longer be seen. As their forms left, so did stillness. The blank nothingness began to stir upward in a violent vortex, and everything else began to fall downward. Down, down, down… Plummeting, until…

Titha slammed onto the ground, her backside landing with an awful thromp. She clinched, rolling over in pain as an awful noise escaped her mouth. She rose slowly, the aches spreading to her entire body as a burning sensation began beneath her feet. She tried to scream, but before she could, horrid flames shot up into the darkness and everything turned to red madness. The same three Elk ran forth from behind the flames, but their fur was fleeting and their flesh rotting. The mightiest of the three fled as two great bone claws destroyed its brethren from behind. Titha gasped as she saw horrid figures arise in their places – one resembling her father, and the other Sigrid. The claws reached out from behind them, ensnaring the remaining mighty Elk by its head as it cried. The shadowy silhouettes of Theole and Sigrid each forced a stone – one of white and one of gold – into the crown of antlers on the Elk's skull. The red madness then engulfed all, and everything perished into fire. Only a crown of antlers, adorned with two jewel-like orbs, remained. It rose above, horrid and all-powerful – hoisted by bone claws.

The red began to fade, but the burning remained. For a while more there was nothing. Life began to return, but only as a thin sliver of vision. A narrow crack of white light flowed like mist against an unknown ground – its surface smooth and clear like a still lake. Huge, heavy sets of stone feet walked the misty grasses to the sides, their footsteps further and further away. Between them, a fair and perfect pair of indigo feet followed – almost gliding – atop the glassy water…

... *"Mother?"*

Titha gasped for air, her mind returning to the world around her like water being poured back into a cup. Her thoughts splashed about as she panicked—looking every direction. But *she* was not there. It was a dream. All of it.

Such powerful emotion echoed across land and air until it awoke two sleeping Lunas in a fit of confusion. A strong, meaningful wind shot through the doors of Roostwood, its breath traveling down the grand halls until it rustled the grass of the knoll at the very center.

Gilly shot up from her flowerbed, the Sun's light gently bouncing off broad white petals. She ran across warm moss, flinging open the beds of her sisters. One revealed Beebee tossing and turning as she cried, her eyes half shut but brimming with tears. The other was empty. Gilly placed her hands on her forehead, her heart heavy with worry as it had been since Titha's departure. She walked back to Beebee's bed, lifting her into the cradle of her arms. There they sat beneath their moonflowers, shielded from the gentle Sunlight in the trees above. Gilly rocked her baby sister gently. Whatever vision had come to them had brought a dreadful feeling of mourning and loss. They sat alone, embracing one another in the pale light.

Gilly sighed. "Where are you, Titha Mae?"

Titha's head continued to throb as it bounced about; the world around her in constant motion. Her body tossed as consciousness returned to her. Finally able to open her eyes a bit, she beheld green for the first time since she had left her sisters and her home. Excited, she sat up, her hands realizing they were in Paw's fur. She gripped to him tightly.

Paw slammed his feet into the grass, halting his run and flinging Titha forward. The enormous bear caught her mid-air, tossing her to the ground and licking her face and nuzzling her uncontrollably. Titha couldn't help but laugh.

"I'm okay, I'm okay!" she cried out, hugging his thick fuzzy neck with her whole body. "Paw!" She yelped, clutching his cheeks and holding him still. "I'm okay…"

Haldor galloped over coming to a dusty stop. He looked tired and worried, his wavy gray fur clumped together. The poor hound still held an extinguished bundle of sticks in his muzzle. Nech jumped down from behind a weary Audun, who too looked much worse for wear.

"Dear child!" he cried, running to Titha. "Oh, dear child... I thought I had lost you both to the darkness!"

"What happened?" Titha asked, squinting.

"The light of the crystals overtook us all, and everything turned to chaos. They fell from the walls—shattering like glass before their blue light extinguished! It was horrid, young one! Rocks and dirt and shards and *oh* it was terrible! You both fell prey to it. Haldor was able to fling Audun astride him with the Sunstone, but Paw and I became stuck and separated from you. It was all we could do to free you from the caving slag. We are very fortunate to have escaped the Druidunes... and oh, my child. I am just overjoyed to see your green eyes once more!" Nech leaned down, his bloody knees resting in the grass. He embraced Titha and Paw, the three of them sharing a tender moment in strange lands. "I am so glad you are alright," he added, unable to stop smiling.

Titha looked over his shoulder. Audun stood gripping Haldor's fur. She brushed passed Nech and walked over to the young boy slowly. His eyes were pink and filled with fear. Slowly his gaze rose to her. He did not smirk, or speak, or move. Titha stood with him staring into his eyes.

"You saw it, too..." she spoke softly.

He nodded, tears welling in his big hazel eyes.

"Saw what?" Nech asked from behind.

"I... don't know how to describe it," Titha replied with heavy words. "But I saw the Elk Kings, the Stones, and many other animals."

"A vision? How fascinating!" Nech shouted. Heavy questions hit his horned-head all at once. "Did you see a location, Titha? Any sort of landmark?" he asked, grabbing her shoulders in an alarming manner. "Did you, my child?" Nech was unusually manic in his inquiry.

"No," Titha replied. Even if she had, she didn't remember now. All she could think of was that fair, wondrous pair of feet after a red, swirling madness. Nech turned from her and gripped Audun, asking the same.

"No!" Audun shouted, too. "There was no place or anything. Just white... and *red*." He collapsed into a fearful agony. Titha rushed to him, cradling her young friend.

"Leave him alone!" Titha shouted. "I know it sounds strange but we saw the same thing, didn't we, Audun?" She held her friend, wiping sweat from his cold forehead with her cloak. "I will tell you what we saw. Let him rest. Audun's not okay."

"I'm fine," the young Viking responded harshly. He was quite used to being babied, but couldn't stand it at home, or now. "I can tell him, too. I'm okay, Titha."

"Let us rest and you may recount the tale together then, my companions," Nech decreed as he walked to the younglings. "For if you truly saw such telling things, then the full details absolutely cannot wait."

CHAPTER TEN

Deathholes and Destiny

"How riveting," Nech spoke, his head shaking. "How utterly fascinating."

They were on the move again after a nice mid-Day rest and meal, both full of the youngling's splendid recounting of their vision. The Sun had become covered by clouds overhead, and all eight paws of their faithful beasts walked steadily into new lands as the Fells' shadows became distant behind them.

"Such a vision from the Druids is only spoken of in grand tales from long ago," the Goblin added. "And for you both to see it as if one and the same? Incredulous. Baffling. Marvelous!" Then Nech fell silent, both thrilled and envious of what the two younglings had described to him in detail. "It would seem much in the history of our lands has led you two to meeting, my young masters. Such a past—and such a future—asks so much of you both… Terrible burdens for such young minds to bear. Yet you venture forth through strife, fear and loss. It is awe-inspiring to such a humble Craglin Scribe. I am amazed at your bravery. And I thank you for it. In time, hopefully-so will all of Gaela."

It was notably colder in the Craglands, a terrain lush with much different greens than Titha or Audun had ever known. The trees were enormous, harshly shaped and hardy. They were evergeens, sure, but thick and jagged with giant needles and strange spiky pink fruits. They reminded Titha of the occasional Cedar trees back in Ythengrey—though these were much drier and much more foreboding. There were no flowers or berries at their roots, either; just starchy grasses full of thick emerald and juniper blades.

Every so often, the earth beneath their feet would reveal a glimpse at what had given the Craglands its name: The vibrant clay soil ran craggy and cracked, and enormous fissures scarred the terrain. From above, the broad flat landscape revealed its true nature: A bird's eye could see the lands peppered with round craters. Some of these craters housed life and evergreens, others were barren but for the steam or water that rested in their bellies. Nech had warned the party of these craters, and advised they steer clear of ever wandering down into one—whether it housed steam or not. "Always traverse the flats," he'd say. It only took one massive explosion of boiling water bursting forth from a steamy crater to show them why. The waters shot straight into the sky as high as the treetops, and then fell back as steam to the flats around it. Hotsprings, the Craglins called them. Titha felt a more appropriate name was needed; something direct like "deathholes" would do. She was utterly fascinated by their unpredictable nature. Some were filled with splendid water, and Titha looked into their deepest depths to find they were layered with every color of the rainbow. Others steamed on quietly, their shallow pools reflecting the trees and skies above. All were, nonetheless, prone to the violent explosions, and whenever one *did* explode, it sent skiddish creatures into a frenzy. Spritely squirrels and enormous crickets would leap terrified from the grasses, and weird howls would echo through the treetops. Titha was confused by this volatile place and its insects being larger than its rodents, and could not figure out why anyone in their right mind would live in such a noisy, unpredictable place; though it *was* beautiful in a dangerous sort of way.

"Now, in these visions," Nech inquired intently, continuing his quest for knowledge, "you are absolutely, definitively positive there was no location revealed to you? No landmarks, or vista? Nothing?"

"Nothing, Nech!" Titha replied, frustrated. "We told you everything we saw. Three times."

"The *animals were* everything," Audun interjected. "We should be looking for animals and not places."

"Hmmm... Perhaps you are right. Fascinating, yet foreboding," Nech scowled. "I may be an expert in lore and legends, but such mythical magick is beyond my writings and studies, younglings. Yes, the magick of Druids is a language of its own—far removed from the etchings of Gaela's mortal peoples in this day and age. If only I could refer to the rest of the Cragoan Scribes for council… but I fear that is impossible. Yes, impossible. Even if so—I am not sure that any of us would be of much help regarding such a fantastical prophesy as the one you two recount. Long have I preferred the teachings of knowledge over the mystics of wisdom, for that is not my domain. The Shaman, however, will know what to make of this. He will know the tongue of this magick. He lies far outside the Craglands into the snowy shadow of Mt. Crag and is no friend to our misguided rulers, so an ally he shall have remained. Yes, to him we must got. We must traverse the entire southern flatland, but the Pine Forest will shield us, and such a journey will take us away from prying eyes. Yes, yes! To the Shaman, then. My old friend will undoubtedly know what to make of all this."

"Well are we there yet, then?" Titha barked sarcas-tically. "There's only so much exploding water and question answering a girl can take."

No sooner did she ask then did the trees give way, and an impressive landscape opened before them. The craggy clay and craters swept into a vast flatland. Trees were a bit more scarce there, and at the center of it all rested the largest crater in all of Cragoa. It was as big as anything Titha or Audun had ever seen. In its heart stood an orange volcano of the most splendid sort. Spiral-sculpted stairs wrapped from the foot of the behemoth formation all the way around to its top where they disappeared into a snow cap—which must have been as high as Mt. Meri. Lavish patterns of yellow, green, and black adorned the entire volcano. Some resembled monstrous bugs, others took the shape of sharp-beaked birds and clawed monkeys. It stood out like a grand monument of nature against the snowy hills behind it.

"We have arrived!" Nech exclaimed. "Welcome, my young friends, to The Craglands of Cragoa—my home."

Titha scoffed, laughing as her green eyes gaped wide. It was a proper reaction, too. Nothing had prepared her for the sight before her, not even the bleakness of Autumnhill. The further she got from home, it seemed, the stranger the world became: Goblins with yellow skin, adorned with brown leather and flat gray iron plates scurried across the bustling crater's cityscape astride enormous black crickets, each carrying a load of… something. The crickets were shiny and loud. *Really* loud. Everything was loud here, and the more she saw and heard, the more bizarre it became, but she did not dare look away.

Small but burly monkeys leaped from tree to tree picking the odd pink fruits Titha had eyed on her way into the Craglands. The monkeys were a grayish brown with pink faces and hands themselves, and their tails were long and expressive. Each had large, wide eyes of amber or yellow or hazel, and they were shockingly fast. The curious beasts worked as hard as the Craglins as they swung from tree to tree, tossing the prickly fruit down to Craglins who would catch them in leather mitts and place them into iron pales. Steam shot into the sky all around the spectacle from cracks in the earth, but the busy beings paid it no mind. Nech, however, had thought long and hard about these sights, how he should never return to them, and whether he missed them at all. In this moment he did not, and as he surveyed the enormous volcanic center of his old homeland he grew increasingly troubled.

"So we are going… in there?" Audun gulped, pointing to the intimidating Volcano.

Nech laughed nervously. "Gracious, no!" he hawed, coughing and clearing his throat. "Goodness me, not in a thousand years would I lead you two sprites through the workfields and spewing hatred of my people into the center of that posessed mountain. That is Mount Crag, and we are to stay as far away from it as possible!"

Audun sighed a huge breath of relief. "Fine with me," he

smiled, wiping dirt from his face. "How do we get to your friend, then? Isn't the Shaman like a Jarl? I thought he was your leader—like my father and mother. I know if I was your Jarl I would live in that mountain."

Nech laughed again, as he sorely needed such youthful naivety to ail his nervousness. "No, no, young one. The Shaman is a Shaman as I am a Scribe. I dare say neither is more glamorous than the other but one deals in history and the other, the Shaman, deals in mystics."

"That's great news," Audun spoke earnestly. "I was afraid you were leading us and the Skallstone straight to some greedy goblin king!" Haldor barked in agreeance.

"I would *never*!" Nech acclaimed harshly. "Nor will I have you thinking such heinous thoughts! And besides; we do not have a King, nor Jarl. No. We have an Emperor. Or we did once..." He rubbed the wide forehead between his small pointed horns. "Humans…" he scoffed before looking over to Titha, who sat calmly atop Paw. "I know our time together has been brief, young master Viking, but I assure you I see no possible good coming of this stone ever reuniting with Vulduun… And I will do everything within my power to stop that eventuality. You have my word."

"We'd better get moving, then," Titha added, still staring into the discord at the heart of Cragoa. "Sitting at the edge of this place is starting to make me anxious. I think now that I've seen it,

I'd rather be rid of it altogether."

"I quite agree, spriteling. I quite agree. Though it is my birthground, I dare say it no longer is a happy place for me, or any other, for that matter," Nech continued, rubbing his forehead before licking one hand and running it back through his thin hair. "Nevertheless—the flatlands continue around the outer edges of Cragoa—we walk upon them now. If we keep this high ground and travel southeasterly along their border, we should be able to remain hidden within the steam and trees, as I mentioned. The Shaman resides in the snowcapped hills beyond to the Northeast in the shadow of Mt. Crag. His hut remains shrouded and distant from Cragoan rule, which is undoubtedly aided by the fierce snow and ice of Wundiberg above it. He has been my friend and confidant for a lifetime, the Shaman. Come, young masters; we make no progress by *talking* of this journey. As Titha Mae said—we must be off!"

This ("of course", as he would say) did not mean Nech would cease talking. As the company traversed the southern edge atop the massive crater, he gabbed and babbled on endlessly of the lore of his people. His inner turmoil became outwardly and abundantly apparent. Nech boasted of "all the exemplary achievements" of his small yellow people, only to immediately follow each tale with how "deplorable and utterly despicable" Craglins were as a whole. Titha laughed at Paw as he reacted to the stories. If her Bear-brother rolled his eyes any harder, they'd get stuck in the back of his head. Audun, though, was captivated. He sat atop Haldor, saddled and cradling the shrouded stone as he hung on every word. Vikingmen never spoke of the Craglins aside from the hiccups in history where they clashed in the Fells. To hear the rest of their lore was of great fascination to the young lad. His ears perked particularly high as Nech made mention of Craga again, their Goddess and protector.

"Some believe she is the very spirit of these lands!" he added, his hands waving in the air as he led the party around the crater's edge. "To them, it is *her* blood and *her* thoughts and teachings that course through the hot-springs up, up, *up* into the majesty of Mt. Crag, our volcanic core. She gives Cragoa life, and sustains it on a whim."

Audun didn't blink. He was ensnared in the tale.

"If we are ever to anger her," Nech continued, "Mt. Crag would *explode!* Bursting into a fiery reign of death and suffering—ending all life in Cragoa as we know it!"

Audun gasped, flying backward off of Haldor. He shot up, climbing his companion's fur back up to his saddle. "*Wow*!" he cried, "She sounds *really* powerful!"

"Oh that she is, youngling, if you believe in such things," Nech proclaimed as he raised his chin triumph-antly to the sky. "Though I will always prefer the teachings of Nature and knowledge, I cannot help but feel drawn to and inspired by Craga's—" Nech cut himself short. A particularly dense thicket of steam laid before them, and he had now seen it shift twice.

"I noticed that, too," Titha sputtered, breaking her silence. The fog shifted again, and out stepped a Cragoan Monkey from the mist. His eyes were wide, yellow and kind. He twitched about, surveying each companion with great curiosity. "Hello little fella!" Titha decreed happily. "Aren't you a precious little rascal? Do you have a name?"

"Do not speak to it!" Nech cautioned. "We know not to whom he returns. Shoo! Shoo hairy'knuckles! Off with you!"

The monkey growled at Nech's words, showing his enormous fangs and snarling ferociously. '*Eeerrrreee-eeeeeeeeek!*' the foul monkey cried, and a horde of Craglin bandits shot forth from the steaming fog! Each brandished a crooked sword and wore the same leather and iron armor seen on the workers below. They howled and moaned and shrieked with the monkey as they surrounded the companions in the mist.

"How may are there?" Audun cried out.

"Eleven," Titha replied without hesitation and much to her friend's amazement; her sharp green eyes able to pierce the dense foggy steam. The young Luna brandished her Feathersword, swinging it once through the air, slicing the fog. She brought it to her side and leaned down to Paw's neck. The bandits laughed at her. They didn't seem at all intimidated by Paw or Haldor, either. No. Their attention was on Nech.

"Look who it is, boyos," one of the bandits cackled. "Just loike the pretty picture plastered on all our walls. We knew you'd come crawling back, ol'timer," The leader and smallest of the band called out. He was short and stout for a Craglin, his armor jagged and his head full of frazzled green hair. "Bossman Emperor said he'd pay a pretty proice for 'yer head if you ever returned 'ere, didd'n'e?"

"We want no trouble, fellows," Nech spoke, his words sincere. "We travel the border of Cragoa only—I dare not go down into the crater of my former homestead! I remain fully conscious of the... alternative to banish-ment. Leave us in peace!"

"Yer fancy words don't sway us, bookrat," The bandit leader decreed, spit flying from behind his pointy speckled teeth. "Banish er no banish, 'eres a lot o'money in it for the fella who sees you tryin'a scurry back anywhere near 'ere after what you pulled."

"We will turn back. You will not see my face again," Nech offered, outstretching his hands.

"Oh but seein'it now will be plenty enough, Nechalec. It's too late for'at."

The companions tensed, both beasts ready to pounce.

"Get 'em, boys!" the marauding leader screamed, and the bandits jumped in on Nech and the others in a flurry of steam and debris. Nech leaped in fear, joining Audun astride Haldor. The mighty wolfhound snarled and attacked first, his outstretched maw immediately biting down on the arm of the leader and throwing him violently into a thick treetrunk. Audun scoffed, Haldor's reigns in one hand and his small axe in the other. He brandished it loosely as he attempted to keep the shrouded stone safe between his knees atop his battling hound.

"Got one!" he screamed as he chucked a hand clean off one of the bandits, the goblin squeaming in pain. Behind them, Paw roared ferociously as he backed into a tree. Six of the bandits had surrounded the bear, each knowing they could never take him on in lesser numbers. The Craglins shambled forward, their blades pointed directly at the young bear as foamy spit left their wide mouths. Paw roared again, rearing up onto his hind legs and slamming forward—crushing two of the marauding goblins under his enormous black claws. Titha swung Feathersword as Paw landed, slicing one of the bandits across his chest, besting his armor. The bandit to his side leapt onto Paw, grabbing Titha. They struggled back and forth, Paw busy swiping at the other bandits to keep them back. Titha screamed, rearing her blade as far back as she could before planting it square into the stomach of the bandit under his iron chestplate. The Craglin made a horrid noise, ooze spilling from his jagged mouth as he fell from Paw's back.

Titha's eyes opened wide, her hands covered in the blood

of another living creature. The world became pale and distant around her as the battle raged on, but she continued to fight, adrenaline coursing through her small arms as she swung her sword again, knocking the same goblin down to his knees with a hard slice across his backside. Only two bandits remained in front of them, and they retreated a few steps to rejoin the others. Haldor and Audun had both dispatched of the leader and his two henchmen, and they turned to trap all four remaining bandits between themselves and Paw. The beasts furled and growled, scaring what was left of the bandit squad into submission.

"Mercy!" one of them cried.

Nech scoffed. "Do not heed their crooked words!" he yelled. "They will make haste for Mt. Crag and our journey thus far will be for not! We will be undone!"

Titha looked to Audun across the battlefield, weary and confused. Neither of them knew what to do. The Luna didn't have it in her to end a creature that begged for mercy, no matter how putrid or vile he was. Audun, however, could not deny his heritage in this moment, and he commanded Haldor forward, the hound making short work of the two bandits.

Paw followed suit, overcome by his instincts, tearing down the last bandits that clinged to life. One managed to slice his side, sending the bear into a terrifying rage that ended the stabber's life in a most gruesome manner. Titha screamed, covering her eyes from the sight, when she heard a clang and patter of footsteps take off down the ridge. The leader had survived being thrown to the tree, and he was running down the crater into Cragoa!

"No!" Nech screamed, his voice heavy. He looked on in despair as the bandit ran further down into his homeland, carrying their fate with him. The old goblin's bones began to ache, and he could not look away… Yet just as the bandit was about to reach the city, a fierce streak of feathers shot down from the sky. Out of nowhere it snapped the bandit leader's head backward, sending his lifeless body tumbling and clanging down the craterside. The mysterious blur retreated as quickly as it had appeared. Nech gasped for air, falling back onto Audun. A great calamity had just been prevented, yet the children were terribly confused by what had prevented it. Titha had guessed it was one of Theole's crows, but she was wrong.

The trees above gave way to a great streak, and the same feathered being tackled Nech away from his companions, tumbling with him back up into the needled foliage overhead. Titha panicked, turning to retrieve her friend until she noticed he was laughing. *Laughing*! At a time like this?

"Can it be?" Nech cried. "Oh, Maya!" he cried out again, hugging the bird. "My beloved colleague! I had given you up!" Titha and Audun were beyond perplexed by what was happening. But the beautiful avian beast, it turned out, was an old friend.

"Oh how I grieved upon banishment. I feared the worst, my darling! I feared the absolute, garish worst! How are you here? How have we been reunited?" Nech cried, purely astonished.

"I know your screams among any, you defenseless old hob!" Maya squawked. She was a Peregrine Falcon with shimmering brown, white, tan, and black markings. A dark faceband of plumage accented her head and eyes, which were a deep rich chestnut, just like Paw's. She was, much to Titha's curiosity, very well-versed in the ways of speech and their common tongue, which found her deep in conversation with Nech.

"It is good to see you again, Nechalec," she spoke gently, her voice carrying significant weight for such a small beast. She grabbed Nech's tattered tunic in her talons, flapping her wings to bring him up out of the grass.

"My dear friends," Nech began, "this is Maya, my oldest and fondest colleague and dearest companion. I never thought I would see her blessed feathers again."

Maya bowed to her new acquaintances in mid-air, then shot down to perch on her old friend's shoulder.

"Yet here I am," she replied, landing. "And here you are, lost without me. How could you possibly think it would be okay to return here? What has gotten into you, old Scribe?"

"You're beautiful!" Titha blurted out interrupting the reunion, in love with Maya's gleaming physique. The white feathers on her underside were particularly remarkable, as were the patterns astride her back and upper wings. "And you can talk! None of the animals in Yythengrey can talk, really. Unless my father counts? But that's not the same… just look at you! Can *we* talk? Together? Can I ask you questions? *I really* love animals, especially birds—and frogs. Frogs are great." Paw harrumphed nudging Titha. "But black bears are my absolute all-time faaaaavorite, aren't they, buddy?" she smirked again, nudging her Bear-Brother back. She looked to Maya, still in disbelief. Sure, Lunas could speak to their forest kin, but they never spoke back! "This is just so wonderful. Please talk more," she continued, "and you really are beautiful, I'm not just being nice."

"Thank you, youngling," Maya chuckled, smirk-ing all the way through the young Luna's rant. "But of course I can talk. I am of the Peregrine Order! A Scholar and Scribe like our Craglin friend here; Just smarter and better looking. We share a love of many things, Nech and I; history, culture, ruins, words and above all—language. Though, for him, this manifests in endless babbling."

"Oh, we've noticed," Titha quipped.

Nech smiled, laughing. "How marvelous that you two may meet. This may be the happiest day I've had in quite some time. What a fortunate turn of events! It delights me to see you so luminous, too, Titha. I dare say Maya is like nothing you will have ever encountered in Ythengrey! To my knowledge, of course," he boasted.

"Well, my father *did* turn into a giant owl and battle the Duskfather…" Titha smirked. "But this is so much more fun! As much as I talk to animals, I've always wanted the animals to talk back to me!" Titha shouted, still elated.

"I would be careful what you wish for," Nech smirked, looking to Maya, who shook her head at the sarcastic comment. "But where are my manners?" he continued. "This is Titha of Ythengrey, Maya. And her friend Audun, Son of the Autumn Realm. We have seen much together, and my do we have much to tell."

"It would seem so," Maya replied. She looked to the children. Even in their happy moment she could see the stress behind their eyes. "Their gazes are heavy for such youth. And to see a child of both Luna and Man so closely bonded… What a rarity. A rarity for any two differing peoples these days, I should say," she replied. "You, too, are a mess, old Scribe, and you never answered my question. How could you be so foolish as to return here? And how did *these two* children both come to your care?"

"At this point, I am not sure whom is caring for whom!" Nech laughed. "Oh, it is a long, arduous tale full of peril," he continued, "one I will happily recount for you upon our way. You will come with us, will you not, my dear? You simply must! It is so wonderful to know you are well and to be reunited! We could greatly use your companionship and skills, as well!" He pleeded wide-eyed.

"I must come with you. At least for now, that is. I have many days and events to recount in return, for the sake of my Order, and your journey too, perhaps."

"You certainly do, indeed!" Nech replied inquisi-tively as they began to walk. "I am ecstatic to see you, but so close to home? How have you remained here after what transpired?"

"I am much too fast for your kind. You know this," Maya spoke with a wink of humorous confidence. "Hard as the False Emperor tried, he could not capture my Order amidst your banishment. We have remained here just out of their revolting reach, but I fear our skill has exhausted to mere luck, which will undoubtedly run its course soon. My Peregrines continue to watch from the flatland trees as our homeland descends into disarray. The days grow frustratingly bleak. Moreso even than the time of your banishment."

"I can't stand it any longer!" Titha cried out, interrupting a very tense monologue. "What did you do, Nech? What did you do that was so awful they kicked you out? Is it that bad? Are *you* that bad? And are you never going to tell me because I'm pretty sick of hearing about it if you're never going to tell me what happened!"

Her scoff caught Nech off guard. He lowered his head.

"He did a great and noble thing, child. Do not hold him in disdain," Maya replied sincere.

"Oh," Titha hiccupped. "So tell me, then!"

"Let's be on the move, and I will do just that," she spoke sternly, motioning for Titha to follow their stride. "We mustn't linger any longer. The beasts nor folk are friendly here as they are in your forest home."

The company dusted themselves off and gathered what they needed from the battlefield, continuing their journey eastward as Maya recounted the tale:

"Nech and I were both Council Scribes for our Emperor's Court," she began. "I was appointed to repre-sent the Peregrine Order—and Nech, one of the most learn'ed and erudite Craglins to ever spawn from Craga's clay, was appointed to represent the dying tradition of Craglin Scribes. In the glory days we raided many ruins and wrote many tomes together... countless adventures. And when I say together, I imply Nech wrote as I flew; the result being, either way, grand expeditions and works full of philosophy and lore and research. Until, that is... our Emperor, Kriggoth, perished. He was rowdy—brash much like most Craglins—but possessed an unusually wise and accepting spirit amidst his flaws. For all his faults, he understood the importance of knowledge, and this alone had allowed the Craglins to rise above all other Goblin civilizations. That's a personal opinion, I suppose, but I digress. Kriggoth was respected by his people, nonetheless, and his death was sudden... greatly grieved. The fallout was paramount. In his wake, many rose to claim the Volcanic Throne, but from beneath Mt. Crag rose the worst possible outcome. Cataclysmic, really. Some say he is more shadow or Ogre than Craglin. He very well may be. His name is Ugar.... and whatever the truth, he is *horrid*. Craglins follow strength and moxie, you see, and Ugar has both in folds. He has used them these past seasons to usurp the throne, sieze the Craglands, and thwart all those who questioned Emperor Kriggoth's untimely passing. It has been utterly dreadful to witness."

"Is Ugar as ugly as he sounds?" Titha asked as they traveled, fascinated.

"Yes, spriteling," Maya hissed. "He is brutish, foul, and sports a horribly unfortunate face. He has used his burnt, craggy hands to pry all of Cragoa from reason or sanity in a relatively short amount of time." She paused, fuming. "Where was I? Right—our friend Nech would not stand for it all and challenged the ignorance Ugar spewed to the people. While others sat complacent and comfortable under Ugar's brash displays of 'protection' and 'power,' Nech fought tooth and claw to bring Craglins the *truth* of what was coming. He refuted Ugar's untimely

"Ugar had killed Kriggoth, hadn't he?" Titha asked.

"Yes, child. But it was far worse than that," Maya frowned. "This foul deed ran much deeper, to the very core of the Ever-war I am sure you are familiar with—and its twisted master. Vulduun, yes. Our once trusted Master of the Dawn had betrayed the creatures of the Day, and by his hand Ugar rose and Kriggoth fell. By the time Nech discovered these vile truths, it was too late. Ugar had swayed too much of Cragoa to his side. The Council was disbanded, and Nech exiled."

"What happened to the rest of the Council?" Titha asked.

"They remain, splintered into new roles beneath Ugar's boots; smug and content that their arses still occupy positions of influence; no matter the price."

"They sound useless," Titha quipped.

"*Below* that, sprite. Far below. Spineless, gutless, cowardly yellowbellies. Every last one of them. Their passivity has cost a once great Mydlan civilization its pride and prosperity. I hate them for it."

Titha furled her brow as Maya grew visibly altered by her anger.

"Mydlan," Audun interrupted, "That's where we are now..." He was holding a leather satchel filled with rolls of crumpled paper.

"Yes it is, child," Maya answered. "What are you doing?"

"Charting our path," Audun replied straight-faced.

"It would seem we have a Scribe in the making!" Nech chirped.

"In that case," Maya added, "to the west, and at the foot of the Fell Mountains, lie the hills of your home from whece you came. Everything from there, your Autumnhill and westward on to Titha's Duskridge home, is known in the Great Lore as Westlyn. Got that?" Audun nodded with a "duh", scribbling furiously with a piece of charcoal he must have found on their journey. "That puts both Titha's Yythengrey and your home there in Westlyn together; a vast expanse of fields, forests and rolling round mountains that stretch far into the Sunsets. Everything to the East of the Fells, until you get to the Svells, is Mydlan—the long, vertical expanse of valleys, craters, caves and canyons we call home. This is, as I said, where we are now. Still follow?"

"What's vertical mean?" Audun asked without breaking his writing spree.

"Up and down. North to South. It is the opposite of horizontal, which is sideways, like the grand Horizon," Maya demonstrated, spreading her wings wide.

Titha could not hear the word 'horizon' without thinking of her father, Vulduun, or the horror that now rose with the Sun. "And everyone in Mydlan will also suffer if Vulduun tries to control them, too… right?" she asked.

"In some ways, we already are," Nech added, "It will only grow worse, my dear child, especially if your precious Night is undone for eternity as Vulduun wishes for it to be. All life depends on the full cycles of both our Sun and Moon, whether said life knows this or not. Sadly, I do not believe Vulduun cares if all creatures are made to suffer and die if it means he can be rid of the Night's horrible hold over his loss and grief."

This sat hard on Titha's mind. She could still hear the screams and smell the smoke from the last hours she spent in Yythengrey. She shook her head, thinking of all the pain, suffering, and loss she had seen, learned of, and dreamed in the short days since her hasty departure. It pained her that she hadn't really taken the time to think about it all—how terribly the world needed *good.* Just that, too—*goodness* and kind people. Such a simple thing to her young mind, it was, yet seemed impossible for most out in the real world.

"The whole world is in turmoil," Titha whispered, "and Lunas sleep in their flowers..." She found comfort, however, by looking to each of her companions. They were the very kindness absent from the lands at large. Nech, Audun & Haldor, Paw of course, and now Maya.

"Is Ugar in the volcano mountain now?" Audun asked, reigniting the conversation and breaking his own furious scribbling.

"Indeed he is," Nech replied as he walked between Paw and Haldor, his head hanging low. "And oh how I wish Craga would blow its top, ridding us all of his fangled face."

"By her grace! If only," Maya replied to her old friend, atop his shoulder. "Cragoa was the last Goblin refuge free of Vulduun's grip. All other Goblin races have risen to his cause during the Ever-war. But now, as his shadow strangles our craggy lands, and Ugar succumbs upon the throne—I fear all of Mydlan will follow into true *madness*." Maya stopped, breathing feverishly. Her words conjured visions of fierce dragonfire in all of their minds. "Only the great expanses of Eastlyn remain untouched by his influence, or so we are told. Our Osprey kin bring whispers from the lands to the East of the Svells and it is said to remain pure. But my Order brings me great and constant worry from every direction within our own lands. They bring frequent whispers that Ugar plans to enslave Cragoa in sacrifice to Vulduun and its fallen people will fulfill the last missing piece of his wretched army."

A hush fell over the party. Nech shook his head. "Such dark magick is unfortunately fitting in such foul times. His hordes lie in secret no more. By his hands, they have ravaged both the sacred forests of Yythengrey and all of the Autumn Realm. Maya, the Order hears whispers of such calamity because you know it to be inevitable! Ugar craves only power, and Vulduun has given it to him in turn for his allegiance! Oh, how very dreadful that so many must suffer from the vanity of one individual!" Nech put his head in his hands in an attempt to stop unavoidable throbbing. "Though it is all much worse than this, Maya. Vulduun now has the Moonstone and Titha's father, Theole The Watcher."

Maya squawked, her neck feathers ruffling into an immediate tizzy. "*This* is the daughter of *The Watcher*?" she cried. "*Why* am I just now hearing of this? You should have led with that information, you old fool!" Maya scoffed. "This is just great. The Drake has reclaimed an Eterna Stone? And The Watcher is forfeit? Bah! Terrible, terrible tidings," Maya cawed as her tail quivered. "So he has succeeded in his first surmounting... Tell me, Nech, tell me he hasn't the Sunstone yet?"

Audun's ears perked up and his arms wrapped tightly around his family's shrouded stone. "No he doesn't," he spoke sternly.

"And this hatchling?" Maya gasped, whipping her head around to Audun. "The 'son of the Autumn Realm'? Nech, you slippery little snake! We are finally reunited for you to tell me not but half-truths? This child is the offspring of Angvar and Sigrid, is he not? Look at the history within his eyes! You old fool!"

"Well, I—" Nech fumbled as Maya continued to cackle over him, "—I hesitate to utter any such revelations within these lands!" he stammered.

"Poppycock!" Maya snapped. "That hallowed Stone's very

light pulses through your veins, doesn't it, child? Do you hold it now? The stone? Have you brought it here so close to Ugar's grasp?"

Audun twitched away, wary. How could this chatty falcon know who he is from a single glance?

Maya smiled, "The Peregrine Order has seen much, Son of Angvar. I do not mean to alarm you. Forgive my… harshness. It is Nech I am angry with, not you," she added, practically glaring a hole through the Goblin's forehead.

Audun did not speak. He turned to Nech, not one to relinquish his trust immediately to a *talking bird*.

Nech smiled, "She is on our side, young master. And yes, my dear, he carries the greatest weight of us all."

"Nech you buffoon!" Maya squawked again, flying right back into her tizzy. "You bring these two heirlings this close to doom? *And with an Eternal Stone*? What in Craga's name has ahold of your brain? Have you grown foolish—no—*stupid*—in my absence, old hob?"

"Now, now, my dear, there is no need for name calling! Though I fear it may soon be justifiable… as I have not told you everything… yet..." Nech's fingers fumbled his leather vest as he looked to the ground. "And this is the gravest of any news I could possibly recount…" he spoke apprehensively. "After my banishment… I set out to travel to Yythengrey and warn their

Watcher of what is, or what was, to come. I thought, as the Lunas are a fair and noble race, he would listen to reason and at least one mighty peoples would rise to challenge Vulduun. I was too late, however, and all of our worst fears have come true, Maya, my dear—"

"—Get to the point, Nechalech!" Maya yelled.

"—It was taken from me! Shortly before I met Titha Mae and our journeys became one, I was brutally ransacked by Reeks and they took it… they took the Eternal-tome! I have no doubt their foul hands have delivered it and our life's work now lays at the claws of Vulduun, and he now holds all the secrets of Gaela condensed into one clump of brilliant text! All that we have discovered, Maya, all of it! His heinous calamity will only hasten with all the forbidden knowledge of our realms now in his hands."

"Are you talking about the Crown of Elk Kings, and the Trinity and the stones and everything else you keep mentioning?" Titha asked. "How would the Dawnfather not know about that already? Isn't he super old and wise and powerful? Why else would he have taken the Moonstone and my father?"

"You are right to a certain degree, child," Maya answered, "but no longer would I call him wise. Powerful? Absolutely. Ancient? Yes, but such a timeworn mind cannot hold onto all the great secrets of an entire Eon. The Elderdrakes did not create Gaela herself, but carved her vistas into liveable, thriving lands with the light of the Sun and Moon. Gaela, our world, is eternal, and she is her own master. Our ancestor's lore tells us she holds other ancient children of creation in the same high regard as the Great Drakes. We believe she only divulged certain information to certain races and to certain deities to keep order and balance. We are all quite different and separate because of it, but perhaps only this has kept such powerful knowledge from becoming all-consuming. Our greatest work, however, the writings in the tome that Nech, shall we say 'misplaced,' charts just that: *all of it.* Everything we have found in any ruin or from any Scholar, Scribe, Bard or Storyteller across the known lands resides in that tome! Many ancient places have we explored to gather such knowledge, but to hold knowledge that deities—even the Elderdrakes themselves—had not known was exhilarating and priceless. And very dangerous too, it would seem."

Titha's eyes were wide with amazement. "Boy, if Nech didn't feel bad before I bet he does now," she smirked as she shot a glance his way.

"Indeed," Maya said, half scowling. "For now Vulduun has access to every bit of recorded knowledge we've gathered concerning the Trinity: The Eternal Stones and the Antler Crown… the Crown of Elk Kings."

"Yet as Titha Mae pointed out, surely he knew previously, Maya," Nech interjected. "His plans to invade Yythengrey and take not just their stone, but their Watcher as well, were already unfolding. He has taken Sigrid too, Maya, Shieldmaiden of Autumnhill. He knows that he himself cannot touch the might of the Eternal Stones, not since he and his love forfeited their light to mortal folk long ago. Vulduun knows he needs their blood and hands to exact his plan! Everything is playing out as if he knew of the Crown and the Stones' united power!"

"Do you think he knew every single song ever sung regarding the Tree of Life, hmm? Of Igdrasil's whereabouts and where she may finally reveal herself? Or all the known passages of the open lands? Do you think he knew the names of all Mydlan's Scribes and Scholars and any others who may oppose him? Because he *does now!* Whatever he *didn't know he sure knows now,* you fool!"

"This squabbling is pointless!" Nech yelled. "My old friend, we must clear our minds and do something constructive for the future—not debate the past! Such misfortune is already extant, whether we wish it to be or not! We are now in a race to find Igdrasil and reach the Elk Kings before Vulduun himself, and we must succeed! For no matter the race nor land, tome or not… the world will always fall as one!"

Titha was unsure if it was Nech's foreboding words or the looming shadow of Mt. Crag, but a great sense of dread washed over their dim path. She gripped Paw's fur tightly as she rode atop him–resisting the call of the darkness. Cringing, she looked up to the Sun, its rays still hidden mid-sky behind thick clouds. "I don't think this is the end," she said softly. "I think there are others who will fight to defend it." She smiled as a beam of light broke through the overcast before being engulfed by the shadow of the mountain. "And if not, then the world still has us."

"I suppose you are right, little Luna," Nech said, looking up from his hands, his eyes smiling back at his young friend. "Your hopeful heart never ceases to amaze me, young one." He looked to the road ahead, pondering a forked path at the end of his sight. As he did, a lone white Fox darted out from behind a great pine tree and made for the left. It immediately caught Titha's eye. Nech's brow furrowed as he eyed the speedy little creature, then Titha. "Isn't that curious?" he said.

"Did you see it, Audun?" Titha asked excitedly. He nodded, their faces alight. "That was a Fox just like the one from our vision! I am sure of it!" she yelled.

"It is a sign, then!" Nech exclaimed. "One that must not be taken lightly, I feel. Our journey takes us in the Fox's direction," he said, his eyes no longer able to see the snowy little fellow off in the distance. "And we must mention this to the Shaman. Undoubtedly it is of the utmost importance."

"Trusting to magicks and superstition now, are we?" Maya frowned.

"Oh, my dear Peregrite," Nech replied. "To what else do we turn in such times, when knowledge has failed us so?"

"Are we headed for the Shaman still?" Audun interjected, "Or the Elk Kings? I think we can beat Vulduun to the Elk Kings and give them at least the Sunstone. That would prevent Vulduun from taking over, right?"

"In theory, yes, absolutely," Maya answered. "To find the Elk Kings, hatchlings, we must first reach the Gates of Igdrasil, and Igdrasil Herself. And no living Falcon, Luna, Man, Beast, Goblin, nor any other knows exactly where those hallowed gates lie. And it is a very big world we live in."

Nech looked to his dear friend, delighted to finally have a positive response for her. "With the Shaman's help we may find Her yet, dearest friend!" he said, "For these two younglings shared a most peculiar vision. Come, Maya! I have not told you everything. Not yet. Let us be on our way to the Shaman and I will explain why we found that snowy Fox most exciting, and why we must now follow Gaela's every whisper and sign. For it is all of great importance."

"Fine. But I do not like that old hermit," Maya scoffed.

"The Shaman?" Nech asked, chuckling. "He is of a unique temperament, sure, but let us not form Titha and Audun's opinions of him before they are acquainted. That would be unwise! Now if I may ask, Maya dear, it may be best if you look to the road ahead, lest we suffer any more surprises," he continued, wary of the white Fox's coinci-dental appearance.

The beautiful falcon nodded and flew above them in silence. Moments passed before she returned as stealth-ily as she had left, darting to Nech's shoulder with a nod of safety.

"Onward, then!" Nech proclaimed.

Titha reached down to him, her face rosy and inviting. Nech climbed aboard Paw, clinging to their supplies astride the Bear-brother.

The friends picked up their pace to a briskful bound. They were off for the dark side of the volcano, one companion greater. The bandits of Cragoa lay slain in the dirt and clay far behind them now—yet amidst that battle's bloody end, their renewed travels eastward, and their wondrous conversation—not a'one had thought to look for the yellow-eyed monkey that started it all.

CHAPTER ELEVEN
Snow Shrouded Secrets

Nothing on their entire journey had been harder to walk through than Cragland snow. It was lovely, sure, but also cold and blank and foreboding. Titha took to riding on Paw at all times, her bare feet were tough but not used to the ice-cold that came with the all-consuming white. Snowflakes, however, she found positively gorgeous. She just didn't want so many at once. Snow was quite rare in Ythengrey's low meadows, and any Luna who dared trek the frosty piles atop their great wandering mountains did so with much preparation.

Audun brushed snow from his button nose, looking back to Cragoa, thinking of its warm oranges and lush greens to keep his mind off the bitter wind. The flatlands had turned to slopes hours ago, and as they climbed higher over the backside-hills of Mt. Crag, the chillier the wind—and the darker Night's hold—became. Haldor and Paw's fur kept them warm, while Nech, and Maya (who seemed much fluffier now), remained tolerant of this part of their homeland. The city behind them was much warmer in climate down deep in its crater, yet neither Scribe was stranger to the dark side of the volcanic mountain. They had friends here. Or Nech did, rather. It wasn't uninhabitable, after all; just bleak and sunless as Mt. Crag's shadow was so great as to allow snow to blanket the ground year-round. This felt quite fitting, as in the grand scheme of their journey, Titha and Audun were further North now than their homelands, and it showed in their disposition.

Nech walked ahead of them with Maya perched atop his shoulder. They led the party down barely- distinguishable snow-trails that wove between enormous evergreen trees, each blanketed in white. There was no pink fruit on trees this side of Mt. Crag, though. This told Titha all she needed to know about this place and its miserable chill. She pulled her cloak tighter still, lowering the hood to cover her face. Up ahead, Maya left Nech's shoulder and darted forward into the foggy flurries. Titha looked to Audun; both had learned to become alert when the falcon darted off. She returned shortly after, however, and Nech motioned to his young companions to hurry forth as they had arrived at their destination.

Faint candlelight shone from tiny round holes on what appeared to be a small hill up ahead. It was a clay mound molded into an intricate labyrinth of small tunnels and rooms, each with its own circular windows. The top was completely covered in snow as were the trees behind it, but strange wooden pikes and figures protruded atop the structure. Some had feathers tied to them with leather cord, others helped hold up a crude chimney that billowed smoke into the diminishing daylight. One of the center windows went dark as a large round head entered its frame.

"Don't just stare, you croakin' moron!" a scraggly voice yelled from within the hut. "Let them in!"

A mound of snow crashed down from atop the structure as a hidden door flung open, revealing what looked like an unpleasant turtle standing upright wearing a ragged canvas apron and wooly'sash.

"Better come 'nside," it groaned. "Cold out 'ere." His tone was baritone and deadpan, much like a reptile's croak. Titha looked to Audun again, each astounded at the sight. They'd never seen nor heard of such a creature before.

"Don't stare," Nech added. "It isn't polite. Come inside!" He motioned from the door, walking in. Titha leaned down to Paw before dismounting underneath some evergreens.

"Are you alright, brother?" she asked. He smiled and

nodded, the cold and snow having benefited the cut on his side. Titha hopped down, plopping into the snow beside the hut. She grabbed two fistfuls and packed them onto Paw's injury, a trick Nech had taught her. "You were so brave, fuzzybut. I love you." She reached over for his maw, grabbing his furry cheeks as she nuzzled her nose against his. "We won't be inside long. Keep Haldor company, okay?" Paw nodded. Haldor lumbered over to the big bear underneath the trees and laid up next to his back, drifting off as the snow gently fell. Audun pulled his blankets from his sack, throwing them over the boys before turning to follow his friend.

Titha squinted inside the hut, her eyes overwhelmed by a hundred tiny candles. As her vision adjusted, she spotted every trinket, bottle and bobble imaginable adorning the walls. Shelves lined the round room, all of them filled to the brim with colorful potions and stacks of scrolls.

"Your bear is hurt, spriteling," a voice called from the next room. "Snow won't do him much good. Grab a bottle of the purple liquid and put it on its wounds. Quickly!"

Titha snapped at the muffled voice and looked to the nearest shelf, her green eyes gleaming with excitement. There were so many pretty bottles! She reached up, her indigo hand landing on a light purple one, its color not dissimilar from the rosiness in her own cheeks.

A stiff little green hand slapped her fingers before she could grab it. "Not 'at one," the wrinkly turtle from earlier croaked. "Blow 'em up, 'at one will," he added before slowly lumbering a few bookcases over and grabbing a much brighter bottle of purple goo. "This one," he gurgled, waddling off into the other room. She tried to hold in her astonishment but couldn't as it finally came bursting out. She knew she had seen much stranger things of late, but nothing quite as satisfying as a turtle-man, or whatever he was. Audun stepped in from outside, coveting his people's shrouded Sunstone. He sat it down momentarily on the wooden floor so he could rub his cold hands together.

"I'll be right back," Titha told him, walking back out into the snow with the potion. Audun picked up the stone and closed the door behind him, turning back to see the same overwhelmingly colorful sight Titha had seen moments before. As he wandered in, Nech appeared from around a corner, rushing to him.

"Whatever you do Audun, do not speak of nor unshroud that stone unless I ask you to. Can you do that for me, young master?"

"Sure," he nodded.

"Good, good. Would you also mind, in fact, not speaking at all unless I specifically ask it of you?" Audun frowned at this. "A precaution, of course, as our host can be quite… volatile."

The young Viking complied, slightly amused by Nech's

nervousness.

"Good, good," he blurted again. "This way, then, youngling," Nech smiled, rounding the same corner.

Audun followed down a short hallway into a room of decent size with a long table and a warm fireplace on the far side. The strange turtle creature stood beside it, tending to the fire and a pot of stew hanging above it. None of the young Viking's books made mention of turtle people or any of the strange trinkets before him. He was entranced. Nech walked by him, still nervous. The old Scribe took a seat, and Maya flew in from a window, perching atop his chair. Audun, though, could not stop staring at the funny little creature stirring the stew.

"That's Gupper, boy. And it's not polite to stare. Don't expect a human to know better, though," a cragly old voice blurted out. A feeble Goblin turned slowly in his chair opposite them all, revealing a severely aged Craglin with one eye missing and the longest nose Audun had ever seen on a... *person*. His ears were equally long and saggy, and the ancient Craglin sported a thin green moustache that trailed all the way down to his belt and sash. He covered himself in layers of tattered robes of deep purple, orange, and mossy green. Audun was fully taken aback by the old-timer's harsh appearance until the turtle-man (or Gupper, rather) waddled to grab other ingredients for his stew. A hiccupping laugh escaped Audun before he could clasp his mouth shut with one hand—the other still clutching to the shrouded Sunstone. The room fell silent. No one was speaking. Audun, as he always did, broke the tension with a few well-placed words.

"Are you a turtle?" Audun asked. Nech sighed, reaching out in an attempt to stop any sort of exchange between the boy and the ancient Shaman. He was unsuccessful.

"He is a Torgle!" the raggedy elder interjected in a thick accent.

"That's what I said! A Turtle!" Audun replied, confused yet delighted.

"Not a turtle, you milkborn brat! A Torgle! T-O-R-G-L—"

"I believe he understands, wise friend! Surely he does!" Nech interrupted, jumping in to save Audun from the brash tongue of the visibly furious (and hilarious, in the young child's opinion) old sod. Nech darted up as fussy as ever. "Please, Audun, do not speak unless I ask it of you?" he whispered harshly. Nech took a deep breath before addressing the room as the tension was unbearable to him. "… May I say again how marvelous it is too see you, my old friend?" The tension did not lessen. His knees began to knock together under the table. "And it has been far too long since I have indulged in your splendid cooking, Sir Gupper!"

"A turtle that cooks!" Audun yelled, thrilled. He could barely contain himself in the chair he had finally settled into.

The elder Goblin slammed his hands down on the table,

outraged. "You think that's funny, do you brat?" the elder decreed, spit flying from his mouth.

"Wouldn't anybody? He looks like a turtle but he's cooking like a person…" Audun mumbled.

The creaky old Shaman stopped, pondering. "I… I suppose 'at is funny, isn't it?" Slowly, a chuckle began to emerge from his ancient mouth. Nech's jaw dropped. A few more chortling chuckles escaped the Shaman before he turned to full out belly-laughing. He was now hysterical at the thought. Audun began laughing with him, but Nech and Maysa sat silent, flabbergasted. Then, just as suddenly as the old timer's outburst of laughter had begun, it ceased. He furled his brow intensely. The one-eyed goblin looked to each body in the room, his eye darting about. A few words disguised as huffs and gargles left his mouth as he rearranged the table in front of him. Then, in a flash, his entire demeanor changed again.

"I am Zazzek," the old goblin grumbled from out of nowhere, "mightiest Shaman in all of Cragoa!" His words turned to a coughing fit as he crumpled over the table. "My full title, boy, is Zazzekarec, Chief Shaman of the First Eon, but no one utters my full name but my mother and Nech, and unfortunately only one of them is dead!" The ancient Shaman's gaze shot over to Nech like a dart. He paused, then burst out into another fit of uncontrollable laughter. Nech choked then blurted a fit of anxious laughter so forced he blew a candle out on the table. Audun chuckled, elated with the strange and moody old hermit.

"I like this child!" the Shaman exclaimed, his old body shifting underneath his tattered robes.

"As for you-" he continued, his eye fixated again on Nech, "Spit it out." The Shaman gargled. "I know you need something, you snoopish old bookrat. Why else would you risk coming back here?"

"We seek only your wisdom and council, old friend," Nech replied, attempting to regain at least some of his composure. "Much has happened these past few cycles of the sky and I am unable to surmount it all with but the humble knowledge of a Scribe."

"Still can't get to the point after all these years," Zazzek huffed. "Don't have time for unimportant details, do we now? Only a fool would return to Cragoa after banishment."

The tension mounted. Audun began to realize the situation was a bit more serious than he wished it to be.

Without warning Titha bounced through the doorway, bursting the awkwardness like a bubble. "It worked!" she shouted, waving an empty bottle.

"Of course it worked!" The Shaman blurted defiantly. "All my bloody potions work, why else would I-" His mumbling ceased as his one eye shifted to the hallway, meeting Titha's face.

Her violet hood came down, revealing her shimmering white hair and rare indigo skin. Her youthful green eyes shone in the dimly candlelit room.

"You…" Zazzek muttered. "Come here."

Titha paused, then complied. She walked through the crowded, messy room slowly, her two eyes locked to the Shaman's one. As she approached him, he grew calm. "By my eye… It has been a full age since I've been in the presence of your kind, little one."

"It's nice to meet you," Titha replied sweetly. The Shaman's edginess disappeared as he slowly reached out his hand. Titha took it gently.

"It cannot be. Yet here you stand, Luna child." His one eye shone with wonderment. He looked into Titha's own gaze deeply, as if he was searching for something. All fell silent but the fire, which began to whisp and churn intensely. Zazzek gasped.

"*What did you see*?"

Titha froze. The fireplace raged out of nowhere and became one with her thoughts. She had no time to be overwhelmed; everything happened quicker than quick. Nech, more nervous and trembling than ever before, cried out to his young companion, seizing the moment as it were. "Tell him of your vision, Titha!" he shouted. "You can trust him! Tell him now!" Titha was not sure of this, hearing Nech's own words from the Barren Fields bouncing in her head… but tell him she did.

Zazzek whipped 'round to the hearth, flinging a leather satchel and all of its contents into the brazen flames. Gupper fumbled backward, his head retreating into his shell as flames of every color shot forth entrancing all in their midst. Titha held nothing back, her heart spilling outward into Zazzek's gaze.

Her vision, and Audun's, became real to all in the room, fiercely alive in the flames as she recounted each graceful step of the Elk Kings, their tumultuous transformations into Bear, Wolf, Fox, Salmon, Snake, and Eagle alike—before her mind fell into the *red madness*… When it did, the fireplace took the forms of her taken father, Theole, and Sigrid as they placed the sacred, coveted stones into what appeared to be the skull of a Grand Elk King. Yet it was not these portions of her visions in the flame that brought her to tears. That was reserved for the recounting of the footsteps at the end of her dream... She watched again as the enormous, rocky pairs of feet walked to each side of a fair, unmistakable Luna. Titha closed her eyes from the firelight, unable to watch the figure walk away again. The Fireplace let loose of its roar, retreating with a great whoosh from the company.

The party stood astonished. Titha sunk, sobbing in her chair. Zazzek fluttered as he reached out, extin-guishing what was left of the flames with a wave of his hands. He sighed, shaking his head.

"This was no vision," he finally spoke. "This was *Druid speak.*"

Nech and Maya looked to one another.

"And they had company."

Titha burst forth from her chair, running around the table to the Shaman. "Was it my mother?" she cried out though her tears. "Was it her?"

"Yes," Zazzek replied sternly. "Your mother, Celtica of Ythengrey, or Thea Mae, whatever you knew her by… She walked with the Druids as they spoke to you." Zazzek could see the hope in her green eyes. "She watches over you and your kin, but do not look for her return. Your mother is no longer of this realm, young Luna… But she is the very reason why the Druids spoke to you and your companion boy. She trusts and loves you, unconditionally. I could feel it through the flames." He reached out, placing his hands upon Titha's weighted shoulders. "Her footsteps, the breaking light… what you saw during those last steps was not in your head. That was your journey back to us. Back to our realm."

This destroyed Titha. Was she truly with her mother again in that moment? If she was, it made the pain all the worse, as her young mind had never truly given her up for good—nor had her father, she didn't think. But the Shaman was the first to ever speak to her with such clarity, and with the whole truth: that her mother was never to return. For the first time, she believed it.

"Why was she walking away from me?" Titha shriveled into tears, inconsolable. "Why would she ever walk away?"

Zazzek buckled into the emotional moment. He looked to the others, each of them colored with hope-lessness. Titha's mind raced with overpowering thoughts; her mother had spoken to her? What would her father think of all this? What would her *sisters* think? Oh, how she longed to tell them. She tried hard to think of her family—of her father who needed her, and her resolve to never give up on him. She looked about, wiping thick tears from her eyes as she peered to Audun, who seemed to be elsewhere. He had recounted his vision in the fire as well, for his own part. Zazzek turned to him.

"They spoke to the boy, too," the Shaman continued. "His heart was also in the fire. Such a weight," he decreed, "Such a *terrible* weight. It would seem the fate of the world is on the shoulders of these two ittie-bitties."

Titha had given her vision much thought since it transpired and was sure of what the *red madness* represented: Vulduun's plan. That had now been clarified, as had the footstep-filled ending, but the beginning—with all its twisted and shapeshifting animals—was still a complete mystery. All was about to become clear.

"The end of their first vision," Zazzek began again, "remains the answer to what you seek, Nechalec, and represents what will happen if your company succeeds. If the Elk Kings are granted the Sun and Moonstones they will become their new keepers, merging with Gaela and our very Time and existence to keep balance and order. The *red madness*, however… shall become very real… if you fail."

"I… *we* understand," Nech gulped, knowing this to be true.

Maya shook her head, still struggling with this new reality. Finally, she spoke up. "But what of the animals? Are they not the most prominent part of this vision?" she asked.

"Yes," Zazzek replied, "and they are *Totems*. Each representing the path you must take—and have unknowingly already taken. Follow these totems and Gaela will guide you to the Elk Kings. To Igdrasil! The Eternal Stone's keepers hold the key to opening Her Gates—and only there can you succeed. But you must follow the Totems!" The Shaman paused, his eye twitching as the air in the room changed. An unsure look overtook his face. "It would be a shame if Vulduun were to gather the Sunstone as well..." The companions looked to each other—and in an instant the Shaman's goodwill vanished.

"You never should have come here," he gurgled.

Audun's attention suddenly snapped to the window across from him. A small snowy figure seemed to be peering in, its eyes glowing *yellow*. He squinted harder and harder until he could make out thick, ice-matted fur. "Monkey!" Audun screamed. A piercing shriek met Audun's own as the beast in the window disappeared.

"Monkey?" Maya screeched. "Oh no… They know we are here!" She darted out the window. The ground began to rumble as more shrieks and shrills were heard outside.

"This cannot be…" Nech decreed, Titha and Audun jumping to his side. The doors behind them slammed shut, startling all but Zazzek. "I am sorry, old friend," he mumbled, his ancient hands quaking.

Nech took a deep breath, turning slowly to his once esteemed colleague. "You knew?"

Just then, Maya flocked back into the room in a tizzy.

"Bandits!" she squawked. "Marauders! Dozens of them!"

Nech snapped, his eyes reverting to a primal red as he jumped across the table, sending objects flying every-which-way.

"*How could you do this*?" he screamed, spit flying as his hands choked Zazzek's frail neck.

"I—do not—do this willingly!" Zazzek gurgled through Nech's crippling grip.

"Yet you do it all the same!" Nech spat, tightening his grip.

Maya flew to him, snatching his tunic and pulling him backward. "We must leave! *Now*!" she spat.

Titha grabbed Audun's hand, jerking him under the table. She looked for Feathersword, but it remained in her belongings outside with Paw.

"What do we do?" Audun whispered as the thundering pound of footsteps grew outside. Titha took a deep breath.

"Whatever happens, do not let go of your stone or my hand, okay? You heard the Shaman, we have to get to the Elk Kings: to Igdrasil!"

Her voice was unwavering. She stooped down to the floor, looking past the table above them to the furthest window across from the hearth, then to the jarred, rumbling door. "We're not getting out that way," she thought, looking back to the open window.

Audun's breath grew frantic. "The Tree of Life?" Audun asked amid the chaos. "We can't go there! It's not for us!" he shrieked. "It is for the Gods and Heavens!"

"We both had the same vision, Audun!" Titha barked back. "Our parent's blood runs through our veins and we chose to do something! We chose to fight, not hide! We must be the ones to do this and I refuse to let us die in this crazy old Goblin's shack! Now let's *go*!"

Above them, Zazzek struggled to escape Nech's grip, taking another satchel from his pockets and throwing it into the fire. Its flames erupted once more, sending the room into deepened chaos. Gupper cowered in the corner, his head and limbs withdrawn into a quivering shell. The cragly Shaman mustered all of his strength, headbutting Nech and knocking him back onto the table. Maya screeched, tending to Nech and his bleeding, horned scalp as Zazzek slowly stepped backward into the fire.

"Come, Gupper!" the old Goblin cried out, motioning for his companion to join him. Gupper waddled, dodging rumbling artifacts as he covered his withdrawn head. Zazzek grabbed him, throwing him into the fire—and Gupper was engulfed, disappearing. The Shaman looked down to Titha below the table, his eye wet and twitching. "The totems, girl!" he screamed over the flames, his voice cracking. "Follow the totems!" With a raging whoosh of the fire, Zazzek vanished.

Titha had no time to contemplate his words amidst the shock of what was happening. "Come on!" she commanded, jerking Audun with her from their hiding place. She bolted for the window, pushing wooden chairs and stools from her path. She let loose of Audun, swiping books and scrolls from the bookcase in front of the window until it was as clear as a stairway. She climbed it, her body halfway into the snow as she turned back.

"What about Nech?" Audun cried out.

"I will get him—you have to get the stone out of here!" She shouted back, her friend's silhouette trembling in the flaming room.

Audun climbed slowly, one of his arms cradling the shrouded Sunstone.

"Get to Haldor as fast as you can—hurry!" Titha cried, looking back. She turned to the wilderness and gasped, screaming as the horrid face of a Craglin bandit leaped right at her. She flung her fist forward without so much as a wince, punching the Goblin square in his gnashing teeth. It cried horribly, falling to the base of the window. "Haha!" Titha boasted. That boast, however, quickly turned to shock as bandits began to flood in from all sides. She ducked, flinging herself back onto Audun and crashing them both onto the floor inside.

"We're trapped!" She yelled. A bandit reached into the window, climbing ontop of the bookcase as it brandished its crooked sword. Maya let loose a fierce cry and swooped over talons first, making short work of the Goblin and pushing his body back out the window atop the other unknowing bandits. They snorted and snarled as they tumbled down into an angry pile. A huge *thwomp* shook the other side of the room, followed by one of greater intensity that brought half the ceiling down. Wind and snow crashed down onto the party as a terrifying Ogre stood above them. With one hand it knocked the debris from its path, grabbing Nech from the table with the other. Maya screeched and cawed, shooting directly for the gigantic Ogre's face. The monster would not have it, and swatted her like a bug. Maya hit the stone hearth with a terrible *thud,* falling to the ground beneath it.

The Ogre looked to Titha and Audun, who froze. Titha

stepped in front of Audun, covering him and the stone from sight. But the Ogre showed no interest. It grunted, then turned from them, having its prize already in hand. The young pair watched helplessly as the gigantic creature took an unconscious Nech from them, disappearing into the swirling fog.

Suddenly the doors crashed in, and Paw spilled forth covered in bandits. He reared up, thrashing about, sending the Goblins flying like ragdolls. The robust bear roared loudly, signaling for Titha and Audun to come to him. Audun lept, stone in arm, to the bear immediately. Titha scrambled to the other side of the table, scooping a barely conscious Maya into her cloak. The trio climbed aboard Paw and ducked down as he made his way through the narrow, broken rooms of the hut. Like thunder he burst back out into the wilderness, his thick matted paws barreling through blood-stained snow. Ahead, Haldor had a bandit in his maw, thrashing it back and forth until sending it swirling into the trees. A last wave of marauders came from behind the hut, but were shortly dispatched by the two beasts. If Titha didn't know she'd be long lost without her Bear-brother before, she desperately knew it now.

As suddenly as the chaos had begun, it ceased. Paw's rump thumped backward into the snow as he hung his head low. Haldor walked over, lowering his muzzle beside his friend's. Titha and Audun slid down, standing beside them. For a while they stood still in a pure white circle, surrounded on all sides by blood and ash.

Nech was gone.

"How did this happen?" Titha wimpered, Audun in shock beside her. She cradled Maya, who was now unconscious. Paw rubbed his fuzzy maw into his Luna-sister's side. She leaned into him, shivering as she placed Maya between them. "Nech, you stupid, stupid Goblin" She whispered, slightly frustrated but mostly grieving. His words rang between her ears as flurries began to trickle down from the sky. "Trust is much like glass," he'd say. "Worth the effort for its beauty, but forever fragile…"

Snow bustled in the bushline beside them, breaking the silence. A Snowy Fox poked its head out from behind a root, raising its nose to the air for a sniff before darting off to the East. Titha's sharp eyes spotted equally white prey in front of it, the hunter pursuing it into the distance. "Did you see that?" she shouted with all the energy she had left. "That was our Fox! He's chasing a rabbit down into that valley!" Titha exclaimed, holding Maya evertighter against Paw.

"There it goes!" Audun yelled. "Titha it's a totem, I know it's a totem! We have to follow it again! Haldor, get up!" But his hound did not budge, exhausted from the past day's battles. "Get *up* snaggletooth!" Audun yelled again, but to no avail.

Titha looked down to Maya. Paw took a deep breath, doing

all he could to cover her fragile body.

"She's barely breathing," Titha shook. "We have to get her out of the cold," she added with wet, caring eyes. "Birds don't do well in frigid weather, Audun. At least not any of the ones in Yythengrey." She grew angry lingering on Maya's fading breath. "That Shaman... That trickster Shaman! Nech trusted him, and so did we. And now look at us. What's left of us. Well thanks to him those stupid bandits have what they came for, right? They have our friend. But we… we still have the Sunstone, right?"

Audun nodded, pushing the orb underneath Haldor beside him.

"Thank goodness," Titha added. "So we should be safe in that old double-crosser's hut for the night. Haldor looks exhausted, Audun. Paw is too, though he's too stubborn to tell me, aren't you, yah big showoff?" She leaned into Paw, pushing her forehead against his as they exchanged a loving glance. "Let's get some rest and food in one of the rooms that's not totally destroyed. And maybe some of that gooey purple potion is left for Maya. Paw didn't seem to like it much, but it helped, and anything is better than being out in this endless snow. Come inside and in the morning we will head down into that valley and follow the path of our Fox. Okay?"

"Okay," Audun replied. "Maybe the turtle-man left some of his stew. I'm hungry."

Inside they went and warm their bodies became, but restless was the companions' stay. Half of the hut still stood, while the other half laid utterly decimated. This destruction, much to their dismay, included the entry room's beautiful walls of glorious potions. Their vials laid shattered across the wreckage, their contents coloring splattered floors and snow. Since no help would come from what was left behind, Titha placed Maya close to the fire, swaddled in a Cragoan tapestry found laying about. Audun fell fast into dreams atop Haldor as they held the stone, both of their mouths wet from Gupper's leftovers. But Paw and Titha could not eat, nor sleep. Their minds, whether in waking thought or in drifting dreams, were on Nech.

CHAPTER TWELVE

Messengers of Hope

The companions traded snow for rain. Fortunately, an uneventful Dawn had passed and the Shaman's hut was now far to the west behind them. Titha had grown quite accustomed to sleeping during the dark hours, which surprised her greatly. She had been raised to believe the Day and Night could not be more different, yet she was finding this to be far from true. She trekked on with her friends, using her keen vision to follow the tracks of the Snowy Fox and rabbit's deadly pursuit. The snowfall had stopped overnight, thankfully, or else the trail her friends had to follow would've surely vanished.

What blind luck they afforded the meaning of their totems now led them down, down some more, and then off through valleys to the east, once more. A bit of rest and food were good for Audun, Haldor, and Paw's spirits, but Titha's stomach gurgled on. Each beast had a spring in their step and carried their loved ones as hardily as ever. Down they slid for miles from the Craglands and into the Valley of the Svells, which encased the young companions in a damp forest. The Svell Mountains rose like teeth of the world around them, their range mirroring the Fells back across Cragoa to the West. Evergreen trees were no longer sparse, but thick and suffocating. The children loosened their cloaks as the air grew wet and humid. What little light made it to the muddy soil was tinted deep like evening twilight. Everything was damp, including the tiny frogs that leapt from puddle to puddle, which Titha absolutely adored. They came in all colors but were far too quick to catch.

"You *don't* want to catch those, youngling," a stern yet fragile voice finally interjected. It was Maya's! She had awoken!

"Oh, Maya!" Titha squealed, then sighed with delight. "I am so glad to hear your cranky voice!"

"Seriously, child, do not touch the frogs!" Maya warned in a harsh tone, interrupting. Titha paused, noticing her friend's disdain. Audun whipped out his papers, trying desperately to guard them from the rain as he did.

"Are they venomous?" he asked, his eyes alight and his charcoal-clad hand a'flutter.

"No—poisonous," Titha answered, following a jumping blur of purple and yellow. "Things that bite you are venomous. Like snakes and spiders. I bet these little guys are poisonous, so when bigger things try to eat them—*blegh*!" She made a horrible sound that caused Audun to burst out in laughter. He slapped his knees, chuckling hysterically. "Write that down!" she laughed looking to Maya, but there was still no joy to be found in the falcon's face. Maya shook her head, hanging it lower. Titha sighed.

"I'm only trying to keep him happy," she replied sincere. "We miss Nech, too. This isn't easy for any of us. We thought we might lose you, as well."

Maya did not respond. The younglings hadn't lived an aged-enough life to form the sort of bond Maya and Nech held, nor to understand how it felt for her to wake after failing him yet again. The expanses of the Svell Valley didn't help her mindset, either. Her heavy heart was complemented by the roaring of the rain, which was doubly-matched by the Lesser Svell River barreling through the crevasse of the valley. Maya quite admired the strength of the river's rapids, and knew quite well where they lead. It had been many years since she traveled this far out of her native forests in Cragoa, and such a journey was never light of task. Every sight she beheld reminded her of her dear friend, who was in great danger now. And she was unable to help him. *Again.* Trees, low mountains and raindrops blurred together as she became lost in grief and thought.

When Maya came back to her senses, Titha had found a quieter refuge under a cliff's overhang. They were now in the heart of the Svell Valley; the point where it turned either straight North or South with the River it fed, effectively ending their Easterly walk. Titha had wandered a bit off their path to find such refuge, but the quietness about it was sorely needed. Maya looked around. They seemed to be just Northwest of a small stream that careened off the Lesser Svell River. Their rocky, serene shelter jutted out and over a mossy flat that rolled down into a gentle streamside. Each of the companions welcomed the safehaven and settled in to dry off, being careful not to step on or touch any of the colorful frogs still leaping about them. Titha spotted an unusually bright red and blue one and could not resist its hopping. Mimicking its bounds, she frolicked along behind it as Audun pulled out his papers to document each color combination he saw: orange and black, green and yellow, purple and green, black and blue, and most importantly Titha's new red and blue pal.

Paw licked his wounds behind Titha's romping, his fur worse for wear after the past day's fierce battles. Each of them had managed to get a bit of rest under the stone roof, but Maya was still not faring well. She believed one of her wings to be broken, or at least sprained and unusable, which she could not bear the thought of. Titha couldn't stand to see the falcon despairing so, either, and approached her to see if she could help. It turned out she could, and under Maya's tutelage she assembled a makeshift splint from twigs and rootvine.

Neither spoke as they worked, and Audun remained sketching and scribing, his legs all tucked up with the Sunstone into a watchful Haldor toward the back of their encampment. Whether in writing thoughts or shallow daydreams, however, each of their minds was still on the loss of Nech. Titha tried to shake the overbearing thought, rubbing the mud from her hands onto the rock walls and looking out into the one tiny break in the needled foliage above. All she could see was the Svells' sharp and harsh mountains that lacked any of the gentle charm of her homeland's rounded, stoic form-ations. Her eyes followed them through the rare breaks in the evergreen trees. They sloped down from the North into the valley where they were, then shot right back up on the Southside, continuing their march down the land-scape. Back down on the streamside, a turtle appeared from the water, and Titha slipped in her tending to Maya as she became distracted by its shell's golden yellow pattern, and the highly amusing thought of whether or not this turtle was a relative of ol' Gupper. Maya nudged her in an effort to cease her neverending curiosity, but all this did was put the Luna in every bit a foul mood as the falcon. They were wet, cold and far, *far* from home. Titha returned to her task, more frustrated than before, and angrily finished tying the last rootvine knot on Maya's splint.

"Careful!" Maya squealed, flinching away from Titha's hands. Her shout echoed through the quiet hollow and the turtle scampered into the water, disappearing.

"I'm sorry, I didn't mean to," she replied, her gaze pointed to the ground. Maya sighed, then grunted before letting out a full ear piercing skwawk. She breathed in, composing herself, then lifted the youngling's chin with her good wing.

"I miss him, too," she said. "And he's tougher than you think, child. He will be just fine—as will your father. You will see in the end."

Paw lumbered over, harrumphing as he plopped his entire fuzzy body down beside Titha, nuzzling his nose into her back. She smiled, reaching behind to fuzzle his cheek.

Many moments passed as the companions stared into the trees, counted frogs, rested, argued, whined, or listened to the brook's soothing language. After an hour or so the babbling let loose a single violent splash to break the serenity (or tension, depending on who you asked). Paw's head shot up, his chestnut eyes surveying each wave, but he saw nothing.

"It's just the rain, fuzzybutt," Titha assured him. "Just this never-ending, super-annoying rain." She sat down beside him, breathing a deep breath as she tried not to let her thoughts run wild again. "How much longer do we have to wait?" she quipped, breaking the silence.

"Until my Order shows, child," Maya replied, her impatience returning.

"Which is when?"

"For the twelfth time I do not have an exact answer, Titha Mae! Now let us continue to be productive in our waiting!"

"When is waiting *ever* productive?" Titha huffed impatiently.

"Right now," Maya hissed. "It is productive right now. Soon a fellow Peregrite will answer my call and come to my aid. They have never failed me, and I do not anticipate now to be the first time."

"And then what?"

"I will return to our sanctuary to be healed. You will be safe here in this cavern until help returns."

Titha leaned back, her brow heavy. "What?" she scoffed, "You're leaving us?"

"I have no choice, Titha. This forest is kind, it will shield you from harm. I cannot thank you enough for tending to me this past nightfall, but it will take much more skill than you will ever possess to right my broken wing. We are in Mammoth's Respite, I believe, and my Order knows its location. They will come to us and one of them who is capable will lead you forward. I promise."

"Do any of the others know all the things you wrote with

Nech in your tome together? Do they know the way through this place?"

Maya paused. Titha Mae, as she was learning, was not to be fooled. "No," she replied deftly.

"Then please stop making promises you can't keep," Titha replied.

"Listen to me, young one; I am of no use to anyone like… like *this*." Maya shook her head, raising her splinted wing. "I must heal, and to do this I must return to my sanctuary! Your mission is to rescue your father, yes? Then you must understand that mine is now to rescue Nech and I cannot do it like this. Or out here. Do you not wish for him to be free?"

"Of course I do."

"Then our paths lead in different directions! You must understand this. I turn back for the good of my… of *our* friend."

"You turn back because you're afraid," Titha spoke sternly.

"Afraid?" Maya squawked. "Why, I, I have raided *hundreds* of tombs and been prey to perils much more dire than *frogs and rain*, youngling!"

"But you never broke a wing, did you Maya? This is a first for you, right? You're terrified and I get it. You can't fly, you've lost Nech *again*, you're out of the Craglands away from the safety of your Order, we don't know where Igdrasil lies and we're about to face whatever is ahead and it scares you. I am scared, too! But

I'm not turning back, not now or ever. Nech wouldn't want me to. He wouldn't want you to either and you know it."

"So what would you have me do, spriteling, hmm? What should I do? Tell me!" Maya asked sharply.

"Keep calling to your friends. I hope that they answer," Titha replied. "But when they do, send them to Yythengrey and to Autumnhill and to Cragoa and have them deliver a message for us all instead, not just you. Send for *our* journey, so we can keep moving forward!"

"And what message would that be?"

"Really? To stand against Vulduun, as father would say! To rise up! To fight for good and for hope! We still have the Sunstone, right? As long as we do, Vulduun can't control the Day and Night and he knows it. If we can fight him off and meet him with more armies, that will give us enough time to make it to the Elk Kings! He may have taken my father and Audun's mother but our peoples stopped him, Maya. We drove him away! We can do it again! We can help Nech and the Craglands and stop Vulduun from getting to us before we reach the Kings!"

"Your people, Audun's people, they do not know my Order and they will not answer their plees. Your heart is true, Titha Mae. I will give you that. And it gives you strength and courage far beyond your years. But what you ask is preposterous. It is nothing more than a dream."

"*You're wrong*!" Titha cried. "A few Moons ago Audun and I were just sprouts—sproutlings no one *ever* took seriously because we had nothing to offer our parents—but here we are now as two friends that can make things change! Maybe the only ones who can make this happen—and we are right in front of you! We need your help, Maya. We've come this far because of Nech's help and our vision and the Totems and I know... I *know* it was not chance that we met you too, Maya. You must help us! So what if no one knows where the Tree of Life is exactly? I bet you have a much better idea than we do, right? I know The Elk Kings live with Her—the tree—I know it from songs and tales sung in Yythengrey—but I do not know how to even begin getting there. You do! We found you and you have seen so much, Maya, and you have written about it. We need to know what you know! If you leave us... if you leave us now after we have come so far this will all have been for nothing, and the *red madness* wins. You must help us, for the sake of all the world!"

Titha stopped for breath. Maya looked to be deep in thought. Not wanting to lose her momentum, Titha continued. "Maya, please... it will work. The leader of my people's soldiers, Cypress, is like a second father to me. If you speak of me he will come to aid us in this—I know it. And Audun, his older brother Rainer now leads the Vikings in his mother's absence. If the falcons speak of Audun, his brother will surely come to his aid no matter the cost. They have seen Vulduun. They have watched their own houses burn! They know what is at stake and they will leave the safety of their homes and rise up and we will be so much closer to beating Vulduun in this awful race!"

Maya gave pause. Titha's words made some sense, but more importantly they rang sincere.

"I will return to my Order to heal," she replied. "Then I will have my kin deliver these messages."

"*Liar*!" Titha yelled, her voice hard. "You are a *coward*! You hid when Nech was banished and now you run to hide again! I cannot *believe* I trusted you!"

"*So I hid*, child!" Maya screamed and screeched. "I flocked and I hid and it has haunted me every Sun and Moon since! But that is exactly why I must return! I must rescue Nech and mend this wrong. I must right my greatest failure! I do not expect one as young as you to understand. You have grown wiser, Titha Mae… but you are still *just a girl*. Just a girl with fanciful dreams and petulant questions!"

Everything went quiet. Titha's ears rang as she was hit with a wave of anger, or was it grief? She couldn't tell. She wiped her mud-matted tunic off and took a deep breath.

"Nech may be too kind to think you really just fled, just *left him in fear*… but I know someone just like you," she started, choking on her words as she struggled to continue, "My older sister, Gilly, is just like you. She is fair and can be kind and I know she loves me but she is also stubborn, and hurt, and *afraid*. She thinks *exactly* the way you do. She'd make the smartest decision for *her*… the *safest* one. But she would be wrong, too. She would also have the same look on her face when I told her how wrong she was that you do now. I am young, yes. I get it. And I am… *just a girl*. But so what? What's wrong with that? What does that even mean? I've come halfway across the world it feels like, and not being a boy or a Man or a warrior or whatever hasn't stopped me from doing anything! Not one thing! And I've thought a lot about this plan, Maya. I didn't just make it up! Cypress, my father, my mother… they taught me a lot and I know it will help us and it will work. Vulduun doesn't know where we are or we would not still be alive. Right? His Sunrises have not come for us in days, not since Autumnhill. Nothing has stopped us since then and we've been through a lot… Like *a lot* a lot and I have come farther than anyone else I've met on this crazy journey and I will not stop until I find my father—but to do that we have to save him from Vulduun and get to the Tree of Life!"

Maya was truly at a loss for thought. She looked up to Titha, whose breathing had grown frantic as she raved. Audun looked over to her from deep in the cavern.

Titha took a moment, calming herself, and smiled to Audun. Much of her strength came from tending to her younger companion. He smiled back at her, as he always did. She leaned down and wiped clean the splint on Maya's injured wing. "Even if you did make it back to Nech, what would he think when you showed up without us?"

Another great splash interrupted their argument, but this one was followed by many more. The brook outside their cavern fast became white with waves. Paw shot up, his nostrils wide and pointed directly at the stream as he darted for its shore. He leapt head-first into the brimming waters, thrashing his snout back and forth until he resurfaced with a slender gray fish in his mouth.

"Salmon!" Audun cried from behind them all. "Paw caught a salmon!" Many more great gray fish began to jump from the shallow water, arching their bodies to reveal shimmering pink underbellies. "It's the next totem!" Audun yelled, sitting the shrouded stone down for the first time in hours and sprinting for the waterside. He turned back, his body shaking with excitement. Titha and Maya sat still. "Weren't either of you listening? The Salmon is our next totem and we've gotta follow them! We must have gone the right way with the Fox!"

"Looks like Paw would rather eat our totems," Titha replied.

"Listen to me!" Audun yelled. "We follow the salmon, Titha! They are all in order! I figured it out!" Audun rushed over to his friend with an excitement she hadn't seen in him before.

"The first animal we saw in our vision was a big black bear, right? That's not a coincidence, none of it is! The black bear is your totem, Titha. Your *people's* totem—for your Bear-brothers! The red wolf is for my people, the Vikings, the Houndsmen, and the wolves we raised into dogs! We followed the white Fox down out of the Craglands and now here we are in the Svell Mountains with salmon! Lots and lots of salmon to follow!" Audun skipped and laughed as he clapped his hands together, thrilled with his findings. "All that's left is a snake and an eagle!"

"Well duh," Titha replied, deadpan. "For a vision I would say it was pretty obvious." The young friends paused, before bursting back into laughter together that Titha sorely needed. Beside them, Paw chowed down on one of the huge fish like he hadn't eaten a day in his life.

Maya hopped to the shoreline, snipping the scraps from his rabid mess but washing them thoroughly before she'd eat them. She turned full-beaked back to the younglings. "I would suggest you two follow suit. This as good a feast as we are likely to see in the near future. Your people do eat fish, I hope."

Titha gagged at the thought of eating an animal, let alone a live one.

"Sure... we eat fish..." she hesitated. "So do bears, hawks, otters, snakes, and snappers, so why not Lunas?" She gulped. Titha was an unusually good sport when it came to trying new things, but like some of her folk she had never really taken to eating animals she also considered friends. Audun, though, did not hesitate. He let Haldor know it was okay, signaling for his pup to join him. Haldor became every bit as ravenous as Paw, and the two splashed and wriggled about with the salmon, tossing what they chose not to scarf down onto the shore for the others. Audun shrugged, snapping a smaller fish in half and digging in. It wasn't the worst thing he had eaten. By far.

Titha tip-toed back into their shelter before rummaging through her sack, and sure enough her fruits, fibers, and berries were running low. A tiny, familiar red frog hopped by her bag and stopped, looking up at her. "Don't you judge me," she said, wagging her finger at the precious amphibian. "Stop looking at me with those big black eyes! I'm all out of food, little frog!" The tiny guy hopped away, and Titha could swear she saw him shake his head. "Hope none of these fish are your friends, red," She groaned, turning away in defeat as her tummy gurgled and growled. With a mighty sigh, she met her friends by the brook, snapped open a small fish, and bit into it.

She then threw up immediately. Twice.

Audun laughed and hollered, checking on his friend who shoo'd him away in embarrassment. He chuckled, wiping his face as he watched the gray and pink fishes' path. Those that managed to escape Paw and Haldor went with the river up the stream toward where the companions had come down, then swam off toward where the Lesser River met the Greater. "We've got to go back once we're done!" he yelled over the stream. "Back up hill! We've got to follow the salmon and go back that way to the big river! Is that North, Maya?"

"Yes," she replied, deadpan, with a beakful of fish.

The next few moments, however, were filled with far more exciting reactions, as amidst the party's merri-ment, feathered streaks began to whisp between the trees. Out of the grey sky shot several sleek forms, and nearby perches and logs became adorned with falcons of differing markings and colors in an instant. Together they formed a circle around the companions, amidst whom only Maya was smiling.

Her Peregrine Order had arrived.

CHAPTER THIRTEEN

The Peregrine Order

"Are you in need of assistance, Harbinger?" the largest falcon asked. His feathers were sturdy, stark, and bore the marks of many great adventures.

"Wow," Titha exclaimed as she washed her hands in the stream; the wave of salmon beginning to settle. Slowly she looked up, her eyes meeting each falcon, big and small, with great wonder.

Maya looked to her young friend, then back to the larger falcon, but did not offer him an answer just yet. She walked slowly to Titha first, who looked down to her with pleading eyes.

A moment passed. Then Maya bowed, giving the authority of decision over to Titha Mae; an offer that, if Nech were present, would've flabbergasted the old hob. Maya was certain Titha was familiar with the gesture—but she vastly underestimated the remoteness of the Luna's forested, sanctuary-like home.

"You are supposed to bow to me in return," Maya whispered, tugging on Titha's tunic with her good wing.

Titha cocked an eyebrow.

"Bow, sprite!" Maya chirped. "Do not embarrass me in front of my Order..."

"Oh, right," Titha hiccuped before tripping over her own feet into a clumbsy bow.

And with it, Maya lowered fully to Titha.

"I am your Harbinger *no longer*, Torai," Maya replied to the largest falcon. "Titha Mae of Ythengrey, Daughter of Theole the Watcher and Thea Celtica Mae of Mother Nature, is your Harbinger now."

The rain gave its first pause in hours as each falcon bowed in 'round, their heads all held low in unquestioning respect of Maya's wishes.

Titha grinned from ear to ear, her feet tapping with delight. "Does this mean you are staying?" she asked, still half-bowed.

Maya bowed again. She would stay.

To say Titha was overcome with emotion would be an understatement, and the two friends embraced, all but forgetting their earlier, coarse exchange. Until said embrace began to squeeze

Maya's crippled wing, that is.

"What would you ask of us, Harbinger?" Torai spoke to the young Luna, his eyes cocked at her foreign visage. He was almost twice Maya's size and bore a scar across his left eye that trailed down the bridge of his beak.

"What would I ask?" Titha questioned. She pittled her finger on her chin. "What would I ask… Well, what is a Harbinger, for starters?"

Torai cleared his throat. "That is your task for us? To explain to the… Harbinger… what a Harbinger… *is*?"

"Correct," Titha answered, stonefaced.

Maya stepped up and interrupted Torai's sure-to-be-harsh reply. "The Harbinger is one who has earned the respect of her kin, Titha, and leads those worthy to follow," Maya interrupted.

"Oh," Titha replied, muttering. "Well can I ask them something else?"

Maya tried not to laugh. "You may," she replied, stepping to Titha. The beautiful falcon stretched her good wing upward. "You may ask as many questions as you'd like. I… am sorry for what I said earlier. I acted in fear and in doubt and should not have taken it out on you." She lowered her head before continuing. "Never stop asking questions. Curiosity is the brightest flame of a brilliant mind, and anyone who tries to snuff it out is *afraid* of it. Many will try; but it is they who need your curiosity most, even if they never know it." Maya heeded her own words as she spoke them to Titha. "Will you forgive my stubbornness?"

Titha hugged her again. Maya took a deep breath into the embrace.

"It's alright," Titha replied softly. "And I think I understand. But I also think I've been pretty lucky so far."

"Luck has nothing to do with it, young lady. Do not confuse your *conviction* with chance, for they are never one and the same." Maya looked out to her Order as she spoke, being sure they observed the truth in her words. "Your devotion to the love of your family is pure, and the courage it has given you just may save us all." The falcon rose, misty-eyed and much lighter of shoulders. "Our newest Harbinger has a great task for the Peregrine Order," she said, motioning for Titha to step center. "One far greater than any we have seen in our lifetimes."

Titha stood center. She fought off the enormous grin from her face and tried her absolute hardest not to be distracted by the beautiful little red and black frog that hopped behind Torai.

"Right," she began. "Let's do this. I have heard really good things about you guys, so don't let me down, okay?" The circle of falcons stood silent as statues. "Good answer," Titha smirked. "Because we really need your help."

Titha's heart was at its purest and brightest as she skipped about, recounting the tale of how she came to leave her home, survive a dragon—*twice*—befriend an old goblin, a Viking boy and his dog, meet Druids, traverse the Craglands, meet talking birds (which the Order did not find funny) and escape a twisted Shaman; all to end up here before them with Audun and the Sunstone on a quest to beat the Last Elderdrake to the Tree of Life. Her green eyes were alight as her hands and feet danced, the resulting tale of Sacred Stones and the Crown of Elk Kings as grand as any song that had ever been sung within their kind. She told them of her people, her family, and of Audun's, and how they must stop Vulduun from retrie-ving the Trinity, and how they can only do so with the Peregrine Order's help. She didn't know it until this day, but this plan was their only hope. *Everyone's* only hope. And she was really proud of herself for thinking of this part of it.

"I have heard enough," Torai exclaimed.

Maya looked to him sharply.

"Enough to know our new Harbinger is beyond worthy of our devotion," he finished with a smile.

Maya let her guard down, smirking at Torai. "We will see it done, then," she replied.

Titha and Audun cheered, leaping into each other's embrace. All of the Order remained still except for Torai, who flew to meet Maya, urgent words escaping before he could even land.

"The news I bring you cannot be coincidence," he offered. "The False Emperor—Ugar has Nech. He is being held in the center dungeon below Mt. Cra, and he is *alive*, but not for long."

Maya breathed a sigh of relief. "Just to know he is alive brings me such comfort. Thank you, dear," she responded. "Send Ira to Yythengrey. She is our fastest and most persuasive—we will need her cunning and wit to convince the Lunas to leave their borders and rise to this fight. Azra is to deliver the message to Autumnhill. He is hardy and brash like the Vikingmen; they will appreciate his directness."

"You mean *dimness*," Torai retorted.

"You are to return to Mt. Crag, my friend. Other races must rise to the cause, but I fear the Craglins are lost to Ugar. Nech, however… we cannot fail him again. Send the others to buy us precious time, but for Nech I send you, Torai. Only you. For this I trust in you, and you alone. Save him, please."

"What of you? Will you return to the Sanctuary to heal?" Torai asked, noting her splint'ed wing.

"I can't leave these younglings now. Not in these last steps of their journey. Our journey." Maya turned, looking to her two companions. "If anything, any foul forces should try to lead them astray… I must be with them. It is the only way."

"Maya, your condition…" Torai spoke with great concern. "You will not survive finding, let alone approaching the Gates of Igdrasil like this!"

"Give me more credit than that!" she squawked. Maya

attempted to be lighthearted in her reply, but her gut told her Torai was right.

"If you will not seek healing, then I wish you Craga's swiftness through the lands ahead. But must I be the one to fetch Nech? Send my sister!" Torai pleaded.

Maya doubled back, not at all used to Torai cowering in any manner.

"Send Lorai," he continued. "They get along, her and Nech. Always have! I do not need to explain to you that we do not. You are sending me on a fool's errand! He does not trust me and will not trust my arrival. We have never seen eye to eye and now is not the time to test this! He will not listen to me, Maya." Torai stopped, imme-diately regretful of his tone. "Forgive me," he bowed. His sister, Lorai, shook her head in frustration behind him.

"These are different times, Peregrite," Maya explained. "Nech will heed your words. Regardless of your... *sorted* past, if there is the slightest chance of reversing the damage Ugar has done or helping Titha Mae, Nech will rise to the challenge. He will know why you have come." Maya lowered her tone and leaned into Torai. "We cannot be too careful, my brother," she whispered. "I must send you. Do you understand?"

"I do," Torai grumbled. "Torai saving Nech from a dungeon... These truly are the end times."

"Not if we have anything to say about it!" Titha pipped

back, her hand clasped to Audun's.

"Have faith in Nech, Torai," Maya replied. "He will listen to you. I had feared his trust had been broken in me as well; in all of us. I am lucky he took me back before his capture. We never should have abandoned him the first time."

"If we had not left during the uprising we would not be here now to play our part, we would be rotting in *bird cages* beneath the mountain. We did what had to be done."

"Perhaps you are right," Maya sighed. "Never-theless, I will guide the young ones on. I wish you Craga's Grace, brother."

Torai bowed. "And you, Harbin—er, Maya… The rest of us will depart swiftly. We will not fail you."

As quickly as they had arrived, the Peregrine Order vanished. Maya held her gaze upward, praying to Craga she had made the right decision. As her eyes met Titha's, however, she believed she had. Titha leaned down, gently hugging her friend; a silent 'thank you'.

"Can we go now?" Audun spoke, fulfilling his customary breaking of silences. He stood still under the shelter of the rocky overhang, the light of his family's shrouded stone muffled within his arms.

"That would be wise, young Viking," Maya smiled. "Gather the rest of your things as we must be off to follow your salmon. We have more totems to find if we are to locate Igdrasil."

Titha squealed. "To go where the Elk Kings live—I can't believe we're going to meet them and get to see The Tree."

"I hope that we do, spriteling," Maya replied. "Do you have enough food to last you another Day?"

Titha nodded. "Yes, but not much longer," she replied as she checked her bag. "I picked up a lot of the pink fruits in Cragoa but they'll start smelling bad soon if they're anything like the fruit from back home."

"Look for mushrooms in the valley ahead," Maya replied. "They will be plentiful here. But *only eat the brown ones.* No white ones, or red ones! If you are even slightly doubtful of the color, I will be happy to point out which ones taste great and which ones will bring about a horrible and most gruesome death."

Titha gulped. "That's reassuring," she thought to herself, then looked to Audun who was stuffing fish wrapped in leaves into his pack as their beast companions sniffed each and every one.

"That settles it, then," Maya proclaimed. "Pack your things, and let's be off. That means you, too, Paw!" She shouted before flapping up with her good wing to land on Titha's shoulder. "You are stuck with me now."

Titha chuckled and threw her satchel over her other shoulder. She turned to place it on Paw, but he wasn't where she'd left him. "Paw!" She shouted. "Where did you—" before she could finish she spotted an enormous back'end as it bounced from side to side on the stream's shore. Paw's head shot around, his eyes wide as saucers as salmon fell from his overstuffed cheeks.

"Such a fatty!" Titha yelled. "Let's go before I have to *roll* you out of this valley!"

Paw gulped, smiled, and galloped for his Luna-sister. Audun and Haldor were upstream already, determined to follow the salmon's direction.

The spawning fish were headed for the Great Svell River. It's waters were an oddity of Nature, as it flowed North, prompting many of Gaela's "magick-fearing" peoples to stay clear of its influence, for mostly all rivers flow South in the world. But the Great Svell River was unlike any other, and the companions would come to find this out for themselves.

After a bit of backtracking up the Lesser Svell stream they returned to noisier, boisterous white waters; still completely shrouded from above by evergreens competing for Sunlight.

Haldor licked Paw's face as the companions traveled, making sure to get every bit of fish left on his friend's whiskers. Titha and Audun found this hilarious, but Maya, beyond disgusted with the slurping mammals, sought to change the subject. The jolting rhythm of Paw's bumbling stride was not kind to her broken wing, either. She was in pain, so any further nauseating sounds emitted from tongues and jowls were detestingly unwelcomed. Her mind was already heavy with the loud river, and her dear Nech was still lost to her; prisoner under Mt. Crag.

"What else do you both know of Igdrasil?" she finally asked her young companions. She spoke loudly above the grinding waters as its waves echoed through the thick trees & mossy grounds. "We must recount all we know if we are to find Her majesty by path of the totems."

"Only what's in the song Father used to sing to me as a sprout," Titha replied first.

"I know it's where all life came from and it connects our world to the Northern Sky. But no Viking-man has ever really seen it, or knows exactly where it is," Audun added. "Mother always said it was both nowhere, and everywhere. Which makes no sense to me at all."

"Very good!" Maya replied. "Toward the Northern Sky is exactly the direction our salmon have led us, too, Audun. I very nearly would have taken us to the South, to the Highlands upstream, as I'm inclined to think Igdrasil would reside at the highest, most unexplored region of our Gaela. But the flames of your vision still burn harshly in my mind's eye. The Totems were unmistakable, and as such we should heed their guidance. So heed we shall, and North we go. I'm impressed by your deeper knowledge of Igdrasil, Audun, You have an eager appetite for learning."

"He likes books," Titha added. "He has a ton of them in his

room."

"True," Audun responded. "And I miss them, so I started making new ones while we ride. I think I want to be a Scribe like you and Nech. My father won't like that, but…" He stopped… He hadn't really had a chance to think of his late father in days. So much had happened sinc—since he died...

Titha, ever Audun's guardian, jumped in immediately. "I loved seeing all of your books, Audun," she said, hoping to distract. "They were wonderful. One of them had all the songs about the Tree of Life in it! One song was even from my people, and it's my favorite song: *The Elk Kings Three*. Well, besides *The Festival of Dawn*… but that song has kind of been ruined for me now, though, so *The Elk Kings Three* is definitely my favorite from now on."

"You should sing it for us," Maya requested, also seeking to cheer up Audun. "And your father would be proud of you, Audun. Beyond so. Nech told me of his valiant sacrifice. Though Angvar was a great warrior, his father's father was a *Skald*, did you know that? Er, do you know what a Skald is, child? A poet! A storyteller. This is where your great hall gets its name, and it is undoubtedly where your thrist for knowledge and history comes from, as well!"

Audun was utterly amazed. He had no idea!

"But that is a tale for another time," Maya continued. "For

now… we must… continue on… through this never-ending valley." She was not accustomed to such slow travel, and found the process grueling, so she asked Titha Mae once more to sing the song she knew.

"Yes! Sing it, please!" Audun shouted, a slight smile working its way onto his face.

"Alright," Titha responded, secretly thrilled with the proposition. She cleared her throat and scratched Paw's cheek as they continued up the riverside, their journey now taking them to the North by Maya's lead. The waters quieted a bit, and she began:

Between the sky and ground below
Where all North's river's waters flow
Her roots dig deep and leaves stand tall
To keep life's bounty for us all

Igdrasil Proud, O' Tree of Life
May no death come 'er fire nor strife
No Winter's Bane nor Summer's Heat
Shall hope for cause of Her Defeat

For Strong and True both Day and Night
The Elk Kings Three Stand Guard Your Might
All crowns of gold and chains of mail
Pail to each King their Glory Hail

Pure Hearts within their Kingdom grow
Vict'ry the foul shall never know
With Sun and Moon their Stars Ignite
Eternal Bound to Dark and Light

"And then that second to last verse repeats," Titha finished.

Audun clapped astride Haldor, being the only other companion now with hands to do so.

"That it does, Titha Mae," Maya smiled, quite pleased with the unexpectedly beautiful tune of the Lunish version. "You have a wonderful voice, my child. I did not expect such a melodious rendition," She praised. Her small brow furrowed in thought. "I've always thought the first verse to be a riddle, a riddle that would disclose the location of the Tree. I still believe it is, but north is a relative term when in travel—for what is south of us now was once north mere steps ago. And so She, the Tree, remains ever-illusive. Igdrasil shrouds Herself in ethereal mist and shadow, legends tell, and though eternally enormous, makes herself scarce to all unworthy of the divine. For our sake, I sincerely hope She finds Vulduun to be as unworthy as we do. But the song is more important than any have realized in generations, I think. It exists in both your cultures and all our grandest tomes for a reason, and it guides only the pure of heart upon the Path to Igdrasil—for only the pure of heart shall ever behold Her majesty. To that effect, perhaps She had a hand in your Totemic vision Herself. What a revelation that would be." Maya looked forward, the skies still blotted by a million foliage-filled obstacles. "Nech and I have never been able to see her for our own, not even with all the knowledge we gathered for the Eternal-tome. An unbelievably pompous name for a book, by the way, but Nech insisted on naming everything, so I let it be."

The song and Maya's knowledge had left Titha stronger, she felt. The verses meant nothing more than their melody to her as a small child, yet now they rang out loud in the valley they traversed, full of vigor and purpose. She pondered Maya's interpretation of the words, searching for more meaning now that she not only sung its words, but lived them.

As the last echo of Titha's song disappeared, the world opened up before her. The Great Svell River's northernly, winding path dipped down into a massive, breathtaking canyon as the trees finally gave way. Such splendor was like nothing the younglings had seen before. The jagged Svells sloped down from both the West and East until smoothing into moss-spotted, rolling boulderhills intertwined with brooks that the river split off to at the basin. To each side of them the towering, sharp Svell peaks carved the walls of the valley up north until, at their joining, the mountains pointed like an arrow to where their river ended and the Horizon began.

"Behold Svellvanyon, younglings, in all its splendor," Maya boasted. "An incredibly gorgeous, yet historically treacherous, canyon. Oh! And welcome to Eastlyn, also. We now leave Mydlan behind."

None of the younger companions had stepped foot in

Eastlyn before. It was the name their ancestors had given to all lands beyond the Western Svells, and its landmarks were largely unknown to each friend, even Maya, as its landscape was largely void of peoples and their histories. She, too, was uncertain of what awaited them. A great look of concern washed over her, and Titha, ever observant, took notice.

"What's wrong?" she asked.

"I just remembered the next totem is a snake," Maya growled. "I *hate* snakes."

Titha laughed. "They're just misunderstood, I think. We have some truly gorgeous ones in the Dusk-ridge. Just don't put your hands or feet toward the end with eyes and you'll be alright."

"Right," Maya exhaled. "I dare say, though, that Nech hates snakes even more than I do, which is saying something—so perhaps it is best he's not here for this leg of our trip."

"Do you think he is alright?" Audun asked Maya.

"I know he is," she replied, confident in speech but uncertain at heart. "Nech has been through much in his long life. Besides, Torai will not let me down. He is fiercely loyal and the strongest of our order. The fastest, too, if you ask him and not myself or his sister. Though tonight I sincerely wish him to be such. We should look for his return, and the others, at next Dawn. For now, many boulders, streams, and unknowns will attempt to hinder us—but we will not be halted by land nor creature!

Especially the Wargles."

"Wargles?" Titha asked. "That's the best thing you've said yet! We have Wargles at home! They are the cutest little buggers in the *wooooooorld*! Oh please tell me we can expect to spot a few for a good chase. I could use their squishy little faces right about now."

"Yes, they are quite precious," Maya replied. "And that is exactly their danger, child! Do not wish for such things!" She spoke, completely serious. "I find their cuteness most unneeded and wholly distracting; as do any who know their true nature! They exist only to deter the lesser from sacred places, Titha, like your Yythengrey and Igdrasil, too, I would imagine—and they deter mortals with said cuteness—an artform they have mastered over all of Time itself. *Such* masters of hide and seek, they are, that they may surprise us at any time. If you see one, do not indulge it!"

Audun cocked his eyebrows. He had heard a lot of weird things on their journey so far, but avoiding cute little creatures as if they were monstrous ogres was by far, in his opinion, the weirdest of them all.

"Continue north along the Western side of the river, Paw and Haldor," Maya continued. "And if you see any crevice, avoid it. Legends tell of many endless pits in Svellvanyon. In this, the coming darkness is our enemy, but it is also an ally in shielding us from any prying eyes, or a Wargle's annoyance via distraction."

"Not for me," Titha grinned mischievously.

Maya shot a sharp look at her, staring a hole straight through her, it felt like.

"I won't chase them! Geez," Titha mumbled, "just like Gilly, this bird is…"

With that, the companions continued north in search of further totems—full of anticipation for the Sunset and their destinies; both of which now rested on the Horizon.

CHAPTER FOURTEEN
Of Blood and Ash

Smoke and embers billowed from atop volcanic Mt. Crag. The mountain was angry.

Deep below its disjointed, craggy crest sat Nech—aching and barely alive. He had been tortured for information all through the night, and his body was close to breaking. The old Craglin propped himself up in the far corner of his dungeon cell against its orange clay blocks. Steam shot from crevices between the slender stalactites on the tall ceiling above him, emptying into the seemingly bottomless pit that fell off to the other side of the dungeon's walking path. The mountain continued to stir as Nech shook his head slowly, still in disbelief and stooped in sorrow. Yet even this slight motion pained him. A faint "ow" left his dry mouth, and a whip sounded from down the hall. Footsteps started up at the end of the corridor outside his prison's rusty gate. He flinched with each smattering of feet against the dungeon's hot floor. Before long a snorting and drooling Craglin guard stood in front of the enclosure, his body as wide as the door. The oversized wretch scratched his potbelly (that hung clear over his tattered breeches) before smacking it so it would jiggle as he laughed a horrid, spit-gurgling laugh. Nech looked him in the eyes, speaking defiantly.

"Back for another round of rousing conversation, are we?" he said with a smirk.

The guard laughed again before slamming his huge hairy-knuckled hands onto the rusty gate. "Nope. Done with 'ew, I am," he gurgled.

Nech smiled prematurely.

"Chief Bossman wants a go at yeh now, bookrat." The guard smiled as he wiped saliva from his mouth.

Nech's knees shot together. "Chief? Bossman?" he thought to himself before blurting aloud. "Ugar..."

The guard's smile widened, and he turned to walk away.

Nech grew nervous. He knew this old foe would be his end. The last confrontation held with Ugar (and all before it) was dreadfully unpleasant and resulted in his banishment. The old Scribe always did what he believed to be right—he would not bow to Ugar then, and no matter how hard his knees were knocking—

he would not do it now, either. A muffled clamor began from the opposite hall and Nech's hands balled into fists. What sounded like a shriek from one of the guards echoed before being silenced. Nech's eyelids shot closed as he braced himself; this was it, he thought. But no noise followed, save for the steam above. He waited another moment—and still nothing.

"Open your eyes, you loon," a gruff voice spoke to him from close to the ground.

Nech popped one eye open and peered through the gate. It was Torai!

"You?" Nech clamored. "Where is Maya? I certainly hope she has sent you, otherwise what in Craga's name are you doing here?"

"Saving your ungrateful hide. Get up, old hob. More guards will arrive any minute."

"We cannot leave now!" Nech whispered force-fully. "Ugar is on his way down—I can feel his footsteps! There is only one way up and it is unlikely that we may pass *through* him!"

"That's a risk we have to take. Besides, you have me now."

"You remain arrogant, I see," Nech spoke dryly. "Splendid."

Torai rolled his dark eyes and stepped backward, using his beak to undo the leather binding around his left leg. He tossed it aside, revealing a lockpick beneath. The stout falcon swooped up and began working on the lock with haste. Nech watched, agitated.

"I suppose it would be too much to ask for you to hasten your disastrous rescue attempt?" he quipped.

Torai stopped, glaring at the goblin as his beak twirled the pick inside the lock's gears.

Nech's foot began to tap. "If Maya were here that lock would already be—" *Pop*! The lock opened.

Torai spit the pick through the bars, hitting Nech straight between the horns. "Maya is the only reason I'm here, goblin. And you can *believe* that."

Nech gawfed at the gesture, rubbing his forehead and silently cursing his old rival (a fierce rival for Maya's time, devotion, and friendship, at that). Torai clasped his talons onto the middle bar of the gate and flapped his large brown wings, thrusting himself and it backward to open. Nech hesitated before stepping out. "

We have never liked each other," he began, "and perhaps we never will. But thank you, Torai. Sincerely."

"Save your thanks for the first breath of fresh air," Torai replied. "I can hardly breathe in this place." He swooped down, latching onto Nech's tattered green tunic to help him stand. As he did, a sudden racket began to echo down the southern hallway.

"See! He is coming! I told you he was coming!" Nech

shouted. "Hide, Torai! Quickly! And shut me back in! *Do as I say!*"

Torai complied, hoping the old Craglin had a plan. One swift stroke of a guard's sword would be the end of either of them. Torai shoved Nech down, kicking up soot, and slammed the gate—but the lock did not click. He darted upward, roosting behind a hanging stalactite. From above he watched as guard after guard piled in; each a more slovenly yellow Craglin than the last. As the thirteenth guard piled in, a shadow fell over the hallway that spread into the dungeon and up to the ceilings. The guards stood back, almost falling off the cliff behind them just to make way.

An enormous, craggy creature walked in the heart of the shadow. His silhouette was gigantic, each edge of him filled with protruding spikes. The False Emperor had arrived, and he made the guards look like piglets. His shoulders were as wide as the cell's barred front, and the four horns atop his head rose out into a jutting crown above his bald head. Strange, ash-like black markings covered his entire deep yellow skin, each jutting in different patterns that lead up to blood red pupils amidst veiny, sunken eyes. He wore only a pair of ashen trousers with a deep, burnt-orange sash made from something that once lived.

Nech stood slowly, his joints cracking from the pain and pressure. "Ugar..." the old Scribe muttered, the very name spoiling his mouth with a vile, sour hatred. Still rubbing his forehead, he motioned to speak again, but no sound came out. The monstrous Ugar stepped forward.

"Where is the stone?" Ugar asked, his voice deep and rough like the rumbling of an earthquake. Nech tried to swallow but his mouth had been so dry that his throat simply closed tighter. His words were usually his only defense against this demonic brute of a being, but even they failed him presently.

"Not speaking at all now?" Ugar growled. "Unusual for you, but fine. I will make you *sing instead.*"

The ground began to rumble beneath their feet. Nech shook, his limbs helpless. Chips of dry clay began to crack and fall from the ceiling as the very shadows in the room danced about. Ugar focused his stare on the old Scribe, his body still while all else 'round him quaked. Nech's muscles began to spasm as confusion swelled within him. What was happening? Some sort of foul magick? Had Ugar grown stronger in his absence?

It was magick; and he had indeed.

Nech's head shot backward as his spine knotted, his mouth wide open. Ugar clenched his jaw and fist, leaning toward Nech.

"Where is the stone?" he asked. "Where… is it?" he repeated slowly with growling intensity. This was not the oafish brute Nech mouthed off to mere seasons ago. This was a new and horrifying Ugar, one with great power that could only have been granted to him by Vulduun. A slight grin revealed the brute's devilish fangs as he twisted his fist, which twisted Nech's back in return. Awful gurgling noises left the old goblin's mouth before the words began to spill out.

"*Sing,*" Ugar growled.

Torai watched from above in horror as Nech's twisted body blurted out everything: Titha and Audun, their parentage, and the shrouded Sunstone, one half of the two *Eternal Stones.* Tears streamed down Nech's face as he forcibly spoke of the children's vision and its Totems, their current path, and ultimate plan to deliver their stone to the Elk Kings before Vulduun could ever reach it.

Ugar's smirk vanished, and Nech dropped to the floor a drooling, twisted mess. Torai's mind raced above. If the poor goblin had a plan, it surely wasn't this. He shook his head and sighed. Before he could stop himself, Torai bolted into action. The large falcon shot down like an arrow, talons bared. One by one he slashed the faces and skulls of the guards, each flailing backward off the cliff behind their heels—save for one, who managed to grab the overhang. Squeals and shrieks echoed through the dungeon as the rest plummeted to their deaths. It was a terrible racket and over in a flash. Torai landed hard on a clay mound in front of the southern hall. He looked up to see Nech still on the ground.

"Nech!" he cried out. "You must get up!" But Nech did not budge. He remained twisted in the dirt. "Get up!" Torai pleaded.

"For Maya! For the world… For *Titha Mae*!"

Fuming, Ugar stomped toward Torai. His fists were clenched and his teeth locked. Halfway to, he swiped his clawed hand down to the ridge, grabbing the remaining guard and flinging him up onto the path. "*You*," Ugar barked. "We must send word to Master. Fetch the horn. *Go*!"

The guard took off like a whimpering piglet up the southern hall. Ugar turned to inflict his wrath upon Torai, but the falcon was too fast. He looked about with his red eyes.

"Where are you, bird?" Ugar shouted. "You are wise to hide! I will enjoy plucking each feather from your tiny, frail body."

Torai hid behind another large stalactite. His scarred eyes were full of dust, as were his lungs. Ugar did not scare him, but his own failing breath did. He looked to Nech's cell gate, which was still shut. Torai knew then the only way they were both getting out alive was for him to lead Ugar away, as he was not strong enough to overpower him bird to beast. But the clever Falcon knew, as did all in Cragoa, that their False Emperor was prideful and vain to the extreme. This in mind, he took another deep breath, wheezing as he reared back. Without a sound he darted down to Ugar, latching his talons to the brute's jagged horns, tossing the wretch's head side to side. Ugar roared, swatting at Torai aimlessly.

"Let's see how beautiful you feel without these, ash-breath!" Torai cawed with a grin.

With one hearty swoop and pull, Torai's mighty talons snapped the two largest ashen horns from the center of Ugar's broad brow. The ugly monster roared backward, his hands grasping the two broken stumps on his forehead. A terrible mix of screams and growls left his fanged mouth. Torai took his chance, flocking up the hallway.

"Good luck, Nech!" he wished as he left, the two crown horns still in hold.

Ugar screamed, the sound booming like thunder as he took off up the southern hall after the falcon and his missing dignity.

Slowly Nech began to stir amidst the commotion. He placed his old hands onto the clay floor, barely able to hoist himself up. He looked out of his cell to emptiness; no Torai, no Ugar, and no guards. The old Scribe attempted to stand a few times to no avail, sinking back down to the floor; positive it was to be his deathbed. Sadness passed, and a swell of anger stirred inside him. He thought of his companions, his homeland, his people and all he had fought for. He refused to rot in a cell under Ugar's command! Knees quaking, he tried once more to stand and grip the rusty bars of his prison. He flung his hands forward to meet them and *plop*—the gate flung wide open. It was unlocked! He grinned for the first time in what felt like ages.

Hobbling forward he exited the cell, looking both directions. Without a soul in sight, he stepped out into the middle of the path; but which way had they gone? Nech looked to the ground, spotting Ugar's clawed footprints. They traveled from, and then back to, the southern passage, but not to the northern behind him. "Even his tracks are grotesque," he mused to himself as he followed them up the southern hall, only to discover an endless flight of stairs. "I should have expected this," he thought. Nech took off up the clay stairs as fast as his weakened body would allow, knowing full well that he was entirely too old for such a flights of fancy.

The chamber at the end of the stairs above was absolute chaos. Guards and servant goblins flung spears, shot arrows, and even threw chairs at Torai amid the orange ceiling—not one of them fast enough to hit him. Ugar barreled through them all, huffing and puffing with his hands still covering his stubby little broken horns so none would see his defiled crown.

"Kill the bird!" he screamed as he stepped over each bumbling goblin, "and get my hor—those *artifacts* back from him! They are *mine*!"

Making it to the other side of the room, he ripped open the doors in front of him, breaking them loose of their hinges to reveal a balcony astride the side of the volcano. All of the Northern Craglands laid before him. He stepped out to furious hot winds, eyeing his Master's Horizon. From the corner of the balcony a cowering, stout goblin lifted up a large bone instrument to Ugar:

the Dragonshorn. Ugar snatched the relic, sucking all the hot air his lungs could muster. Placing the Dragonshorn to his cracked lips, he let loose a garish and brutal trumpeting. It was an unmistakable Dragon's call… from one to another.

Vulduun would soon rise again.

The rest of the companions drudged on far to the east of Mt. Crag and it's dungeons. The sharp walls of Svellvanyon rose ever higher around them; the mountain peaks disappearing into strangely dark clouds in an even darker midnight sky. Titha looked to her feet, her bare toes dirty and puffy.

"Not a single Wargle," she huffed, disappointed that the darkest Night had come without any sightings at all. They hadn't seen much of anything living in hours, really, save the changing trees. Suddenly, the palm of her foot met a pointed rock as if it was thrown beneath her feet. She thought nothing of it, until the very same thing happened not twice—but three times more!

"That's it!" She screamed, stopping in her tracks. She slammed her other foot into the mossy dirt beneath her and shot daggers with her eyes over to Paw.

"I don't care how 'sore' your shoulders are, you big baby, I am riding on them! These rocks keep jumping out of nowhere and if I step on another I swear I'll—" Before she could finish, another rock jumped out of nowhere. This one hit her on the knee. "Ouch!" She cried out in both pain and surprise. Maya, however, knew exactly what was happening. Once Titha caught wind of her falcon friend's disdain she lit up like a starry sky. "Wargles!?" She squealed.

"Wargles..." Maya scoffed. Titha squealed in delight! Maya opened her beak to sternly warn the younglings not to join its mischief, but there was no use. Two small bottoms romped in the air as Audun and Titha's chins met the ground, each scouring for the cutest of all Gaela's creatures. Not a glimpse of hide nor hair came to Audun, but Titha was not to give up. Her green eyes glowed in the darkness as she peeled the landscape —every blade of grass and every rock by the river—until she came to a fork in the river. Both of its paths led far into different strokes of darkness. Maya took great issue with this, and the Companions halted.

"Can you see which river'path is less dangerous, Titha?" Maya asked.

"No, they both lead down into crevassess I can't see!" she shouted in reply. "You think it's dark up here, my eyes can't even make out what's down *there*!"

She continued to peel the night with her vision until—aha! There it was! A *Wargle*! She squealed again, so high pitched Audun had to cover his ears. A tiny fuzzball with a big round snout and two teeny button-black eyes popped out from behind a tree on the left path of the river's divide. It wore a budding acorn cap atop its frazzled head and hopped about on two big flat bunny-like feet. As it bounded and sputtered about it made the most adorable sound, making it immediately clear where the name 'Wargle' came from.

"Titha Mae don't you dare follow that Wargle!" Maya hissed, "We must continue forward and have no time for distractions!" She flapped her good wing in disapproval from atop Paw, who was wholly invested in Titha and Audun catching the Wargle. Slowly his huge round paws crept toward his Luna-sister.

"Paw! Cease this!" Maya cried, but it was no use.

Haldor and Paw both were now sniffing about for acorn-capped creatures. Titha and her Bear-brother, having done this at home, were practically experts at Wargle-sniping.

"Hah! I've almost got you!" Titha squeamed, her cheeks rosy with delight as she bounded down the left riverbed. "I'm gonna squish each of your little cheeks until you love me like your own mother!"

She wiggled about as she tip-toed toward the thick line of trees on the western edge of Svellvanyon, creeping along the path of the Wargle and quietly snickering as it led her closer and closer to the forest's edge; cooing and wargling all the way.

"Titha! Don't!" Maya shouted harshly. "Come back here at once!"

But she did not listen. As the young Luna neared the trees, a green glow met that of her eyes. Two glisten-ing green orbs swayed in the dark, their gaze hypnotizing. The Wargle let out one last squirmy sound, then *poofed* into nothingness before the strange, gazing green orbs. Titha took one more step toward the eyes in the forest. She could not help but approach them. Was it a fellow Luna? Whatever it was, it had her absolutely enchanted and entranced. As her foot met the patchy soil, her heel snapped a crispy branch, and the dead quiet of the canyon echoed with its sound.

Alerted, the bearer of the great green orbs let out a nasty *hisssss* into the midnight before them. Titha's heart skipped a beat in her chest. Slowly the set of glowing eyes raised higher, then higher still until they sat halfway into the treetops. As quickly as they had appeared, they snuffed out. Another deep *hissssss* slithered out from between the trees, and the companions became paralyzed at the sound. Haldor let out a barreling growl from his chest, and the curly gray hair on the back of his neck stood straight up. Paw crepped forward, ready to pounce. Another seething serpentine call engulfed them, sending goosebumps up Titha's arms. Paw was poised and ready to attack when a hefty *rattling* resonated out from the shadows. Titha's mouth opened wide as if a scream wanted to escape, but no sound came.

With all the speed of a raging river an enormous Serpent's head splintered through the foliage; its slanted green eyes glowing ever-brighter as its pointed brown and black jaws gaped wide. Two deadly fangs dripped with venom, their length poised and darting directly for Titha Mae at the edge of the forest. Paw anticipated the strike, however, lunging past Titha and onto the gigantic snake's neck, lashing into its diamond-patterned scales with tooth and claw. Maya flapped backward, and Audun rushed to catch her. The horrific reptile bristled and moaned before them, flailing its thick body side to side. Paw's grip loosened, and he flew to the ground beside Titha and Audun, hitting the soil with a hard *thud.*

Suddenly the ground itself began to shift, and the girth of the diamondback serpent's length became known as it uncoiled from beneath the grass—surrounding the companions as it rattled its tail once more. Haldor growled at the sight, stepping backward to protect the others. As Paw rolled over, the gleam of Titha's Feather-sword caught her eye, and she jumped to retrieve it. Out of the air behind her the rattlesnake's tail shot like a spear, slamming the young Luna from her path and to the ground. Haldor barked furiously, finally charging forward to bite down on the slithering tail. A pain-filled *hisssss* echoed through Svellvanyon, and Titha leaped for her sword again, her mud-covered indigo hands outstretched like wings. Paw rose to his Luna-sister, and her grasp met Feathersword's silver sheen for the first time in what felt like (or had truly been) many days. With great determination she swung it around and revealed its splendor to the serpent. It seethed at the sight, recoiling and lowering its arrow-shaped head as the blade gleamed in the Moonlight.

More and more the sword's sheen grew as it absorbed light from the Night sky above, and with each twinkle the snake would twitch and flinch. Titha's keen eyes took note of this, and she stepped forward, her eyebrows pressed down as far as they'd go. She swung the sword once, Paw behind her, and the serpent recoiled further. She swung it again, its great glistening form cutting through the midnight, and the snake slithered back even further. Titha placed both her hands on the stem of the feather, raising it above her head as a scream she did not know was coming left her lips. The green shine disappeared from the snake's eyes, and it retreated. Its mass slinked down into the riverbed before vanishing into the Great Svell River below.

Maya watched its dark shadow like a hawk (or a falcon, rather) and clenched her broken wing in frus-tration. She followed the dreadful shape with her eyes as best she could until it came to the fork in the river ahead. Without hesitation, the snake swam up the eastern-right fork of the stream, abandoning the current of the western-left. Slowly its enormous silhouette merged with the Great Svell River as the churning waters slithered on northward through the canyon, much like a serpent itself.

Titha's vision went blurry and she fell backwards into the grass. Paw and Haldor rushed to her, licking her face with what surely was both thanks and love. Audun popped over with Maya atop his shoulder.

"That was amazing!" he cried out. "That was the most amazing thing *ever*!"—little hands waving with glee.

Titha laid silent. Her face held an expression somewhere between amazement and arrogance.

"I think we found the snake," she spoke. Her stillness slowly turned to laughter, as it was all she felt like doing in such a triumphant yet terrifying moment.

"I believe *you* found it, you mischevious young-ling!" Maya scoffed, holding her injured wing. "And though it is the first of your Totems to try and *kill* us, it has revealed the next leg of our journey all the same. Abandon the leftward stream. Along the Easterly river-fork we must travel! To the right!"

Yet their contagious mirth did not last long. Paw looked up from his Luna-sister, his expression imme-diately changing to fear;

one she was not accustomed to seeing on his face. His chestnut eyes began to glow with the reflections of an ever-burning flame. Her heart sank. The others paused with the burst of light. An intense heat overtook their backsides. Slowly they turned to the Western Svells, knowing exactly what—or who, rather—such events heralded. "Vulduun…" Titha whispered. "Do you think he knows where we are now?" she asked Maya, her throat dry and scratchy.

"Yes," Maya said after hesitating. "It has begun."

"Should we run?" Audun shouted.

Maya's eyes were saucers. She stood straight up, perched on Titha's belongings astride Paw as her gaze stayed glued to the blazing mountains. Orange overtook red… yellow engulfed the orange… and then blinding white took all sight. Masses of birds, some making horrid noises, made themselves known for the first time as they fled surrounding treetops into the disorienting light.

"I can't see!" Audun yelled, his voice cracking. Fear washed over the tiny young Viking, as if the weight of their peril suddenly appeared before him for the first time. He stuffed his papers down into his sack, staring into the blazing midnight sky. "I'm scared, Titha!"

Titha grabbed Paw's fur, holding it tight as the light washed over and crashed into them like waves. "We'll be okay, Audun! I promise! Just hold onto Haldor! Everything will be okay!

Everything will be—"

Her voice broke as the light dimmed down; the blinding white subsiding over the crests of the Western Svells. And as suddenly as it had begun, the inferno ceased, its heat no longer advancing as it sought to change directions.

"He is headed for Cragoa!" Maya squawked abruptly. "Not for us, but for Mt. Crag! Nech and Torai! Hah! They must have done something stupid! Bless them!" She hopped from their bags to Titha's shoulder. "Run, child! We must *run*! Swiftly! Our friends have given us a precious diversion and we cannot waste it. Swiftness take us up the river! Follow the path of the vile serpent! To Igdrasil!"

CHAPTER FIFTEEN

Shadows of Evil

The doors to the balcony flung open as a mob of sweaty, bloodied Craglins stumbled out from the chambers of Mt. Crag and into the ashen air. Slowly they stepped aside, revealing Nech battered and bruised, a worn scowl on his tired face—his arms clasped by the claws of his former brethren. There was no wiggling out of this predicament, nor any sign of Torai. Here he was... caught yet again.

Ugar the Terrible stood staring into the blazing horizon, not even bothering to turn to his old nemesis. "You have failed. Again," he grumbled, his cracking voice deep and faulted. "It is what you do, it seems. Fail. And now you will watch your ultimate failure as my master takes your people for his own before turning his sights to your poor little friends."

"These are your people too, Ugar," Nech spat back, his words tired yet pointed. "You may think you are above us—and Vulduun may have twisted you far beyond recognition—but I know what you really are... *Welp!*"

Ugar's body shot around, his massive, clawed hand swiping away the guards holding Nech. He gripped Nech's throat with the other as he lifted the old Scribe above his broken horns. Slowly Ugar's face turned, his red eyes burning and bulging from beneath his hot, cracked skin. Nech kicked and gurgled, but there was nothing he could do. Ugar turned his much smaller enemy around, forcing him to look outward from the balcony and into the dry North Craglands beneath his feet. Nech's eyes widened as he beheld that which he had never seen before. There on the horizon was the last Elderdrake: Vulduun, in a ghastly new state. The Great Day Drake-Dragon of Old and Dawnfather to some—Herald of the Sun—was directly upon them and *rotting* with rage.

Ugar stretched his long, thick arm out so Nech could watch as the Craglins below, his own people, either bowed before Vulduun's fire or became engulfed by it. It was a gruesome, heartbreaking torrent of blood and ash. Flames checkered the landscape as all who resisted his order perished into raging, sparking infernos. As his supreme power became evident, few others rebelled against the Great Drake's onslaught, and soon all of Cragoa was his. He stomped his golden feet, keeping one clutched; the other three's mass and breadth kicking up clay'mounds and soot. The grand creature shook ash from his wide crown, its jagged and swirled horns gleaming in the flames—their length now marked with black cracks. Vulduun dug his tremendous feet deep into the orange earth below him and paused, sniffing the air as he pulled his clutched hand into his chest. He surveyed the Craglands for a moment, then froze. His enormous head jolted as his nostrils flared. With a quick snort he cleared them, and his expression turned deeply sour.

Nech froze as the Dragon's maw shot over, pointing to him like a poised spear. Two dead red eyes locked onto him as every golden scale on the massive deity flexed and hardened.

"YOU," Vulduun thundered. His voice parted the air in front of him, its sheer power crumbing everything before it, straight up to Nech. The entire mountain shook, a fissure cracking through the clay and up Mt. Crag. "I smell... *Luna,"* the grand beast growled.

Nech froze, his hands still grasping Ugar's grip just enough for him to breathe. His heart pounded so hard in his chest he felt as if he surely would burst or fall apart. Or both. Vulduun's claws popped up and his head lowered. His massive wings swooped down to his side as he streamlined himself. The dragon stomped toward the balcony, his gaze fixated on Nech as he trampled the ruins before him. Ugar began to laugh as his master neared, if from nothing more than nervous fear.

The full girth of Vulduun's behemoth, golden frame stood before them. Slowly, his thick neck raised to the height of the balcony like a serpent, nostrils twitching. Two humongous, deep-seated red eyes surrounded by black pits rose over the railing to meet Nech. The old Scribe's body quivered, then froze. Ugar held him in place, his strength unwavering. Vulduun lowered his snout, pointing his gaze down his wide-bridged maw directly at the Craglin.

"This is him, Master. He is the one," Ugar blurted to his overlord.

Then he spoke.

"*So I have you to thank?*" Vulduun decreed, his voice booming like a thunderstorm. "*You write lovely tomes, Goblin Scribe, and I thank you for your contributions to my cause.*" The twisted Drake let out a demeaning laugh.

Nech's stomach dropped into his knees; His greatest failure realized. The stolen book… the Eternal-tome... had given Vulduun what he had not known before. Nech began to shake.

"*Come now, Goblin. You shall be remembered as a herald of knowledge during my Eternal Sunlight! Relish in knowing you played a pivotal role in bringing about the Eon of Day.*" A twisted, toothy smile broke through Vulduun's unfathomably deep voice, which rumbled in tandem with Mt. Crag. *"Now answer me this, Scribe. What business do you have with... Lunas?"*

Nech blurted back immediately, his mind far from clear. "That is a rather broad question. Perhaps you could be more specific, oh mighty one?" he quipped before realizing what he had said, followed by a slow *gulp*.

"I ask nothing twice!" the Great Drake shouted, erupting like a volcano. *"And I absolutely detest riddles. Speak plainly!"* His gargantuan right claw remained low and clutched, ever-close to his golden breast. He raised it a bit as he spoke again, revealing more blackening cracks in his scaled armor. *"I grow impatient, imp. What business do you have with those wretched Night Children? Answer me!"*

Ugar's grip tightened on the back of Nech's neck. The twisted servant of Vulduun pushed his arm even further, bringing his captive mere inches from the steaming sheen of the Dragon's maw. Nech's toes curled back as they burned from the radiating heat.

"I will tell you nothing else, Vulduun, for I already wish for death having fed you such precious, pure knowledge with my Elder-tome," he gargled through Ugar's grip. "And it breaks my heart to finally behold your majesty... only to see how black and vile you've become. Meriduun would be ashamed!"

The air smashed to pieces as Vulduun screamed, throwing

his head into the air—spouting fire so hot it singed the swirling soot around them all. He slammed his front foot into the earth and tightened his clutched hand.

"*Do not speak her name!*" he decreed violently. "*No one is to ever speak her name again*!" he cried out, his tail lashing back and forth. "*I will find my Sunstone, Goblin! I will claim my eternal right from the piles of the dead and I will burn all who have aided you alive*!"

"Master!" Ugar shouted in an attempt to break Vulduun's rage.

"*What*?" the Dragon swiftly thundered back.

"I pulled everything from this fool for you, my Master! The Luna you speak of is but a child! A *girl* no less! She is the Daughter of Theole and she flees with a Viking child companion and your Sunstone—"

Every scale and muscle of Vulduun's massive being flexed in all-consuming anger. A deep breath inflated his hate-filled lungs. "*Out with the rest*! *Now*!" he commanded.

"They traverse the lands to Igdrasil, my Lord! To the Tree of Life! They aim to take your Sunstone to them… to the Elk Kings Three!"

Vulduun's egregious tantrum grew in ferocity as every part of him curled and coiled in rage. The black underbelly of his girth began to pulsate with horrific fiery veins as his twisted mind came to terms with such an unexpected revalation. He would not, *could* not be bested in his quest to claim the Crown of Elk Kings and the power of the United Trinity for himself! Monumentous wings whipped and whirled in the thick air astride Mt. Crag as the Elderdrake's hatred grew into a deep, fearful loathing. His wrath was, however, cut short.

From the pines to the West a piercing goat'horn call shot through the Craglands. The very Fells seemed to rumble in the red night as trees wavered and cracked. Hundreds of hooves galloped like a hurricane through the cratered lands westward. It was the advance of the Vikingmen; the Song of Skaldhall! They had come! They had answered the Peregrine Order's plea!

Vulduun let out an awful cry somewhere betwixt a lion's roar and a mammoth's shrill trumpeting as his neck recoiled and his wings shot out even farther into the midnight sky; their golden sheen ablaze. The entire Night, too, was alight as the Dawnfather turned for *war* with the Men of Autumnhill—which neither he, nor the Craglins, were prepared for.

Ugar faltered, his grip slipping. Nech yelped as he looked down hundreds of feet to the dark ground below. Vulduun's shoulders raised and he flapped his wings, lifting himself into the air. Briefly, he turned back to the balcony.

"*Gather what remains and lead this miserable race against the Vikings! Cleanse this land of Men!*" he commanded. "*They have turned against me in full! I will not have them best me again! Defeat them in battle, or I shall have your head on a pike and see this entire crater burn in eternal flames!"*

Vulduun was unusually manic. He had not counted on anyone being cunning enough to bring the other stone, *his* Sunstone, to the Elk Kings. *He* possessed the Eternal-tome now, not the enemy! This was utter blasphemy! And the only army of Men to ever best him—his own former Children of Day, at that—had returned! Through this all-consuming obsession and madness, it became clear what was causing his once marvelous hide to turn black, and his golden scales to crumble.

"What of him? What of the Scribe?" Ugar asked his master, raising Nech before the Dragon.

Vulduun smiled, his red eyes glowing.

"Drop him."

There was no hesitation between these words and the loosening of Ugar's grip. Darkness and flame swirled in Nech's eyes as his arms and legs flailed. It felt like an eternity as he fell into Cragoa. His eyes shut and his breath ceased. Yet no ground nor end met him. Slowly he opened one eye, peeking about. "Am I dead?" he pondered as his body rose upward. He felt a hard tugging at his back, and looked up. "Torai!" he shouted. "Oh I have never been so glad to see you!"

Torai had caught him mid-air, and was hastily flying away from Ugar and his guards. "Not even in the dungeons of Mt.

Crag?" Torai yelled back above the sound of swift winds.

"Perhaps it is a tie!" Nech replied, still in disbelief whilst catching his breath. "You are full of miraculous feats, my Peregrine friend!"

"It was nothing," said Torai. "I perched above the balcony and waited, is all. I knew that imbecile would toss your fragile old body eventually!"

"Marvelous!" Nech spouted. "Simply splendid! And do I hear that horn'ed call correctly, Torai? Do the Vikingmen approach?"

"They do!" Torai replied as he swooped upward and around to point them westward. An arrow shot close by them—a little *too* close—so Torai flew higher to continue to speak. "Maya chose to honor your path. She is with Titha Mae and the Viking child of Sigrid and Angvar. She is guiding them to the Tree as best she can, by their Totems and to the Elk Kings! To hand over the Sunstone and rid ourselves of its peril and thwart Vulduun's Eternal Day! Maya also sent the best of our order to gather the peoples of the West to rise against Vulduun, though it was Titha Mae's idea. A clever young girl, that Luna! And speaking of—The Vikingmen now approach—but where are the forest kin of Yythengrey? Do they not also come?"

Torai's infallible eyes scanned the night and the flame-riddled landscape below. The first of the Houndsmen burst forth from the pine forest, their enormous longhaired horses stampeding down Cragoa's steep crater walls—but no Lunas followed. A wall of giant insect-mounted Craglin soldiers, workers, and startled citizens began to form at the crater floor's edge. They snorted and cackled as they pushed each other into formation, their leather padding and iron armor burnt and worn. They were a makeshift army of Ugar's sloppy design and Vulduun's crippling influence. Before them rolled the opposite: a charge of willing, hearty, and lethal warriors. Slowly their tide parted, and from the ranks rode out a white horse, its mane braided and magni-ficent. Astride it rode an equally handsome Man—Rainer, Son of Angvar and new Jarl of Autumnhill—and there on his shoulder sat Azra of the Peregrine Order. The leader of the Houndsmen (and Audun's older brother) let loose a bloodcurdling *HRAH* as he and his white horse, Kelliah, barreled ahead of their fierce fellow warmen & maidens. The Craglins stood firm below and the Houndsmen did not stop. Certain bloodshed flooded every mind.

Back by Mt. Crag, Vulduun swooped and barreled through the air creating whirlwinds of flame beneath him, both claws now clutched tight up against his glowing chest. He powered away from the volcano in a blind rage that was pointed directly at the Houndsmen.

"*Attack*!" he commanded from far behind his newly

assembled Craglin forces, their boots quaking with both fear and anticipation. Slowly they began to approach the stampeding Vikingmen, while nearer and nearer Vulduun flew to the battlefield. There he beheld a white stallion and the young rider astride her. The Great Dragon's maw filled with flame as he became blinded by murderous wrath. He climbed higher and higher into the air, his mind consumed with thoughts of consuming Rainer and his horse alive.

Rainer smirked, his scruffy, freckly-handsome face alight with confidence. He stared directly into the gleam of the Great Drake, a once proud symbol of his family and heritage. A deep breath left his lips as he unsheathed two broadswords, raising one into the air.

"*ATLAGA*!" he screamed, his voice piercing the helmets of every Houndsman. Without hesitation each warrior's horse rampaged into an unbelievable haste, and carnage overtook the Craglands. The armor of Cragoa's enormous insects was thick, but their Craglin-riders astride were no match for the broad shoulders of each warman and maiden. Like lightning through clouds the Vikings sliced each and every Craglin down from their paths. Limbs left every insect (be it giant cricket, ant or grasshopper) and death took countless Craglin soldiers by Rainer's double blades.

Vulduun, now high above the battlefield, shot forth a thunderous call. "*Ogres*!" he cried out, and the ground began to quake. From massive holes at the pit of each crater came gigantic hairy ogres, each stomping directly on or over the failing Craglins before them. A few larger Craglins wielding longspears managed to down Vikingmen as surprise took them; Ogres sweeping the front ranks. Their huge, fur-clad knuckles grabbed the throats of galloping horses and tossed them aside, dismounting their riders. No form or tactic controlled the battle now. It was pure chaos.

Torai began to tire in the skies between Mt. Crag and the battle. He was unusually large and strong for a Peregrine, but even that could not warrant endless flight with a Goblin in tow. "The Great Dragon's forces are unorganized, and he's startled!" he cried out to Nech. "Now Orgres emerge from the craterous ground, but I still see no sign of Lunas! They are nowhere my eyes can see! If they do not show soon, the battle's tide may turn for our worse!"

"They will come!" Nech decreed with certainty. "They will come. Just a little longer..."

Torai hoped Nech was right. He had no experience with Lunas. Below, either way, his cautioning words rang true as the Ogres tipped the carnage in Vulduun's favor. Few creatures could match the strength of a Viking, but Ogres were one such behemoth. Weaponless, their hands smashed through the Houndsmen like boulders as cries left both Man and horse. From behind the Houndsmen's ranks, however, a new sound emerged. Melodious Howling and the snapping of jaws overtook the

Moonlit night. Rainer raised his sword again, dead center of the battle.

"Hounds! *Atlaga*!" he commanded, his eyes shooting up to Vulduun. He smiled as behind him large wolfhounds shot forth from between the trees, their clawed paws racing down the craterside as foaming slobber left their maws. They were domesticated wolves, somewhere between the sweet yet strong Haldor's make and the brazen, unpredictable manes of their wild brethren. Their amber and brown hair stealthily swept down to the battlefield as they mauled any Craglins in their path. The lunging movements of the hounds and the Houndsmen became one.

It was a great display of strength worthy of any legend. Five or six hounds attacked the Ogres at a time, latching onto the giants with their steel-trap-like jaws and fangs. Maidens bashed their skull-clad shields into the frail bodies of Craglins as warmen cut down insect and goblin alike.

Vulduun spat fire, huffing and hawing. He had now been taken by surprise three times by those he once claimed as his own worshippers. His ancient mind raced and fought on the edge of panic. Below him, Rainer galloped toward his underbelly—Kelliah's pale hooves smashing fallen goblins.

"By my family's honor and my father's helm shall I *end you*!" The young man shouted into the night sky. "I am Rainer, Son of Angvar and Sigrid and New Jarl of Autumnhill—and the Men of the Day no longer worship you, *Worm*! You hold no power in the West!"

Rainer drew back a broadsword, flipped it, then flung it like a lance directly toward Vulduun's chest. The Great Drake jerked himself sideways, guarding his bare blackening breast with his clutched hands, loosening his grip for the first time. A muffled sheen of Moonlight let loose from between his fingers. Locks of white and blonde hair trickled down betwixt the gleam. Rainer squinted, narrowing his gaze as Kelliah galloped closer.

There, in Vulduun's guarded grasp, lay his mother, Sigrid, Theole the Watcher, and the Moonstone together; the parents unconscious. Surrounding them, he could now see the twisted Drake's hide for what it was—old and putrid, rotting beneath glorious golden scales from ages of anxious hatred. Rainer could not believe it!

"The Dragon must know this is it!" he thought aloud. "He must be nearing his and all ends! This is the battle to end our Eon! He has each of his prizes in tow! *Mother*!" he cried out, but there was no answer.

Comfort was taken, however, in his knowledge of their bloodline, and that she would need to remain very much *alive* in order for the Dawnfather to enact his power-hungry plot. That or

the Dragon would have to take him, which he would die before allowing. Vulduun, as if he felt Rainer's probing thoughts, tightened his grip and con-cealed his captives. With one huge, hot breath, he took in all of the surrounding dark air and let forth a raging inferno. Rainer pulled back on Kelliah's reigns, reaching to his own back for a shield to protect them from the blaze and raised it just in time. He lowered it, however, not to a reprise of fire but to the Dragon's backside—Vulduun had been made vulnerable and was fleeing yet again!

"*Mother*!" Rainer cried out again, but his words were swallowed by the violence swirling 'round him. He watched as Vulduun flew off into the distant Svells with his beloved mother's fate. A berserker's ferocity overtook him, and he slashed and hacked every living enemy his blade could reach. Hounds circled and protected him, fending off splintered spears and arrows; crooked swords and jagged daggers. As Vulduun left sight, a great roar echoed from the dragon's throat, and the earth began to shake again. Slithering Reeks emerged from the same holes from which the Ogres had ambushed the Hounds-men! The Lizardmen jumped into battle, scantily-armored and wielding long curved swords and claws. Behind them more foes arose; other foul races of the Day—emerald Moglins from Southlyn's Unreachable Swamps emerged alongside reddish-gray Slaglins from Eastlyn's rocky Boulderlands: all Children of Day swayed under Vulduun's malcontent, and races those so close to the Horizon had rarely (if ever) seen before. It was with this the Great Drake's forces were all accounted for. With the Lizardmen and Goblin's claws added to the fray, the Vikings were finally outmatched. Rainer fought harder and harder, then looked to his men, their horses and their hounds now falling in greater numbers. The Great Drake disappeared into the Svells eastward. Rainer's eyes darted north, then east, then south and west, surveying the carnage as waves of twisted minions overcame the Houndsmen. He refused to lose what remained of his people to a rogue war in the pits of Cragoa.

"*HEIMTA*!" he shouted to his warriors. "Heimta, Houndsmen! *Retreat*! Retreat to the high ground with your hearts still beating! To me, Houndsmen! *To me*!"

Vulduun ignored their plight, his gaze and flight pointed eastward towards Svellvanyon. If his ancient mind was right, its peaks were now the only thing standing between him, Igdrasil, and this accursed Luna girl.

CHAPTER SIXTEEN

The Tree of Life

The Svells were *a'blaze.* Paw ran through Svellvanyon as fast as his huge feet would carry him. Haldor was faster, but the two had grown close, and the hound slowed himself to keep an eye out for his friend. Titha adored their kinship, and held it as one of a million reasons that failure was not an option.

She leaned forth on her Bear-brother, the early morning darkness sweeping through her white hair as tinges of Vulduun's fiery siege highlighted it with gold. Audun, however, did not share her urgency to be nearer to doom. His eyes were wet. As the beasts ran, a low wimper escaped from Audun's mouth and Halor came to an alarming halt. The hound's head nuzzled his master as the lad's lips began to quiver. Precious Audun began to weep.

"I—I don't know if I can do this," he muttered, pitifully.

The companions came to a full halt. "I thought I could be brave but I don't want to see—see *him* again."

She frowned and leaned back, yanking Paw's hair and directing him toward Audun.

"You *are* brave!" Titha shouted in reply. "Look how far we've come! Look where we are, Audun! We are almost to Igdrasil. I can feel it, can't you? I know you can! I never would have made it this far without you. You've been very brave, and even if you don't think you are, the rest of us absolutely do—and that's all that matters. Not to mention your smarts! Who has pushed us on and on to follow our totems and our vision without fail? You! Think of it, Audun. Think of all of the things you have written down and *will* write—books of your own based on all the amazing things you've seen and done! Think of all we've done together, silly! You are so very brave to me."

"That's what scares me!" he replied, a lump in his throat. "I can feel him coming for me. I can—I can feel his hot breath and see the red death in his eyes! *He killed my father*! He killed him, Titha! I feel it now. I feel it. It feels real now, Titha, and I'm scared. I'm scared of Vulduun!"

Audun's breathing had grown frantic and his skin clammy. None of his friends had seen him this way before. Something awful was happening underneath his curly locks and the words kept coming. "He killed my father, Titha! Vulduun killed him! My father was so brave and was the best warrior Autumnhill had ever seen and Vulduun killed him! My father failed and I can't be brave if he wasn't. I can't even breathe. I'm not brave. I can't breathe! *I can't breathe*!"

Titha jumped from Paw and rushed to Audun, taking his hands and enclosing them within her own. "Deep breaths, Beebee. Deep breaths," she breathed as she held his hands. "Slowly in—then out. In—and out."

Audun took to her pattern and followed suit with deep, calming breaths; his demeanor changing with his friend's touch. He breathed slower and slower until his fingers began to calm, and his eyes focused on Titha.

"What did you call me?" he asked.

Titha looked right into his hazel gaze, still holding his hands. "What did I call you? Oh! Beebee, you mean?" she laughed. "It just came out, I'm sorry. Beebee is my little sister. She has trouble breathing sometimes when she gets scared, too. Whenever it happens I—I hold her hands and breathe with her and it makes us both feel better. Happens to me, too. So don't worry those pretty little curls." She looked down to her bare feet, barely able to see them between the thick grasses.

Audun took another deep breath, taking his hands back to pull his tattered brown cloak tighter around him. He took a moment and realized he did feel better, but that Titha may be scared, too. "You miss your family, I think," he said.

"Yes, I do," she replied. "My father, my sisters, and always my mother. She taught me that—to breathe in the moment. She used to do it with me, too, when I was tiny. I think. And oh, how I miss them all right now... more than anything. You do too, right? Miss home?"

"A lot," Audun replied quietly, his lip quivering again.

"I know it's hard. This is all hard. Nothing has been easy since we met, really. Not since we looked at your paper books or played with your stuffy animals."

Audun laughed with the joy of the memory and her mispronunciation of 'stuffed'.

"But that's why we're doing this, right? Our families! And you're so right: It is real. This is all *really* real," she continued. "It's not in books or drawings or the walls of your big stone house. You *are* brave, Audun. I promise. You are the bravest boy I have ever met! All the boys I know back home would be whining inside a flower by now—little pansyblossoms, they all are. But not you! Not you Audun, Son of Angvar! Not you."

Audun's expression turned dour again at the sound of his father's name. Titha frowned. "You know what my own father used to tell me?" she asked. "He always told me that being brave doesn't mean you're *not afraid*—it means you are willing to do something *about* being afraid. It's okay to be afraid! I am. I am awfully scared by a lot of this. But I am going to *do* something about it, because I want to be strong for my family. I can be… I am. And so are you. More than anything, I want to hear my father's stories again… and see my sisters' faces. Beebee. Gilly. I know you want your mother back too, right? And to save your brother and the rest of your family back home?"

"Yes," Audun whispered.

"Then let's be brave for them," she smiled. "For our families, and for us too." She took Audun's hands and placed them around the shrouded Sunstone resting in his lap. "This is what we were meant to do, Audun," she said proudly. "This is our family's responsibility. And now it's our destiny."

Audun gazed down at the cloaked stone. His young mind thought for a moment, then looked back up to his friend. He smiled to Titha. "Okay," he said meekly, his hands clutching the Sunstone.

"You truly are extraordinary children," Maya added, bowing her head. "I am in awe of your selfless-ness. It is beyond clear to me why Nech cherished you so. But the niceties must end, and we cannot stay idle any longer. We are running out of time! Straight ahead and swift we must be with the stone! We have a Tree to find!"

Paw roared in compliance, his enormous claws digging into the moist earth below. His eyes hadn't left the Horizon.

Haldor barked to his friend, and the companions shared a glance. Titha mounted Paw, making sure all of their bags were tied shut and Feathersword was secure. She smacked Paw's side and looked back to Audun. "Ready?" she asked. He smiled, then nodded. With that they were off, and Paw roared once more as he lunged forward into a gallop. Haldor matched his stride, and together the five companions thundered deeper into the heart of the canyon in a desperate attempt to beat the next fiery Sunrise. Surely it was to be dawn soon, but if light was breaking over the Horizon, something blocked its glow.

"Has anyone seen an eagle?" Audun asked as they ran northward, still out of breath.

"A snake and now we must find an Eagle," Maya thought to herself. "Something, or someone, is truly testing me with these totems." The falcon shook her head once more, loathing the thought.

"I can understand snakes but you don't like eagles, either?" Audun added, confused. "An eagle is our last totem, so we really should be finding one whether you like them or not. The totems have led us in all the right directions, and we made it past a giant snake! How could an eagle be worse?"

"Eagles are violent, impetuous, reckless beings, child. They do not share a Peregrine's love for lore. All talons and no thoughts, those bludgeons, and I would rather fight a hundred snakes than bare the company of an eagle." Maya attempted to shed her disdain as they galloped. "It is too dim to behold any beast at this hour, Audun. Even if it were not, you need no such Avian. You have me. Falcons are far superior to eagles."

"So are you the Eagle, then? From our vision?"

"I most certainly am not!" Maya squawked, wholly offended by such a thought.

There was much history between falcons and eagles, Audun guessed; something he hoped to write about someday, but definitely couldn't in such a hasty sprint. "Okay," he replied for the moment, rolling his eyes. "We have to see one, though, otherwise something is wrong." He clutched the Sunstone tighter in its wrappings. Haldor leaned his head back as they rushed on, brushing his curls up againt Audun's hand, who ruffled him back. "Will you keep an eye out, Titha?"

"You know I will," she replied, her green eyes illuminated in the dark. She meant it, too. Unrivaled eyesight was a gift every Child of Night possessed—especially in darkness, as her friends had learned. Titha particularly enjoyed bird-watching; even, she thought, at a time like this. She looked behind her to watch her things as they jumbled atop her rotund Bear-brother amid his thundering gallop. The gleam of Feathersword caught her eye, reminding her of the serpent.

"I think the worst Svellvanyon has to offer is behind us!"

Titha yelled to her companions, their beast-brethren quickening their pace. "But where do we go next? If we won't find an eagle here, then where will we find one, Maya?"

"Eagles do not reside here, child, and I do not trust them, if you cannot tell," Maya sighed after she spoke, preparing to answer the question. "But where their hatchland lies? I do not know. I do know, however, that they hail from the North… from Beyond the Horizon, as do many foul things. And as much as it pains me to say, our previous totem—that dreadful rattlesnake—slithered into the body of the Great River itself, which I do not think we should ignore. Many have compared the river's path to that of a serpent. I believe my colleagues would denote this as a 'totemic sign'—symbolism, if you will—and symbolism we should follow. Northward along the Svell we must trot as hurried as possible. This, and only this, is our best chance of finding anything of use to us. Keep your eyes sharp, as well, for our eagle may come in the form of another, less straightforward event—if we are so lucky…"

The companions set off up the path of the Great Svell River, Paw and Haldor stopping to drink from its shores every so often. The water was violent yet crystal clear. Though, as they ventured on, an all-too-familiar light began to rise over the Svells behind them, as if the Sun was initiating next Dawn. The time was right, but its cradle was all wrong. The companions knew well at this point that any such light in the West was of Vulduun's making, and their guts hardened. Whatever diversion that had given them another Night's precious time had come to an end, and the Dawnfather rose from Cragoa to meet them.

Swirling, horrible golden light and flame lit up the morning sky. Harsh heat washed down into Svellvanyon and cascaded onto the backs of the running friends, lighting all in their path. Yet as all of the canyon became bright, something they did not expect met their eyes.

Light bounced strangely off a heavy mist on the Horizon at the very point where the Western and Eastern Svells met. At this culmination, tremendous shadows and fog swirled in Svellvanyon's hills before them. As Day overtook the landscape, the hazy, ethereal cloak of fog parted at a snail's pace, revealing something so large that at first it did not make itself known. So enormous was its grayed trunk that all else paled in comparison. Every earthen color imaginable made up the colossal being's bark; and every shade of green, yellow, orange and red peppered its foliage. Its leaves blotted out the sky and produced an ethereal mist that warded off all who were unworthy of her sight. As a giver of life, however, she still let enough light twinkle through for all Gaela's creatures below. The party had come to a complete stop in awe of Her majesty.

There it stood, revealed to them: the Tree of Legend and of Life, *Igdrasil herself.*

She was still far, but the sheer size of the towering tree made her feel near.

"Is everyone else seeing this?" Titha asked with sheer wonderment. Not a response was uttered. "I'll take that as a yes," she huffed. "Wow… She's gorgeous." Her mouth remained wide open, Paw's matching below her. "I… I can't believe it. There she is."

"Believe it, young one," Maya replied. "For all of your life has led to this moment."

Audun, for once, was speechless. He combed the skies for any sign of an eagle or any large bird, but found only Igdrasil and the coming storm of light that lit her greatness.

"I wish Nech was here to see this," Titha spoke gently.

"As do I," Maya replied. "He has seen many other incredible sights, if that brings you comfort. But he would marvel at this… I am without words." A single tear rolled down Maya's face, her mind unable to wrap itself around Igdrasil's pure glory. "All Scribes worth their salt wish to see the sights they write about. If we never do, then what are we, truly?"

"Liars?" Titha quipped.

Maya smirked. "I suppose so," she replied, but it was not lost on her that Vulduun still approached. "As much as I wish to stay, we must be moving" she added. "Wehave lingered too long. Igdrasil may be visible now by the coming light, but there is still ground to cover! Her size only *makes* her look close!"

The others were so lost in the Tree's beauty that this came as a harsh reminder. Turning together, they beheld the abominable rising of the Dawnfather's flames to the west. He was nearly to the Western Svells now, and would soon be directly upon them.

With Igdrasil in sight and the twisted Elderdrake in tow, the companions raced down into the Roothills: billowing slopes of flowering grasses and bush'mounds that grew atop the roots of the Tree of Life. With each turn, perils from legend rang true. Their trajectory had now become a zig-zagging uncertainty as the lands before them either disappeared into nothingness or shot up to insurmountable heights. There was no stopping for rest again, and ss morning set in, Titha's eyelids remembered their usual bedtime. Coupled with her exhaustion, it took over. Her eyes began to shut as she slumped forward onto Paw, her forehead knocking onto the back of the bear's thick skull. She snapped up, shaking her head. Her grip tightened into Paw's fur instinctively.

Haldor was ahead of them with Audun astride, who remained hunched over the Sunstone, clutching it tighly. He turned to look back over his left shoulder. Smoke rose over the Svells to the West of them, and the echoes of a great battle now shook the Roothills, serving as heavy incentive to hasten their pace.

"My thoughts are with your people!" Maya yelled to

Audun above their rushing beasts. "For it looks as if a terrible clash has overtaken Cragoa. It seems nech and Torai may have done something *really* stupid! But they fight for us. They fight for all! You should be proud of your kin!"

The children did not answer. Titha's sight was fixed forward. The old gray and brown bark of Igdrasil seemed to swirl into familiar patterns. At the center of the unfathomably-large trunk was bark that unmistakably resembled her father's face. Beside it, another visage began to make itself known. The bark forming its shapes was much gentler, however; much softer. Moss began to sprout and form everlong locks of hair around the fair face. "Mother?" Titha whispered. Were these shapes real? Or in her mind? All at once a longing yet rageful sound left Titha's lips. She leaned forward, digging her heels into Paw as he intensified his pace. She stared only at the faces, not breaking her focus as her Bear-brother galloped on through Svellvanyon's perilous beauty, traps, and swirling mist. Paw showed great care and uncharacteristic grace as he followed Haldor's lead amidst the brightening canyon. Such a treacherous path of pitfalls and gaping rootholes required finesse and constant dodging. It was exhausting, but necessary, as the last leg of their race against Vulduun was upon them in full fiery, deadly fervor.

The Roothills and crevices began to lessen until they finally gave way. Suddenly the landscape changed, sloping down into the last valley of the canyon. The haze faded completely and Titha could breathe again. The beasts slowed but did not stop. Titha looked to Audun, then down over Paw's snout and into the hillside in front of them. For the first time they could see where the Great Tree met the land below it… and there it stood, plain as Daylight: The Gates of Igdrasil. Maya gasped. The structure was of the tree's roots themselves—each door of the gate an intricate woven pattern of branches, roots, vines, foliage, and earth. Moss and grass covered mounds sloping down from each side. In the middle of each mound a long, curved ivory beam held the Gates in place, locking them together. There was nothing but the Tree of Life behind them, yet nothing beyond the Gates could be made clear to the eye. Maya leaned out, still riding on Titha's right shoulder. She turned to see her young companion's expression.

"We are so close," Titha spoke softly as they rode toward what had once seemed like an unreachable dream. Her companions could not hear her above the sound of their still-galloping beasts. As their eyes met the Gates, however, an abysmal roar, one fueled by hatred and madness, overtook Svellvanyon. Titha turned to Audun, their eyes meeting. They shared a smile together, each secretly hoping it would not be their las,t as the Dragon's horrendous trumpeting muted all other sounds. Audun looked down, bringing the shrouded Sunstone up and close to his chest.

"This is it, younglings!" Maya shouted proudly. "Shall we greet the Gates?"

Titha looked to Audun again, knowing this was a rhetorical question (though she wouldn't have known what the word 'rhetorical' meant if Maya had said it to her). The ground began to quake beneath their feet. Slowly the beasts realized the intense shaking was not of their nor their pace's doing. Behind them smoke still poured into the morning sky above the sharp mountains. As the companions moved closer to the Gates, time seemed to slow around them. It raged on feverishly in the Svells behind them, yet the more they quickened their pace for Igdrasil, the more leisurely and reluctant time became. The strange effect continued until—there they were, even if unknowingly so—right on the Edge of the Horizon.

Suddenly their world became remarkably hot, and flashes of fiery light overtook their sight as a Dragon's unmistakable roar deafened them once more. The surrounding foliage began to singe and wither as the great blindness encapsulated all.

"There are no diversions to save us this time!" Maya shouted as Titha recoiled atop Paw, who's entire body was now poised for conflict.

Audun closed his eyes. "I am brave," he said to himself, his hands deep in Haldor's curled fur. The Dawnfather would be upon them in mere moments.

Another vicious roar echoed in his throat before escaping Vunduun's toothed maw; his beady eyes shining everbrighter with *red madness* as he finally entered Svell-vanyon. Titha hesitated, her hands slipping down to Paw's cheeks as she rubbed his fur in the intensifying heat. Her Bear-brother pressed his face against her hand. Knowing he could wait no longer, the broad bear barreled directly for the Gates ahead. His Luna-sister turned to behold The Great Drake head-on for the first time since he desecrated their homelands and took their parents for his own. Eyes locked from a great distance, fire escaping fVulduun's nostrils as he looked upon Titha Mae and her companions running for The Gates of Igdrasil. She could feel his anger—his complete *rage*.

The Dragon was upon them.

CHAPTER SEVENTEEN

Breaking of the Horizon

Vulduun's weight moved the very air between the mountains, and his fury would not be satiated. The more his timeworn mind raced, the more the *red madness* took him. The expanses of Svellvanyon teetered between him and the companions, but Titha knew their time grew short. She took a deep breath and turned her gaze from the Dragon and set her eyes back onto the bark of the Great Tree. She could see the faces of her family there still, and that was all she needed. Vulduun scoffed as he lost the Luna's attention, driving his vanity over the edge, and hysteria took full control. Flames shot from his snout and maw, the trees below erupting in fire and death. Countless cries escaped from wildlife, each one breaking Titha's heart even more than the last. But she could not turn back. She looked to Audun, who began to glow. It was the Sunstone reacting to Vulduun's presence.

"Hold on, Audun!" She screamed to her beloved young friend as their beasts neared the gate. She looked forward to behold the enormous, mossy gates directly in front of them. Their beasts hastened feverishly. Out of the ground shot roots and vines, snapping up as whipping obstacles. Haldor began to bark furiously as he ran. Paw grew angry at their attack, and roared lividly as he snapped and swiped at the sprouting obstructions. The Gates, it would seem, did not let anyone approach lightly. More and more roots, vines, and branches shot forth from the earth, but the mighty beasts and their companions persisted. This seemed to anger the ground itself, and out from below them shot two mighty roots the size of the Roothills themselves. Try as the boys might, the gargantuan grips of such tendrils stopped the beasts dead in their tracks, sending their riders flying forward into the grass and dirt. Titha, Maya, and Audun hit the ground hard, their necks whipped backward as they landed. Behind them, Vulduun's cackle could be heard above the burning forest. It was a horrid symphony Titha had heard before. The trio immediately looked to each other in worry—but each had landed fine, the soft ground preventing any injury. But Audun succumbed to panic.

"Where is my stone?" he cried out, its shrouded weight not within his grasp for the first time in many Moons. The stone had flown ahead! His eyes franticly scanned the grass beneath them. He began to shake... Finally—there it was! He spotted it, halfway unwrapped, mere inches from the Gates. Titha scrambled onto her hands and feet, jolting toward Audun. She looked back for Maya.

"I will be fine!" Maya shouted. "To the Gates! Hurry!"

"I can't leave you!" Titha cried out.

"I can take care of myself, young one—go!" she screamed above Vulduun's approach. "Remember your song, Titha Mae! Remember it well! The Gates will only open for the pure of heart, but if all else fails, look to each other! You both hold the key to—" Before Maya could finish, the blinding heat and light from the fires behind them forced Titha to turn away. Vulduun's rage was all-consuming now, and he could be *felt*. Maya closed her eyes, burying herself deep into the grass. Titha wiped ash from her rosy face and lunged forward grabbing Audun's hand and pulling them both upward. Together they took toward the towering Gates, and a great, displeased roar filled the Svellvanyon.

The children stepped straight up to where the Gates met, tossing their hands onto the moss and wood searching every-which-way for a handle or hole of some kind. Nothing revealed itself but more foliage and bark. Titha struggled, her worn indigo hands patting and pulling everything in sight as the lyrics to *The Elk Kings Three* ran through her head. She looked to her right for Audun, but he was far away down the opposite gate.

"Look!" he cried back to her. The ivory that formed the swooping brace of each Gate protruded from the middle of the mossy hill, then down to the ground at the middle of the Gate before curling up into the heart of each. At the middle point within the ivory's circle rested an indention, and Audun's eyes lit up. It was the shape of a hand! "Titha Mae!" he screamed, rubbing his right hand up against it's groove. Its impression was much larger than his tiny hand, but it felt purposeful—and *right*—to his young mind. Titha heeded his example and ran off to the left until she reached the middle of the Gate's ivory brace.

"*Stop at once!*" Vulduun's enormous voice boomed from behind them, its girth accompanied by raging flames. "*I am your Master*!" he hissed, frightened and furious. "*I am all that is, and will ever be, from this Day forth! I command you to stop*!" His enormous frame began to swoop down, poised to engulf the children as his terror grew.

Titha's left hand searched the ivory before finally finding a mirrored imprint—its impression also much larger than her own hand. Thinking nothing of it, she pushed her palm into the groove... but nothing happened. Vulduun shot flames behind them. He was now so close the fibers on the backs of their tunics began to curl and singe. "I don't understand!" she shouted, pushing again. "I think we need to hold hands? But we are so far from each other! Maybe our blood will do it?"

Audun's mind raced. His Gate would not budge either! They had to get the Sunstone to the Elk Kings or this was all for nothing! They turned to look at one another, full of despair. Yet in that moment, something clicked inside of them *and* the gates. Their hearts swelled with a loving, deep friendship; time and space not allowing their gaze to unlock. As their eyes held to one another, they pushed inward in tandem. Slowly the grand, mossy hills to each side of the gate began to move and shake. Dirt and grass crumpled away as long, shaggy brown fur revealed itself within the mound. The two hills moved in toward the gate, their ivory braces rocking inward. Two of the grand roots of the gates revealed themselves as trunks as more and more foliage gave way to massive tufts of thick, matted fur. The children looked up in wonder as the Gates themselves were manned not by hills—but by age-old Mammoths—their mighty tusks serving as the curled ivory hearts of the Gates of Igdrasil. Bowing, the two behemoths continued to turn their moss-covered heads inward to the Tree of Life. But it was too late. Vulduun had arrived.

The Great Drake's hands clutched tighter as he dove down to snag the children in his massive maw. They looked again to each other, slowly backing from the Gates while time slugged about. A grand, prismatic light over-took their sight before seizing everything before it. Titha and Audun finally closed their eyes, giving in to what they assumed was Vulduun's inferno… but no flame took them. The very Gates themselves unearthed, and the two titanic, mossy Mammoths threw their tusks overhead of the younglings—driving their blunted curls directly into Vulduun's girth. Screaming and hawing, the Dragon flinched and flailed at the display of strength. The mighty Mammoths turned to Vulduun, meeting his onslaught with unbreakable ivory. The Eons-old beasts clashed, and Vulduun shuttered, recoiled, and landed on his back. As his spines hit the dirt, the force shook his entire body and surrounding lands, forcing his clutched, craggy hands to open upon impact.

Out fell Theole of Yythengrey to the left, and Sigrid of Autumnhill to the right. Their bodies hit the soft ground to each side of their captor. And there it was, too: The Moonstone! It rolled from beneath Theole's deep blue robes out into the grass, unraveled and shimmering brilliantly. Audun's Sunstone matched it with golden orange light, and he turned back with Titha. There lay their parents… forfeit on the hills.

Titha's body shook, her eyes wide and trembling. "*Father*!" she shouted as she began to run for him in disbelief. Audun ran for his mother in turn, but the stirring of Vulduun forced them to stop.

He grunted and growled as he rose, his thick serpentine

neck rolling up and his wide wings violently spreading out, allowing him to lunge forth. With one hurricane swoop, he stood upright. Before him towered the two ancient Mammoth Guardians, flanked by the tiny children of his pawns. He snarled, flames shooting from his nostrils. A gleam caught his left eye—the Moonstone! His hand shot out to grab Theole, but the Mammoths lunged into battle, their tusks locking with Vulduun's grip. Oh, it was a terrific, titanic struggle to behold. Titha and Audun stumbled backward as the three colossal creatures ebbed and flowed in conflict; their sheer mass shaking all of Svellvanyon and blocking out the skies above.

Through tumbling limbs and clashing claws, Titha beheld Moonlight: the Moonstone! She took off, running and zagging between thunderous, slamming feet, madly dashing for her family's stone without a single second thought. Vulduun screeched, lowering his head and letting loose a terrible inferno. The left Mammoth lunged forward, the brunt of the horrible Drake's flames overtaking his moss-and-fur-clad hide. A painful trumpet left the Mammoth's trunk as it held firm, shielding the tiny Luna from Vulduun's scorching hate. She jumped forward, her arms outstretched. Time slowed around her as her two hands slid directly onto the sides of the smooth, beautiful gleaming Moonstone. As it rested into her grip no harm came to her—as she was, after all, her father's daughter.

Audun watched in amazement, still clutching to the hills where the Gates once stood. Thoughts of their journey, his books, and Nech's teachings swirled in his mind as he watched Titha rise with her family's stone. His young mind had learned so much, and his equally young body had come tremendously far. Though as everything hit him at once, he did not panic. Not again. The young Viking, Son of Sigrid and Angvar of Autumnhill, knew what had to be done. What *he* had to do. Reaching down beside him, he removed the shroud from his stone completely, releasing its full amber sheen. He placed his hands onto each side of the perfectly smooth stone as an entire galaxy of warm colors swirled inside of it. He raised it above his head triumphantly as its shine blasted the surrounding valley. The Sunstone's warm light met the cold glimmer of Titha's Moonstone, and Vulduun screeched violently. His tail swooped around, but the Mammoth Guardians were too fierce and hardy. The scorched one locked Vulduun's left wing and tail into his tusks, while the right Guardian managed the same on the Dragon's opposite side. There they held Vulduun in place as he squirmed and screamed, revealing more of his charred black hide beneath his armor.

Each Mammoth, their titanic weight holding the Dawnfather in place, looked down to Titha. No words left their mouths, yet she understood. The last verses of her favorite song played through her head once more:

Pure Hearts within their Kingdom grow
Vict'ry the foul shall never know
With Sun and Moon their Stars Ignite
Eternal Bound to Dark and Light

"Both stones!" she screamed aloud, her hands lifting the Moonstone to her chest. With all the haste of a Peregrine Falcon she took off for the opening before Igdrasil, and Audun turned to meet her. As she drew closer, Vulduun spat flames to her back and onto the Mammoths, but they did not budge, protecting her still. Her feet quickened as did her pulse. Vulduun's fury grew in kind, and in his hatred his hide churned with such vile thoughts that he became as much foul-black as he was gold.

Titha reached Audun and the opening before Igdrasil, and as she did, the eternal shine of the Moon-stone blended perfectly with the sheen of the Sunstone. The two companions shared another glance, triumphant in their moment. Yet before they could ponder what the universe would do next, the Stones were pulled back-ward, and a great gallop overtook the sweeping meadow before the Tree of Life. The children held to their family's stones and would not let go amongst the ripping tide of time. Its pull was too great, however, and the stones slipped from their care and into the torrent behind them. Three ethereal shapes careened forward, their whisping forms shining like prisms.

The Elk Kings had arrived, summoned by the call of the two Eternal Stones and their bloodlines.

Vulduun panicked. He grabbed the tusks of his captors, pulling them into him as he screamed a vile breath of fire upon their faces. The Mammoths weakened, but still would not budge—not even through their horrid trumpeting pain.

"*You will not take the Stones from me*!" the Drake howled savagely. "*They belong to me! I am the Sun! I am the Light! I am the Day itself*!" Vulduun's thundering tone began to crack and quiver. He was afraid... and he knew only *one* of these stones *rightfully* was his. "*False Kings*!" he screamed into the night-filled canyon. "*False Kings*!"

Before him galloped the opposite of his insults—The Elk Kings Three; Eldest Children of the Wild and indeed the truest of Kings. Titha and Audun let loose an audible "wow" as they passed by, their hooves treading thin air itself. As the Elk Kings descended into the valley, they parted. The largest, most grand of the Three careened forward, his massive crown of antlers pointed directly at Vulduun's exposed underbelly. His two kin split to the left and right with the Stones, their orbs becoming part of the Elk's very essence. The younglings could not look away. They watched as Vulduun's red eyes darted, searching every which way for any form of escape or deceit.

Enraged and exasperated, his flailing madness intensified. He screamed thundering calls and roared forth flames, his pure strength beginning to overpower the weakened Mammoth Guardians. As the Grandest Elk King drew closer, in a full charge with his pointed Crown of Antlers, Vulduun panicked and lashed out. His enormous serpentine neck shot forth and he drove his fangs deep into the neck of the left Mammoth, lashing and tearing violently. The Mammoth's trumpeting cries were silenced, and it fell hard to the ground below. Vulduun swooped around, locking claws with the tusks of the remaining Guardian. They rocked back and forth, their strength almost matched. The Great Drake was too vile in his fury, however, and he thrashed the Mammoth's tusks to the side, slamming its full weight into the grassy soil beneath them. With a terrible roar Vulduun threw a massive clawed hand down into the Mammoth's throat and ended the last of the Guardians. His wide, golden-black crown of horns raised into the morning sky as he trumpeted a proud, victorious call. Yet his vain moment cost him precious seconds, and the Grandest Elk King's antlers drove deep into his side. Vulduun screeched, wasting no time in swatting the Elk King away. The Dragon's malice blinded him to any goal or plan, and he lashed out immediately at the Grand Elk King; completely unaware of the flanking two brethren behind their leader. Vulduun grabbed the Crown of Antlers atop his foe's head and began to tear it side to side, violently ravaging the divine Elk's very being.

"*Your crown shall be mine*!" He screeched with wrath. As his singular rage continued, the other two Elk Kings split off in front of him to the left and to the right; one glowing of blue and the other of gold. With a matching pair of regal calls, they leapt up into the air, then dove down into the earth—disappearing. Or so it seemed.

Slowly, two illuminated beings rose from their grassy cradles where the Elks met the soil. One was of Man, the other Luna. It was Sigrid and Theole! Their drained bodies lay motionless moments before, but now rose, full of the Light of both Elk Kings and Eternal Stones. Their eyes shot open in tandem, and shimmering *life* returned. The royal pair raised their heads to each side of the terrible struggle, a great rush of ancient knowledge spreading through their souls. Their entire bodies became luminous, and they ascended further above the wet ground.

Theole inhaled deeply. He looked about, first to the smoke billowing above the pointed Svells, then to Vulduun. The Dragon's hot red eyes burned upon him once more, as the former Dawnfather locked himself in ferocious battle with the Grandest of Elk Kings. Theole then looked to the Tree of Life… and there *she* stood. His precious daughter. His eyes welled with tears as he rose higher, the spirit of Elk Kings empowering him.

"Oh, my daughter," he spoke gently, his white beard waving in the wind. "My precious Titha Mae."

His words swept over the valley all the way to Titha. Immediately, she collapsed into a joyous yet heartbreaking sob. The brave little Luna could not believe her ears… it was really the voice of her father. Oh, how she had longed to hear it again and to hug his sweet, bearded face. He was here! They had found each other! Not in a dream or a vision or a wish, but his true voice and self. A smile spread from ear to ear across Titha's indigo face as a light returned to her green eyes not seen since Theole's capture. But there was no time for a proper reunion. Vulduun's age-ending battle with the Grandest Elk King still raged on before them.

"My son," soon echoed forth from Sigrid's teary gaze, and Audun collapsed beside Titha Mae. He sniffled, wiping crocodile tears from his eyes as he beheld the brilliance of his mother. Titha rushed to him, quicker than quick.

"We have done our parts, my dear Audun. Now our parents must do theirs!"

Before them, clumps of roots and vines began to stir. Rumbling barks and growls escaped from the earthy mounds as fur of both black and gray shot forth from the hills. It was Paw and Haldor, their release granted by an earth that recognized the side of the righteous.

"We're coming, boys!" Titha shouted as she took off toward them, Audun in hand. The children rushed forward and leapt for the mounds, pulling and swiping away any earthly entrapments they could. Paw's large head burst forth in a spray of soil and he shook his thick black mane. Immediately his tongue met Titha's face as he licked her uncontrollably. She chortled gleefully, grabb-ing his face as her green eyes locked with his loving chestnut gaze. Haldor's upper body broke free of the vines beside them and Audun tightly wrapped his arms around his hound's neck. The pair mounted their freed beasts.

"Wait!" Audun shouted. "Where's Maya?"

"I haven't seen her!" Titha replied.

"We can't just forget her, Titha!" he screamed.

"We will find her Audun!"

Vulduun's mighty struggle with the Grand Elk King showed no sign of ceasing. Never before had the Dragon witnessed such a show of strength in direct contest of his own physical prowess. He looked to his left and right, the embodiments of Theole and Sigrid hovering beside him. As he beheld their luminous forms, it finally hit him. They had become one with the Stones. An atrocious gurgling spilled from his jaws as the Dragon came to terms with what he saw.

"You will both watch as I remove the Crown from this false king's head!" the Elder-drake roared in madness. *"I will drive it through both your hearts, and then I will take both Stones for my own and rid this world of your precious Night and all you took from me – my beloved Meriduun! Then, then I shall have peace once and for all!"*

The Great Drake raised his body upward, placing all of his weight onto his forearms as he pressed down on the Elk King's antlers. The King welped, letting loose a pitiful cry. Vulduun laughed, his deep booming chuckle overtaking his demeanor. He prepared to remove the Crown of Antlers from its host's head, just as he would have done had his plan gone his own way. Yet before he could, each of his eyes seperately beheld the sheen of the Stones shining everbrighter from within his former captives. His beady gaze widened as another horrified gurgle left his throat.

Sigrid looked to her son, and Theole to his daughter. As the eyes of families met, the winds raged and the skies rumbled. Vulduun let loose of the Elk King as his body sluggishly struggled outward in each direction toward the shining cores of Theole and Sigrid, trying desperately to claw at both of them. He was not successful.

Beams of Moon and Sunlight shot from the royal pair's cores, creating a line of shimmering pale blue and warm amber light from the children to their mother and father, and to each other until all of Svellvanyon was alight with their energy. As the Moonlight washed over Theole, his body began to twist and sprout upward. Gleaming silver feathers burst forth from his robes and his eyes lit up with the light of a thousand blue stars. Titha knew this transformation now. She watched as her father became The Grand Silver Owl once more.

What happened next, however, she did not expect—and neither did Audun. His gaze remained locked onto his mother, and as the Sunlight hit her— something very similar to Theole's transformation—yet distinctly different—began to happen within Sigrid. The wolf pelt around her shoulders began to change from fur to brilliant amber feathers. Her armor crumbled and fell to the ground below as royal talons and regal wings spread forth from limbs. Her neck cracked and creaked outward, thickening into the brazen, feathered red mane of an enormous, glorious bird of prey.

There before the younglings towered the last piece of their vision, and their last totem: their Eagle. Sigrid was reborn not as Shieldmaiden of Autumnhill, but as the Glorious Red Eagle: a being of the Firstblood, the right of her ancestors tied to the very fate of the Sunstone. She was another Grand Avian to match a Great Drake, and she was marvelous.

An extravagant energy swirled around the trio of Elder-beasts alight in Red, Gold, and Silver. Vulduun shrieked, throwing the Grandest Elk King violently to the ground. He turned to meet the Grand Avians with flame, but they were not to be tested. Their wings spread wide as each uttered a terrific beam of Moon and Sunlight. The flailing Dragon spat more embers, but the Sun and Moonbeams perished their heat before any harm could come. The terrified Drake screamed again, but his flames again shot into nothingness. Desperately, he began to lash out—but he could do

nothing. Rearing back, Theole and Sigrid poised their shimmering, Eternal Stones down-ward. Their beings now harnessed relentless, unmatched energy.

With two magnificent Avian cries, they focused their birthrights into beams of horrible power, and Vulduun shrilled and moaned as what was left of his golden scales began to fragment. One by one they burst,
revealing his bruised and rotting hide beneath. His decayed, timeworn form singed under the catastrophic onslaught of the Eternal Stones until all his armor completely deteriorated.

The Dawnfather's wailing began to diminish. His splendor depleted and his skin was exposed; decaying. With one last gasp of flames and his last great blinding flash of light, Vulduun erupted into malicious rage, but his form could no longer hold such hatred. Within it, he met his own demise—erupting into a fiery inferno before dissolving into Svellvanyon forever.

Titha and Audun ran forth, their eyes wet with tears as the terrible tyrant disappeared into nonexistence. Theole and Sigrid, still in their Grand and Glorious forms, returned to the ground with their stones. They lowered their enormous heads, bowing and weeping as their children ran through Igdrasil's Meadow to meet them.

Theole's sharp silver feathers softened as he knelt before his daughter. She wrapped her arms around his neck, burying her face into his down. "Father..." she wept, her heart swelling. "I found you."

"No, my precious flower," he replied, "you *saved* me."

Tears fell from his shimmering blue eyes, running down soft silver feathers until joining with the wet soil below. Audun held his mother's softened red mane tightly beside them, his sobbing much less beautiful and quite adorably-sloppy. He was in shambles, but abso-lutely elated. Sigrid sat back, her amber feathers waving in the wind as she wrapped her glorious wings around her beloved son, holding him.

Titha looked to her dear friend's uncontrollable sobbing, now laughing alongside her joyous weeping. She attempted to gather her composure. "I missed you so much," she smiled to her father.

"Not as much as I missed you, my tadpole."

"We have so much to tell you," she spoke softly looking up to her father through very wet eyes.

"And I cannot wait to hear it, sweet daughter. Though a grand adventure it may have been, none of it will compare to this moment. For I have returned to you–and there will never be a greater joy," he replied, embracing her once more.

Slowly before their loving reunion the remaining Elk King rose, his Crown bloodied but intact. His hooves ascended from the earth and carried him forward. The companions and their parents looked on in astonishment, wiping their tears and bowing before the King's majesty. Without words or sound, the King shook his head. The family looked up, confused. Then the Grand Elk King bowed to *them.* He held his gesture in place, out of respect and gratitude, of course—but also out of necessity.

Theole, the Great Owl, walked forth, manifesting the Moonstone from within. Sigrid the Glorious Red Eagle rose to join him, the Sunstone appearing in her beak. Together they reached out, placing their family's Eternal Stones into each swaddling-side of the Elk King's Crown of Antlers. Their glistening, swirling light left them and became one with the King's splendid form, and he bowed further to them. Looking up one last time, the King made sure to make thankful eye contact with each companion before turning from them forever—his duty taking him t'ward the Horizon.

A great rush of thundering discord began to shake the walls of Svellvanyon. One by one, beautiful yet turbulent waterfalls burst over the mountaintops and canyon walls, rushing down into the valley as The Elk King walked away. The landscape was transforming— every crevice between mountains becoming a chorus of churning waters. Soon the companions were surrounded by flowing, life-giving streams on each side, and a river began to form at the lowest valley before the Tree of Life. The slain Mammoth Guardians became one with the Earth again, their bodies molding into memorial mounds that framed the entrance of the new river's mouth. Four tusks protruded from the changing landscape; pillars of an Eon that would never be again.

As the gaping crevassess of the canyon filled with water, the Grand Svell River met this new River of Life, and together they roared on. The Grand Elk King walked across the River's mouth, his hooves gliding atop its waters as he entered the Meadow before Igdrasil. As he passed where its Gates once stood, the Eternal Stones emitted a swirling light from his Crown the likes of which their time and existence had never known. The Tree of Life and everything within her let loose a tremendous exhale. She then burst into a million colors of fragmented light, each slowly trickling down within her own misty skies onto the Horizon.

As the shadow of Igdrasil passed, she took the memory of Vulduun with her—and the Sun took its rightful position in the height of the afternoon sky for the first time in many cycles.

The Horizon had broken, yet was now restored; born a'new. The companions stood together, staring into the first truly-blue sky they had beheld in what felt like a full Eon. There, in their triumphant moment they embraced not as heroes, but as family.

It was a spark in time they had doubted would come, but would've lived in forever.

CHAPTER EIGHTEEN

The Second Eon

The two river's rage grew tenfold. Svellvanyon's burgeoning waterfalls continued to hammer down into the valley. Not a single flow ceased, and in short time the canyon came to more closely resemble a singular, raging river. Titha, weary of the rising rapids, looked to her Owl-father, who then looked to Sigrid. The parents were surprised to behold each other still in their Grand Avian forms! Perhaps they had kept some of the power of the stones and their family legacies, or perhaps it was a gift of thanks from the Elk Kings. It mattered not why—for they were eternally grateful for the power to save their kin, nonetheless.

"Where is she?" Titha cried out above the churning. "Where is our last companion?" Looking about, the waters grew more threatening to her by the moment. "Maya?" she shouted in terror. "*Where are you*?"

Up out of the river's mouth shot a seemingly insignificant brown, wet, struggling creature. Gulping and gasping for air, its wings splashed violently in an effort to escape the raging waters. "*Maya*!" Titha cried out again, both worried and elated. "Can you get to her, father? Sigrid? Please, we've got to save our friend!"

Both Grand Avian beings heeded her words without hesitation, much to Titha's astonishment. In a flash both had taken to the air, unrivaled wings of Silver and Amber filling the skies as they plucked the waters for Maya. Splashes overtook the echoes of the canyon as the children watched from atop their hill with hopeful angst. Paw's chestnut eyes darted to each splurge of water, Haldor huddled beside him panting. Audun's little hands shook as he gripped tightly to the hound's neck.

"I have her!" Sigrid cried out! A mountain's worth of breath escaped the companions' lungs as Sigrid shot upward from the river with one talon clenched. She flew to the bank of the Roothills where friends awaited, and Theole landed beside her. Slowly Sigrid unfurled her enormous talon, and a wet, pitiful-looking bird rolled out. Coughing and choking, Maya flipped over, water escaping her beak in a most alarming quantity. As she came to, she looked to the heavens not to behold a grand sky but an enormous Eagle. Her coughing intensified as she hacked and

scraped backward. Sigrid's glorious feathered head cocked in confusion.

"*E-e-Eagle*!" Maya screeched, petrified and barely coherent. "*Eagle*!" she shouted again, still scraping away
from the enormous silhouette above her. "Begone you brute!"

"Oh you tough bird! You're okay! You're alright!" Titha screamed, jolting down to her friend. "That is Sigrid, Maya,

Audun's mother! She is an Avian, too! Breathe–breathe! I just am so glad you are alive!"

Maya took several deep breaths, calming herself as she returned from what surely would've been, ironically, death by River of Life. Dispersing one last round of water, she turned to Audun, then his Eagle-mother, then back to the children. Sigrid bowed, lowering her enormous head to the companion. "It would seem you found your eagle," Maya finally spoke, a faint smile filling her dark beak.

Audun laughed, overjoyed. "We have to get her to her order so she can heal!" he shouted to his mother.

"We all must flee Svellvanyon," Sigrid replied, "or its waters will overtake us!" She looked to Theole, who nodded his silver feathers to her. He looked down to his daughter and Paw, still unable to wipe the smile from his own beak.

"Are you ready to return home, my daughter?" He spoke, both age and emotion wavering his voice.

"With you? Yes, father," she replied.

"I shall never leave your side again so long as I live. Nor will any Child of Night. All of Gaela is in debt to you, my daughter. Your compassion, your brightness and your bravery saved our world from a horrid, burning Eternal Day. There are no words to express the gratitude we all surely feel for you, Titha Lilly Mae."

With this, all the companions joined Theole's bow, and the

waters raged on beneath them. The river splashed against Sigrid's tail, and her worry grew.

"Your father speaks what we all feel, Titha, but we truly must leave at once!" she shouted as the waters met her talons amid their hillside. "Children, mount your beasts. And beasts—I am afraid I must ask you to mount *us*. It shall be a sight this world has never seen!"

Paw and Haldor looked to each other as their beloved friends climbed aboard them, Maya cradled in Titha's arms. Paw harrumphed, shaking his head. He lumbered to Theole who cupped his wings to greet the wet black bear. What followed was a hilarious display of wabbling limbs and shedding feathers as two large fuzzy beasts climbed atop the backs of grand, majestic Avians. The companions were stacked, and it truly was a sight unlike any other.

They took to the skies, Theole and Sigrid carrying their families with ease. As the kin rose above the canyon their eyes beheld a completely changed landscape. Gone were the sharp, sloping walls and crevasses of Svell-vanyon and the majesty of Igdrasil. A churning, beautiful and crystal clear river raged in their wake, filling the breadth between the Svells.

Theole took one last look, amazed with the furiously altered landscape. "May Igdrasil's glory continue to guide us through the birth of this daughter, The River of Life," Theole spoke as his wings glided upon the sky. "Gone are the Great Drakes and Tree, givers of land and life. With them goes the First Eon Gaela has known… and everything must change. A new Eon has begun; and it is an Eon for Promise."

The Horizon was behind them, and the Svells pointed sharply beneath their path. Titha and Audun beheld the world as it changed rapidly until returning to more familiar sights. The Svells, as ancient as the First Eon, stood unchanged. The inseparable friends looked about and to each other, beholding places they had been before. Sigrid's focus took to Titha as her sharp green eyes continued to scout about.

"Where must we head first, Titha Mae?" she asked. Titha could not believe that *Sigrid* was asking *her* for direction, but her heart held an immediate answer as she swaddled Maya.

"We must land in the Craglands!" Titha shouted. "So much has happened—I'll explain it on the way!"

Sigrid and Theole nodded and lowered their gaze, darting through the winds as they overtook the Svells at her command.

Snow appeared, the cold pelting each companion as they came to Mydlan and Cragoa's northern passages. The vistas below grew harsh and white, mountains jutting up beside frigid valleys. Titha's keen eyesight beheld a strange mountainous region with icy cottages jutting from mountainsides. "Where is that, father?" she asked. "We didn't go through there! It looks amazing!"

"That is Wundiberg," he responded. "It is the only Gnomehold of Cragoa."

"Did you hear that, Audun?" she shouted across the winds. He nodded, his smile turning to a frown as he realized he could not write this down amidst churning air. Underneath the landscape changed again, and Mt. Crag resurfaced into their lives. She seemed calmer, however; a less vile, strangely tender smoke billowing from her top. "Land down there!" Titha commanded, pointing to a most crowded scene at the foot of Mt. Crag. Their descent brought about drier, crisper air in the deep crater.

Upon landing, however, no words were uttered. It was a most abhorrent sight and smell. Titha's hands shot to her mouth as a lump the size of a bullfrog filled her throat. Slowly their atmosphere stilled, and a grizzly battlefield immersed their senses. The orange clay had been turned to black and red; bodies of a dozen different races scattered throughout the crater. Maya closed her eyes in respect, but Sigrid could not break her astonish-ment. Many of the slain belonged to her own kin; the proud armors of Autumhill littering the landscape alongside smattered Ogres and mamed Craglins, Moglins, Reeks, and Slaglins. As her eyes filled with carnage, so did Theole's. A strange smile filled her face, however, once her eagle-eyed scan of the slain was completed—and her beloved eldest son Rainer, nor his beautiful white horse Kelliah, were *not* among the dead.

"Such sacrifice. Such pure, honorable sacrifice… without which all lands would now be asunder," Sigrid spoke softly. "Yet fate has been kind to us all, and to us, Audun. I feared the worst for my sons within our horrid capture amidst Vulduun's lair. To have you safe with me, and feel in my heart that Rainer is alive and well… I… I can never know a greater joy. Your father—" she paused, unable to speak as her throat swelled at the memory of her slain beloved. "—he would be so furiously proud of you, littlest one. And I know he is even in death, as he watches over us both from the halls of our fathers."

In this, a great song of their people, "To Skies, All Sail" swelled inside of her as Angvar smiled down upon her from the heavens above. She pulled Audun in tightly beside her as she honored the fallen with melody, the words and beauty of her song ensuring those lost here would find their way within their afterlives.

Breathe no fright. Skald holds, none fell.
Fjords take all. To Skies, all sail.
Fist hold mighty, Sword burn brightly
To Skies, all sail.

Shields will crack. Bone splinter, heart fail.
Fjords take all. To Skies, all sail.
Sunlight greet you, Dragon lift you
To Skies, all sail.

Men n'er break. Soul walks, ever hail.
Fjords take all. To Skies, all sail.
***Fóðr's making**, Val-hall waiting*
To Skies, all sail.

Theole's eyes reopened after his dear friend's song. He had heard it once before—in the abysmal fires on the other side of the Horizon. It had brought him hope in their captivity, yet such a feeling now faded as he glimpsed the bloodshed once more. The more he looked about, the more a seeded, suspicious terror grew within. Armors of many peoples laid at his talons; all but the one he strangely—yet appropriately—hoped to be present. He stopped, clearing his throat.

"You sent the Peregrine Order to our Duskridge, yes?" he asked. Titha and Maya nodded, but no answer came from any, for they had all had the same revalation. Theole stood with a broken heart. "I see no fallen Lunas," he spoke, his voice cracking. His head turned to more and more sacrifice. "They did not come?"

Dense rattling broke the tension, its racket echoing throughout the deathly-silent craterscape. Two pointed cowls shot up from slain remnants far ahead of the companions. Their fabrics were of deep red but covered in clay and ash.

"Nech? Torai?" Titha and Maya yelped together, hoping for any sign of life to be their dear friends. At once the companions rushed toward the commotion, hurdling fallen causalties. They neared the ruckus to behold not familiar faces, but two very small, strange beings.

A pair of tiny bearded munchkins squabbled and slapped one another over a most glorious silver object. Such sheen was unlike anything else in the carnage; tailored to a perfect leafen pattern that shimmered brilliantly. Titha and Theole knew it immediately: it was *Lunish armor*! Theole leapt to the artifact, his wings spread fierce and wide. The two tiny scavengers crumbled into themselves, shrieking as they held the treasured plating above their pointed hats in pure shock. Their screams and pleading fell upon deaf ears, however, as none in either family could understand a single word they said. Theole backed down, listening for a moment to their foreign tongue. He then knew exactly what these tinies were. Much to their surprise he shot down, grabbing the silver plate with his black beak. The pair froze under their pointed, stitched cowls.

"Please unt forgiven us'n?" one squabbled, stepping forward. The cowering fellow behind him looked to Theole, and could not believe what his Gnomish eyes beheld: an indigo Luna riding a black bear riding a giant silver owl.

"Where did you come across this armor?" Theole commanded.

"It un'speak'ns!" each munchkin cried out in unison from

beneath beards. Their words were mangled by a thick, harsh accent; further muffled by brown and gray beards the thickness of winter shrubs. "Please you vill forgiven us'n! Unt armor is yours if'n required!" they pleaded.

"Gnomes…" Theole growled.

"Scavengers! Thieves!" Maya cried out, her good wing flapping amidst Titha's embrace.

"Please'n!" the pepper-bearded, cowering Gnome replied from behind his partner. They were nearly identical, but this one stood just a hair shorter and sported a much whiter beard above his coat of goat'hide. "Ve are here vis permission from unt friend!" he cried out. "He vill be here soon, you vill see!"

"Who gives permission for such defiling of the dead?" Theole scowled, lowering his enormous head as he stomped toward the tiny being's quivering frame. "And you did not answer me, Gnomes. Where did you come across this armor? Out with it! I do not wish to grow angry with you—"

"He retrieved it from the edge of the battlefield, oh Mighty Watcher," a familiar voice decreed from behind them all. "And it was I who sent him there to find it."

Paw and Haldor's ears shot straight up—they knew that quibbling old voice among any. Each family turned to behold a beaten, bloody yellow Craglin with a war'stained green tunic and a rather large Peregrine falcon on his shoulder; also much worse for wear. Maya broke free of Titha's arms, falling with one wing through the air onto both beings, knocking them to the ground. The three rolled around for a moment before Sigrid finally interrupted.

"What is going on?" She asked through a very curious eagle-beak, "Why does she attack the unarmed? Should we stop her? Falcon, cease this!"

Titha and Audun jumped down from their Avian parents and ran to the rolling pile, jumping into what now to be an embrace, rather than a tussle. Theole and Sigrid were flabbergasted.

Titha popped her head up amongst them. "This is Nech!" she shouted, "My friend! The Scribe! My amazing, smart, kind and very talkative friend, Nechalec, I told you so much about on our way! Without him we never would have made it! We travelled all the way here together before—well—so much happened—but he is here!"

"Oh, my dear friends!" Nech shouted amidst his laughter and the onslaught of hugs. "How I have missed you all! I am tickled beyond count of joy to see you all alive and well." Slowly they disbanded, but their mirth continued. Nech stood up, dusting off his knobby knees before gasping in the full majesty of the two Grand Avians before him as the air settled around their feathers. "Master Theole," he decreed. "Sire, tt is an honor to finally stand in your presence. I have written many tomes concerning your Days—or, Nights, I should say. And who is this phenomenal Red Eagle beside you?"

"That's my mother!" Audun cried out with pride and love as he hugged Nech's side.

"Bless my bones!" Nech's eyes widened. "Sigrid of Autumhill? You too take such a grand Avian form? I would like to say I am surprised by this, but I am not at'all! Why this makes perfect sense! Here stand the Guardians inherent of the Eternal Stones as Avians, side by side—both of first'bloodlines. My, it is such an honor to behold you both in such splendor."

"The honor is ours, Nech," Sigrid spoke, bowing her feathered amber mane. "Thank you for looking after our children. Thank you for everything."

Theole bowed beside her before exchanging a glance with Titha. "He *is* talkative, isn't he?" He joked, his daughter laughing in turn.

"No, no I insist all honor humbly stays with me!" Nech replied to Sigrid, insighting laughter from both families. "For it truly is that. All of my formidable years have been spent weaving the both of you into epics, epochs, tomes, scrolls, and all the lore of Gaela. To think I would have the—the *priviledge* of helping your extra-ordinary younglings reunite with you and subsequently heal our very world… I am beside myself. Truly wondrous, it is."

"Nech," Maya interjected, "what has become of Ugar?"

Torai looked to the old Goblin, the two sharing a grim glance. "He has vanished," Torai finally answered, his voice heavy, "We have seen no sign of him since the battle was won and the Gnomes have found no trace of him here."

"Then he still lives," Maya replied, "Undoubtedly cowering back into the darkness like the yellow bellied welp he is."

"Let us hope he stays there," Nech added, shaking his head. "A worser fate awaits him should he rise to face these companions once more!" The light crunching of small footsteps crackled behind him as the two Gnomes waddled forward.

"Nech'n, sir?" They inquired.

"Ah, of course my friends, of course!" Nech replied, fumbling over to the tinies. "Please allow me to introduce a most estute Gnome duo, Sirs Willamar and Waldemar of snowy Wundiberg."

The two Gnomes bowed, still slightly petrified. "Unt your serwice!" they replied in unison, none of the foreighners quite understanding.

"Unt it is Vundiberg, Nech'n," the brown-bearded Willamar added.

"Villamar, Valdemar, unt Vundiberg!" Waldemar followed.

Everyone nodded and squinched their faces, looking to eachother to give the Gnomes a polite affir-mation of their pronunciations

"Of course, of course, sirs. Apologies," Nech replied. "We Cragoans have long worked in tandem with the Gnomes of Wundi—ah—v—Vundiberg, excuse me, to our snowfilled Northeast. And if it were not for their unique abilities, I dare say we never would have found her."

"Found who?" Titha and Theole asked at the same time.

"Ah..." Nech hesitated. "Please, Sires... Follow me." He spoke grimly, looking to the armor Theole still held.

Nech walked the companions away from their current wartorn landscape. As they respectfully traversed the fallen, Maya and Torai rode atop Paw, perching upon Titha's provisions and huddling together; elated to see one another alive.

The families came to the edge of the crater. There laid a single body lay slain in the ashen clay. She was beautiful and of fair indigo skin, her tunic stained with purple blood.

Theole screamed out, launching himself forward to her. "Aspen!" he cried.

Nech bowed his head, followed by the others. "She would not let us move her, my Lord," he told Theole. "She awaited only you."

The exquisite, yet now frail soldier slowly turned her head

upward to the sky as a familiar silhouette filled her fading vision. "I knew you would come for me, my Watcher," she muttered; filled with the splendor of Theole in his Grand Owl form.

"Please, Aspen, my child," Theole spoke, barely able to contain his sorrow, "you must tell me what happened! Where are our people? How are you all that has come? Were there no others as brave as you, my fallen angel? Why would none fight for our beloved Nightfall?"

Aspen's eyes welled with tears. She laid teetering somewhere between a mortal's death and the last breaths of an immortal's wounds. "They could not, my lord… they could not come," she spoke softly, her mouth dark. "We tried to raise… them… but in vain. He… He stopped us. He stopped all of us… I was all that escaped, my Lord… Ythen…grey is… held captive…"

Theole's great, ice-blue eyes widened. "Who stopped you?" he commanded. "Who has done this?" A strange anger welled in his gut that wrestled with sorrow as Aspen faded in his wingtips. "Aspen! You must tell me! Who could have done this?"

But no more words came from her. Finally at peace, she passed from Gaela in the embrace of her Watcher. Theole lowered his head, pressing it to hers. As he did, the companions all fell silent, honoring her life and last breath. A whispering melody trailed from Theole as he gently passed his silver wing over all that remained of the once proud and beautiful Aspen of Yythengrey.

May the Green of Gaela take you
May Oathera's Dim forsake you
With Root and Soil and Stream you sleep
Your soul in Mother Nature's keep

Titha stepped forward to her father, placing herself upon the side of his broad neck. "We must go now, father," she spoke. "We have to go home to our people. They need us."

"Vulduun is perished," Theole replied, addressing his daughter and all the companions. "We beheld his demise with our own eyes! Who else would dare hold my Lunas hostage? There is no greater evil left in this world yet my heart aches now more than ever. We must go. Titha is right. To our people with haste! I am sorry, Sigrid, but we must bare straight past your realm to our Duskridge! To Yythengrey!"

Sigrid nodded in agreeance. "You, Craglin!" she shouted, picking Nech out from the companions. "My son, Rainer. Did he lead our peoples here? I see much of the Houndsmen's armor, yet thankfully I have seen nothing of his own."

"Correct, my Lord!" Nech decreed. "He bested Vulduun and drove him from these very lands, retreating with his young life and what was left of your brave warriors. Last we saw, they passed back through the Druidunes—er, the Abyss—to your hills westward of the Fells. For all Torai and I know he holds Autumnhill securely."

"*Fóðr's grace*!" Sigrid cried, her breath heavy. She leaned her head back to nuzzle Audun who too was elated with the confirmation of their hearts' hopes. Ironically, in days past they would have thanked Vulduun for any such victory, but to the best of their knowledge the Eon of the Great Drakes was now fully behind them.

"If my eldest son lives, my people are guarded," she spoke after heavy thought. "Theole, my darling friend, we have been Beyond the Horizon and back together. With my realm safe, even if not, I could never forsake you now. We are with you, Watcher! We accompany you to Yythengrey; to help in whatever way we can."

The two Grand Avians shared an empassioned, deep gaze as all of the past Moon's perils danced within their timeworn minds.

"I think I could get used to this," Titha thought to herself, admiring the sight and Sigrid's declaration. Here stood her father with the awe-inspiring Eagle-mother of Autumnhill, their hearts and minds in sync. Never had she known such a time for Lunas and Men, nor did she ever expect to. The young Luna looked to Audun as she always did, and they shared a wonderful smile at their parents' bond. "Are you okay to come with us, Audun?" she asked. "You can go home if you want to. Its okay, I promise. We just need to do this one last thing."

Audun did not pause. He walked to Titha and wrapped his little arms all the way around her. "You are my home," the precious boy replied. Titha buckled into her dearest friend, their tender moment alighting each companion's heart.

Nech stumbled up behind them with the Gnomes. "Willamar and Waldemar, sirs; this is where we part. Please continue your services and bring any beings found alive to Mt. Crag for healing, no matter their race or creed. In exchange, you may keep any treasures you find here on this battlefield. My esteemed fellow Craglin Scribes of the former Council shall aid you and all citizens of Cragoa in repair and rehabilitation; I have seen to this. For my place—my place is also with my companions."

The Gnomes lit up, their eyes looking straight to the rare Luna armor plating Theole still held.

"Except that! Except that," Nech quacked. "You may not have that. Now off with you, sirs!" Nech shouted as the two tinies waddled off to their hired duty.

"You've a strange lot of friends, wart," Torai spoke up, his sharp eyes beholding each of the group one by one. "What a lot, indeed."

A laugh was shared, and they all mounted their rides; Nech

finally able to rejoin Titha and Maya astride Paw, then Theole. Audun and Torai boarded Haldor and Sigrid beside them.

"Let's go save our home," Titha spoke, her father nodding. Before taking off, however, he stepped back. Lowering his head once more, he scooped the now lifeless body of Aspen into his talons and spread his great wings. With a gargantuan *whush* of swirling air, the two Avians left the ground, kicking up ash and armor below them.

CHAPTER NINETEEN

A Time for Promise

The Companions (now capitalized, for they were Gaela's saviors, after all) left Cragoa behind them and passed over the Fells into Westlyn, the land from which both great families hailed. Pine trees gave way to sharp, snow-capped mountains of golden amber, every vista painted with warm colors. The Grand Avians made short work of the Fells' breadth, and below them the massive circular border of Autumnhill rolled into sight. Audun smiled, frazzling Haldor's hair as they passed over their home. He kicked and hopped excitedly aboard his hound and mother as they beheld cheering Vikingmen below; each outstretched in delight and praise as their saviors flew overhead.

Autumnhill was in shambles from the Ever-war, but showed signs of a great rebirth. There, at the center of the Skaldhall steps, stood Rainer. He smirked, raising his father's goat'horn to the air—letting loose its triumphant call as the Companions cut through the afternoon sky.

Herds of Woolly Rhinos parted amidst the Barren Fields as the journey tread westward. Titha shouted and pointed to the Autumn Trail, showing her father where she and Nech had first met. She looked about for the hole his kart was in, but could barely make out anything amidst the stampeding megafauna below. Slowly, the vistas turned from warm bronzes and ambers to deep blues and grays. They were almost to the Duskridge, the mountain range that cradled Yythengrey.

As the Companions finally landed, the forest in front of them was eerily quiet. No birds or trees sang in the wind. The Wood Gate stood firm and shut. Titha and Paw dismounted Theole, his breath still. In all his peril, all he had dreamt of was the joy of his return. For Yythengrey and his family he yearned and kept himself alive (if that is what it could be called). Titha had returned to him; rescued him. But a foreboding energy now stood between him, his home, and the rest of his family. He had not dreamed his return to be so sterile… so quiet… so *foreign*.

Slowly Theole stepped forward, his talons brushing against the calm sage grasses. He had hoped to shed his Grand

Owl form once returning to his beloved home, but now he knew not what awaited him. His Wood Gate remained cold and closed at his approach. Beside him Sigrid followed, her family still astride her. She looked to Theole with great concern. The air was absolutely still. Between their enormous talons, Titha hopped forward, less wary than her elders. Her green eyes sparkled as they filled with the trees of her home. She began to jog joyously, scampering all the way to the Wood Gate before placing her outstretched arms upon it with glee. She was *home*. Home with her father, and nothing could keep them out now—surely.

"Step back from the Gate!" a shrill voice comm-anded from the shadows amidst the treetops.

"What?" Titha barked, completely caught off guard. "Who is that?"

"By order of the Cedarguard, child! Step back at once—or be struck!"

Theole's silver form blasted with anger and light, each feather turning fiercely sharp as Moonlight escaped every ounce of his being.

"*You threaten my daughter*?" he shouted, his voice barreling into the Wood Gate like a hurricane. "*You dare incite harm upon the Daughter of Theole, Watcher of Ythengrey?*" He was furious, and any curiosity he held now shattered beneath outrage. "*Open this gate at once – or I shall open it myself!*"

"We cannot," the voice replied. "Our Lord com-mands it stay shut to all outsiders. Please step back or we will be forced to strike." The voice grew much more shrill and shriek, as if the words it emitted were of fear and not of its own.

"Outsiders?" Titha questioned, looking up to her father. But Theole took quarrel with a different word.

"*Lord*?" he scowled. "*Your Lord? Who is this Lord you speak of but I? I am your Sire! Your Lord, Your Watcher! You will open these gates and reveal my eldest and youngest daughters safely to me, guardsmen, or I shall be the one to strike! This is my last prompt*!" Theole barreled again, his voice terrible.

Titha stepped back, unsettled both by the Gate and her father's unbridled anger. The treetop voice did not respond, yet the stillness was broken by a *slice* and a delayed thump on the ground. The Companions took one step forth, all sharing a glance. As they did, the Wood Gate gave forth a great creak and crack. Suddenly it opened, if just enough for one shadowed figure to come forth.

Out stepped an unexpected, yet familiar stout and portly frame; armored and armed to the teeth. He carried himself with great poise, yet low to the ground, like a fierce wild boar. His silver plated garb shone through a deep cloak of midnight blue. From beneath its hood, a mustached and grave voice finally made itself known to all.

"So good to see you, my old friend," the husky Luna decreed.

Titha's face scrunched. She stepped forth, leaning down and cocking her head to try and get a look under the shroud.

"And you, young Luna," the voice continued, "So good to see you returned to us. Please join me in greeting your sisters. *Welcome home.*"

Titha did not budge. Theole poised his sharp feathers forward in shock.

"*Cypress*?" he asked.

The dense figure did not reply. Instead, it lowered its hood to reveal rosy cheeks, thick white hair, mutton chops, and a curled mustache beneath a round nose.

"Please, Theole, come inside. We have much to discuss upon your return." It replied. And 'it' was Cypress, indeed.

Titha scoffed. "I should say we do!" she interrupted, budding with anger. "Where are my sisters? Why do the guards threaten? Why won't you open the Gates to us?"

"Please, please, Titha Mae. One question at a time! Your sisters are safe and secure, as they have ever been with me. Does your trust in me waiver?"

"*Mine certainly does,*" Theole barked. "What is the meaning of this? Stand down, old friend, and reveal my girls to me. We have returned from great peril—and hear foul whispers of our people being held hostage. I do not wish it to be true. Please do not give such foul words weight."

"Hostage? That rings a bit harsh, does it not?" he chuckled. "What some may call hostage I simply call… *Safe*. Who would say such a thing; 'hostage'?"

Theole spread his wings at this, arming his sharp feathers as his cold eyes blazed. His one clenched talon unfurled, and the lifeless body of Aspen rolled out onto the cold ground.

Cypress' harsh eyes twitched. His hand left his sword's hilt as he beheld the fairest of his Cedarguard dead in front of him.

Theole lowered his head, a mighty owl poised to strike with a heart that was close to breaking.

"Explain this to me, Cypress," he commanded. "Explain to me why Aspen *alone* lay slain in the dirt of Cragoa. Explain to me why she fell amongst many brethren of many realms, yet no other were of her and our kin? Explain how this *battle to end an Eon* was championed by all but the mightiest Children of Night?"

Cypress did not return any words. His hard demeanor had broken at the sight of Aspen, his *cara*… his beloved, astonishingly fair friend. He looked away, hiding her lifeless body from his gaze. A callous, staunch posture overtook him again, and no words followed.

Theole's massive brow clenched. "What have you done, Cypress?" he asked, his voice deep and threatening. "What has become of Yythengrey?"

Cypress scoffed and rose his head once more. He snapped his thick fingers, and at his command two guards rushed from the opening in Wood Gate to retrieve Aspen's body. Gently and respectfully they lifted her, carrying her away to eternal slumber within Yythengrey. Cypress watched her exit from him a last time, then clenched his fists.

"What has happened, you ask me?" he finally replied to Theole. "In your absence I have kept this sacred realm safe, old friend. I and I alone have ensured the survival of our people. The last Children of Night remain *alive* because I willed it; because I chose to protect them and guard them and not fall prey to the entrapments of Day, its kin, and… *Men*." He shot a furious glare to Audun.

"Do not defile our people's existence with your ignorance! Your selfishness!" Theole yelled, furious. "You would ignore the suffering of all outside our gate and let the world burn in Eternal Day? How dare you claim such a deed in the name of all Lunas—in the name of all Children of Night! *Coward*!"

"Coward?" Cypress barked, "Ignorance?" he scoffed. His hand slipped back to the hilt of his glistening sword. "Folly, these words," he replied deftly, a strange calm composing him. "As I have seen this past Moon, your party has stopped such a calamity from happening, so there is no more need to worry, correct? The

Dawnfather is slain, is he not? And we are all most grateful for it. Indeed, we are elated upon your return. Now please, Theole, step inside and we will discuss… *everything*."

Titha looked to her father, each offput by the offer. With no other option than bloodshed presenting itself, however, the Companions stepped forth together to enter Yythengrey and *discuss*. Together.

"I am afraid I must not have been clear," Cypress interrupted harshly, halting their stride as he ordered his guards to point their spears. "I ask only for my kin to re-enter. The rest of you are not welcome here."

Theole's heart burned with rage. Titha let go of his leg and stomped forward, her own heart shocked and heavy. "How dare you!" she screamed.

Theole hissed behind his daughter. He stepped forward to protect her from a Luna he never thought he'd have to. "How dare he indeed, Titha Mae," he scowled. "You speak to champions, Cypress. You deny entry to heroes of all races: Gaela's Saviors! How dare you deny them entry when it is not yours to deny? Those that stand before you have sacrificed *everything* for us, for *all*, and in turn we will *forever* do the same. Sigrid and her kin are welcome in Yythengrey from now until the end of all Time! Now, I am only going to ask you this one last time, my old friend… Stand. Down. And let us enter to my daughters and our land."

"Or what?" Cypress barked, finally shattering his calm demeanor. "You'll succumb to your own gluttonous power as the Great Drakes did? *Hmm*? And *smite me*? *Strike me down*? *Obliterate me before your own daughter, casting me down in wrath and ruin—sending me into the oblivion of the Otherworld*? Will you become another *fallen deity* here before us, Theole? *Will you*?"

Theole stopped, shaking as his rage did indeed consume him.

Cypress spat, laughing in Theole's face. "Much thought have I given our plight in your absence, Sire. Much, indeed—and a curious thought plagued my mind with every step. I had buried it deep, you see; shadowed it with our bond and our friendship and love. Yet these recent events have shattered any such shroud and it has all come crashing to the surface of my mind!" He threw his cloak off, its weight swishing to the ground. "None of this—*None* of this Ever-war would have happened had you not sought *her*. *All* of Gaela would live on unscarred if you had not gifted your precious *Thea* with the Moonstone… Am I right, old friend? *Am I not right*? Or have you forgotten your greatest failure? So why should I bend to you now? Again? Why am I in the wrong for the *dispatching* of that *prying Peregrine* that came knocking on our gate and choosing instead to keep our people safe? Hmm? Safe and far from the edges of war? Are we all to look to you, Aspen, and Titha in such times? Reckless vagabonds who flee even further from our traditions, our *bloodrights*, to sacrifice ourselves for *who*? Races who would as fast spit on our precious realm as they would *cut it down*? And now you wish to bring more Goblins, that *freak* of an unnatural hound and… and *Vikingmen* into Yythengrey? *Men*, Theole? *Think of where you stand!* Think of our fallen, our *slaughtered* Bear-brothers and *torched* trees never to rise in these Barren Fields again because of *Men*! *Men* who *murder* our forest-kin to adorn their foul homes with their once-living skin… *Men* who forgot our once-precious Duskmother and *forsook* her Festival long ago! *Men* who continued to cling to their mad Dawnfather long after the tides of the Ever-war began! *Men who dismissed Vulduun's crimes as folly*! You wish to bring these treacherous, vile defilers into *my* home *and I am the one who needs to stand down*?"

Theole lowered his head, looking away from both Cypress and Titha. Slowly his Silver feathers softened before molting and falling to the ground. His beak disappeared into a white and silver beard, and the crown of his head balded once again as thick eyebrows grew over sunken eyes. Midnight and sage robes folded about him, and his bare, wrinked indigo feet met the grasses before Yythengrey once more.

"We both are to stand down," he finally spoke to a fuming Cypress. "I yield my power, Cypress. In this you are right, and I yield."

Cypress did not move his hand from his hilt, his sight still burning with a seething wrath. Theole shook his head and continued.

"But please." he said, "I beg of you to heed my words now—not as The Watcher, but as your oldest friend. Not a Night unfolds that I do not think of my greatest mistake and the terrible losses this Ever-war has brought. Not a single Moonrise comes that I do not wish for my Thea Celtica Mae to follow it. In this, I do understand and pity Vulduun's fall. His tragedy. But in all else we differ. Meriduun had grown restless far before the Ever-war, Cypress, this you *know* to be true. I simply thought the Stone would be safer with Thea… I… I thought it would be wise to keep it from our restless Duskmother. I was wrong."

Titha hugged her father's robes tight, burying her head into his warmth.

Theole placed his hands upon her back. "I am but myself in this moment, Cypress; no power, no stone, no trickery. Now please, you too must yield to *reason*! Sigrid and I were held captive for many Moons together by the twisted and maddened Vulduun. Now he is gone, forever, but this would not be so without Titha's strength of will, nor the rest of our Companions of many kins and bloods. Least of which this brave, incredible child of Man! Audun! To these two spritelings do we owe *everything*, Cypress. They saw no color of skin nor borders of lands and rode together with beasts and Goblins alike for the good of *all* Gaela. We must heed their teachings, Cypress. We must! We are old and have worn many titles in this world but we still, as I have found, have much to learn. My daughter has opened this to me. Audun's mother, Sigrid… she too has revealed much I never thought I would know or feel. See reason, oldest friend. A new Eon is upon us, and it is ours *together*. Together in the promise of a land united. Bring my daughters to me, and we shall all—"

"—*No*!" Cypress yelled ferociously, interrupting. "There is no *all*, Theole! There will be no *together*! I will not allow you to put our people at risk again! I will not bow to the whims of a fallen, *fallible Lord* or a *child* and I will never, *never* defile our sacred home with the footsteps of *Men* again! Be gone with you! All of you! *Cedarguard*!" he called out gruffly, hesitating no longer. The Wood Gate opened behind Cypress, and out poured the full strength of the Lunish armed forces. "Remove these traitors from our doorstep at once," he commanded to his guard. Each Luna looked to each other, and then out into the grasslands before Yythengrey. There in front of them stood their beloved and kindhearted Watcher, Theole. Beside him his most rambunctious child, Titha, the light of their Meadow, stepped to his side as Paw, her familiar Bear-brother poised behind them. To his left stood Haldor with Audun astride, Maya of the Peregrine Order perched atop his shoulder. Afront stood Nech, the Craglin Scribe of Cragoa, with Torai. Then, the last of the Companions rose proudly: Sigrid landed, wrapped in brown and red wolvesfur as her amber feathers shed and glistening blonde hair returned: braided and flowing down each side of her freckled, fair face.

"You hesitate?" Cypress scoffed to his guard. "Remove them at once! Do as I say!" He barked again, but the Cedarguard did not move, each of them absolutely bewildered by the true splendor of the Companions. The soldiers fidgeted nervously, but not a one managed to step forth. From between the Wood Gate two pairs of eyes peeped out into the standoff; one a set of bright yellow and another of wild violet. They stared at the Com-panions, combing their splendor until they spotted their own kind. Silence fell across the field.

"Titha?" a tiny voice called out.

Titha's knees gave way. A pair of beanpoles rushed out of the woods carrying the sweetest bundle of joy any Luna had ever known. Two Children of Yythen-grey burst from between the Cedarguard and across the grasslands. As they appeared Titha screamed out, her heart swelling and tears welling. She knew what was happening yet could not fully process it, as her emotions took all control. Tears poured from her eyes as the faces became clear. Theole staggered, placing his hand on Titha's shoulder. She cried out for the two running Lunas, but was tackled to the ground before any words could escape her lumped throat.

There between such wanton bickering embraced three

sisters, each hugging and screaming and crying as they squeezed tighter and tighter. No words could be uttered, just sounds and squeals mixed with love and longing. Titha tried to wipe her eyes but could not pull her arms from her sisters.

"Is it really you, Beebee?" she finally cried out. "Begonia Bee Mae is it really you? My baby Bee?" Titha couldn't manage any more words before bursting into another deep sob, Beebee's arms wrapped tightly around her neck. Titha looked up as a much taller Luna cradled them both, the Sun shining behind her head for the first time in their relatively young lives. It was Gilly, and she looked just like their mother as her deep silver hair shimmered in the Daylight.

"Don't you ever leave me again, you hear me little sister?" Gilly cried, fighting more tears. "Don't you ever, *ever* leave me again," she grieved, cradling her two siblings as she rocked them in the grass, her chin placed atop their heads. Paw romped over, bursting into their embrace as he licked salty tears from all of their rosy faces, each sister giggling and crying into his warm black fur.

"I have so much to tell you, Gilly," Titha spoke, her throat tight and eyes watering.

Theole walked forward, leaning down to his family. He fell to his knees, wrapping his arms around them as he too met them with salted eyes. "My daughters, oh my precious daughters. How I love you so."

Not a dry gaze existed amongst either side, except Cypress. As Theole embraced his beloved children, a few Guards stepped forward. Looking to their Watcher and his daughters they dropped their weapons and leafshields to the grass. Theole smiled, his ancient demeanor alight with relief. More followed suit, and more after that, until each Guard was unarmed, forming a protective circle with the Companions around the Mae Family of Ythengrey. Cypress stumbled backward, clambering for his Guards to heed his order—but no such eventuality came. Roaring and spewing vile words the likes of which Titha had never heard, he drew his sword, stomping toward the guarded circle. Every Cedarguard resumed their defensive stances, weapons or not, without hesi-tation. Their once proud commander stopped, raising his sword in a threatening manner. No soldier flinched, ready to fend him off from Titha and her Companions 'til death.

"*Fools*!" Cypress shouted. "I have done nothing but *protect and serve* you! *Without fail,* all my life! I have guarded you and led you all to prosperous times! And you would draw your blades to *my* throat?"

Not a single Luna waivered, all still holding firm between Cypress and what once was a family of his own. Titha finally managed to pull herself from her sisters and stepped up onto her dirty feet. She turned to Cypress, walking past the guards and out to meet him in the sage grass.

"I think you should leave now," she spoke, a great confidence behind her voice as she stood alone against this tyrant she had loved as a child. But a child she was no more. "This is a new age, Cypress. One we all fought hard and travelled very far for. One where my friends and family can be together, no matter where they're from or the colors of their skin. All of Gaela's people can share in both Day and Night as one, Cypress—and you will not take that from us."

As she spoke, each of the guards and Companions stepped up behind her, the eyes of Lunas, Vikings, Beasts, and Goblins alike burning right into Cypress' very soul. He scowled, furrowing his heavy brow as hard as it would furrow before a guttural growl left his throat. Slowly he turned his back from the display of unity. As his cloak became all that was visible of his form, a slight yet violent movement shook its cape. Like a lion he flipped around, throwing a dagger from his shrouded form straight past Titha. It brazed her arm, cutting her deep, yet continued to fly as she fell—its path headed into the Companions. The dagger shot over a Guard's helmet, removing it before darting directly to Sigrid. She flinched, but not in fear. Her shield was too fast and her skill too great, for she splintered its hateful aim before it could cause further harm.

Cypress gurgled and yelled, his utter loathing of her and her kind spewing forth. Theole barreled out from the Companions to his bleeding daughter, her left arm brazed and sporting purple. A terrific, terrible sound of anger leapt from beneath his thick white beard as his right hand shot into the air, summoning a swirl of air from above and a mass of ground below. The elements whirled into the center of a vortex at the Watcher's gray hand, and in it materialized a new Ozark Staff from the very elements themselves. It bared not Meriduun's fallen Moonstone, but the light he shared with his daughters; for their love was more powerful than any ancient stone. He twirled it once, hoisting it with both hands before swinging its rooted, shimmering end directly down onto Cypress' jaw. A great *crack* let loose, and Cypress slammed head first into the soil below. Theole pointed the end of the Ozark Staff onto his old friend's throat, pressing him hard against the blades of grass.

"*You* are no longer welcome in these lands, Cypress Sylvanus Byle," Theole growled from behind his teeth. "Take yourself wherever you wish to go—but never again will it be here." He pushed Cypress deeper into the earth, extending his left hand to shield Titha. "Be grateful I leave you with your *life*, old friend, as my daughter kneels before us bleeding by the treachery of *your* blade."

Cypress reached up, swatting the Ozark Staff from his throat. He rose to his feet, brushing his regal swadd-lings of soil as he looked to the Cedarguard with disdain. "*Look at you,*" he snarled. "*All of you*! Abandon your Commander now? *Disgrace*!"

"You are the disgrace!" Titha barked, stepping forward of her father's protective hand. "And if I had Feathersword right now I'd give you a worser wound!" Theole reached forward, pulling the ferocity of his daughter backward.

Cypress scowled. There was no emotion, no reaction left within him. "So be it. I shall leave," he decreed, "but know that you shall *rue* this day. When the tree walls splinter and the *hateful fires and blades of Men* have cleared our lands of all beasts and flowers that remain… *you will rue this day*." He raised his hood to place his face in shadow once more. "Enjoy your fairy tale while it lasts."

The once beloved Commander of the Cedarguard surveyed his soldiers a last time, but none budged or rose to join him. None but one. A fellow stocky, sturdily- armored Luna stepped forth to Cypress's side. They shared a firm handshake and grip, both planting large hands on the other's shoulder. Cypress smirked.

"It is good to see the Line of Byle still holds true, at least," he spoke.

"As it ever has, my cousin," the stout guard replied.

Cypress slapped his kin on the back, and pushed him on Southward before turning himself to Theole.

"Goodbye, old friend," he spoke quiety from beneath his

gown. "*Until we meet again.*"

The former Commander walked from his home-land and out into the wide grasslands to the South. He did not turn back and he did not waiver, as his path was clear. The Companions did not know where he headed, but Cypress knew full well.

Titha turned, wrapping her arms around her father's waist and squeezed him tight. He embraced her, and as he did she peeked around his arm to behold their family and friends all marveling at one another; smiling and embracing. Sigrid held Beebee up into the Sunlight, smiling and nuzzling her nose against the tiny Luna's indigo cheeks. Gilly patted Haldor curiously atop his curly head as Maya and Torai's fascination drew them to a tall guard. Nech and Audun walked past their ranks with Paw in tow. As they approached Titha and Theole, their arms opened.

"Thank you, my friends," Theole spoke with deep compassion and truth. "Sincerely. Your devotion to each other, and to my daughter's cause, has saved us all. And my gratitude for your kindess will never cease. Before me stand races I have never truly understood, and have stopped myself from doing so through ignorance and bigotry." He ceased, placing a hand on Audun's head and Nech's shoulder as he looked past them to Sigrid, who cradled Beebee and conversed with Gilly. "I believe my daughter is right, my new friends. This is indeed the Dawn of a new Eon, the likes of which Gaela has never seen before."

Cheers of mirth rung from all Companions; the Cedar-guard smiling and shaking hands, paws, and wings with all of their new compatriots.

"A new land is born!" Theole decreed, "One where we shall all live together under the Moon and Sun and prosper not from behind cold walls or harsh words, but side by side in bountiful fields and swaddling mountains!"

Titha jumped up in glee. "Together!" she shouted.

"Together!" the Companions cried out in reply.

Theole leaned down to Titha, Audun, and Nech, who stood side by side, their arms on each other's backs as Paw licked the back of his Luna-sister's head. "And we all have you to thank for this, Companions. The brave hearts and unwavering friendships we see here: Luna, Man, Beast, and Goblin."

Sigrid walked forth as he spoke, Beebee in her arms and Gilly astride behind her. Theole smiled, opening his arms to Sigrid and his youngest daughter who could not, for the life of her, stop giggling.

"Such promise," Sigrid spoke, overjoyed. "My heart eagerly looks to this new land joined in tandem." Her blonde hair began to waiver in the wind as its breeze returned after a long silence.

"What a truly marvelous day!" Nech smiled, looking to all. "I daresay I have always dreamed of a place built on such ideals;

such blindess of color and openness of heart. If you will have me, I will be happy to assist in any way I can."

"And I," Maya added.

"And I," spoke Torai after her, both riding forth upon Haldor's back.

"Me too, I think," Audun added laughing as he hugged Nech beside him. The brave young lad held a few of his scrunched papers in his hand. "But what will we call it?" he asked, his precious young voice spritely and curious. "A new land has to have a name if I am to write about it in my books." He looked to Nech, dead serious, who grinned from pointed ear to pointed ear.

"I believe you are right, my apprentice!" Nech replied.

Audun's hazel eyes lit up with the fires of his ancestors at the thought of being a Scribe's apprentice. Beside him, Titha grinned, thrilled with his happiness and the proposition. As her laugh met the wind, a warm rush lifted her chin, the breeze gently kissing her cheeks.

"I know you…" she spoke softly. "*Thea Celtica Mae,*" Titha whispered amidst the breeze's familiar embrace. "Celtica… Yes. For you, mother. For your memory and spirit, your help and your totems… for your *love*… we will call it *Celtica*." One last tear for that day rolled down her cheek, escaping her green eyes as she closed them and met the sky with her face. "Thank you, Mother. For everything," she spoke gently, her words carried off into the glen by a warm whisp. Theole leaned down to his daughter, emotional yet delighted at the thought.

"It is perfect," he spoke, cradling all three of his daughters into his arms. Thoughts of his beautiful, graceful Thea Celtica Mae danced through his head as he turned with them, the wideness of the Wood Gate finally welcoming them with full breadth. Titha stepped out from her father, looking back for Paw. Her Bear-brother galloped and harrumphed to her, barreling uncontroll-ably to reach her. He smiled as only a bear could, his entire wide and fuzzy face lighting her life as he licked her forehead. He nuzzled Titha's chin with his soft wet nose. She squeezed his neck tight, then climbed atop his shoulders.

"We did it, fuzzybutt," she spoke to him softly, squishing his ears in her hands. "And look... We're *home*. We're home."

Turning, her green eyes gleamed in the Sunlight. "Come on!" she yelled to her Companions, each standing outside the gate. "All are welcome here now! Especially *family*."

Together the Companions walked into Yythen-grey, some entering the misty canopy of the Duskridge's sacred forests for the first time—others longing to return to the shadowed embrace of its foliage. Yet even those who returned stepped into a *new* land, one changed and much greater for it. As the Wood Gate creaked closed, the family of heroes beheld The Meadow and all its wond-erous white Moonflowers in tandem. Curious Lunas peaked their heads out from their slumbering petals as excited whispers overtook the trees.

With those footsteps of many colors, the First Eon, and the only age their lands had ever known, ended – giving way to a new one: The Time for Promise; ***The Second Eon***. Titha Mae and her Companions had seized peace for all of Gaela, and would see it through to the next cycle of their world. Realms of Luna, Man, Beast, and Goblin united as one, the great expanses of Westlyn rising under a new banner. It was to be:

Map
N
W
E
S
The
Snowy Fells
FRORORA
Duskridge
Mountains
Northfjord
Fell River
FELLS
Loch Daenu
Mt. Meri
The Abyss
Ythengrey
Autumnhill
Barren Fields
The River Daenu
WESTLYN
Mouth of MYDLAN
Ruins of Byle

the
IGDRASIL
Snowy Svells
SVELLS
Gates of Igdrasil
Wundiberg
Roothills
SVELLVANYON
Svell Valley
SVELLS
Mammoth's Respite
SVELLS
Great Svell River
EASTLYN
Gaela Falls
Highlands

Her Ballad may be over, but the adventures of Titha Mae have just begun. Look for **Book Two,** ***The Dawn of Celtica,*** on Amazon and with your favorite book retailers.

Full color illustrations are available in Hardcover editions of the Titha Mae Series. For more on the world of Titha and her companions, including series updates and signed copies, visit **tithamae.com**.

Glossary:

Henceforth you'll find, hopefully, any and all terms you may wish to have help in defining, pronouncing, or just want to see one more time.

The Abyss: A deep, swallowing system of caverns and caves underneath the **Fells** - the furthest depths of which are completely unknown. Many had ventured in never to return.

Aldin: The first Bear-brother of Cypress Byle, sibling of Boldin and a fierce warrior of Luna legend.

Jarl Angvar: (pronounced Yarl Ang-var, with 'Ang' as in angle and 'var' as in 'jar') Ruler of Autumnhill alongside his wife, Sigrid Shieldmaiden, Angvar is a steady and hardy Jarl (king amongst Vikingmen) whose skill in battle is only matched by Sigrid herself.

Arbor: An elder, grizzly-looking forest bear with shaggy, long grayed fur and many scars. He is Bear-brother of Cypress Byle, and son of Aldin, Cypress' first Bear-kin.

Aspen: Captain of the Cedarguard and a long trusted friend of Cypress and Theole. She was swift and gifted, and her word was greatly respected in Yythengrey, right up to her valiant self-sacrifice.

Asra the Falcon: A brash, hardy male of the Peregrine Order who carried Titha's message to the Vikingmen in a great hour of need.

"**Atlaga**": Ancient-Viking word, meaning "Attack".

Audun Angvarson: (pronounced Aw-dune, as in 'aw' isn't he cute, and dune like a sand dune) The youngest son of Sigrid and Angvar, Audun is an avidly curious reader and very intelligent at a mere seven years of age (during the time of ***The Ballad***).

<u>**Autumnhill:**</u> The first and largest homestead of the **Vikingmen**, **Autumnhill** is an impressive stone stronghold housed by the Boulderwall, a massive wall built from ancient stones seemingly too large to move. At the center of the many houses, workshops, and stables was **Skaldhall**, ancestral home of the **Jarl** and **Shieldmaiden**.

<u>**Ballad**</u>: An epic, lyrical story passed down from one generation to the next as part of a land's folklore.

<u>**Barren Fields:**</u> The expansive fields and prairies that make up these barren lands are mostly void of trees and covered by thick golden grasses, wheats, and weeds instead. Despite much of the land being scarred from battles long ago, large grazing animals such as Buffalo and Wooly Rhinos happily make their homes there.

<u>**Bear-brother:**</u> The oldest companions of the Lunas of Yythengrey, these bears are all of the Forest Bear race, also referred to as Black Bears or Forest Black Bears.

<u>**Beebee Mae**</u> (short for **Begonia Bee Mae**, pronounced Bee-bee like the honey-making insects): The youngest (and by far the most adorable) Mae sister of only three forest-years at the time of ***The Ballad***.

<u>**Boldin:**</u> The first and only Bear-brother of Theole the Watcher, and brother to Aldin. After Boldin's passing, Theole could not bare to suffer losing another Bear-kin and never took another.

<u>**Breaking of the Horizon**</u>: The catastrophic clash that took place between the treacherous Vulduun, The Elk Kings, and the Companions on the edge of the known lands beneath the now vanished Tree of Life.

<u>**Cedarguard:**</u> (Or Cedar Guard) Protectors of Yythengrey since the beginning of the First Eon, all were under the command of Cypress Byle before his exile. They stand guard at the ***Wood Gate***.

Celtica: The name many races gave to Thea Mae upon her rising, and the name Titha and her Companions chose to name a new land of cooperation between themselves and the world of Day.

The Companions: The band of heroes who came to Gaela's aid at the end of the First Eon. They are comprised of Titha Mae and Paw, Audun and Haldor, Nech and Maya, Theole and Sigrid.

Craga: The Goddess of the Craglins and their homeland of Cragoa. She is said to be one with Mt. Crag and all surrounding lands, and her mood is the temperament of the volcano itself.

Craglin: A short, yellow-skinned race of Goblins originating in Cragoa. Males sport two small bony horns on their foreheads and long, pointed ears.

The Craglands: Home of the Craglin Goblins, situated around Mt. Crag in its immense crater and comprised of dense clay huts.

Cragoa: A northern region of Mydlan covered in huge, dangerous craters and enormous pine trees.

Crown of Elk Kings: A crown only spoken of in the oldest known lore, said to be made up of the very Crown of the mightiest Elk King's skull and antlers. If said antlers were made to house the Moonstone and Sunstone, whoever possessed the united Crown would wield control over the rise and fall of the Sun, Moon, and Time itself.

Cypress Sylvanus Byle: (pronounced Sy-press, like the cypress tree) Cypress was Theole's Squire, closest confidante, and Commander of the Cedarguard before his exile.

Dawnfather: The Luna race's name for Vulduun.

Dragonshorn: (pronounced Dragons-horn) A large horn made from a discarded Dragon's horn.

Druidunes: Large, cavernous holes that extend into the deepest bowels of Gaela in areas of great importance. Each race has different names for them, such as The Abyss for the Vikingmen.

<u>Druids:</u> The bridge between the land and life, these ancient beings are both part of the living and of the soil, rock, and roots of Gaela. They are said to know all the secrets the world had to offer, but guard them well, and will only pass on their vast wisdom to those who seek it with pure intentions.

<u>Duskmother:</u> The Luna race's name for Meriduun.

<u>Duskridge:</u> The Duskridge is the oldest mountain range in Gaela, its peaks rounded by the erosion of time. It formed the western-most border of the known lands of Gaela, and is home to the elusive ***Lunas***.

<u>Eastlyn:</u> The furthest land East in the known parts of Gaela. The Svells form its border with Mydlan.

<u>The Elk Kings:</u> The first Children of Mother Nature, and the reigning rulers of her kingdom. They were said to protect all that is sacred to Gaela and her daughter Igdrasil, the Tree of Life, before becoming one with the Horizon after their battle with Vulduun at the end of the ***First Eon***.

<u>Eon:</u> A vast expanse of time, only defined by those who record it.

<u>Eternal Stones:</u> Used to refer to the Orbs of Power, such as the Moonstone and Sunstone.

<u>Ever-War:</u> The scholarly name for the secret war Vulduun raged against the people of Gaela.

<u>Feathersword:</u> A single, sharp-edged feather from Theole's Grand Silver Owl form that Titha takes as her own weapon of choice.

<u>Fell River:</u> This winding river is given life by the **Northfjord** and runs through the deepest valleys of the **Fells** all the way to **Mydlan**. It forms the basis of the first stronghold of Westlyn's humans, the ***Vikingmen***.

<u>The Fells:</u> The dominant mountain range of the West, the **Fells** are harshly steep and rocky mountains covered by sparse, dry vegetation. They form the east border of **Westlyn**. Their enormous presence across the landscape is deeply rooted in the legends and lore of many peoples, but none moreso than the ***Vikingmen of Autumnhill*** that make their home in their foothills.

Festival of Dawn: A Yythengrey festival once held on the Summer Solstice (longest day of the year) to celebrate the Dawnfather and the life his Sun gave to the plants and animals of the world during Day. Needless to say, it is not celebrated anymore.

First Eon: The first period of recorded history in Galea, accounted for by Scribes and scholars such as Nech and Maya and their predecessors. The First Eon began with civilization, and ended with the ***Breaking of the Horizon***.

Fóðr: Ancient-Viking word for "Father".

Frorora: An ancient, mysterious civilization carved from ice that was important enough to put on the Map of the First Eon, but not featured in ***The Ballad***.

Gaela: (pronounced Gay-lah) The name used to describe all that is, was, and will be of the land, earth, and sky.

Gaela Falls: The massive waterfall that flowed forth from the Great Svell River into the Unknown Lands.

Gates of Igdrasil: Ancient gates said to lead to the Tree of Life herself, built upon the sacrifice of the Svell Mammoths long ago.

Gillian "Gilly" Rose Mae: (pronounced Gill-ian, like the gill of a fish, and you know the rest) Titha's older, lankier, and supposedly more "mature" sister of roughly 16 forest-years at the time of ***The Ballad***. She is poised to become the Watcher after her father's time.

Grand Avian(s): A legendary form only beings of great power and influence can change into. Their existence is said to be tied to the first bloodline of each race in Gaela, and the orbs associated with them. Theole is capable of transforming into the ***Grand Silver Owl*** and Sigrid the ***Glorious Red Eagle***.

Gupper: (pronounced, for once, just like it looks!) Gupper is a strange turtle-person, known as a *Torgle*, which is something no one else in this Ballad has ever heard of before. Regardless of peculiarity, he is known to whip up a mean stew.

Haldor the Wolfhound: (pronounced Hal-door, with 'Hal' as in hallelujah and door like a front door) Audun's fiercely loyal, unusually large, and prone-to-face-licking best friend and dog.

Harbinger: A respected individual elected to serve as leader of a group, such as the Peregrine Order.

"**Hondla**": Ancient-Viking word, which meant "heed my command" or "ready", only issuable by a person of status.

The Horizon: The edge of the known world of Gaela, where the lands of Westlyn, Mydlan, and Eastlyn end. It holds great importance to the people below its influence, as it rose and settled both the Sun and Moon, and nothing beyond it has been explored in recorded history (The First Eon).

Igdrasil: The Tree of Life herself; an indescribably large tree of Legend said to resemble an Oak tree of many colors. The vast waters of Svellvanyon and Mydlan were said to have flowed both in and out of her enormous roots. She existed before any other Nature in Gaela, and was regarded as the daughter of Gaela (the world) herself. Igdrasil became one with the Horizon after the ***Breaking***.

Ira the Falcon: She was the fastest and brightest of the Peregrine Order according to Maya, and delivered Titha's message to the Lunas in their most desperate hour.

Jarl: The ruler of Vikingmen, holding a similar position to a King or Emperor, but equal in power to the ***Shieldmaiden***.

Kelliah: (pronounced Kell-I-ah) The most brilliant white mare (female horse) ever born to Autumn-hill's stables, and the noble steed of Rainer Angvarson.

Kriggoth: The former Emperor of Cragoa, betrayed and murdered by

Ugar the Terrible.

Luna: The oldest known Children of the Night, and once Meriduun's most devoted kin. Their skin is a pale indigo and their hair white or silver. They harbor a deep connection with their forest home, ***Ythengrey***, and form lifelong relationships with the Forest Bears that share their lands.

Mammoth's Respite: The ancient wetlands where the winding Lesser Svell River meets the Great Svell River. Mammoths used it as a watering hole during the Time before the First Eon.

Maple: A small, spectacled and shy Luna girl and one of Titha's only friends in Yythengrey.

Maya the Peregrine Falcon: (pronounced Mai-ah, like the traditional name Maya) Head of the Peregrine Order and Nech's oldest friend & colleague, she is fiercely smart and independent to a fault.

Meriduun: (pronounced 'Merih', followed by dune like a sand dune) One of the two Great Drakes responsible for shaping the lands of Gaela. She was the Duskmother and former love and light of Vulduun, and was worshipped by all creatures of Night, including Lunas, long before the time of Titha Mae.

Moonstone: One of two orbs older than time that were deeply connected to the origin of the Great Drakes and the ***Moon*** herself, who was seen as a deity by the Lunas. The Moonstone was trusted to Theole's bloodline after Meriduun forfeited its power.

Monk: A devoted follower of a practice or religion, typically robed or cloaked in a covered manner.

Mount Meri: The highest peak of the Duskridge Mountains that forms the center of Yythengrey.

Mount Crag: A dormant volcano, the largest in all of Gaela. It slumbers in the middle of Cragoa adorned with the carvings of beasts revered by the Craglins.

Mouth of Mydlan: An enormous cliff that drops South from the Pine Forests of Mydlan. At its bottom rests a lake sharing the same name.

Mydlan: The great expanse of land between the Fells and Svells, populated by Craglins, Gnomes, and countless fantastical species.

Nechalec (Nech) the Scribe (pronounced with a hard CH sound commonly found in Hebrew speech, closer to 'Nec-hh' than 'Neck') A well-learned and once-prosperous Craglin Scribe from the Craglands. In short: one very old and talkative Goblin.

Northfjord: A mighty fjord* that creates the border between the Duskridge and the mighty Fell mountains, the Northfjord has served as a port for seafaring Vikingmen since the dawn of civilization. *Geologically, a **fjord** (pronounced fiord) is a long, narrow inlet with steep sides marked by cliffs or mountains, created by a glacier.

Oathera: If Gaela is one side of a coin, think of Oathera as the other—the shadow cast by Gaela's being. It is another realm, the Realm of Mist and Shadow, and a dreadful place the living do not dare tread.

Ogre: A massive, brutish race covered in sparse, greasy hair and inclined to not-so-nice deeds.

Otherworld: The name given to the Realm of Mist and Shadow by the common tongue, a foreign, dark realm where certain souls travel after death.

Ozark Staff: Theole's staff made from the splintered spear of Thea and the Moonstone itself. It was destroyed by Vulduun during his invasion of Ythengrey, but a new one was summoned by Theole after the end of the Ever-war.

Paw the Black Bear: (pronounced like the paw of a bear) Titha's Bear-brother and best friend in the entire world. Paw is a rambunctious (and enormous) young forest black bear.

Pine Forests: Usually refers to the dense forests of harsh pines that dominated Mydlan's mid-landscape.

Rainer Angvarson (pronounced Rain-ehr, with 'Rain' as in water falling from the sky) The oldest son of Jarl Angvar and Shieldmaiden Sigrid of Autumnhill. Commander of the Houndsmen and devilishly handsome.

Reeks: A race of mostly-intelligent lizard people whos devotion to Vulduun has twisted their scaly appearance into something foul and putrid.

"**Rhofo**": Ancient Viking-speech for "open".

The River Daenu: This mighty river flows southward from **Loch Daenu** straight through the heart of **Ythengrey**. Its waters give life to all creatures who live there.

Roostwood: The home of Theole and his daughters that sits atop Mt. Meri in Ythengrey. It is of the finest wooden craftsmanship and only accessible from the Grand Steps that lead up from the Meadow.

Roothills: Massive hills formed by the very roots of The Tree of Life, Igdrasil. They were said, in legend, to come alive and fend off any who would invade her sanctity.

Ruins of Byle: A timeworn ruin from the age before the **First Eon**, left untouched for centuries.

Scribe: An ancient writer, keeper, and recorder of events, things, and persons important to history.

Shaman: A master of the magic, mystical, and dark arts who serves as a spiritual guide for their society.

Sigrid Shieldmaiden: (pronounced See-grid, as in look, 'see'! A 'grid'!) Sigrid is ruler of Autumnhill alongside her husband Jarl Angvar. She is mother to Audun and Rainer, and a stoic yet gracefully beautiful warrior of fair hair. She is, undoubtedly, destined for even greater things.

Skaldhall: The ancient home of Sigrid's Vikingmen ancestors, made to house the Sunstone and her people's power within Autumnhill.

Snowy Fells: The snow-covered mountains that make up the northernmost portion of the **Fells**.

Snowy Lands & Snowy Svells: The northernmost, snow-covered lands at the end of the Svells.

Squire: An armor-bearing individual of high status, who is in service to a master, or ***sire***, and is considered second-in-command.

"**Stodva**": Ancient-Viking word, meaning "Stop".

Sunstone: One of two ancient Orbs, the Sunstone was entrusted to Sigrid's bloodline after Vulduun forfeited its power and entrusted its keeping to the Vikingmen of Westlyn. It was deeply connected to the birth of the Great Drakes and the ***Sun*** itself, seen as a deity by Day-kin (also called the ***Skaldstone***).

Svells: The Great Svell Mountains; harsh peaks that form the border between Mydlan and Eastlyn. It is said that the 'V' in their name came from the V-shape they form around Svellvanyon, the vast canyon in-between.

Svell Valley: A large valley in the Western Svells that houses the Winding Wundi River down out of Cragoa into Mammoth's Respite.

Svellvanyon: The massive, deep canyon in the 'V' of the Svells that dominated the landscape of Northern Eastlyn. Legend tells that Svellvanyon held the Gates of Igdrasil that led to the Tree of Life herself.

Thea Celtica Mae: Mother of Gilly, Titha, and Beebee, and the fallen Lady of Yythengrey. She was said to have been unmatched in her beauty, and shared a peculiar kinship with Gaela. None miss her more than her daughters and the soulmate she left behind, Theole.

Theole the Watcher: (pronounced The-Ohl, with 'The' as in Theodore) Father of Titha, Gilly, and Beebee Mae and the great protector of Yythengrey. His better half, Thea, was taken from him many moons ago in a great battle. Theole houses great, ancient power, and is capable of taking the form of the ***Grand Silver Owl***.

Titha Lilly Mae: (pronounced Tih-tha Lilly May, with the 'Ti' sound as in 'tip', Lilly like the flower, and May like the month) Aged almost 11 forest-years at the time of ***The Ballad,*** Titha Mae is the adventurous middle child of Theole the Watcher and Thea Celtica Mae. She shares a deep love of all her forest home's kin, but none moreso than her Bear-brother, Paw.

Torai (pronounced Tor-eye) The largest member of the Peregrine Order and Maya's right-wing man.

Torgle: A very odd mixture of person and turtle with an affinity for cooking and servitude.

Totem: An object, living or otherwise, embued with importance or purpose. A symbol.

Ugar the Terrible: (pronounced Oo-gahr, with the 'Oo' as in tool, and 'gar' like the fang-toothed fish) A horrid foe who might as well be the combination of all bad and ugly things in Gaela. His hideously scarred form shielded many secrets.

Unknown Lands: These are the lands… that were unknown… and have yet to be explored!

Vikingmen: The humans of Northern Gaela, their main stronghold being Autumnhill. ***Vulduun*** cherished them as the hardiest Children of Day before his betrayal.

Vulduun: (pronounced Vuhl-dune, with 'Vul' as in Vulcan and 'dune' like a sand dune) Vulduun was the last surviving Great Drake (Dragon, or ***Elderdrake)***. He was known by many names: Dawnfather to the Lunas, Great Day Drake, and Herald of the Sun. He was also shaper of the lands of Gaela alongside his fallen mate, Meriduun. Vulduun was driven mad by the death of Meriduun and turned on the very world he shaped before perishing during the ***Breaking***.

Wargles: The fuzziest, most adorable little creatures to ever spawn from Gaela. They use their infamous cuteness to lure people into peculiar, magical places. Any who have seen them say they are tiny enough to wear an acorn cap on their head.

The Watcher/Watchress: The ancient position of leadership in Yythengrey, in which a Luna is entrusted with watchful protection and guidance, rather than all-powerful rulership.

Welp: A hateful term used to describe smaller, weaker creatures in Cragoa.

Westlyn: The expanse of land west of the Fells that holds everything from the Duskridge Mountains and Yythengrey to the Barren Fields and Autumnhill. It is home to the Cradle of Civilization, where the first great organizations of divine races came to be organized under banners and names in history.

Sirs Willamar and Waldemar: A duo of scrappy Gnomes from Wundiberg, both old acquaintances of Nech's. They are most skilled in scavenging and scouting, but most find it too hard to get past their incredibly thick accents (and bickering) to hire them.

The Winding Wundi: A twisting, turning river that flows through the Snowy Svells down into the Svell Valley; an offshoot of the Seas at the Horizon.

Wooly Rhioncerous: Also known as Wooly Rhinos, these enormous rhinos are covered in long, thick hair and are peaceful until challenged. They reside in the Barren Fields where they graze on the tall, dry grasses.

Wundiberg: Home of the Gnomes in the North, comprised of intricate tunnels, houses, and roads nestled into the Svell Mountains.

Yythengrey: (pronounced Yee-thin-grey) Home of the **Lunas**, **Yythengrey** is an ancient forest from the time of creation. Here, time passed slowly and peacefully during the First Eon. The center is formed by the Meadow and the **Duskridge**'s highest peak, **Mt. Meri**. Yythengrey housed many things seen nowhere else in Gaela, including enormous white ***Flowerbeds*** and the ***Lunas*** themselves.

Zazzec: (pronounced Zaz-zeck, with 'Zaz' as in pizzazz) The unmentionably old Craglin Shaman of Cragoa, prone to age-appropriate mood swings.

Jonbdalvy.com

I am indebted to my better half, my Brandee love, for her tireless eyes, heart, and hands. Without them, the Lunas would still be lost to the Dark.

- *Jon B. Dalvy*

Raised in Knoxville, Tennessee, Jon crafted ***The Ballad of Titha Mae*** from his youth in the Great Smoky Mountains and love of the fantasy genre, historical mythology, and his Celtic heritage. ***Titha Mae*** was born from these passions, as well as bedtime stories created for his three little sisters and two younger brothers.

A lifelong storyteller, natural history enthusiast, and outdoorsman, Jon returned to his birthplace to study zoology and wildlife with the Nashville Zoo after graduating from Middle Tennessee State University with degrees in both communications and performance. He's been enraptured with his love of character creation and world building ever since, the crafting of the Titha Mae Series becoming a constant between inspirational trips to Ireland, Iceland, Israel, and Japan (you get it) with his beloved wife, Brandee. We cannot thank you enough for coming along on these adventures with us, and hope you've found the same immense joy within their pages.

All the best,

Nechalec Press

www.ingramcontent.com/pod-product-compliance
Lightning Source LLC
Chambersburg PA
CBHW060612310726
48982CB00003B/528